Soft Focus

BOOKS BY JACK GUNTER

Wally Winchester Adventures:

Original Finish

The Egg Rocker

Mother of God

Soft Focus

A Pictorial History of the Pacific Northwest Including the Future

The Gunter Papers

Soft Focus

JACK GUNTER

A WALLY WINCHESTER ADVENTURE

Flying Pig Publications
Camano Island, Washington
flyngpig@camano.net

This novel is a work of fiction. Names, characters, places, and incidents either are products of the author's imagination or are products of historical record or geographic descriptions used fictitiously. Any resemblance to actual persons, living or dead,
is pure coincidence.

ISBN 13: 978-0-9841841-3-2
ISBN 10: 0-9841841-3-98

Printed in the United States of America by Ingram Books

Cover design from an original painting by Jack Gunter

Acknowledgements

In 1972 Robert Wyatt plucked me out of a junior science lab where I was writing my own material for my eighth graders. He turned the mimeographed lessons into "The Gunter Papers," Avon Books, New York. Thirty years later he taught me how to write a novel. The Wally Winchester series was created under his thoughtful guidance.

Suzanne Livingston took fifteen notebooks scribbled in longhand and waded through cross-outs, false starts and misspellings to produce a typed manuscript. Three attorneys, Frank Butler, Michael Keller, and J. Robert Leach, helped me with the trial questions. An unnamed ex-policeman who used to work on the meat wagon squad on Chicago's east side was my law enforcement consultant.

Gus Bostrom, Ed Farrey, Neil Hall, Nathan Collver, and especially David Manard were my first readers. They improved the book with their observations. John Dean performed the final edit and trimmed with a firm but delicate hand.

Thanks also to Peter Copeland for post-edit suggestions that gave "Soft Focus" a beautiful polish.

Chapter One

Camano Island, Washington

Wally Winchester sat in front of his new flat-screen monitor at 2:00 in the morning, junk mailbox open, skimming captured SPAM, on the lookout for a real message hidden amid the male enhancement ads. He hesitated on a subject line that read, "I want to give you $150,000 for your car," then scrolled to the bottom of the list of rejected emails before returning. The sender had the tag, *Cobra 157*. Wally opened it, as he happened to own a hundred fifty thousand dollar car, a Shelby Cobra.

Soft light from an old art glass lampshade flooded his dark brown oak desk. It was a trestle-based library table, an early Gustav Stickley design with the red box around the name on the label.

From the living room, Tom Waits sang "Waltzing Matilda" on the college radio station that filled in as a companion in the cliffside cabin these days with Rae gone, off to find a less chaotic life, she said. Wally heard echoes of the familiar gravelly voice, a whiskey-soaked victim of smoke-filled bars, delivering an emotional weather forecast.

Wally nodded to the invisible singer as he looked out the window at a string of street lamps twinkling through the blackness of a Pacific Northwest overcast night from Whidbey Island, half a mile west across the water. He opened the email message, half expecting to read a Nigerian heiress's proposal to send her fortune to his bank account.

The message read, "Mr. Winchester: It has come to my attention that you own a Shelby Cobra automobile. I am interested in this car for my collection. I believe that $150,000 is a fair price for your vehicle, delivered to my garage in Boston, Massachusetts by June. This is a serious offer. Please reply."

Wally, wearing shorts and wool stockings with a Red Sox jersey, carried the last of the evening bottle of a local red in his juice glass through a hall, barely lit by a green glass lamp glowing from the bathroom. A framed turn-of-the-century chromolithograph on the wall offered five-cent relief for stomach discomfort. Dark shapes of beefy reclining chairs and side tables met him in the living room, backlit by the dim glow of a 2:00 a.m. cloud over Whidbey. He reached under a leaded glass lampshade and tugged on an acorn-tipped chain. The framed photo of Rae emerging from a sports car, a low, blue two-seater, reflected the yellow and green glass squares of the prairie school pattern above it. Wally tilted the photo, gazed at the blonde's long legs as she exited the sleek roadster, parked precariously at the edge of Chuckanut Drive, distant grey islands at her back.

"Damn," Wally said to the dark corners. The two true treasures in my life. One gone. Some fool willing to pay a king's ransom for the other. If I sell the car, I'll have nothing. Some cash, sure. A lot of cash, but nothing of value – no love, no magic – nothing but a pile of filthy money.

At the computer again, he typed, "My Cobra is one of the 40th anniversary aluminum bodies. Horsepower—500 plus. Comes with the side oiler. Hand-signed on the visor by the man himself. I value it at $200,000 at least, but I'll take $175,000." He yawned and sent it off as a reply. Fuck a bunch of happiness, he thought. He drained the last of his wine and shut down the computer.

Tired, he looked down the dark hallway at his bedroom, a million miles away, where there was too much room in the empty bed and lost dreams lurking in the pillows. He chose the office sofa again and slipped under a Native American blanket to ward off the 3:00 a.m. chill.

Chapter Two

Everett, Washington

Late morning in the city of Everett, two blocks inland from the naval base, Wally drove the brick canyon of Hewitt Avenue in a funk, one eye on the three-story destination looming on his left, the other on the lookout for yard sale arrows. The faded vintage sign above the door read, *MacAvoy's Garage.*

Wally parked across the street. In the past, he had tried unsuccessfully to buy the sign from old man MacAvoy, grandson of the original owner, a Ford dealer back when the company offered only one model, the "T." The soft squeal of rubber tires, protesting a tight corner, floated down to the street through open stone arches on the second story. He looked up at the bricked-in windows above the upper floor arches to the long-term storage floor where his car sat safely out of the weather for sixty bucks a month.

Inside the garage, he noticed a new face behind the reception desk. Behind her, on the wall, were yellowed photos of the MacAvoy heydays before the Great Depression. He said, "Hello, you're not Glenda." It was all he had, taken by surprise by the olive-eyed Latina. "Hello, señor," she said through perfect teeth. "I'm not Glenda. That's correct." She held his eyes and smiled. "How can I improve your day?"

"You already have," Wally said. "I have a car here. On the third floor." He watched her eyebrows arch. "Glenda quit?"

"I never met this Glenda. They tell me of an accident, skiing. I answered an employment ad. Señor MacAvoy hired me to take her place. He asked me if I spoke English. I said I did. He said you start tomorrow."

"I bet he did," said Wally, aware of the old fart's lecherous reputation, "Skiing in June?"

"*Oh, claro*. It was in Chile, the accident. Señor MacAvoy told me she won a trip to Chile in a contest."

"Is she OK?" Wally kept his eyes on her face, aware of the two undone buttons on the white cotton shirt.

"I was hired two weeks ago, Señor, to sit at this desk and answer the phone. How would I know this answer?" The smile returned. "I have many other answers if you have other questions," she said.

"Como se llama?" Wally knew ten Spanish phrases. He planned to use them all.

"Manuelita. My father wanted a boy."

Wally debated placing a kiss on one of her perfect cheeks, the Hispanic greeting he'd learned on his trips south of the border. He stuck his hand out instead. "Walter Winchester, but you can call me Wally," he said.

He watched her smile blossom into a sensuous *Oh*. She stood up and circled her workstation to close the distance between them. She stood close, eyes up into his, a look Wally had rarely seen aimed at him.

"The Cobra man," she said. "Señor MacAvoy showed me the car on my first day. Told me not to let any other cars park near it. Owner's orders."

Her breath smelled like mangos or some fruit he couldn't place. This close, he went for the Hispanic greeting. She offered a tan cheek upward. Wally felt warm, firm skin on his lips. He tasted coconut.

"You surprise me," she said. "You know our greeting. I expected the owner of this car to be ruthless, cold. The owner of a bank, perhaps. An older man."

Wally ran his tongue across his upper front teeth, tasted yesterday's onions. He tilted his head back as though remembering something and aimed his breath at the space above her head. "Won it in a card game," he said.

"No shit," she said and covered her pursed lips with a hand.

Wally watched the blush flood her brown face. "Just kidding," he said. "Actually, I stole it at an auction."

"Ah, a *bandito*, a gangster." She took his arm. "Latinas like the bad man."

"Unfortunately, stealing a prize at an auction means getting it for a cheap price," Wally said. "But I *have* killed a man."

"Really?" she asked, eyes wide.

"No," he said, laughing. "Just kidding. I'm handicapped with a big heart. Lately, I look at it as a curse. I'm afraid I'm one of the good guys. Sorry. Hey, want to see the car with me, Manuelita? I have to sell it. Ever seen a grown man cry?"

"Yes, Señor Wally, I want to see your car with you, and I have seen a man cry." She coiled a strand of coal black hair on a finger. "You will be a rich man. You can buy five cars."

"Broken-hearted and wealthy, yes, at least wealthy. Come on, girl, let's go say goodbye to the last important thing in my life."

Behind the expanding gate that read, *Long Term Storage, No Admittance,* the cavernous upper floor held seven cars, three of them under shaped tarps. A pink Caddie convertible, two 60's Mustangs and a Boxter sat uncovered, lit by shafts of dusty light. Wally sighed as he unbuckled his shroud with *Shelby Racing Team* printed on the side, a $500 luxury he'd allowed halfway through a bottle of wine in a moment of Cobra lust. He lifted it gently. Eighty coats of lacquer glowed blue. Manuelita reached down to stroke the car's flank where it swelled over the rear wheel. Wally said, "Careful, young lady, it has to be perfect," then regretted it.

"I'm sorry, señor." Head down, she withdrew to the shadow of a concrete column.

"It's my paranoia. Come back. You can't hurt it with a caress. Want to take a ride in it? I have to take some photos for the buyer, and I want it in the sunlight for the detail. When is your shift over?"

Arm in Wally's again, she said, "It ended. I just quit. Let's go."

Rubber chirped. The car lurched ahead. Wally begged forgiveness. "Lot of horsepower under the hood in this little bug," he said. "Takes some getting used to. Have to start out in third gear or I'll leave half of the rear tires on the street behind me."

The throb of eight oversized pistons echoed off glass-fronted stores selling fresh fish and nautical gear where Hewitt Avenue met the waterfront. The marina parking lot sat empty, sunlit and steaming, as morning dew on the macadam surface warmed and returned to the air. Wally pulled in and parked. His passenger beamed. She freed herself from the seat belt, leaped with a giggle onto the hot tar surface and slammed the door. "Wheee! I love this car," she said.

"Try not to slam the door next time," Wally said, his attention on the camera. "It's a quality machine. They know how to make doors that close with no effort now."

"I'm a curse to this car," she said, palms out in surrender. "I'll walk home from here. *Manuelita, the Destroyer*, they will call me, a demolition derby in a dress." Deflated, she turned toward town, head down, and walked away in long, slow steps.

"Manuelita, wait." Wally jogged five paces to her back. He snapped a final photograph over his shoulder, the blue classic sitting sun-drenched on an empty lot. "I'll drive you back. I'm just nervous.

The buyer contacted me this morning with a list of conditions. He wants me to drive it to Boston, for Christ's sake, and get it there, unscratched and undented. The final condition will determine the purchase price, and he, the buyer, has the right to refuse it because of damage to original parts incurred on the journey."

Manuelita turned with a tear on her cheek. "Is there not a train that you could put this car onto, a boxcar, a container? Even a boat. You live on the ocean. Boston is on an ocean. They meet. It takes awhile, maybe through the canal, but it gets there."

"I told him exactly that, in a reply this morning. I told him eighteen-wheel car carriers leave Seattle every day, usually empty. I could guarantee a perfect delivery, and I'd pay for it."

"His answer?"

"He answered right away. He said he already owned four Shelby cars. He really didn't need another one, even this one, the 40th anniversary edition. He just wanted to see me do it. Then the car would have a story. I said OK. That's why I'm nervous. Sorry if I was harsh. I'm told it's one of my faults."

"You can take me to my *casa,*" she said. "I'll be more careful with your car. The house I'm staying in is not far from here, perhaps a kilometer."

Wally watched the shape of her mouth and her dark, bouncing curls as she moved to emphasize her words. He thought about the silence that awaited him back on Camano Island. "The sun's still high on the yardarm, as they say, Manuelita. Wanna tag along while I take the car for a spin up I-5?" he said. "The engine needs some rpm's to clean out the gunk."

"My future begins today, señor. Spin away."

"Sorry you quit your job today," Wally shouted over the 80 mile-per-hour airflow with four lanes of interstate highway freedom in front of him as they pierced the hills near Bellingham. He marveled at the car's instant response, a burst of power from a toe movement, and steering that seemed to run on thought.

"I was going to quit soon, anyway," came a faint response through the open-air din. "My sister is having a baby. She wants my help. A few weeks of work are enough for a ticket. I don't have a green card. My jobs end when the paperwork comes back."

"Where does your sister live?"

"In a town called Nashua."

"Nashua, New Hampshire?"

"*Si*. New Hampshire. In a region called New England."

"Nashua is three thousand miles away, girl. How do you plan to get there?"

"A bus perhaps. I don't know. I haven't thought about it yet. Do you know how much this bus will cost, the bus to this place, Nashua?"

"Boston, where I'm taking this car, is only thirty miles from Nashua." Wally stopped. He did the math. No wife. No perfect car. One hundred seventy-five thousand dollars and an empty slate. It was a Wally Winchester version of Zen. He said, "Hey, Manuelita. This is a two-seater. I leave for New England next week. Want the other seat?"

"Si, Señor Wally," the passenger said. "*Gracias*. You can show me your United States."

Chapter Three

Camano Island, Washington

Through the window behind his computer monitor, the last rays of sun lit edges of the Olympic Mountains in purple. He read his mail.

"So you had a choice between inviting me or a pretty Mexican señorita to travel with you across the country in a sexy sports car," the email read. "And you decided on the dame? Why do you call that a choice? You, with a broken heart and a soon-to-be fat checkbook; me, a tired, old Russian fart who's already listened to all your stories – twice. I'd call this decision a mandate, particularly if you carry out the plan you mentioned in your last message – to camp out all the way across the U.S.A. Why are you doing that, by the way, other than for the romance of it? Why drag a tent around when you have the best part of a quarter million dollars in your back pocket? All those greenbacks, you should be in the finest hotels–up to the penthouse. Maybe the bridal suite. As you Americans say, *stay at the Ritz*. You be traveling with a lady, Winchester. Remember to treat her right."

Wally typed back, "My job is to get this perfect car across the US of A without a scratch. Do you expect me to leave it in a Holiday Inn parking lot in Muncie, Indiana on a Saturday night while I sleep somewhere upstairs in an air conditioned interior room with a view of the courtyard and the fucking pool? Not a chance, comrade. Some asshole, leaving the lounge after *last call* or an unemployed autoworker with a chip on his shoulder or a gang-banger with a spray-can and an attitude, could cost me fifty grand. No, Yvgeney, I plan to keep the car in my sight while I sleep, eat, shit, shop for antiques, or screw. Scratch the last phrase, please. Manuelita is just a child. I'm driving her to Nashua, New Hampshire so she can help with her sister's new child."

Yvgeney answered ten minutes later: "This Mexican girl is the same age as Chana, Mr. Reverend Billy Graham. I remember some odd sounds in the Amazon jungle when you and Chana spent time in your tent. The Mexican woman is an adult and you are single. Get over it and do the math."

Wally signed off. He thought about the red-haired Amazon native that he had slept with, fought with, and shared a trans-Siberian train carload of zealots with. She called herself a shaman these days, lived on an island out in Russia's Lake Baikal, two thousand miles east of Moscow.

He tossed off a salute to the most powerful woman he'd ever met and poured another glass of wine.

The phone rang. It was 10:30 p.m., too late for all relationships but three. He picked up the phone and heard a Latina voice.

"Señor Wally, I have a backpack ready for our trip tomorrow."

"A small one, I hope. Not much room in a Cobra for luggage," he said.

"Three shirts, toothbrush, and a spare pair of panties," the voice said. "My sister promises more clothes when I arrive in New Hampshire."

"Pack a bathing suit. We'll be camping every night. It looks like summer weather across the United States in June."

"What's a bathing suit?"

Wally's pulse kicked. "See you at 8:00 a.m.," he said.

Chapter Four

Everett, Washington

The faded paint of the two-story apartment house where Manuelita lived suggested years of neglect. Wally considered himself an expert at looking for antiques inside people's homes. To him, exterior walls were transparent windows. The age of houses was a clue. New neighborhoods are a waste of time. A yard full of children's toys, a stand-up wading pool or trampoline around back, mountain bike racks on the SUV hybrid, or a personal watercraft in the driveway all telegraphed nothing interesting inside. A fertile interior revealed itself by a small barn or an unused chicken coop out back, unmown grass, a brass light fixture above tattered curtains, or a vintage hitching-post Negro statue holding a lantern in the front yard, one whose face had yet to be painted pink.

Wally looked at the North Everett neighborhood of low-income housing, junkie squats, and gang-tagged cinderblock shells of former businesses and knew his x-ray vision would reveal nothing of value inside.

He rumbled, as quietly as four hundred cubic inches of high performance side-oiled engine could, through the housing project and spotted Manuelita waiting on a grey, concrete stoop. He pulled to the edge of the potholed street and parked in front of the house where he'd dropped her off a week before. He pulled forward, leaving a car length of space between the Cobra, a rusty station wagon, and a 70's big-block Chrysler with two living room-sized speakers in the back window. An unshaved thug inside the car nodded to some throbbing base tones as Wally shut the engine down. The tweeker spit out the car window onto the remnants of a sidewalk and narrowed his swollen eyes. Wally remained in the Cobra and honked the horn, chivalry trumped by a two hundred thousand dollar investment.

Manuelita smiled as she crossed the dusty front yard. Wally frowned, noting a large burlap sack on one shoulder and the sparely filled backpack he'd requested on the other.

"Whooeee! *Hola, Señor Wally*," she squealed through fine white teeth.

"What's in the sack, Manny?" he asked.

"Fruit, señor. Fresh mangos, bananas, some of your Pacific Northwest cherries. Food for us on our adventure."

"Where do you suggest we put this bounty, Manuelita? Our reality here is that we're driving across the country in a race car."

Again she withdrew, took three steps back toward home, holding the bag of fruit to her chest.

He said, "Come back, Manuelita! You can bring any supplies that you are comfortable sharing your front seat with."

Brightening, she chose six fruits and scampered back to the front door with the sack. Wally watched as a hard-faced Hispanic giant met her at the door, malice in his demeanor. He pressed a package into her hands and withdrew to the darkness within.

"You don't live alone?" Wally asked as she hopped in, holding a brown bag.

"A cousin," she said and closed down her smile. "He doesn't like *gringos*."

"What did you forget?" Wally asked, looking at the package that she dropped in her opened backpack. She retrieved it and unwrapped a six-inch knife with a serrated top edge.

"Whoa! You didn't tell me you were a Navy SEAL. What do you plan to do with that?"

"Protect myself," she smiled. "Can we go now?"

As the roadster effortlessly pulled Snoqualmie Pass in fifth gear, Wally was beginning to understand the allure of Caroll Shelby's automotive engineering. At 2000 rpm, the motor felt like it was idling at a stoplight instead of hauling them up the long, steep grade on Interstate 90, headed east.

"I have to pee," the girl announced as they passed the ski lodge, open now for tourists and hikers.

Wally eased the Cobra into a service station offering regular gas for $4.79 with one eye on the gas gauge. With over half a tank left, he decided to hold out for the Vantage Bridge Texaco where I-90 crosses the Columbia River, a popular truck stop that could save him ten bucks on a fill-up.

"Hurry, *por favor*," the girl said. Wally drove up to the restrooms and let the motor idle as she leapt out and ran for the ladies' room.

He watched as she pulled the doorknob, then yanked and shook it, cursing in Spanish.

"You have to get the key," Wally said, watching her efforts. "In the *store*. They have keys to the restrooms." He pointed to the convenience store around the corner. "*Mierda*," she said with visible discomfort. "Why would somebody lock the bathroom? There's nothing to steal."

Driving the mountain's east downgrade, Wally said, "Sorry about bossing you around at the rest stop."

"Yeah, señor. What was that about?"

"For the next five days, my job is to protect this car. With you on board, this job is not so daunting."

"What is 'daunting'?"

"The word means difficult or nearly impossible. The point is, Manuelita, that with two of us, one can go pee, or shop for tropical fruit, or check out a yard sale while the other stays with the car. That way the Cobra is never unattended and no accidents, or acts of God, or drunk assholes with a chips on their shoulders will mess with these perfect eighty coats of lacquer."

"One of us stays with the car at all times all the way to Boston, *si?"*

"Si."

"*Claro*." You didn't want to take me to this Nashua, New Hampshire, Señor Wally, you wanted a baby watcher, a guard."

"I love the idea of company," Wally said. "You'll have an air conditioned seat for a ride across the great United States, young lady, for no charge at all. My only request is that we work as a team to keep everyone away from this car till I turn the son-of-a-bitch over to the new owner in Massachusetts. Two of us make this easy; are you OK with that?"

"*Si*, Wally. I'll be your back-up."

Thirty miles before Spokane Wally exited the interstate.

"There's a campground near a fabulous waterfall south of here," he said.

"But the sun is still high in the sky," she pointed out.

"There's a few places I want to hit in Spokane. See what's been turning up," Wally explained. "Five o'clock is closing time for antique shops around here, so we missed them today."

Manuelita smiled, opened her eyes wider and looked out at a landscape that seemed to be missing its soil. She pointed to a rolling, boulder-strewn hillside and asked, "Why does nothing live out here? Is this what you call a desert? Is there a large mine for gold nearby? In

Mexico, there are many gold mines. Around them is a zone of death. They say it is the cyanide."

"This wild soil-less region is not man-made. Story is, there was a flood out here ten thousand years ago. A wall of water – some say five hundred feet high – swept across eastern Washington. Scoured the land down to the bedrock. All the topsoil was stripped off and ended up in the Pacific Ocean. They call this area the scablands today."

"*Mierda*."

"Geologists claim there was an ice dam up north in Idaho that had a lake behind it as big as Lake Michigan. It was at the end of the last Ice Age, you know, and half of North America was covered with a mile-thick layer of ice – all melting at the same time."

"In Mexico, there is little talk of this Ice Age."

Her hand touched Wally's knee as she spoke.

Wally felt a current of heat radiate from the contact and chased the thought away. He left the macadam for a dirt road that promised *Palouse Falls 2 miles*, and dropped the speed to a crawl as he remembered the value of the car he was driving on loose stone and gravel.

He pitched his mountain tent and watched Manuelita spread a bedroll under the picnic table. She said, "I like to sleep outside."

Chapter Five

Spokane, Washington

In Spokane the next morning, they passed a pile of objects for sale in front of a once-grand church, now festooned in foreign-looking text on a banner. Wally parked. He opened the door and asked, "Can you wait here in the car, please?"

"Señor, I am getting a free trip across the American land at no cost and in a fancy car. I can be your guard if you wish."

"You can shop at the yard sale after I return."

"What do I want from a church?" she said. "Go on, I'll wait."

Wally noticed a flash of attitude. He looked back as he hustled toward the sale and saw her eyes on him.

A bearded, turbaned man, wearing a western shirt and Dockers, adjusted items on a table. Wally looked over the objects for sale. Telephones, an old spirit duplicator, a group of happy brass elephants and a box of footwear – sandals. He noticed that nothing in the box was made of leather, chalking it up to his vague awareness of Indian religions.

His eyes on the turban, Wally asked, "Are you a Sikh?" He knew a Sikh couple that were regular exhibitors to the LA Modernism show. They dressed weird but always had a booth full of high-end mid-century modern art for sale.

"No," he frowned, then shrugged. "This is a Hindu temple."

"Oops. Is that a rude question? I'm sorry. I'm sort of ignorant about your side of the world."

"Ignorance is no excuse for rudeness. Your apology is accepted."

"Do you have any Indian items?"

"Everything we have is Indian."

"Sorry, I mean American Indian. Blankets? Rugs? Baskets?"

"No." The turbaned elder turned toward other customers.

Way to piss the guy off, Wally chided himself.

"Sir?"

With a sigh, the elder turned back.

Wally asked, "What was this church before you took it over?"

"Methodist."

"When was it built?"

The turbaned man looked to other customers waiting to purchase items in front of them and shook his head. "There is a date on the cornerstone. There." He pointed to the number 1909 raised on the granite block. "If you have no other questions, I would like to help these others." The statement issued from tight lips.

"Actually, I do have another question."

The man's bearded face looked skyward. His eyes returned to Wally's, lids half closed. "What?" he said.

"I buy old things. Old light fixtures, chairs," Wally looked to the colored glass panels flanking the door. "Stained glass windows."

"I have a question for *you*, sir," the man said.

Wally, a veteran of door slams, waited for the wisecrack dismissal. Instead, the man asked, "Can you come with me? I have something to show you."

Wally's heart jumped. Fuck, I love this job, he thought. He glanced down the street toward the Cobra and saw a dark-haired head in the passenger seat, watching back. Wally followed the man to a massive front door, stepping out of his Italian driving loafers when he saw his host untie his running shoes and place them beside the door. No cowhide, of course, Wally thought, remembering that some Indian religions worshipped the cow.

Inside, a cool stillness in the oak-paneled anteroom smelled like money to the trained antique dealer. A pair of brown and green metal wall sconces, flanking the inside door, were missing the glass shades they came with a hundred years before. That, plus the absence of light bulbs, was a good sign to a man who made a living on other people's discarded objects. "Are those lights for sale, sir?" Wally asked.

His Hindu host ignored the question and opened double doors to the main sanctuary. Wally forgot the sconces as he entered a dome-ceilinged hall lit by colored light from huge leaded glass windows.

"Here is my question," the Hindu said. "Can you sell these windows for us? We would like to replace them with other colored glass not so…." He hesitated.

"Christian?" Wally volunteered.

"Yes, exactly. Thank you."

Wally believed he understood. A ten-foot leaded glass scene of Christ's body on the cross was the first of five windows on his right. To his left was a matching window that portrayed the birth of Jesus in a manger. Wally saw related scenes on the rest.

The man said, "We respect the Christian religion, but windows of this size and…topic are," he hesitated again, "distracting to our Hindu prayers."

"You thinking of replacing them with some cow windows and that goddess with six arms?" Wally spoke, remembering a program he'd caught on the History Channel during a slow TV night.

"Please don't speculate on Hindu images, sir. We would like to replace them with geometric glass panels."

"Big stained glass windows with religious pictures on them are tough to sell these days. They don't fit in most homes, you know, and there's not a lot of churches being built these days."

"Can you sell them?"

"Sure, if the price is right. Whadda you think they're worth?" Lesson number one in the picker's bible is: *Make the seller come up with the selling price.* Wally was reading from the playbook. Suggesting a price was the last resort. It limited all the options and risked a lawsuit. Wally's ex-friend, Ed Brown, had once bought a pair of original, unused Titanic crossing tickets for ten grand and spent two years in court after selling them publicly for ten times the price.

"We would be satisfied with enough money to purchase and install simple colored glass to replace them," the man said. "Can you accomplish this?"

"I can," Wally said, "and I even know a guy on Camano Island who can make your new ones. I can get you a special deal. He owes me."

Wally looked up at four fluorescent tubes that hung from the vaulted ceilings on long chains. He asked, "What happened to the original fixtures?"

"There are many lamp parts in the attic," the man said. "But they are old and tarnished. They wouldn't be of much use these days. They weren't powered by electricity, only gas."

"I believe we have a relationship," Wally answered. He offered his hand. "Wally Winchester at your service."

"Baldev Singh," the Hindu said as he squeezed his fingers around Wally's. "I'm lucky that you came by today. Our bank account is low, as you can surmise from our sale outside."

"These lamp parts, can we go up to your attic and look for them now?"

"We are quite busy outside with the sale. Perhaps when you come to purchase the windows."

"I'll help you carry a few of these boxes out to the sidewalk," Wally offered. "Hey, what's this?"

The turbaned gentleman peered into a card box Wally held up from a pile of yet-to-be-offered donations. "Many of our worshipers are from Sri Lanka. It looks like ordinary letters and here's a photograph, an old one. Yes, she looks like a Sri Lankan child from many years ago when it was Ceylon."

Wally lifted an envelope from the box, handed it over, noticing the ancient British stamp and an address in Ceylon of Julia Cameron, a name that scratched at his memory. The photo brought the name into focus.

Julia Margaret Cameron nearly burst from his lips. "How much do you want for this box of old letters?" he asked.

"Probably ten dollars. There could be value in the old stamps."

"Sold," Wally said, as he peeled a Hamilton off a roll of cash in his pocket. He hoped the seller didn't notice his heart thumping under his shirt. He looked at the other items yet to make it to the sidewalk sale and saw junk.

"I can see you're busy, Mr. Singh. I'll take that rain check on the attic lamps till I come back. Should be a couple weeks."

"Very good, sir," the cleric said, as Wally double-timed his exit. "Leave the name of the stained glass window maker before you leave."

"Gotta run," Wally said. He clutched the box to his chest. "We'll talk on the way back. I'll look up the phone number."

"Budda Bing, Budda Bang," was Wally's greeting to Manuelita as he skipped and pranced around the Cobra's front end to get to the driver's seat.

"Did something *bueno* happen at that church?" she asked. "You have nothing but a box in your hands. No antiques."

"I have an appointment in three weeks when I get back from Boston, my Mexican good luck charm. And in this box I have a thousand dollar photograph." He carefully inserted the box into the narrow storage behind the seat. While doing so, he placed a kiss on the lid, said, "If you want to use the bathroom in the church before we leave, I'll wait with the car. It's a nice one. Tell the turbaned man you're with me."

"Thank you, señor, I will," she said as she opened the door of the convertible, careful to not slam it behind her. She grabbed her backpack on the seat.

"You're not going camping, young lady, it's just a pit stop," Wally said.

"It's a ladies thing, señor." Wally's lip buttoned as she sprinted back to the church like a schoolgirl.

Manuelita emerged from the bathroom to find the Hindu waiting to let her out of the temple.

"Sir," she said with an innocent smile. "Are we alone in here?" The cleric seemed perplexed with the question. He answered, "Yes."

"Did my Anglo friend leave you his phone number when he left?"

"Yes," the man answered, pulling a business card from his pocket. "And an email address. He said, use the email."

"Good," she said. The seven-inch knife in her hand shot up under the rib cage, slicing easily through his white shirt as it cut arteries on the way to his heart. The Hindu's eyes widened as he coughed red blood into the air. She stepped aside, feeling a bloody mist that she wiped off her arm with a tissue. He crumpled, eyes unfocused, as she turned the blade to the serrated edge and began sawing on his neck.

Manuelita smiled as she repositioned herself in the passenger seat, careful not to slam the door. She tucked the pack behind the seat.

"I'm ready now for the highway, Señor Wally. Fire up those horses."

Wally noticed a tiny blood spot on her white shorts and decided not to embarrass her by mentioning it. Ladies' issues, he figured, were best left unmentioned.

Chapter Six

Spokane, Washington

LeRoy Thompson and his brother, Billy, heard the deep chortling of the five hundred horsepower Cobra engine trumpeting from the twin exhausts. Billy put down the crack pipe he was hitting on and blew out the match before it burned his fingers. Midday traffic on Division Street was light as they cruised the four-lane boulevard, gangster rap on the radio, no plans for the afternoon except a beer stop for a half-rack at the *Park 'n Shop* ahead at the corner of Fifteenth and Pine.

LeRoy was driving, keeping the speed low because of the dope in the front seat, the cops knowing the car and all. No need to give 'em a peek inside with a probable cause hook.

A sweet, blue Shelby Cobra rumbled by in the left lane, and a pretty *chica* on the passenger side looked them over before turning away.

"When's the last time we jacked a car, Billy?" LeRoy said.

"Been a while, LeRoy. You likin' that Cobra? Don't see many of them motherfuckers in these parts."

"That sure is a nice ride, and it's got a chocolate bar inside for dessert."

LeRoy saw the traffic light turn yellow at Fifteenth. Beer could wait. He pulled his unwashed 4x4 alongside at the traffic light and looked down at the racecar beside him.

"Hey, little *puta*," he growled at the dark-haired passenger. "Want to dump your faggot boyfriend and come to a party?"

She looked up, made a face like she'd tasted something really bad, and pretended to shoot herself in the head with her finger. Wally glanced up and decided to ignore the drunk beside him. As the light changed, he juiced the Cobra to a hundred-yard gap in the space of a breath. The I-90 ramp was up ahead, he figured, and the car was not to be put into harm's way with a carload of hillbillies and no payoff. He checked the rearview mirror for police, saw nothing but a muddy pickup truck gaining speed, and pushed the Shelby to ninety as he hugged the curve of the on-ramp like it was glued to the road. He passed a lumbering semi and saw the hills of Idaho far ahead. He pushed his toe down and felt a couple of G's as the car snapped up to 120 miles an hour.

"Fuck you, rednecks," he shouted into the wind. "We've got five hundred aces under the hood. Let 'em eat dust, is what I say."

Manuelita looked back, thought she could see the dark speck of the drunk Anglos trying to keep up but said nothing. She patted Wally's knee, feeling him jump as she touched him. "You're my hero, Señor Wally," she shouted, laughing. Wally beamed and pushed the Cobra to one-forty for a second as if to acknowledge her praise. He dropped the speed to ninety at the Idaho border. No need to push your luck with the State Patrol. He drove toward late afternoon thunderheads, airbrushed yellow from the setting sun, thinking about the pretty girl's hand on his knee.

Five miles behind the Cobra, LeRoy said to Billy, "Toss that crack pipe out the window, you damn fool; we're doin' ninety-five and the barracks are just ahead at the state line."

"I just bought this pipe, LeRoy."

"You stole that motherfucker at the head shop on State Street last week. I seen you do it. Throw out that last rock, too."

"LeRoy."

"It's a five dollar rock, what's left, and a ten dollar pipe, fuckhead. I don't mind a pop for speeding if the mounties see us; everyone drives fast this side of Spokane. I don't want a possession on my sheet. Can't afford it. Neither can you, you fuckin' criminal."

Both laughed as the drug gear hit the wind and disappeared.

"You think you're going to catch that Shelby, you're crazy," Billy said. "Those things can do a buck fifty all day long. I see it on 'Monster Garage.' Did you know the motherfucker who invented that car writes his name on the visor with a Sharpie?'

"Since when do you learn anything on TV? I think you been too stoned to focus since you got out of Walla Walla."

"Marleen puts it on when I'm banging her ass. I ride her doggy like. I like to kick the sound up. Muffles the screaming. That crazy whore sounds like she's dying half the time. She loves that meat."

"That arrogant little prick's gotta slow down when they get near Coeur d'Alene," LeRoy said. "Lotta traffic around quittin' time. We'll catch him. I may kill him slow for pissin' me off. You can do the Mexican. See if you get some sounds outta her like Marleen."

Lit by the setting sun, the "Welcome to Montana" sign glowed yellow.

"We should try to find a campground after we pass Missoula," Wally announced to his dozing passenger. He silently cursed the State Patrol car ahead that kept him, and the twenty or so vehicles behind, all doing exactly 70 – the speed limit posted on the signs.

"Nobody drives this road at seventy," Wally said, mostly to himself. "There's four lanes each way and nothing out here but mountains and moose. The highway's as straight as a laser beam, and I'm building up carbon deposits on this engine, slow as I'm going."

Manuelita, head back with her left eye closed to the *gringo*, watched the sideview mirror with her right. That truck with the *mal hombres* was back there in the pack that followed. She saw it emerge from behind an eighteen-wheeler and watched it duck back behind as it kept pace. She sent back a small prayer that the pickup would get low on petrol or just get bored of the slow-motion pursuit and return to whatever *barrio* they lived in – bother someone else. Her assignment was complicated enough without stupid drug heads to muck it up.

After passing the four exits to Missoula, Wally declared that the next off-ramp would be it for the day, little enough daylight left to set up a tent with the trooper ahead of them still enjoying the 70 mph traffic jam in his wake. He thought again about the buzz when the *señorita* touched his knee. He thought about how long it had been since he'd held a woman in his arms. Only two times since Rae left, and that weekend, three months ago, seemed years away. He wasn't that much older than her, he thought. Twenty years, tops. She seemed to like him, though being honest, he had to admit, she hadn't said or acted that she was interested in anything more than a ride. The first night in the tent was no indicator, she under the picnic table and he in the tent. She liked to sleep outside, she'd said. He believed her.

The little white bra under her shirt played peek-a-boo as the fabric moved. She stirred in the passenger seat, apparently still sleeping, and her arm fell towards the shifter between them. Wally thought about shifting to a lower gear so maybe their hands would touch. Perhaps her fingers would not move away after contact. That wouldn't mean anything, Wally thought. Two friends holding hands on a road trip.

Wally kept his hands on the steering wheel as he canceled the hand-holding plan. A conversation, he told himself, was necessary before he made any assumptions about touching. He congratulated himself on his grown-up decision.

She stirred again. Her arm angled sideways and brushed his. She opened her eyes and said, "Excuse me. My mother used to tell me I slept like a windmill, arms here and legs there. My sisters refused to sleep with me in the children's bed when I was twelve. Said they preferred the animals in the barn." She patted Wally's arm as if to repair it from a wound that her touch inflicted and sat up, looking around. “Where are we, señor? Did I snore or make noises in my sleep?”

“You were a mouse, Manuelita,” Wally said as he placed a reassuring hand on her leg by the knee, violating his recent pledge, and tapped it twice before he returned it to the steering wheel.

“The next exit should have everything we need,” Wally said. He squeezed a reassuring clench, and she responded with one of her own.

LeRoy kept the pickup behind the semi once they spotted the little blue creampuff with a Mexican pussy inside, stuck behind a smokie who was holding traffic at the limit, no doubt enjoying his game. He watched as the Cobra ignored the Missoula exits on its way east and figured the little fucker driving it was headed all the way across Montana. The gas gauge was nearly on empty, so he was pleased to see the car turn off at Exit 31. He elbowed his brother awake and held back just enough to keep the car in sight. Nighttime would make them invisible, he knew. And nighttime was the right time, he also knew, for rock and roll.

The brothers watched the car gas up at a truck stop. The *chica* entered the restaurant and came out with bags of food, while the yuppie sat in the driver’s seat. LeRoy threw a quick ten dollars of gas into the 4x4 when he saw they were heading for the resort lake to the south. Dark now, they caught the fancy taillights up the road and followed as the meat pulled into a campground.

“We won’t be staying, so I guess we don’t have to register, Billy.” He ignored the unmanned ticket window as he drove in behind them, headlights off.

After popping together the two-man backpacker's tent he carried behind the driver's seat, Wally grabbed the cardboard box from the Hindu church sale and brought it to the picnic table, lit by his battery lantern.

"Fuck, oh dear," he said. "Hey, Manuelita. This is what I bought from that Hindu dude back in Spokane. Got this box of letters and this photograph while I was talking to the man about looking at old chandeliers stashed up in the attic."

Wally's traveling companion pulled her eyes from the surveillance of campsites that circled the lakeshore with a glowing necklace of lanterns and campfires.

A photo that looked ancient in the glare of the lantern showed a dark-skinned subcontinent girl, dressed in ancient white garb. The eyes were black pools that burned fiercely through the old emulsion.

"I know this photographer," Wally said. "My ex collected books that showed this woman's photos. *Julia Margaret Cameron* was her name. Took amazing pictures way back in the 1860's, when the science of photography was still being invented. A packet of old postal envelopes, tied with rotting twine, came loose as the string crumbled in Wally's hands. He held one up to the light. "Damn," he exclaimed. "Julia Cameron. Here's her name on the envelope. Here's an address in Ceylon, British Province. Son-of-a-bitch, Manuelita, here's her home address."

"Señor Wally."

"Yes?"

The Mexican stared out at the dark lakeshore, listened but then focused her attention on the yard-sale box of letters. "I don't understand your excitement for these…letters. If you don't mind my asking, why is an old photo and a hundred year-old address in a region halfway around the world so important?" Did you pay money for this old carton with the letters in it?"

"Ten bucks. I'm calling that a bargain."

"Ten U.S. dollars in Chiapa would feed all my sisters for a month, señor."

"The photo itself could be worth a thousand dollars, girl. Julia Cameron was a big deal in England in 1870. When things quiet down, I want to go through the letters, see who wrote to her and what they said. Autographs can be worth a bundle if there's interesting material attached, and then there's these old British postal stamps."

"A thousand dollars? For a photo?" She lifted the yellowed sheet by its edges, holding it to the light.

Manuelita pursed her lips, hesitated, and said, "I don't believe it. You think this child is an important person?"

"No," Wally answered. "As I remember it, Julia Cameron used anyone she could talk into donning a costume for a photograph: babysitters, servants' children, even her own family. When I get paid for this car, I'm tempted to hop a flight over to India, to Ceylon – it's called Sri Lanka now – and look up this address. Who knows what's still in the attic. I live for door-knocking leads like this."

"I know about Sri Lanka. The Tamil Tigers are a group that has some respect in Mexico."

"They're a bunch of terrorists, Manuelita. Bombers of innocents."

"Fighting for freedom, I'm told, can get messy, señor," Manuelita said, her eyes narrow.

"Hey, look at the time," Wally said as he turned his wrist with the watch on it. "There's room for two in the tent, you know. Chance of rain, they say."

"I prefer the sky above me, Señor Wally, but thank you. The wood table next to the fire pit will protect me from the rain."

"Suit yourself." Wally carried a foam ground-pad under his arm as he ducked under the tent's flap. "Mind if I bring the Coleman lantern with me? I want to look at the Ceylon letters."

"I prefer the safety of the darkness," his companion said.

Manuelita heard the rednecks approaching along the water's edge. Soft muffled snores from the tent told her that Cobra Man was out. With half a moon lighting the backs of small clouds, she closed the distance between the bivouac and her adversaries, shedding garments as she entered the lake without a sound. The light from the moon was important to her plan. Waist-deep in chilly water, she watched two human shapes creep like hunting dogs toward the *gringo's* tent. She playfully splashed the still waters around her and looked upward to the moon-edged clouds – as if innocent, vulnerable and unaware.

Billy saw moonlit titties and put his hand out to signal his partner. "LeRoy," he whispered loud enough to flow across the water surface like a loudspeaker. "There's the *chica puta.* Naked as a bird. Wait here. I'm gonna get me some taco."

"We're here for the Cobra, dumb ass. The Mexican is just dessert."

"LeRoy, once we whack the queen-boy driver, we come back and she's gone." Billy held a baseball bat like Ken Griffey Jr. and took a practice swing.

"Whadda-ya want, a fifty grand car or pussy?"

Billy handed the bat to his brother. He said, "I want both but I gotta do the girl first, else she'll do a fade once the batting starts. I'll just be a minute. She's a little thing."

"Be quiet, for Christ's sake, before you wake up the asshole in the tent." LeRoy hesitated, looked over to the clearing where the sports car was parked. "Don't fall in love. We're not taking prisoners."

Manuelita, her back to the shore, heard small splashes as one of the rednecks entered the water, headed in her direction. She waded deeper, the chilly soup covering her breasts. A glance at the backlit clouds above afforded her a quick view of a dark shape, up to his waist, ten feet from her back. She drew in a big lungful of Montana night air and exhaled, then filled her lungs again and ducked her head under the surface.

Billy cursed quietly when the Mexican girl disappeared. He turned back to look at LeRoy in the dry land shadows but darkness had swallowed him up. In the dim light, he saw nothing but flat, black water, with some ripples, moving outward in slow, widening circles where the Mexican girl had been catching moon rays. His arms pushed through the dark soup, sweeping arcs designed to encounter an underwater nymph. "Time to take a breath, *chicquita*," he said to the empty air. "Then we party."

The cold of the lake shriveled his desire. As he stood, chest deep, clad in a soggy t-shirt and jockeys, he allowed himself momentarily to question the folly of this entire day. He pushed the thought away, amazed his quarry was still underwater.

LeRoy looked at the dark figure of his brother silhouetted by a moonlit lake. Crazy fucker, he thought. Always thinking with his dick. He turned toward the campsite with the Cobra. A yellow pup tent glowed with a light inside. Baseball bat on his shoulder, a Bowie knife on his belt, and a Saturday night special bulging his pocket, he pondered his next move. He didn't need Billy to do this asshole, he told himself. He didn't even need to kill the guy, he thought, but was leaning in that direction because a witness could complicate his future. The gun was out, here in a public campground. The knife meant he had to enter the tent to poke him or lure him out quietly. A baseball swing through the thin tent material seemed a good first step. A good homerun swing, aimed just right, could solve all his victim's problems simultaneously. At least it would slow the fucker down for a *coup de grâce*. As he hefted the bat off his shoulder for a practice chop in the low underbrush near the clearing, he heard a sound behind him. He turned, with a grin, expected his crazy brother in wet undies, done from his lovin', here to help. There was nothing but night breezes fluttering through dark foliage. Holding the baseball bat above his head, he stepped into the campground clearing.

Five minutes in the cold water had sapped all of Billy's interest in the Mexican girl and left him feeling foolish – a grown man standing in his wet underwear in a Montana lake after dark.

He slapped his hand against the surface saying to no one, "What are you, a goddamn fish?" and began to wade ashore.

LeRoy felt the impact of something heavy and soft land hard on his back. A hand covered his mouth, and small legs encircled his waist. He felt a pinprick, a jab of pain, as the flesh in his neck parted, spewing blood outward in heartbeat spurts onto his flailing arms. To his surprise, Le Roy felt no discomfort as his legs gave out and consciousness faded.

Manuelita wiped the blood off the bat handle and headed back to the lakeshore.

Billy was pulling the Carhart two-pocket denim shirt over a wet undershirt, wondering if he wandered out into the lake after a ghost or a mirage when the baseball bat connected with the back of his skull. He heard the aluminum twang as the small cranium collapsed and his brain turned to mush. He felt the biggest boner he'd ever had spring up as darkness covered his awareness.

Wally woke to the sound of movement inside his tent and saw Manuelita switch off the lantern. Pale moonlight lit the little-girl face, a blanket to the chin, beside him. He reached out a groggy hand and she took it, cradling his fingers.

"Your hand is cold," he murmured.

"I took a swim."

"Did I ever tell you about the couple trapped in an ice cave on Mount Hood during a blizzard? They survived by skin-to-skin contact."

"It's almost summer, señor. No one freezes to death in Montana in June."

She pulled his hand back to face level and held his fingers in a friendly, firm embrace.

Chapter Seven

Central Montana

Mountain sunshine hit Manuelita's face as the Cobra emerged from the shadows of a steep, walled canyon at 80 miles an hour. Wally watched dark Mexican hair flutter in the airstream and thought she looked radiant. He told her so.

"I love life in this car," she shouted above the roar of the wind. She reached over and took Wally's hand as the racecar took the curve into a broad valley at 100.

"You seem more alive today," Wally shouted back. "That midnight swim seems to have refreshed you."

"Cold water washes a person inside and outside," she answered with a soft finger pressure.

Wally slowed to 60 and took the exit for Butte without braking, entered a four-lane road that followed a river in spring-melt flood. "There's an asshole south of here," Wally said. "The guy's never taken me seriously as an antique dealer, sends his Stickley finds to some guy in Berkeley. I just want to park this son-of-a-bitch in front of his shop and see what he has for sale."

"I don't understand," Manuelita said. "You will have a great deal of money when you get to Boston, and a great deal to lose if the car gets damaged. Four days of highway, maybe two, the way this car goes, and you're rich. Why risk the uncertainty of side trips?"

"Respect, Manuelita. Respect opens doors. I want to get to the next tier of the Arts and Crafts ladder. All the money in the world doesn't buy that. It's all about how I'm perceived. I'm tired of being this good and not being recognized by the big dogs."

"You will get that respect by parking this car in Butte, Montana?"

"One stop at a time, girl. The ladder to the top is invisible. Every step opens new doors to dealers and collectors."

"I predict you will be famous soon," Manuelita said.

The road sign read, *Butte 90 miles*. Wally said, "From your lips to God's ears," and caressed her fingertips.

Butte, Montana, was a boomtown in the years after the Civil War, Wally explained to his passenger as they cruised a downtown of old brick storefronts, mostly empty. Wally slowed and parked in front of a window that displayed Victorian walnut dressers and leaded glass table lamps. The sign on the door said, *Gone Fishin'*.

"Damn," Wally said. "It's Wednesday. The arrogant bastard. What right does he have to be closed at two in the afternoon?"

Manuelita was amused. "Señor Wally, you wake up when you want and expect the world to operate on a timetable that fits your day."

"The other sign says, *Open*," Wally said. "The son-of-a-bitch should be open."

The back streets of the old mining town offered no other opportunities to buy antiques. Wally cursed the two-hour detour and plotted an eastern route to regain I-90.

Manuelita laughed.

Wally asked, "Are you laughing at me?"

"*Si, señor*. A little."

"What's so funny?"

"You and this car."

"*¿Por qué?* Wally used one of his ten Spanish phrases.

"It reminds me of my friend, Maria, in Mexico City. One day she finds a leather bag, a purse, on the beach. It was a wonderful thing. Gucci leather."

"Good find," Wally said. "Big bucks."

"I know. Everyone knew. Two hundred pesos."

"More."

"She was offered a hundred even on the street. She said, no, I want to show it off. The next day her…manager…"

"Her pimp?"

"*Si.* Her pimp took it from her the next day. Slapped her around. Says what she has belongs to him. Should have sold it the first day. Her sin was pride."

"What's that have to do with me?"

"You have a large sum, a payoff, if you get this racing car to Boston, yet you want to stop and show it off."

Leaving Butte, Wally caught sight of a colorful object on the balcony of a five-story apartment building. He pulled to the curb.

"Why are we stopping?" Manuelita asked.

"It's a *Marshmallow Sofa,*" Wally said as he shielded his eyes, looking up. "I don't believe it." He pulled a U-turn and drove to the door. A wall of mailboxes and a buzzer entry suggested a way in. "We're going to run a game, girl. Will you work with me? We're going to go up and buy that son-of-a-bitch, but, to do it, you have to pretend we're just married."

It was Manuelita's turn to ask, "*¿Por qué?"*

That sofa on the outside deck is one of the coolest of the mid-century, designed by a guy named George Nelson, called a *Marshmallow Sofa* 'cause that's what it looks like. Just go with me on this, Manuelita. You're my new wife. Can you fake it?"

"This is a scam?"

"Yes. Are you in?"

"I can pretend to be anything. I grew up on mean streets."

The old couple on the third floor was surprised but pleased when they opened the door to Wally's soft knocking.

"Hi," Wally said to a short, grey-haired man in a t-shirt and stained pants, held up with suspenders. His wife, a ball of a woman, seemed happy to have some company on a quiet spring afternoon. "My name is Wally and this is my wife, Mary," Wally began. "We just got married. Isn't that right, honey?"

"*Si*, just married. It's my dream come true," she answered.

"Why, isn't that special," the woman said. "Come in. We have so few visitors these days. George, put the water on; we'll have some tea."

They entered a modest living room that smelled, to Wally, like some nursing homes he'd visited. Tired hand-me-down chairs in a 70's orange plush sat on a shag carpet. Thrift store prints in plastic frames, and a pair of gaudy ceramic table lamps on cheesy mahogany tables completed the décor

The mouse of a husband emerged from a kitchenette with a teapot and four mugs. He introduced himself and his wife as he poured thin tea. "We didn't expect visitors today," he told them.

"Well," Wally began. "We just got married yesterday."

"How sweet," the woman said. "What brings you to our door?"

"We've been talking about decorating our new home, right, darling?"

Manuelita pasted on a sweet smile and said, "*Si*. Just married."

"Well, our plan is to decorate in bright colors. Like in the 50's. We call it, mid-century modern, and, driving by, we saw that sofa on your balcony."

"That old thing, it's been out there for twenty years." George said. "Get rid of that ugly sofa. We never sit on it. But we're old. It's a heavy frame. We don't have young people to help carry it away. You like it? Do you want it? What a lucky day for us. If you want to move it, it's yours."

"We'll gladly pay for it," Wally said.

"Nonsense," George answered. "If you can get it out of here, it's yours."

"I want to pay," Wally said. "It wouldn't be right to furnish our home on charity."

"Ten dollars," the woman said, wincing on the hot beverage. "Now you own it, and it's not a handout. Can you take it now? You'll do us a favor."

Wally pulled a ten spot out of his roll and handed it to the husband, who tucked it into a dirty pocket like a thief. He said, "I'll come back in an hour with a little truck."

The deal was done. They thanked the couple and left.

Wally shot his fist in the air on the staircase, sent a thank you to the picker's god, and drove three blocks to a U-Haul store where he parked the Cobra in the rental yard and returned with a ninety-dollar, one-day van.

The carry-out of the Marshmallow Sofa was a bitch. Doorways and staircases required tilting and tipping as they manhandled the heavy frame down to the rental vehicle on the street, the old man useless, despite his wheezing attempts at assistance. Wally assigned him door-opening duties till the treasure sat safely in the van.

Manuelita looked up at the empty back porch, thought about making the excuse to use the couple's bathroom, and decided to let the old Anglo couple live, assignment be damned. She appreciated the tea and chose not to include them in her prime objective – the destruction of the *gringo's* world. There will be plenty of more worthy people to kill on my trip across the United States, she thought.

Chapter Eight

Montana/North Dakota Border

At a campground near the North Dakota border, Wally, still thrilled about the Marshmallow Sofa stashed in a rental storage unit, and Manuelita, feeling OK about the old couple sleeping soundly and safely in their rundown flat, sat in the tent under the six volts of glow from a Coleman lantern.

Wally pulled out the box with the letters sent in 1871 to a British woman living in Ceylon. He glanced over the three pages penned in a crisp, beautiful calligraphy. On the last page, he gasped, "Alfred Lord Tennyson."

"Who is that?" Manuelita asked. She sat on her bedroll, wearing a tight tank top and shorts.

"Alfred Lord Tennyson was famous," Wally said. "A writer, as I remember."

"What did he write?"

"Poems, I think. 'Into the valley of death rode the six hundred …' *The Charge of the Light Brigade* is what I remember from eleventh grade English class."

"He is famous because of a poem?"

"He wrote many. That's the one I remember. Something about British soldiers in the Boer War in Africa, or maybe it was the Crimean War. I was distracted in the eleventh grade."

Manuelita let her attention wander. Wally brought her back. "This letter itself could be worth a lot to autograph collectors. Could be worth thousands just by itself."

"Congratulations," she said, bored.

"Listen to this: *My dearest Julia, The sun in the Brightwater Circle shines less brightly in your absence. The moon has lost its glow...* Wow, this is great stuff."

"I'm going out to check the car," Manuelita said.

"There's more," Wally said as he watched her bottom leaving the tent. He read the letter and opened another.

A cloudless, starry sky lit the campground in dim phosphorescence. Manuelita walked a hundred-foot circle and found three empty fire pits. A pickup truck camper, back by the bathrooms, seemed innocent. The muffled monologue of a baseball broadcast put her at ease. She opened a cell phone and pressed the speed dial.

A man's voice asked in Spanish, "How is your mission, dear?"

"On target, sir," she answered. "Three kills to date."

"I haven't read any news about a string of murders."

"Two of the subjects won't make the news. Drug heads that got in the way, but the links to the *gringo* are there. It will come back to him when the string reaches Boston. The evidence is there. All the dots will connect."

"The other?"

"Watch the news from Spokane."

"Where are you?"

"Somewhere in Montana, near the state called North Dakota."

"When will you act again?"

"It depends on my driver. He drives east in an unpredictable pattern." She detailed the detour to Butte.

"Why did you spare the old couple?" The voice asked, irritated.

"They were not in the victim profile you laid out, sir. Old Anglos without a connection to Winchester's world."

"They've seen your face, give me their address. I'll send someone to silence them."

"Please trust me and my judgment, sir. I know my business. They'll never hear of Wally Winchester's case unless it's reported on *Wheel of Fortune* or the Health Channel."

"It's not like you to contradict me, Manuelita."

"I'll do my job, sir. Please trust me."

Manuelita found Wally sound asleep when she returned to the tent, papers on his chest as he snored. She kissed him on the forehead, an act that surprised her as the tent went dark.

Chapter Nine

Spokane, Washington

To Detective Mike Kelly from the Spokane Police Department, the gruesome murder at the Hindu temple on Division Street made no sense. As he donned paper booties and rubber gloves to approach the body lying in a congealing blood pool, his first thought was hate crime. He remembered the local outcry a year ago when the Hindus moved into the grand structure that had served the Methodists for a hundred years. There had been some threats, two of which he had investigated and found baseless – just the redneck-bitching that was not uncommon this close to the Sand Pointe, Idaho crazies, quiet now but still spewing violent manifestos on the web.

Skinheads came to mind. He circled the body, opened up like a gutted salmon with internal organs spilling out of a ripped, bloody shirt.

The CSI tech called to him, "There's something in his hand, Mike." The tech opened rigored fingers to pull out a business card now crumpled. Kelly held the card by a corner and read: *I buy anything old, contact Wally Winchester, Camano Island, Washington.* "Bag it," he said and thanked the clue gods for sending down a gift.

He circled the carnage on the lookout for bloody footprints. Doc Martin boots, a favorite stomper for the white supremacist crew, had a distinctive pattern. He saw a smeared trail, leading to the grand front door. Close up, he looked for tread pattern but, instead, found circular swirls that suggested the killer had deliberately twisted his steps to obliterate the size and identifying pattern. A smart one, he concluded, not likely the local skinhead crowd that had been known to leave Doc Martin footprints as messages to minorities. And they seemed small.

The turbaned man he interviewed was distraught. His brother had been alone, the crying man said, when they found him.

"Had anyone threatened the dead man?" Kelly asked. "Or your church lately?"

"It's not a church," he was told. "A temple."

"Excuse me, the temple."

"Not more than the usual harassment, some letters, another sprayed swastika last week."

"Do you have the letters?"

"In the office. We have a boxful."

"Any unusual activity this morning?"

"There were people here, out front, all morning. We had a fundraising sidewalk sale."

"Did you see anyone enter the…temple?"

"Earlier, a white man went in with Singh and left. Singh was excited. Something about an answer to his prayers."

"Your brother was alive when the man left?"

"Singh was smiling. He talked about replacing the temple windows."

"Can you describe him?"

"White, forties, unkempt hair. I didn't pay attention."

"Could you pick him out of a line-up?"

"I doubt it. Spokane white people all look alike."

The other temple members who helped that day were no help, though two mentioned a fancy, blue sports car that got a lot of attention when it parked on the next block.

In his office, Kelly called 411 for the number of Wally Winchester of Camano Island, and then he dialed it. The voice message said, "I'll be gone for the next two weeks. Off to make my fortune. Leave a message."

He left a message, asking for a callback, not leaving his name as he recited his cell number.

Another case was new on his desk. Two Spokane men found dead in a campground over into Montana. He knew the names, both tweekers with long records of petty mayhem. He'd arrested one of them a few years back for suspicion of rape, but nothing stuck. He remembered bad teeth and an attitude.

"Good riddance," Kelly thought, glad that the deaths were Montana's problem.

After a cup of the usual shitty coffee, Kelly called the Island County Sheriff's Office to see what they had on Winchester.

Chapter Ten

Fargo, North Dakota

Over a bacon and cheese omelet in a Fargo, North Dakota café, Wally noticed Manuelita avoiding his eyes.

"Hey, babe," he said through half a mouthful of white bread toast. "Did I do anything to offend you last night? Did I snore? Sometimes I fart while I'm sound asleep, I'm told."

She looked up and made an attempt at a smile. "*No señor*. Maybe something I ate."

"I find that hard to believe. You don't eat meat. Your diet seems to be fruit cups or apples from roadside stands. You eat like a bird."

She shrugged and looked out into an early morning street with little traffic, the Cobra parked by the window. Wally went back to reading the local newspaper.

"Hey, check this out, Manuelita. There's an auction outside of town tomorrow. Listen to this." He read, "*Auction Offers Pioneer Relics.*"

Manuelita yawned. "Don't you have a car to deliver?"

"That's money in the bank, girl. It says the North State Asbestos mine is closing after one hundred ten years of operation. All the plant facilities, including machinery and office equipment dating back to the turn of the century, will be offered for public bidding. Hey, it's tomorrow! The preview is scheduled from noon to five this afternoon."

"Where will you carry these things, behind the seat?"

"I'll get them on the way back. All I need is my trusty credit card. I know you don't care. You can stay with the car while I check it out. OK?"

"I know my job."

Five minutes to twelve, Wally drove carefully over loose crushed rock that served as the parking lot to a series of wind-blasted tin structures at the edge of a vast, open pit. Wally silently wondered how many locals caught lung cancer in a hundred years of digging and processing.

A handful of pickup trucks were already in the lot. Manuelita settled down on a grassy patch within spitting distance of the Cobra and watched her *gringo* do a *cha cha* as he entered the main building.

The scene inside reminded Wally of an old western movie combined with the set of *Blade Runner.* Huge fifty-ton mills sat in a gritty, grey cavern. He saw a large, unkempt man with a magnet testing metals on the machines. He saw tables everywhere, massive iron-legged monsters with grimy, oil-soaked wood tops, the rage in New York City now as loft furniture. The lighting was sparse, with a windowed second roof that lit the working area in true turn-of-the-century thrift, for free.

Most of the bidders waited at the far end where a series of offices offered more portable artifacts of a bygone age. Wally got in line as a man with a clipboard opened the doors and announced, "Everything in the buildings will need to be removed on the day of the sale, except, of course, the larger machinery. Cash or certified checks will be the method of payment. No credit cards or personal checks." As a small crowd of previewers entered the rooms, Wally followed.

Inside the smaller rooms, Wally found himself in industrial design heaven.

The main office held three oak roll-tops in good condition, save half-an-inch of non-breathable dust. The desks were high-end, S-rolls, with raised panels. He didn't care. Roll-tops were dead right now, victims of a dot-com collectorate that had no interest in Victorian furnishings. The things that first aroused him were the old signs and advertising on the walls. He drooled over a Starrett Tool advertisement, framed in oak. It pictured the old manufactory in a bird's-eye view. Other framed signs touted the tools themselves with great graphics illustrating drills, hardware, and tools not seen in recent times except in museum collections. A green-domed banker's lamp sat on one of the roll-tops. Wally made a mental note to wash the dust off the shade if he got a chance to own it on the next day.

A wonderfully lettered sign over an interior door read:
NO ADMITTANCE INTO MACHINE SHOP WITHOUT PROTECTIVE EYEWARE,
painted into the shape of a pair of wood goggles. Another wall piece, one that Wally guessed to be World War II vintage, reminded workers to *Close blackout curtains when the alarm sounds*, an easy two hundred dollar item.

The machine shop itself was a Wally Winchester wet dream. The lighting consisted of green metal cones suspended from heavy rubber-coated industrial wire. Looking up, Wally saw the mirrors. "Frink reflectors," he said out loud. "Ye gads." He counted eighteen before he stopped. The milling machines themselves were fitted with adjustable task lights, three knuckles each, with old Benjamin sockets holding green reflector caps, the kind that Wally watched from the sidelines on eBay when the bids topped five hundred dollars on the first day. He checked himself from swooning, realizing that he'd have to buy a two-thousand-pound complex drill press in order to unbolt the cool lamp attached to the work surface.

His inventory shifted to the chairs, curved wooden backs and seats on an Eiffel Tower-shaped base that screamed, *New York City loft.*

Wally pondered the logistics of this sale and concluded that, even returning in a week in a van, he couldn't hope to carry half of the things he wanted back to Seattle. Then there were the sale conditions he'd just received, *items must be removed on the day of the sale*, and him with a sports car, a Mexican cutie, and an 1,800-mile trip ahead.

As he returned to the car, he made a mental note to find a cash machine in Fargo while he formulated a distasteful plan.

At a riverside campground north of town, Wally called a person he didn't like to offer him a chance to make a bunch of money.

"Winchester," a familiar voice said, "Why are you calling me? Are you out of funds again?"

"No, Piccard, money's not the problem. I hate to do this, but I'm calling to offer you a chance to get into a great score I just made."

Manuelita listened to Wally's side of the conversation, looked him in the eyes, and batted her eyelashes like a coquette. She grabbed her own crotch as if to say, "What a pussy you are."

Wally shook his head and mouthed the words, "Trust me, I know what I'm doing."

She shrugged and walked down to the river.

"Here's the story, Piccard," Wally continued. "There's an auction tomorrow in the town I'm in tonight. A shit-load of industrial design, tables, signs, chairs, and lots of lights. I've seen the people at the preview and can tell you all this great stuff is going to be sold for a song."

He listened and answered, "No, I won't tell you where until we come to an agreement."

Piccard said, "If I wait long enough, the little guys in the business, like you, always end up at the door to my shop with their tail in the air and a sheepish look on their face. Are you acknowledging that, Winchester? Do you expect a tip if I like what you found for me?"

"Fuck no, you arrogant bastard. I could buy all of this and make a fortune, but I'm on my way to Boston and I'm traveling light. Plus there's a time constraint. They want it gone the day of the sale, tomorrow. If you or I don't buy this shit, it'll end up in some farmer's barn where it will be found someday on that picker TV show."

"What do you want from me, small change?"

"You can have all of this lot, and it's going to sell for nothing," Wally said. "For that, you owe me a favor someday. I want the lights. Promise me you'll not bid on the lighting and agree to truck them back to Seattle when you pack the eighteen-wheeler. I'll pick them up later."

Piccard took the hook. "So, if I agree not to bid against you on some lighting, you'll tell me what the fuck you're talking about."

"Exactly."

"OK. I agree."

"The auction is in Fargo, North Dakota," Wally told him. "You should fly out here early tomorrow morning with a pocketful of cash. They want cash. And you better have some guys and a rented truck. You won't find this one on the internet. Buy what you want. I'll stay out of your play; you stay out of mine."

"You better not be jerking me around, Winchester."

"Trust me Piccard," Wally ended. "I have bigger fish to fry."

Wally added another log to the riverside fire pit. Manuelita walked back to the campsite, coming out of darkness from the direction of the river, wearing a towel. She returned his shampoo and soap. "Thank you," she said, and sat on the ground beside him.

"What do you think of this adventure?" Wally asked. He kept his eyes on the fire, aware of her draped nakedness, trying to be a gentleman.

"You are an interesting man, Señor Wally," she said. "You like to play like a little child."

"Yeah," he said. "I call myself lucky."

"Have you ever had a job?"

"I have a job, a good one, I think, though it seems difficult in this line of work to keep a woman."

"I mean a real job. Go to work. Get a paycheck. Watch TV. A North American job."

"Sure, I've had many of those. It was difficult for me to stay in one place for eight hours a day with a boss looking over my shoulder. How about you? What did you do for work in Mexico City?"

Manuelita adjusted the towel, Wally trying his best not to notice, but failing. His eyes caught the flicker of firelight off small, high breasts. She answered, "I have done many things, driven trucks, cleaned people's houses, sold phone cards on the street, some other things I would rather not mention. Life in Mexico City is a gamble."

"So you're just like me."

She shuddered.

"Do you have family back in Mexico, that is, besides your sister?"

"I have cousins in Chiapas, in the south. That's where I was born."

"Parents still live there?"

"Dead. My father was killed by the government during the unrest."

"Was he a rebel?"

She nodded with a small smile and said, "*Si.* Were you an American when Bush was the leader?"

"Of course," Wally answered.

"How did you like it?"

"I couldn't believe we voted him back a second time," Wally said.

"Then you understand my father."

"Your mom?" Wally asked.

"Raped by the same crew of soldiers. My sisters, too."

"Your sisters. Even the one in New Hampshire, the one having a baby?"

Manuelita stared into the fire and pinched a frown into a neutral mask. She said, "She got over it. We all do."

"Wow," Wally said, "That's a shitty hand of cards you drew as a child. Sorry."

"Look at me," Manuelita said. She held the towel tightly around her body. "Up here," she said with attitude. "My face."

Wally looked into dark eyes that burned into his. "I'm here in North America," she said, "riding around in a fancy car, my tummy full, and a kind man for company. My life is more than OK."

Wally watched her attempt a smile that didn't work. She began to readjust the towel but thought better of it and withdrew to the shadows to get dressed.

"Tell me about your younger days, señor," came her voice from the darkness. "Did you eat peanut butter and jelly on white bread?"

"Sometimes."

"Did you get your first bicycle when you were five years old?"

"Four, actually." Wally watched the intriguing woman walk, fully dressed, back into the firelight. "But I was five when I took off the training wheels."

"I got my first bicycle when I was nine. I stole it," she said. "Sold it a week later for food."

Wally walked over to the Cobra, pulled a paper bag from behind his seat, and returned with a flat pint bottle "You like Scotch?" he asked.

"Is that whiskey?"

"Yes, it's a single malt. Out of a little distillery in the…"

"Sure," she said. Wally handed her the bottle, uncorked. She took a pull and coughed.

"You seem pretty smart," Wally said after his sip. "How much schooling do you have?"

"Schooling? If that means sitting at a desk in a classroom and the teacher writes on the blackboard, the answer is none. In Mexico City, when you were beaten, robbed, or worse, we called that another degree from the University of the Streets. I did take a class…about computers…a school for street rats like myself."

"I saw some schools for street kids down in Manaus and in Brazilia," Wally said. "Called themselves *Future Clubs*, dodgy places, run by a whack job who believed he was Hitler's son, if you can believe that."

"Sounds terrible." Manuelita edged closer, stretched and yawned, her chest pressing against the thin fabric of her shirt. "Tell me about your schooling. You have many words, and you know the value of everything. It's like you have a whole library in your head."

"I have a college degree, I admit, Manuelita, but most of what I know I learned the way you did. The college of hard knocks."

"Are you married, Señor Wally?"

"I spent a lot of years with a woman I loved. I miss her. How about you?"

She answered. "I don't expect a little yard and children and a dog in my life. My feet gather no moss."

"That's a bleak outlook, Manuelita," Wally said.

"I love my life, Señor Wally. It is a journey of surprises, just like yours."

Her leg made contact with Wally's as she yawned and looked at the little pup tent with the blue Cobra behind it.

With the 10:00 a.m. auction looming, Wally parked the sports car on a patch of grass where the road met the crushed-stone parking lot.

"Should be a couple hours, Manuelita." Wally tossed the words over his shoulder as he sprinted like a school kid for his appointment with a roomful of mirrored industrial lampshades. Manuelita kept a neutral face and spread a blanket on the dewy grass to wait.

Inside, Wally recognized a few of the old machinists he'd seen at the preview, plus a lot of new faces, among them, Piccard. His Seattle rival was bent over the top of a beefy steel-topped workbench, the kind that Wally saw on East Coast vintage industrial design websites for eight to twelve hundred. Without Wally's competition, he knew Piccard would only have to outbid weekend hobbyists who wanted another table for their garage woodshop.

Piccard looked up and said, "This is what you made me fly fifteen hundred miles for, Winchester? When are you going to learn good stuff from great stuff? This boondoggle is a complete waste of my time."

"But since you're here, you're going to stick around and bid on all these mediocre pieces of crap, right?"

"I've rented a truck and hired two drunks from Fargo already, listening to your advice, Winchester. Thanks to you, I'm already out four hundred bucks plus airfare. Might as well get my money's worth. But if you think I owe you a favor for the tip, you're dreaming."

"Just stay away from the lights. That was the deal."

"They're the only things out here in this God-forsaken desert that're worth anything."

"Does that mean you're not bidding on the signs and the Toledo Metal Furniture adjustable chairs?"

"Got to fill the truck up with something. Excuse me. You're in my light."

Wally left the room as Piccard scuttled over to another metal table.

The sun warmed the grass next to the Cobra. Manuelita was pleased to find she didn't mind the guard duty today. Something about last evening had put a human face on her assignment that both pleased and troubled her assassin's brain. There'd be no murder today, not in a roomful of bib-overalled, fat, retired *gringos*, nothing that would point the finger at her charge, the hapless dreamer. Poor guy, she mused. He had no clue about the airtight box she formed around him, an insect stuck to the spider web – soon to be entombed in a cocoon of silk. It bothered her that she liked him.

A beat-up pickup rumbled down the street, two boys in front, two in the bed, drinking beer. She looked up to see a can arching through the air as they passed, a missile with Wally's car at the end of its trajectory.

On her feet in a heartbeat, she caught it still full, a kilo of damage in flight. Raucous laughter and catcalls echoed down the road. One finger in the air, she watched their truck get small and disappear over a far-off rise. She invited the young assholes back to play and sent the thought into the noonday North Dakota air.

Eight cast-iron monsters were first in the sale and surprised Wally when they realized six- to eight-thousand dollars each. He figured it was cheap for thirty tons of scrap iron.

Piccard was busy, snagging three tables and all the chairs for about twenty bucks apiece. Wally kept his head down and let his competitor score each item on a single bid.

Worthless, my ass.

The office bidding was more brisk, the cool, framed ephemera purchased by Piccard for a couple hundred each. Even in North Dakota, Wally mused, old boys like their vintage tools - on a bench or in a frame.

He sat back when the roll-tops sold for seven hundred each to local dealers, half the price of the 1980's when the world still cared about these things.

In the machine shop, the auctioneer told the crowd he was going to sell all the lighting in an auction he called *choice* – highest bidder wins the choice of the one, or the ones, he wants. Then the lot goes up again for the next round of bids, usually, Wally knew, for a little less, until everything was gone. He looked over at Piccard and fingered the roll of hundred dollar bills he'd withdrawn from the Wells Fargo bank that morning.

Manuelita smiled when the distant rumble morphed into the old pickup truck with the assholes inside. She surveyed her position: a grove of trees and dense underbrush to the north, the parking lot, full of auction bidders' vehicles to the west, and the four-lane black top beside her. She liked her playing field just fine.

Ten yards across the grassy knoll, the truck skidded to a stop at the edge of the road. Manuelita watched as two thugs leaped from the bed with baseball bats while the driver and the passenger played the radio at full blast, laughing.

"Hey, taco meat," the tall, pimple-faced farm boy yelled. "Where'd you steal that fancy ride?"

"Please drive away, boys," she said in a voice designed to show fear. Her internal voice told the bullies it's not wise to bring a baseball bat to a knife fight. She took a hesitant step toward the wooded area and worked on a strategy to draw the driver out.

"We have twenty old tin hanging reflectors that have mirrors inside. Darnedest things I've ever seen," the auctioneer announced in a friendly country twang. "Put 'em over your pool table. Use 'em in your woodshop. Ought to be worth thirty or forty bucks apiece. Remember, you're bidding for one, but the winner has the choice of more for that price. Get the perfect ones. Leave the rest. What am I bid? Do I have thirty dollars?"

Nothing. Wally, who planned to sell them for $250 each on eBay, held back.

"Do I have twenty? Remember, this is *choice.*"

Silence.

"Ten dollars, I have."

Wally looked at Piccard. His bidding number was folded in his shirt pocket.

"Fifteen," Wally said. He looked at the thirty faces in the spacious room, saw a gaggle of locals, a dealer or two maybe, and wondered who would have a market for these tin whacker's fancies out there in Bumfuckville? Piccard wasn't bidding, as promised.

He saw a bidding card rise when the auctioneer asked for twenty. The other bidder, a bearded man wearing a shirt too nice for a machine shop auction, looked directly at the auctioneer, then up at the reflectors above his head. Wally raised his number, while watching his competitor's eyes, when the auctioneer asked for thirty. They were downcast. He wasn't looking to Piccard, the bastard, Wally thought. What's his angle, eBay?

"Thirty, I have," the auctioneer said. "Do I hear forty? That's for each one, folks," he added. "Not the lot."

The competitor raised his number.

"Damn it," Wally said out loud. Twenty reflectors at forty bucks each was eight hundred dollars. His pocket held only a little more in cash.

"Fifty," Wally shouted. He'd been in many auctions where a bold move like that caved the competition.

"Sixty," the stranger shouted back.

The auctioneer said into the mike, "Well, I guess I'm not needed here." The crowd laughed nervously. The auctioneer continued, "Why don't you two boys fight it out? If you need an auctioneer, I'll come back in to tell you who won."

"Seventy-five," Wally shouted. He risked a glance at Piccard, saw that he was not paying attention, maybe checking something on his cell at his waist. Wally looked back to the bidder, also looking down.

"One hundred each," the guy declared.

The bastard, Piccard, Wally screamed internally. The asshole was texting. So was the son-of-a-bitch across the room.

A dilemma loomed as Wally pondered the betrayal. He saw his choices clearly: Bid the bastard up and stick the shades up Piccard's ass so even he, the back-stabbing bastard, couldn't make a dime; or jump off now while there was still some profit left in the lamps and then show up at Piccard's shop and bitche the motherfucker out for using a shill and a lie.

"Do I have one hundred twenty-five?" The auctioneer jumped back in as Wally bit his lip and kept mum. "The bid is one-hundred dollars for the choice of shades or all twenty. That's two thousand dollars if you want them all. You sure you understand that, sir?"

The stranger nodded and looked at Wally in a taunt.

"Five hundred dollars," Wally shouted, and took four long strides into the crowd to stand in front of Piccard, who put his cell phone in his pocket as Winchester looked him in the eyes, his back to the action.

"Five hundred dollars? This is for the choice of *one* shade, sir," the auctioneer said to Wally's back as all five-foot-five inches of his nemesis looked up at him, outraged with beady crow eyes.

"Do I have any advance on the bid of five hundred dollars for the choice of one shade?"

Piccard stood, frozen by Wally's face-to-face, his hands at his side. Wally waited. "Go on, asshole," he whispered. "Tell him what to do."

Piccard glared, immobile.

Silence.

"All in, all done for five hundred dollars."

The auctioneer paused. "Sold to…" Wally held up a paper number while violating Piccard's personal space. "*Ninety-Seven.* Congratulations, sir. How many do you want?"

Wally refused to break eye contact with Piccard. "One," he said.

At his back he heard the auctioneer ask, "Which one do you choose?"

"I don't care." Wally spoke without looking at the man with the microphone behind him. "Choose one, and start the bidding again."

The voice of the auctioneer was clearly rattled. “All right,” he said, “Does the underbidder want any of the remaining nineteen shades for five hundred dollars each?”

“Start it again,” Wally, eyes still on Piccard, said over his shoulder.

“These shades seem to be better than anyone imagined,” the auctioneer’s voice said from the speakers in the room. “Let’s start them up again at one hundred dollars apiece, choice, like before.”

Wally dared Piccard to pull out his phone and text instructions to his shill. The man stood immobile, hatred and embarrassment in his eyes. The room was silent.

“Start them up at five dollars again,” Wally shouted behind him to the man with the microphone.

“Do we have a five-dollar bid for choice of the remaining nineteen, clearly valuable, tin reflector shades?” the auctioneer said, meekly.

Wally raised his card.

“Five dollars, we have. How about ten?”

Wally watched Piccard’s eyes and kept the bastard’s hands in the periphery of his sight.

Silence.

“Seven dollars and fifty cents? Any bidders?”

Silence.

“Sold. For five dollars, choice, to number…” Wally’s hand shot up with the card. “Ninety-seven. How many do you want?”

“All of them,” Wally said as he turned to smile at the guy with the beard scowling across the room.

“Do you want to inspect them, sir? There is some mirror damage in a few. They’re old, you know.”

“I want them all.” Wally walked from the room to pay the cashier five hundred dollars for the first one, and ninety-five dollars total for the other nineteen. As he left the room, he looked at Piccard and said, “Thanks for taking these home for me, bitch. I’ll pick them up in a couple of weeks. Pack them carefully. They’re worth a fortune.”

Manuelita seemed to be in a better mood when he rejoined her at the car.

“How did the auction go, Señor Wally?” she asked. “I gave out some of your business cards.” She pointed to the stack near the shifter.

“I appreciate your promotional efforts, girl. I kicked ass in there,” Wally said. “How did your day go out here, Manuelita?”

“The same,” she said. “Let’s hit the road and sell this bitch.”

She closed the passenger door gently, just as she’d been trained.

One foot stuck out of the bushes near the abandoned truck on the road beside them. Beside it was a card that read, *I buy anything old. Contact Wally Winchester, Camano Island, Washington.* Blood obscured the email address and phone number.

Chapter Eleven

Camano Island, Washington

During the six-hour drive from Spokane to Camano Island, Detective Mike Kelly pondered the murder in the Hindu temple. The autopsy had concluded the cause of death as exsanguination from a knife wound to the abdomen, followed by an upward, tearing thrust to the heart and lungs. According to the medical examiner, the weapon was a seven-inch knife with a serrated blade, similar to a Navy SEAL issue. A professional assassination, Kelly felt. He made a note to look into Winchester's military record.

The absence of a murder weapon didn't help Kelly's road trip to Camano Island. He carried no search warrant, just a Q&A agenda: interviews, and a walk-around in case Winchester wasn't home. If he *was* at home and allowed the detective inside, so much the better.

Peter Falk's *Columbo* voice on the dashboard GPS told Kelly to cross the bridge to the island on SR 532 and bear left on East Camano Drive, then drive ten miles to Winchester's address which he had found on the internet.

"Ah, I hope you don't mind my saying this, but you should take a right on Forest Street one-tenth of a mile ahead," the GPS voice said.

Five miles before his destination, Kelly spotted the Island County Sheriff's Office and turned into the parking lot to follow protocol.

The GPS wasn't pleased. Peter Falk's polite, understated voice told him, "Ah, I hope you don't mind my saying this, but I am recalculating. Take a U-turn and go right on East Camano Drive."

"Got to take a detour," Kelly said to the dashboard tracker.

"I don't know how to put this," the Garmin speaker said, "but if I were you I'd take a U-turn to East Camano Drive and turn right."

"Got to check in with the locals," Kelly talked back to the machine on his windshield. He walked into a bright office interior and introduced himself to the desk sergeant.

"Winchester," the trim young man said. Kelly took him as a recent veteran by his military bearing. "He's a character. Drives an older van. I see it on the road frequently on Saturday mornings – yard sale day. Why are you interested?"

"Just checking out a case," Kelly said as he displayed his badge. "Found his business card at a crime scene in Spokane, a murder."

"Murder, eh? Winchester? That would surprise me. Robbery, maybe. The guy likes old stuff. Doesn't seem to have a job, yet he lives in a nice waterfront cabin. Don't know how he makes a living, but that's not unusual down on the south end of the island. Lot of unemployed down there, living in their grandpas' cabins. Land was cheap out here in the 40's and 50's. Now it's waterfront property, Microsoft executives' second-homes, or third."

"Ever been down to Winchester's place?"

"Never had cause. Nailed him for a DUI last year, my collar. He claimed he was a designated driver, but he blew a .81. Got to admit, the passengers in his old van were a lot drunker than him."

"Half the population of Spokane drives around with two drinks in them," Kelly said. "What's over the limit out here?"

"This side of the Cascades, it's a blue state," the sergeant said. "Politically correct. MADD gets a vote."

"MADD?"

"Mothers Against Drunk Drivers," the sergeant said. "You boys in the Palouse don't know the Mothers?"

"I'm a homicide detective," Kelly said.

"You want directions to Winchester's cabin? I've followed his van to the driveway, waiting for him to cross the fog line, but never had cause to drive down and sniff his breath."

"I do," Kelly said. "Want to join me?"

"I'd love to see how that son-of-a-bitch makes a living. My shift here ends in five minutes."

Kelly let Peter Falk tell him directions to Winchester's driveway to the beach to amuse the local lawman. "There's a handful of creeps on the south end," the seargeant said, as Columbo's voice advised, *One more thing, turn right in one-tenth of a mile.* "Tweekers, a couple of meth kitchens waiting for probable cause, a handful of junkies, Christ, half of the people south of the state park probably smoke pot, but I wouldn't put Winchester into that group. He's a goofball, no doubt, but I'd be surprised if he was a murderer."

"A lot of murderers are surprised that they are murderers is what I've found," Kelly said. "All I got is a dead guy with Winchester's business card in a bloody hand."

A bumpy gravel drive toward the cliff edge opened to a cabin with outbuildings and a parked van.

"Got a warrant?" the local asked.

"Just want to ask some questions at this point," Kelly said. He felt the hood of the van and found it cold.

"Let me knock on the door," the sergeant said. "He'll recognize me."

Kelly stood beside him and unbuttoned the strap on his holster. No one answered. He put his face against the kitchen window, saw a dark interior, one green lamp burning in a hallway, and a pile of mail on the other side of the door.

Kelly turned the doorknob. It moved.

"We have no business inside," the local said. "You find anything, you can't use it."

"I know." Kelly opened the door and sniffed. "Do you smell marijuana?"

"Honestly, no, unless it's really important we get in. Is there something about the case you haven't told me?"

"Actually, no," Kelly said, closing the door. "It's not like I'm chasing a serial killer. I wonder what the meter reader sees." He strolled on the side of the cabin with its two living room windows. He saw a couple of oak recliners, reminding him of some family heirlooms. The sight of leaded glass lamps and bookcases filled with pottery caused him to ask, "All these antiques and the guy doesn't lock his door? His vehicle's here, there's some lights on. Do you think he might be inside injured, maybe a heart attack? I'm concerned for his safety."

"No," the sergeant said.

"Can you provide a list of his friends that I can interview while I'm six hours from home?"

"I'd try the antique shop in Stanwood. I see his van there a lot. And try a gal named Rae Roberts. I think that's the name of Winchester's ex."

Rae Roberts was in the phone book. Kelly called. The woman who answered told him she hadn't shared a word with Wally Winchester in eight months and that was fine with her.

The antique store was more helpful. A friendly bear in a plaid shirt and suspenders told him that Winchester was on a road trip to New England. Driving a fancy racing car, he told Kelly, a Shelby. Driving it to its new owner in Boston. Should be gone for about three weeks.

Kelly remembered the Spokane witness who reported a fancy sports car at the scene and made a note of it in Wally's jacket. Heading east, he pondered, thinking about the two Spokane tweekers found dead in a Montana campground.

As he filled up with gas for the long drive home, he called Missoula, Montana police, and got hold of the detective who caught the case. He heard the gruesome details without tears, knowing the creeps, but pulled over to the side of I-5 when the detail of a business card, found on the scene, was added, almost as an afterthought. The name on the card was *Wally Winchester.*

Chapter Twelve

Northern Minnesota

When Wally heard the sound of the snake rattle, he turned to warn Manuelita. It was too late. He watched the viper's head whip forward and clamp onto her calf muscle. She shook her leg to dislodge the six-foot attacker but the snake held on till Wally kicked it free and pulled her from the retreating reptile.

"I feel a great numbness below my knee," Manuelita reported.

"Does it hurt?" Wally asked.

"I would rather that it did," she answered. An attempt at walking failed. Wally referred to his data bank of Animal Planet TV shows and decided not to move her – keep the poison localized.

"Got your knife on you, hon?" he asked. She pulled the sheath from her pack and released the wicked blade. Wally knelt by her foot and said, "This is going to hurt. Do you want some whiskey?"

"Yes," she answered.

"Gotta hurry," he said and sprinted to the bottle of Scotch behind the seat.

After two pulls from Wally's hidden flask, Manuelita didn't flinch as Wally cut X's into her flesh at the two puncture points. He flooded the area with *Glenfidich* and put his lips to the wound.

He tasted aged peat and blood as he formed a vortex with his cheeks, negative pressure to coax the poison out.

It felt like an exercise. Wally focused. He remembered mother's milk. He closed his eyes and sucked with the intention to pull liquid into his mouth.

Manuelita shuddered. Wally put all of his energy on pulling the nectar into his mouth.

A bitter metallic taste overwhelmed his taste buds. Blood metal, but odd. He spit it out and went for more. Wally's lips felt numb as he spit a mouthful of blood and venom and Scotland's finest onto the grass. "We have to get you to the car, Manuelita," he said.

She stood up on wobbly feet. Wally strapped her in.

He reached under the seat and pulled out the Garmin, found the plug-in, and sought a hospital.

A friendly British female told Wally that the nearest hospital was twenty miles away. He turned right onto Route 30, on the instructions of a woman stuck on his windshield with a suction cup.

She scolded him as he did ninety on deserted stretches as city lights glowed on the horizon.

The GPS screen showed 1.5 miles and then a left. Traffic stalled.

I'm out here in the badlands, Wally thought. It's six o'clock at night and I'm caught in a traffic jam. He pulled the GPS from its mount and eventually found an alternate route button.

The left turn into steady traffic was unnerving to the driver of a hand-rubbed, eighty-coat paint job. The woman on the dash reminded him to take a left. The traffic said, no way.

He gunned a gap like an easterner would, leaving rubber at the turn when he made the narrow lane.

He gained an alley that ran behind a city block of closed or badly advertised storefronts. Wally negotiated dumpsters as he made his way forward, finally coming to a blockage.

He exited the car and pushed at one of the dumpsters. Despite its size, it moved easily. Wally shoved it to the side and saw a group of farm boys smiling.

This can't be happening, Wally thought. This is the United States of America.

"This is a toll road," a young, long-boned youngster said. He held a tire iron.

Jesus Christ, Wally said to himself, is this Minnesota, or am I in *Tron?*

"The GPS says this is a road, sonny," he shouted. He mustered all the bravado he had. "Move these containers out of my way."

"Make me," the taller one said. "The toll is one hundred dollars, cash."

"Let me deal with them, señor." A voice behind Wally startled him.

Manuelita looked like death. She limped as she stepped forward, the SEAL knife in her hand. Her tan face was ashen. Wally went to her side, in case she fell.

"Open this passage," she said to the farm boys on heroin. "Or I'll kill you. One at a time."

Wally maintained his best deranged-killer face, holding eye contact with the hooligans as he reached for Manuelita's hand. "Give me the knife, Manuelita," he said. "Get back to your seat. You shouldn't be moving." He felt the warm handle as she pressed it into his hand.

"I'm going to kill the little guy first," Wally announced over his shoulder. He lunged and released a deep-throated scream that scattered the youthful thugs who turned and fled. Wally cursed as black dumpster slime coated his fingers. He pulled three containers to the side. Rough bricks on the backside of a darkened clothing store served as Wally's washcloth as he climbed into the Shelby and gripped the steering wheel with reddened palms.

Manuelita was unconscious when Wally parked the Cobra by the ambulance entrance to the emergency room. He ran inside and shouted, "I've got a snakebite victim in the car. She's out cold."

Two attendants pushed a gurney out the automatic doors. They returned with a still form under a blanket and came to a halt in the corridor, their path blocked by an imposing woman wearing nurse's garb. She looked down at a clipboard in front of her ample bosom, and then at Wally, who looked past her at the waiting treatment rooms.

"There's an intake procedure, buster. Is this girl one of your employees? I'll have to ask her to fill out this questionnaire and show me her green card."

"She got bit by a monster rattle snake!" Wally put his ear to Manuelita's chest. "She could be dying. Can't we do this later?"

"Does she have a green card? I'll have to see it."

"Sure she does," Wally manufactured the answer to open the roadblock. "I think she just stopped breathing. Can't you give her a shot of some anti-venom medicine right here on the gurney?"

"Paperwork first. Why don't you go out and find her purse?" She looked down at the Latina face. "Or her paper bag or whatever she carries documents in."

"Why don't you get your head out of your ass and save this woman's life. Isn't that what you do here?"

"What's your relationship with this Mexican? As an employer you're required to…"

"She's my wife."

"What do you take me for? A fool?"

Wally said, "I'd like to revisit that discussion, Nurse Ratchett, but right now my wife's in danger. Oh, and by the way, I have health insurance – *we* do, Manny and me."

"I'll need to see your identification card."

Wally fished out his wallet and extracted his health insurance card. He stuck it in the woman's face and pushed the gurney into her middle until she gave way.

Manuelita woke up in a hospital bed with an IV drip taped to her arm. She saw the *gringo* sitting beside her.

"Welcome back," he said. "You had me worried."

"What is this place?" She attempted to lift her head but gave up.

A hospital, run by the Wicked Witch of the West." Wally leaned close and whispered, "If anyone asks, remember to tell them you are my wife."

"¿Por qúe?"

"Do you have a green card?"

"What is a green card?"

"Never mind. Pretend you and I are married. If you sign your name on any forms, write *Manuelita Winchester*.

"Twice now I have a husband," she said weakly, smiling. "You saved my life three times today it seems, señor, from the snake poison, the gang, and this nurse. *Gracias."*

"De nada."

Chapter Thirteen

Eau Claire, Wisconsin

“We have to buy a gun,” Manuelita announced in Wisconsin as they approached multiple exits for Eau Claire. Wally chose the first off-ramp and cruised from outlying farmland into a zone of tired roadside businesses at the edge of the downtown core.

A pistol-shaped neon sign read, “Guns and Ammo” in red tubing. Wally turned into the parking lot, but stayed in the car. “We gotta talk,” he said. “Why is it that you think we need a gun?”

“We are headed for big cities. This car is a magnet. You disappear into shops or auctions and leave me in charge of a half million dollar toy, left in the street. Many people, both good and creepy, are drawn to the car. It’s my job to keep them away. The streets ahead are meaner than in North Dakota or Minnesota.

“I don’t mean to put you in danger when you watch the car. I’m sorry.”

“I don’t mind harm’s way if it’s a fair fight. We need a firearm, Señor Wally. Only you can purchase it. You, a citizen. It will save your car.”

“What’s one of these guns going to cost, Manuelita?”

“Two hundred to five hundred,” she said.

“I won’t know what to buy. Will you come in with me, help me choose?”

“Of course,” she said as she opened the door, “I’m your wife. I must have a vote.”

Wally was no stranger to a roomful of objects, but the selection of guns was daunting. A large, mustachioed man in a cowboy hat welcomed them.

"I need a weapon for self-defense," Wally announced. Manuelita made a face.

"Something for the home, a holster, for the car? Lots of choices here," Cowboy Hat asked as he eyed Manuelita with an ill-conceived frown.

"I like this one, honey," she said, standing in front of a glass showcase. "Can I see that one, sir?" She aimed the question at the cowboy. "The Glock 17."

He pulled the weapon out and handed it over. His mouth twitched as he placed it in the small brown hand.

"Do you stock 9-millimeter Lugar cartridges for this gun?"

"Of course."

"How much is the price?"

"Five hundred sixty."

"Do you have a used model for sale for less money?"

The owner looked at Wally, said, "Who's buying this gun? You, or the chiquita? You, I'd sell it to. Her, no."

Wally put his head close to the cowboy hat.

"Look, buddy," he said. "We're married. She treats me right. Guns are her hobby. Let her choose. I got a license."

"A permit to carry?"

"No, a driver's license. I figure I have to have ID and fill out a form."

"There's a 24-hour waiting period for new customers, sir. The Feds have to run your numbers. It's the law."

"Long-shot question," Wally interjected. "Are there any gun shows nearby this weekend?"

"Funny you should ask." The cowboy desk clerk pulled a flyer from a stack on the counter. "There's a knife and gun show that started this morning. Out at the Holiday Inn by the interstate." As he ushered the couple out of his store, the cowboy said to Wally, "Good luck with that one."

Wally whispered back, "She makes a great taco."

As they wandered past tables of vendors peddling weapons of all types, Manuelita spotted the Glock 17 she wanted on a table with five other guns, all more important.

She picked up an HK P7M8 pistol, admired the thumb-style mag release and looked at the price: $1,400. She put it down sadly.

A polished nickel Desert Eagle 50 was out of Wally's range. She looked at the price, $1,550, and wished she was rich. She picked up the Glock. It felt familiar. She ejected the clip. Smelled the interior and decided it had been well cared for.

"How much is this one?" Manuelita asked. She grabbed Wally's hand and brought him into the conversation, *him*, the buyer.

"Got that as part of a trade yesterday. It's a nice one. How about two fifty, cash?"

"Oh, buy it for me, honey," she said to the man on her arm.

"How about one fifty?" Wally said back.

"One seventy-five," the dealer said to sell a gun he didn't want to own. "I'll throw in some ammo."

"OK," Wally said. He peeled off a handful of twenties. Took a five back. Where's the paperwork?" he asked.

"Give me your name and address and I'll take care of the rest. See you later," the dealer said. "You need a receipt?"

"No."

"Well, there you go. Have a wonderful day."

Wally walked toward the exit to the parking lot, holding a paper bag with a gun inside. Manuelita walked, head down, as she mentally fed bullets into the empty clips and followed her husband to the car. That's when he gave her the wedding ring.

"I got a pair of them at a jewelry booth at the gun show, the simplest rings they sold. One for me and a smaller one for you."

Manuelita's head clouded in a warm rush of blood. She refocused on Wally's hand, offering a ring of gold.

"Try it on," Wally said. "Third finger, left hand."

It fit. The feeling of warmth remained.

She looked at the ring's mate on the *gringo*'s finger. A swell in the heart was the last thing she expected.

"What does this mean, these rings?"

"They solve the green card question till I get you to New Hampshire, for one thing. As my wife, a lot of bigoted middle Americans we'll run into on this trip will have to accept you as their equal. Is it wrong to want that?"

"Thank you for thinking about my feelings, Señor Wally," she said as she fingered the gold band. "No. You are right on target. I enjoy bending the mind of a bigot."

"I'm just glad it fits."

"So, Señor Wally, the rings don't mean we're married. That's not what you're asking. Me to be your wife for real?"

"Heavens, no, Manuelita. Why would you want to marry a crazy old picker like me? The rings are a prop."

She touched his ring and felt the broad gold band.

"Just out of curiosity, did you think I was asking you to marry me when I gave you the ring?" Wally asked.

"I wasn't sure. I can tell you that my heart raced."

"What would your answer have been if I had asked you to marry me with these rings?" His fingers played with hers in the dark cockpit of the Cobra.

"Ask me that question when we get to Boston," Manuelita said. She put her hand out and found his face, pulled him to her lips, felt his softness and didn't want it to end.

Chapter Fourteen

Spokane, Washington

Spokane Homicide Detective Mike Kelly had a bug up his ass. On a computer screen, he looked at a Google map of the most likely route from Seattle to Boston. He was cross-checking the cities on the map with recent murders.

He found a connection in Fargo, North Dakota. Four youths killed near an old asbestos plant.

He clicked on the story. "Four victims of a knife attack were found on the outskirts of the old asbestos plant north of Fargo, North Dakota. Details follow."

He dialed the Fargo Police Department. Got an answering machine. Pressed zero. Got a tired voice. "Can you put me through to the detective on the asbestos factory murders?" he asked.

"You want Zingarelli," the desk woman said. "Hold on." The phone filled with the worst elevator music Kelly had ever heard. He was fiddling with the volume settings when a voice came up. "Yo," it said.

"I'm Mike Kelly, Spokane Homicide. Who have I got?"

"Frenchy Zingarelli. Call me Frenchy. They all do. You got something for my case?"

"Maybe," Kelly said. "I'm working on a Spokane homicide. The information I have on the suspect suggests he's traveling across the country in a sports car. He's connected with a double homicide in Montana. I'm Googling my way down I-90 and I-94, looking for more."

"What's this feller's name?"

"The guy I'm interested in is Wally Winchester."

"Why, that's right here on this business card with blood on it."

"Wally's card?"

"Seems he was looking for old things. Hard to read in this condition."

"Tell me the details of the deaths," Kelly said.

Chapter Fifteen

Eau Claire, Wisconsin

When the Cobra passed an upholstery shop on the strip of small businesses east of Eau Claire, Wally turned the wheel hard and pulled up to the front door. Manuelita said nothing.

Inside, the smell of leather and glue and furniture polish reminded him of his Camano home. A bent shape of a man, wearing yellow tape like a necktie, looked up from a fabric cut.

"Who buys Stickley furniture around here?" Wally said as a greeting.

"You don't want to know," the upholsterer said and returned to his work.

"There's no mission oak collector in the world I don't want to know," Wally said to his back.

The deeply-lined face looked up. "There's a big time Stickley collector east of here, thirty miles. I do his cushions. He's a private man with a capital P."

"Can I call him from here?"

"Hell, no."

"If you give me his phone number," Wally said, "I could just call him, tell him I'm a fellow collector, and I happen to be in town. You're out of it, and you're a hero."

"Being a hero and two dollars gets you a cup of coffee."

"If you have a favorite charity," Wally said, hand in his pocket, "I have a fifty-dollar donation." He pulled a fifty off the top and held it out.

The old craftsman looked up from his work, placed the fifty in his pocket, and wrote a number on a scrap of brown paper.

"You didn't get this from me," he said.

The man who answered the phone had a loud voice. Wally dialed the volume down. The voice repeated, "Who are you, and how did you get this number?"

Wally said, "I'm here in Eau Claire, and I'm a Stickley collector. I thought we could get together. See if we had anything the other guy wants."

"I don't sell my collection. Is that clear enough for you?"

Wally had played this chess game before. He knew he had to sacrifice the queen. He answered, "I have a set of eight Thornden chairs, original finish with the old rush seats. Two arm chairs with the big through-tenons."

"You're telling me you have them for sale? Do you have them with you?"

"No," Wally said, "I'm driving east in a sports car, a Shelby Cobra. The Thornden chairs are back in Puget Sound. They've never been for sale until this phone call. Are you a serious collector?"

"You have no idea, young man," the voice said. "How much are you asking for your chairs?"

Wally said, "I'd like to tell you face-to-face."

"All right," the voice said, "You've intrigued me sufficiently to invite you and your Shelby to my farm. Where are you now?"

"In the center of town, by City Hall," Wally lied. "I can leave right now if you like."

Wally scribbled directions on a pad of paper Manuelita provided and started the car. The instant power that rumbled under his feet was a shock of delight, again, just like all the other times. He eased the little car into the street and headed for the interstate.

Manuelita said nothing. Wally consulted his notes and took the next exit, headed east with the sunset at his back.

The fence said *Private Property, Keep Out*. Wally pushed it aside, as the collector had instructed, and drove inside. The gate fell back into place behind him.

The high center of the country path down to the valley made scraping sounds on the undercarriage that caused Wally to wince on each telegraphed contact. He slowed to a crawl. The road flattened to a clearing where a gatehouse barred the way.

At the barrier, Wally idled as a camo-clad soldier, carrying an automatic weapon, walked up to his open window.

Wally looked again at his instructions, then said, “Condition Orange.”

The boy dressed up like a soldier looked at Manuelita in the passenger seat. He said, “They’re letting this beaner in?”

“She’s my wife,” Wally said. He created the maddest face he could. “You got a problem with that?”

“No, sir,” the boy in the camo suit said. He opened the gate. Wally drove through it, stone-faced.

The road turned into asphalt and opened to a spectacular valley view and a monster log house.

Wally pulled in by the front door under a steep snow roof. “Stay put till I open the door for you, Manuelita,” he said. “We’re going to make a dignified entrance.”

He inspected the front end for road damage, found none, not counting a hundred dead bugs. He opened Manuelita’s door, helped her out, and walked her to the front door.

Automatic weapons fire echoed up the glen. It continued for half a minute and stopped.

Manuelita recognized the bark of Kalashnikovs.

A massive bog oak door that looked like it came from a castle opened up to a shaven-head tough, wearing a tan shirt, crisp chinos, shiny shoes, and a holster.

"Gotta pat you down," he said to Wally, ignoring Manuelita.

"Suit yourself," Wally said. He raised his arms and took a wide stance, felt rough hands on his ankles, inside thighs, lower back and armpits.

"You can enter," the point man said. "The Mexican girl waits outside."

"She's my wife. She goes where I go."

"No, sir. Not in here."

Wally said, "I'm leaving now. I'll call your boss from the road and tell him the deal for the set of chairs is off."

Wally was opening the door of the Cobra for Manuelita when a booming voice said; "You're not getting out of that Thornden chair deal that easy. Come on back in. Of course, you can bring your wife. Don't mind Carl. He does a good job of keeping the property secure."

A big hand reached toward Wally. He shook it, looking into cold eyes on a chiseled face that suggested ex-marine.

"Conroy Lincoln."

"Wally Winchester. This is Manuelita, my wife."

"Carl," the big man barked. "Come out here and keep an eye on this fine race car while I entertain these people inside."

The skinhead frowned and obeyed. A glare at Manuelita followed her into the spacious home. "Keep your fingerprints off the finish. It's an expensive car," Wally warned, smiling a fuck-you grin.

The entry hall held a matched pair of Gustav Stickley hall seats. Wally noted butterfly tenon joinery and gave each a small salute. "Get those at that Rangle estate sale in the 90's?" Wally asked.

"That would be telling," his host beamed. "Needed something for the mud room."

Manuelita looked down at a colorful tile floor and guessed that mud never touched these stones. Wally looked up at a series of leaded glass boxes, hung from the ceiling. He said, "Purcell and Elmslie."

"Good, son. You know your prairie school."

Another burst of automatic weapons fire echoed outside.

"Don't mind the boys," Lincoln said. "They just got a new set of Obama targets. Got the entire cabinet. They like the secretary of state pop-up. We're almost out of her silhouettes already."

Wally kept his mouth shut, his attention on a giant American flag that covered a huge wall in the living room. "Nice flag," he said.

"Bought that son-of-a-bitch from that good American down in Georgia at a car dealership. The commie bastards down there made him take it down. Said it was too big. Can you imagine that? How can the symbol of the most powerful nation in the world be too big?"

"Sounds un-American to me."

"Damn right. The country's going to the dogs. Where's J. Edgar Hoover when you need him?"

"Probably in the closet," Wally risked.

"What's that?"

'I love the big Stickley rugs," Wally said. "I see you like the Arts and Crafts."

"Old Stickley got it right. He built his pieces to last with no inferior woods. He had the vision to keep things simple, all the bare bones exposed. Like this nation used to be before the Kennedys got a hold of it."

"What's your favorite object?"

"That's easy. Look over there in the corner."

Wally did. He saw the huge ball of beaten copper that Frank Lloyd Wright called an urn. "Holy shit," he said. "I've never seen one in person. Good for you."

"Come over and touch it," Lincoln said.

Wally stood beside a Gus Stickley Morris chair and put his hand on a repoussé globe that looked like it was not from this planet, an artifact from the movie, *Alien.*

"It's warm."

"It's always warm. No one can figure it out. A buddy says it's probably radioactive."

Manuelita wandered in the vast hall with a view of the valley. She looked for exits, counted three doors to the outside and a corridor leading into the interior of the house. At the front door, she looked out the sidelight to see the young soldier staring back. She gave him the finger and watched his eyes widen in anger.

"Before we talk about my Thornden chairs," Wally said. "Do you have anything for sale?"

"I told you I don't sell my goods. I'm a collector."

"Don't you have a barn full of pieces you're not using?"

"Of course I do, but that doesn't mean I'm selling them."

"Where are you placing the Thornden chairs if I decide to sell them?"

"Around a director's table. In the formal dining room." He pointed into the darkened hallway.

"What's around the table now?" Wally asked.

"V-backs, early models with the rush seats. I hear you. All right, Winchester, let's take a stroll down to the bunkhouse."

"My wife isn't that interested. Can she hang out on one of your settees till we get back? We've been camping out with the car, roughing it…"

"Sure," Lincoln said. He walked Wally to the big front door, shouted to his boy, "Go inside and make the young lady a cup of coffee or tea or cocoa."

"Me? Make her coffee?"

"It's an order, sergeant."

The skinhead glared at Manuelita and ignored her beverage request. He gave her his back, sat down at a computer station and logged on. She strolled over and caught a glimpse over his shoulder before he noticed her behind him and darkened the monitor.

"I'd like milk and sugar in my tea," she said.

"Make your own fuckin' tea, Mrs. Wetback. I don't wait on Mexicans."

"I see you were looking at the *Anarchist's Cookbook,"* she said to his back.

"This one's in English, Consuela. You wouldn't understand it. You're a long way from the border, cupcake. I'm surprised Jake let you in back at the guardhouse."

"My husband is a collector of important things. I go where he goes." She stuck her ring finger in his face, gestured to the Shelby outside. "He's an equal to your boss. I am his wife. You work for him, you work for me."

"Try giving me an order, beaner bitch, and we'll see how that works."

"I order you to take another breath," she answered. She watched him struggle with that logic.

He smiled. "You're a clever little wetback. When's the last time you got the bitch slapping you deserve? By the way, until your pimp husband gets back, try not to touch anything. Old man Lincoln's antiques are worth a mint. Taco sauce is hell to get out of leather."

The computer monitor opened now to the mechanical blow-up of an M-16.

"What's it like being a terrorist in your own country?" she asked.

"There's a change in the wind coming, sweetheart. A prudent American is one who is prepared to weather the approaching storm."

Wally showed up at the big front door and told Manuelita it was time to hit the road. Lincoln was busy with some details down at the barn, he said.

"I'll be right with you, my husband," Manuelita said. "I should go pee." She smiled at the sergeant and asked for directions to the bathroom as Wally headed for the car.

"Try not to touch the seat with your brown ass or I'll have to hire your sister to clean it up." He pointed to the second door in the dark hallway.

"I'll leave the door open," she said in a scary sweet voice. "You can watch me hover.

He stood in the hall and watched her step out of her pants and panties. His eyes were on her as she squatted. "Think your big boss will be back to this house soon?" she asked, watching his eyes take in her nakedness.

"Probably not. What's it to you?"

"Too bad," she said. "I wanted to say goodbye to each of you personally."

She stood up and made no effort to cover herself. "Can you hand me my backpack, please? I have a treat for you, even though you were not friendly."

As he nervously eyed her bottom, the man passed her the canvas bag. She thanked him and put her hand inside on the knife handle.

"Did you hear that?" She looked past his ear. He turned. She sliced an ear-to-ear smile across his throat and pulled him onto the bathroom tiles. She pulled a boot off the gurgling form and sawed through his big toe as the body tried to recoil from another painful insult. He lay still. She watched bubbles of deeper lung air pop and open in the bloody mouth that she inserted the toe into, gave him a kiss on the nose and washed her hands.

She reached the Cobra with the hop and skip of a schoolgirl and jumped in. “Leave me some of that famous rubber, Pancho,” she said. “We got a country to see. I love America.”

Chapter Sixteen

Spokane, Washington

The view from Detective Kelly's cubicle was a tan building across a wet, potholed street. Musculo's Pizza was dark this early in the morning. The storefront beside the pizza parlor displayed a tired collection of old things that had not changed in the five years Kelly had worked homicide in Spokane.

On the computer monitor, he scrolled a list of recent homicides on the Indiana State Patrol home page. He found one death by knife, an eighty-two year-old woman apparently done in by her ninety year-old husband. Minnesota and Wisconsin had been murder-free yesterday, according to their shared information, even Milwaukee and Chicago's north shore.

Chicago proper took some time. Of the six murders where a knife wound was the cause of death, four were gang-related, one was a prostitute and one was killed in a home invasion. Since five of Winchester's six victims had criminal records, he had to check them all with phone calls to the lead detective on each case. None of them, he concluded, could be connected with a middle-aged antiques dealer and an expensive sports car.

He went back to the Fargo murders and redialed the detective who caught the case. He asked if anyone questioned mentioned a Mexican girl. No one at the asbestos factory auction mentioned any Mexican, though all of them remembered the blue car at the edge of the parking lot.

The coroner's report of the Fargo deaths suggested a skilled attacker using a large knife, consistent with the other cases. The business card, found in a bloody hand, yielded no usable prints other than the victim's bloody mark.

On a hunch, he called a friend who worked for the Washington State Department of Fish and Wildlife to see if Winchester had a hunting license, something to suggest he could field dress a deer or a Hindu cleric or a pair of tweekers near a Montana lake. The records indicated that Winchester liked fishing but never went into the woods for large game.

Kelly opened a police inquiry to the Armed Forces database in D.C. He found no evidence that the suspect had served in the military.

A shadow crossed his desk. He turned, startled to look up at the face of his boss. "Don't sneak up on me like that, Frank," Kelly said. "I nearly plugged you like a cardboard cutout from the shooting range."

"The lady with a loaf of bread in a shopping bag, I hope, Kelly. Word is you shot her twice in the last interdepartmental shoot off."

"She was holding a handful of processed wheat flour. Carbohydrates can be deadly to an Irishman," Kelly answered.

"How's the Hindu case going? I'm feeling some pressure to put someone in jail. Hate crimes can escalate."

Kelly brought him up to date and concluded that Winchester was linked to all the I-90 / I-94 murders up to Fargo, but he seemed an unlikely assassin, owned no registered weapons, and didn't have a motive.

"Charles Starkweather had no motive."

"Who?"

"Killed eleven people on a shooting spree in 1958 through Nebraska and Wyoming. You never heard of him?

"I wasn't born in 1958, boss. Of course, I know of crazy Charlie and his girlfriend, Caril. I took a course on serial killers awhile back at Quantico."

"You hint there is a woman involved in this case, Kelly."

"Only a woman sighted near the Hindu temple crime scene, boss. Montana and North Dakota scenes have no witnesses except the dead."

"What's your best guess as to his whereabouts?"

"Somewhere in the Midwest, on the way to Massachusetts according to a Stanwood antiques dealer who knew about the trip."

"Driving a two hundred thousand dollar Shelby, he shouldn't be hard to miss."

"You'd think so," Kelly said. "You'd think so."

Chapter Seventeen

Shipshewana, Indiana

"There's a flea market ahead, Manuelita. We're gonna stop. Maybe spend a few days."

"*¿Por qúe?*"

"I was at this place once before, years ago on a junket with an auctioneer named Brown from Tacoma. They have a mega country auction every Wednesday in a huge county fair pole barn. Ten auctioneers working at the same time. A crazy house for buyers."

Manuelita looked puzzled. "I don't understand anything you said."

"OK. Here's how it goes at this place," Wally said. "Every Wednesday, there's an all-day auction in this big-assed exhibition hall. On Monday, the hangar doors open. I've watched it. Farm trucks, piled with family heirlooms, line up at the entrance where they're assigned a space on the floor. After off-loading the family truck at a designated area, dad drives home to milk cows and leaves a teenager with an iPod and a foam pad to camp out amid the family treasures till Wednesday – auction day. The auctioneers, ten of them all at the same time, walk from space to space with a microphone and try to get everything to go away. For me, it's a great place to see if anything great shows up this week."

"It's Monday, Wally."

"Guess we'll have to hang out for a couple of days."

"I'm confused, señor. I thought you wanted to get this Cobra car to Boston. So much *dinero* waits for you. So much danger hangs over your perfect car, and yet you are in no hurry to complete this delivery."

"They say great things turn up at this Wednesday auction, Manuelita. I heard a Gus Stickley director's table got snatched up here last year for six hundred bucks, sold later for twenty grand."

"It's so weird. You antique guys and your furniture. Do you hear about everything old that is sold? How can you know a table was sold here last year when you live on an island three thousand kilometers away?"

"Networking, Manuelita. I'll give you an example. You know when you go to a beauty shop and all the gals are chatting, dishing on each other's sex life, the kids, rumors, the more vicious the better?"

"I've never been inside a beauty shop."

"No shit?"

"No shit."

Wally said, "Career antique dealers are like those chatty Kathies with their heads under the dryers. Stories, rumors, and lies are a big part of the business."

The Shipshewana exit took them through a colorful village where horse-drawn wagons outnumbered the cars. Men in dark hats and suspenders sported chin beards. Women strolled in bonnets and long dresses.

"What kind of place is this?" Manuelita asked.

"We're in Amish country, girl."

"Perhaps my English is not so good. I don't have the words, Amish country."

"The Amish people belong to a religious group that rejects the machine. No cars, no television, no computers even. They don't play card games or dance. I saw the movie. See the suspenders? To the Amish, even trouser belts are machines. It's less offensive to them to hang pants from shoulder straps."

"Weird *gringos*." She locked eyes with a pair of light-skinned teenage girls who stopped walking to stare at the shiny sports car as it growled a low-gear melody.

She flicked her tongue through two fingers in a licking gesture, a *puta* greeting, learned on meaner streets in Mexico. The pedestrians stared back with innocent, blank expressions. She made a gesture with her middle finger. They waved.

Five blocks of rural charm dissolved into fields of young corn and a flat horizon, broken only by distant grain elevators. Wally cruised the two-lane blacktop at a leisurely pace and passed a line of one-horsepower wagons, headed out of town. One youthful driver wrestled with the reins as the big Cobra engine spooked his horse. He spat in Wally's direction and raised his middle finger while a string of inaudible curses erupted from snarling lips.

"Finally, someone in this region who speaks English," Manuelita said to no one in particular. "Teach that one to your sister," she shouted out the window. "She thinks it means *hello.*"

At the fairgrounds, Wally slowed to a crawl in a dusty parking lot.

Manuelita said, "Are you asking me to sit in this terrible place while you spend two days waiting for a farmer to bring another dictator table for the Wednesday auction?"

"That's *director's* table, Manuelita, and don't sweat it, we have another option."

At a tin building, sporting a *Fairgrounds Office* sign in the window, he hopped out, leaving the engine running, and disappeared inside. Manuelita noted the smile lines in her *gringo's* eyes as he pasted on the innocent face she'd seen him adopt when he wanted something.

"Can I help you?" a matronly manager asked as she watched Wally pull out his wallet.

"I want to rent a flea market space through Wednesday."

She looked out the window at the tiny roadster. She said, "Mister, if you're looking for a safe place to park your fancy car, you can park it here, in the space behind the office."

"No. I want a flea market space."

"What exactly are you selling, sir?"

"Stamps."

Flea Market Space #41 was up against a fence. Wally liked that. Space #40 was also vacant. He liked that a lot, and parked the Cobra up near the back line of his plot of land. Twelve feet of open space for tables or a tent lay between the car and the dirt driveway that circled the market. Wally had no tables. He didn't care. One hundred twenty bucks had given him a safe place for the Cobra and a much more interesting environment for Manuelita to babysit than a dusty lot. The grassy spot to pitch the tent was a bonus.

"Let's get the tent set up here, behind the car," Wally said. "That would give you privacy. The restrooms are up by the office."

Manuelita leaned against the back fence, her feet near the front tire. She looked up at a yellowing sunset and decided she liked this place, guarded by a boundary and a car. She watched as a large bird, a hawk, was harassed by tiny sparrows. It was a lesson she knew well.

Alerted to the sound of a footfall, she leaped up from behind the car, mindful of the new Glock in her pack by her ankle. She knew a straight drop would place her hand on the zipper that held the weapon. Dip. Pull. Grab. A technique taught her by Claus Braun himself. She saw two teenagers, attracted by the shiny Cobra. She chased them off.

As Wally entered the vast space of the auction barn, he saw the quilt booth first. The quilts already on the display boards were beautiful but new. Wally's interest sagged. He wandered deeper into the cavernous hall.

A tall oak dresser caught his eye. It sat among an island of interesting items in auction space #72. A twelve-year-old lounged in a claw-foot Morris chair.

Eyes closed, ear-plugged to an MP3 player in her hand, she took no notice. He circled her family's offering to the auction gods on quiet feet, peering into a truckload of some family's history, sacrificed by indifference, a mortgage call on the family farm, another kid in college, or time to take a cruise.

He saw nice old things, a sweet oak wall phone, a fancy, carved Victorian bookcase, nothing for him. He walked toward dusky light that flooded the entrance and piles of family treasures, silhouetted on concrete like islands in an archipelago.

He spotted a small table under a stack of old board games.

"Can I see that table, son?" Wally asked a pimpled fourteen year-old who looked like he wanted to be anywhere but there.

The youth moved aside two early *Monopoly* boxes and handed Wally the piece, a foot-and-a-half of quarter-sawn, dark oak with a clipped corner top. On the arched cross stretcher, he spotted the L.&J.G. Stickley logo and passed it back, recording the space number on the palm of his hand with a Sharpie. Wally had experienced this auction a few years ago. He knew the drill. Multiple auctioneers, all working at the same time, meant a guy had to carefully monitor each selling station simultaneously, dashing from one auctioneer to another. Timing was crucial. By the time Wednesday rolled around and the vast hall was full, he would have identified the location of everything he wanted to bid on so he could map out the bidding strategy when a chorus of amplified voices began to sell off their assigned spaces.

Outside, through the hangar door, he saw thunderheads building in the late afternoon sky.

Manuelita hadn't killed in a day and a half and didn't expect she'd get the chance to follow another *gringo* purchase with a murder anytime soon, not in this public place. She texted a summary of her progress to her employer and had planted her feet on the fence to take another nap when a loud roar jolted her to her feet. A dust-covered cargo van barreled down the gravel access lane, headed for the empty selling space next to theirs. The driver lurched left into the slot and skidded to a stop three feet from the Cobra. The Mexican girl weighed the option of shooting the asshole through the windshield just for waking her up.

She watched the driver's door swing open. A hard-faced woman leaped out. The stranger took two steps to be next to the fence, pulled her pants down as she squatted, and let out an audible sigh while a growing puddle of urine reached a low spot and flowed down to the front tire. Manuelita couldn't help but notice the oval brown birthmark on her bottom.

The woman looked up and saw Manuelita. "Whee-o," she exclaimed, "I've had to pee for two hours, but the fucking traffic on the interstate kept me boxed in until the Shipshewana exit."

"You almost hit this car," Manuelita said with no emotion.

"Not a chance, honey," the woman said as she zipped up and redid the belt. "I've got 400K on this rig and I ain't hit nothing yet."

I think you need a good bitch slap, Manuelita thought. She said, "That mark on your *cullo*. I saw a mark like that on a piece of wallboard in Nogales."

"I hear that a lot, hon. I'm told it looks like a plywood plug. There's a carpenter in St. Louis that calls me his laminated lover."

Manuelita made a face that caused the conversation to cease. The new arrival opened the van doors to inspect the contents. Blues music rose from the interior, then the sound of a blender. Smiling again, the renter of space #40 approached the Cobra, Manuelita leaning on the fence behind it. She carried two frosty glasses.

"Let's start over. We're going to be neighbors. It's a hot day. You want a margarita? My name is Stacie Morningstar. Call me Stacie. What's yours?"

"Manuelita."

Stacie waited and said, "That's enough for me." She looked over the sports car. "What are you going to sell here, stamps?"

"The owner of this car chose this space as a safe parking place."

"That explains the look in your eyes as I slid in. Sorry, hon, when you're on the road alone for a week or so it makes you crazy."

"*De nada*." Manuelita tasted citrus and tequila. It reminded her of Mexico. She felt herself relax, an unexpected sensation.

As they sipped the drinks in silence, Manuelita watched a neighborhood of vendors prepare their booths for a day of sales.

"You gotta love these guys," Stacie offered. "I stop in here on my way east a couple of times a year, but these folks around us are full-timers. Seven days a week at the Shipshewana market. See that guy across the way?" She pointed to a van with a table in front of it. "Balloon animals on sticks are his trade. I see this guy, Gary, his name is, every time I come through Indiana. He's here all week, making a living blowing up balloons. Amazing. I respect him."

Manuelita ran her tongue across the salty rim, thinking of Mexico City, as the *gringa* talked.

"See that stand over there?" She pointed to a tented kiosk with candy pieces in tall, clear bins. "They get the sweepings from the Saint Louis candy factories, clean the rat drippings out, or not, and sell it cheap here by the pound. If you've got the munchies, an M&M's an M&M."

"Can you make another of these?" Manuelita said, holding up her glass.

"Sure enough, Manuelita. Can't wait to see your stamps."

Wally wandered through a sad field of permanent exhibitors in the substantial flea market that had grown around the auction. Nothing he could profit from caught his eye on the way to the Cobra. He found the offerings depressing.

A dust covered van now occupied the space beside the Cobra. Wally saw nothing in front but an empty table. He walked behind his car to find Manuelita sipping frozen cocktails with another woman. Her posture got his attention. A natural confidence hovered around her as she talked. The conversation ceased as he approached.

"This is our neighbor," Manuelita said. "She is OK."

Wally turned to a dusty blonde with a pretty, weathered face and beautiful eyes. A trim figure registered on his side-scan radar as he locked irises.

"Nice van," he said. "Wally Winchester."

"Stacie Morningstar. Four hundred thousand miles and still rolling," she said, smiling. Nodding at the Cobra, she added, "This your everyday flea market car or are you goin' somewhere special?"

"Nope. Just takin' her to market…back east. Gonna miss this car."

"You sellin' it?"

"Damn it."

"Let me guess the price."

"You know Shelbys?"

"I know quality. I'd say one seventy-five."

"I got him up to two hundred," Wally lied.

"Good job. Wanna help me unpack my stuff? It's going to be a boring couple of days till Wednesday." Wally followed her around to the back of the van.

"By the way," she asked, her fingers on the back door latch, "What are you selling in your space next door?"

"Stamps," Wally said. Want to see some? I can show you a nice set from Ceylon, 1871."

"That's all right. Can you help me unload? I've got a desk that's heavy as a motherfucker."

"What kind of stuff are you selling?"

"Arts and Crafts shit."

"First dibs," Wally said. Through the open back doors, he saw blanket-wrapped furniture. "Check this out," Stacie announced as she pulled the packing cloth off a Charles Rohlfs tall chair.

"Holy Harmonica!" Wally exclaimed.

"This is the third version of this chair I've owned; probably the best."

"You've had three of these chairs?"

"Yup."

"How'd you do with the other ones?"

"I did all right," she said. "I've got a bigshot stockbroker in New York who's crazy for Rolhfs."

"I guess I can't afford it," Wally said.

"I seem to have a knack for stumbling onto Charles Rohlfs furniture," she said. "Some people call me the Rohlfs Queen."

"I'm your new best friend," Wally said. "Let's get the blankets off these things and help you with your setup."

Manuelita held back, watching the *gringo* lose his composure in the presence of this renegade white woman. She reminded herself of her mission.

The desk under the packing cloth was indeed heavy. Wally recognized it by the red leather top.

"Molesworth?" he asked.

"Out of a Cleveland hunting club. I've got a guy in Wyoming who buys Molesworth furniture. No one here in Indiana will have a clue about its value, but since I'm here for the auction, I might as well unload for a day. See what I find on Wednesday."

On the grass, Wally saw an Arts and Crafts folk art masterpiece sixty inches long and forty inches wide, six drawers hung under red cowhide with brass buttons around the edge, a hundred saplings cut in half and nailed to the exterior. Red-stained leather on each end depicted an Indian Chief in the tooling. Wally was in love.

"I figure nine grand," she said.

"I'm guessing fifteen. Got any Stickley in your load? There's an L.&J.G. taboret in the auction. Are we going to butt heads?"

Stacie said, "It might depend on what's there, but here's a news flash, Mr. Collector. I just put a Gus No. 332 Morris chair in my living room, and that's for sale."

"How much?"

"Original finish, dark. Missing one of the back pin adjustors. Forty-five hundred, today."

"I'm going to come in to a lot of money in a few days. Does that price work next week?"

"Call me," she said, and reached into her back pocket for a card.

Wally was amazed by the quality of Stacie's load. They unpacked a Frank Lloyd Wright coffee table, the commercial line, offered by Heritage-Henredon. Wally asked her the price. She said fifteen hundred. She was right. He went back to the van. No buying in this booth. He'd met his match. A female version of himself.

The next thing under the blankets was a lounge chair, the chrome and wood version by the architect, *Le Corbusier.*

"Is this an old one or a new one?" Wally asked.

"Nineteen twenties," she said, "I bought it from Germany on eBay."

"We gotta talk," Wally said. "Mind if I ask the price?"

"Twelve to twenty thousand is what I figure. I bought it cheap the other day from a former dot-com millionaire in Berlin, poor bastard. He had a lot of money in Lehman Brothers. Poor guy's scared to death. Buying from him is like going to a museum yard sale."

"Ever heard of Josef Hoffman?" Wally asked as they uncovered deeper treasures in her load. Wally wondered what impact these intellectual objects would have on the chin-bearded farmers who came to the flea market to buy a poodle-dog-twisted balloon, but kept his question to himself.

Manuelita set up the tent in the space between the car and the fence. She watched a towering cumulus cloud grow higher and darker into a slow motion technicolor explosion as it drifted eastward and covered the setting sun. A sharp gust of cool air spun tiny dust devils and rustled the loose papers in the Cameron photo box that Wally carried inside.

She crawled through the tent flap carrying a striped Mexican-weave blanket she bought for three dollars on her own sojurn into the flea market and her backpack. As the sun slipped under the prairie horizon, a cool zephyr followed her into the tent.

"That backpack follows you everywhere, Manuelita."

"It holds our gun. Good not to leave it out, do you not agree?"

"If you use it as a pillow, best put the safety on or you might shoot me with your ear."

"Or shoot an *hombre* in my dreams."

Wally hung their battery powered Coleman from an *S*-hook looped onto the tent pole. He turned it on and reached for the box of letters with the killer photo inside.

"Ever seen a ten thousand dollar photo?"

"No. I thought you said it was worth one thousand."

"I think it's better than that now. Wikipedia reported that our Julia Margaret Cameron was criticized by fellow photographers for sloppy technique. She'd put her hand right into the developer bath and warm up the photo emulsion to get more action. See, on this picture?" He held the photo in front of the lantern. "There, a dark blur, it almost looks like a fingerprint. How cool; if one had Julia's fingerprint, this smudge would be better than a signature. Looks like a child who lived over there in Ceylon. They call it Sri Lanka now. Didn't know she made photos there. Wikipedia said she quit when she moved to Ceylon from England around 1870."

Manuelita looked at the handful of letters. She examined the stamps.

Wally repositioned the photo in the bottom of the cardboard container to keep it from getting scratched. Manuelita handed a letter to him. Said it had a pretty stamp. The address on the envelope was *Cameron Plantation, Kalutara Province, c/o Colombo, Ceylon.* Wally's countenance brightened. "If I was to go to Sri Lanka after I sell the Cobra, I bet I could track down this tea plantation and door-knock it – maybe find a stash of Julia's photos in the attic."

"You're a funny *hombre*," Manuelita said. "To fly to the other side of the earth to see if you can find some old pictures."

"At ten grand a photo, it might be a huge score." He opened the letter inside, penned in a crisp formal hand. The signature at the end was Alfred Tennyson.

"Alfred Lord Tennyson; he was a famous guy. This letter itself is worth a bundle, Manuelita. Listen to what he says. *Dearest Julia, our circle is bright no more with you away from the Isle of Wight. I heard your plea for more developing fluids and glass plates and have sent a trunk with the necessary chemistry inside to your plantation. The boat that brings you this missive has it in the hold. I wish you to send my fondest regards to Charles."*

"She ran out of developer, for Christ's sake. No wonder she quit working! This settles it, girl. After I sell the car, I'm on the next flight to India. Wanna come with?"

"My sister in New Hampshire is waiting."

"Sure, I wasn't thinking. I have to admit, I like your company.

"I also enjoy this…road trip…is that the English word?"

"That works."

Manuelita leaned over and kissed him on the lips. The taste was neutral and little bit salty. Wally encircled her in an arm and she pulled away, face of stone. Filtered through yellow tenting, the twilight looked to Wally like sunlight filtered through a Tiffany window as it covered her face with gold hues.

She said, "This false wedding ring does not give you husband privileges, señor. That was a kiss of happiness, not love."

"In my country, love usually comes before marriage."

"In my country, getting to know someone usually comes before love." She reached down and took his hand with hers. *"Buenas noches, amigo,"* she said. "Sleep well."

Music from the Rohlfs Queen in the next space throbbed into the warm night outside the tent. *Riders on the Storm* by the Doors. Wally closed his eyes, fingers interlaced with a small Mexican hand. A woman picker, he thought smiling in the dark. Where have you been all my life?

Dawn arrived with the promise of a cold front to the west. Tall cumulus pillows rose from a dark wedge of Canadian air that hung over the horizon like a chisel blade. Manuelita left the tent at first light to visit the fairground bathrooms and to forage for something to eat at the snack bar. With a menu that offered a hamburger, a hot dog, egg sandwich, and three varieties of corn dogs, she was pleased to discover a banana and an apple to start her day.

Wally and the neighbor *gringa* were sitting on two of her fat armchairs, drinking coffee heated on a camp stove, when she returned.

Wally said, "I'm glad you're back, Manuelita. We're headed over to the auction barn to preview the new arrivals. Will you keep an eye on her items while we're gone?"

"Of course, señor. What if a person wants to buy these things? Is there a list of values?"

"Don't worry, hon," the Rohlfs Queen said. "I guarantee that none of these rubes is going to spring real money for a Charles Rohlfs chair."

"I don't understand, señorita. Why do you display these things if there are no buyers?"

"It's a flea market, sweetie. Just like you folks, I'm using this space as a parking spot to pick the Wednesday auction. The furniture is more likely to attract a seller. One of these Mennonites could recognize a Stickley chair here on the grass that looks like the one at grandma's house. Pricing these pieces would be not only a waste of time but it would give the locals a big heads-up on the value of something they own. If anyone offers to sell something, take their name and number."

As they strolled over to the auction hangar, Stacie said, "She's a nice kid. You two a couple?"

"She needed a ride to New England. I needed a second set of eyes on the Cobra, someone to keep thieves and curious assholes with greasy fingers away from my investment. How about you? Do you always travel alone?"

"It's a bitch getting someone to share the driving, especially another gal."

"Boy howdy," Wally said. "It's a lonely highway."

In the cavernous hangar, Wally said, "There's an L.&J.G. drink stand that came in yesterday. You gonna let me buy it?"

"I'm into mission too, as you know. You want to work something out, an agreement?"

Wally said, "Tell you what, any Charles Rohlfs items show up here, they're all yours. Any Stickley is mine. OK?"

"That ain't gonna work, Einstein. Nice try. How about all the Stickley is mine and you can bid on the Roycroft and Limbert?"

"Like we're going to see Roycroft furniture here," Wally said. "I say we make a mini-auction pool – you and me. No one bids against one another at the sale, we'll have our own auction, see who goes home with the furniture and who goes on with a pocketful of cash."

"Realistically, Wally, I know this auction well. With a bunch of auctions all selling at once, chances are something's going to get away from us way-the-fuck and gone, across the way. Let's split up and try to cover as many of the auctions as we can. We'll see who gets what."

"That sounds like a no," Wally said.

"Call it every woman for herself," she said, smiling.

In the hall, filled with family offerings, Wally pointed out a small Limbert rocker. Stacie saw a generic Morris chair, an off-brand, a beginning collector's piece, five hundred, tops. Halfway across the hangar, they watched a farmer lift a spindle-slatted cube chair from his truck and hand it down to his children. Wally wrote the floor space number on his hand.

"I think I'll be around here when the auction starts," Wally said. "It's sort of in the middle. A guy could see most of the auctioneers from here."

"Sure, if you're ten feet tall. Where will you put this chair if you buy it, in the trunk?"

"I was thinking of hiring you to deliver it to Washington State. You'd like Camano Island. Lots of Charles Rohlfs out there."

"What, in books?"

As she dozed in an oversized rocker that she'd dragged behind the neighbor's van, Manuelita heard a woman's voice: "Excuse me," it said. She opened one eye, saw an overweight white woman with her hand on the tall chair that made her *gringo* so jealous.

Manuelita remembered the pricing conversation. She asked, "Do you have one of these chairs in your grandmother's house?"

"No, I just want to know how much you're asking for it."

"You can't afford it," Manuelita answered. "Take a hike."

"This is a flea market, young lady. You have to tell me the price."

"We're closed."

"You can't be closed. You're at the flea market."

"A thousand dollars," Manuelita said, making up a huge price for a chair.

"How about five hundred dollars, cash?"

"The owner will be back soon."

"Did she tell you a price for the chair?"

"She told me that no one here would want to buy it." Manuelita found herself annoyed by this pushy woman.

"All right, I'll pay the thousand." She pulled a roll of hundreds out of her purse.

"I'm sorry. We're closed." It was all she had to escape this terrible conversation, other than luring her behind the van and cutting her throat, a thought rapidly escalating into first place.

"You can't be closed. We're in the middle of a business transaction. I have a thousand dollars, cash. You quoted me one thousand dollars. Take the money and let me have my chair."

Manuelita said, "I have another chair like this that you might like. It's back here, behind the van. Do you want to see it?"

"That's what I'm here for, Consuelo," the pushy woman said, watching the Mexican girl stoop to retrieve her backpack.

"Hey, Silvia," a female voice said. "Long way from Long Island. What brings you to God's country?"

"Hello, Stacie," the pushy woman said. "Are these your things? I just purchased your Rohlfs chair for a thousand dollars. Priced a bit under the market for this model, don't you think?"

"I didn't sell you that chair."

"Your assistant did. I have the money here in my hand."

Stacie said, "Did this woman give you any money for this chair?"

"I told her we were closed."

"You did right, honey," she said to Manuelita. To the woman, she said, "The girl's right. We're closed. None of this furniture is for sale. If you want to make an appointment to see my merchandise, you have my number. I'll make time for you. I can send jpegs of anything I have for sale."

"It's a flea market. You had stuff out. I purchased that chair from your hired help. I have the money right here in my hand," Silvia whined.

Stacie said, “Exactly where it belongs. Get the fuck out of my booth. We’re closed.”

“This could jeopardize a fruitful relationship, you know, my dear.”

“Silvia,” Stacie said, “The next time I have something that you want, we’re going to be best friends. Now get your ass off my private property. We’re going to have a meeting.”

“This is a flea market.”

“Call ya,” Stacie said, her thumb and finger making a phone. “Now scoot.”

She watched an unhappy client waddle away.

Wally was impressed. “Back-talking a buyer is a delicious option that one always has when you’re standing behind a table of objects for sale in a booth,” he said to his neighbor. “I don’t use it enough.”

“It’s fun to fuck with these bottom feeders who believe they can whine their way to a lower price,” Stacie said.

Wally said, “In my New England days, I would purposely purchase cracked and damaged vases by Roseville, and other mid-range potteries, for pennies. At my booth at whatever flea market I found myself on a Sunday morning, I’d put a price tag of five dollars on the fifty dollar vase with a rim chip. It didn’t matter if I made or lost money. The five dollar price tag was part of the game. My targets were the whiners, the complainers, trying to push the price down by trash-talking my product. I waited for a skinflint to point out the chip or crack in a product that was nearly free. I’d take the wounded piece back and stomp it to death on the ground. Just to see the look on their face.”

“You’re a man after my own heart,” Stacie said.

Wally said, “Be careful what you wish for.”

On a Tuesday afternoon, few shoppers walked the dirt paths of the market. Wally figured most of those were sellers or buyers in tomorrow's auction out for a meander on a sunny day. Other than a pushy New York City client, her prediction that no one would be interested in her high-end objects was proving true.

A blender whined and stopped. Stacie carried three tall frosted glasses over to the Cobra.

"This a good market for a fifteen thousand dollar chair?" Wally asked as he squeezed the lime slice into his drink.

"I put the chair out front in case a collector of mine wanted to find me here," Stacie said. "It worked, didn't it? Unfortunately, that spoiled bitch from Long Island was not the person I wanted to see."

"The market around us is that bad?"

"It's all about the auction, Wally. The regulars here, Balloon Man, the bulk candy folks across the way, the guy with the Nike socks for 79 cents a pair, they all scrape a living out of this hell hole 'cause they have no overhead. The Nike sock dude has a silkscreen printer in the Joe Palooka trailer – he lives in that box. I suspect this field is his home. Doesn't want to be arrested with a stash of counterfeit footwear, so he prints only what he figures to sell on the next day. Balloon Man's inventory is a box of balloons and some wood dowels. Five dollars for a week's worth of twisted, inflated dachshunds on a stick."

"This field is a rogue's gallery," Wally said. "Ever sell anything here?"

"Not to the locals, no." She looked to the van and continued. "I'll prove it."

From the back, she pulled out a small mission desk and several Tupperware storage tubs and muscled them out to the dusty path where the sellers set up tables for their wares. Wally thought she handled the heavy piece like a road pro. "I can help," he said.

"Got it, chief. Thanks." She covered the desk with a white sheet, pulled a fat Sharpie out of her tool chest and marked "*FREE,*" in thick, black letters, on a cardboard fragment. A moment's fishing in one of the cartons produced a colorful vase, which she placed on the free table.

"I don't buy Roseville myself unless it's early," Wally said.

"Neither do I. It came in a box lot that I wanted last week at the auction. That's why I'm giving it away."

More rummaging produced a single Roycroft bookend missing its mate, a nickel-plated brass over-the-tub soap dish, and a faded Maxfield Parrish *Daybreak* print with a crack in the glass.

"I might like that soap dish," Wally said, looking at the name *Brasscrafters,* stamped on the back. "I have a claw foot tub at home."

"You can't play at the free table, Wally; the free table is just for the rubes. It will be cheaper entertainment than going out to a movie."

Wally ran a mental checklist on the meager inventory he carried in the sports car and concluded he didn't have anything to add to the free table.

"I'm going shopping," he announced to no one.

He waved at the Balloon Man and headed for the smattering of vendors set up on a Tuesday afternoon.

He returned later carrying a Victorian rocker over his shoulder and swinging a heavy shopping bag.

"Did you go foraging for the Free Table offerings?" Stacie asked.

Wally said, "I did. Got the rocker for twelve bucks. Look what else I found."

He unwrapped an ancient, well-loved teddy bear. Stacie twisted the head and made the arms move. "Steiff?" she asked.

"Didn't feel a button in the ear," Wally said. "It was priced right for your experiment." He placed it on the free table with its threadbare back against the Roseville vase.

"Find anything else out there?" Stacie asked. "I'm here a lot but don't bother to check out the tired inventory that bakes here in the sun seven days a week."

"I found a big-assed, flat holophane shade, sixteen inches across. Not for your experiment. I can fit it behind my seat."

Wally reached into the bag. "But look at this." He produced a handmade box in the shape of an outhouse. A glass window displayed a corncob. In old fashioned lettering, it read, *Welcome to the Ozarks. In case of emergency, break glass.*

"I used to collect this weird stuff," Wally said. "Today I think it's perfect for your table."

Manuelita watched the interaction from the late afternoon shade behind the Cobra. She pressed *Send* on a text message she'd typed in Spanish to her employer describing the last two days.

An answer appeared. "You are my sword, Manuelita. This is not a vacation. Please resume your duties. Have you identified a subject at your location whose death will be linked to Winchester?"

She typed back, "There are a number of people at this market that deserve killing. One sells American candy mixed with rat droppings to unsuspecting locals. That pleases me, actually. They've had no contact with Señor Winchester – just neighbors at the market. A *gringa* is parked in the next space. Winchester seems fascinated by her. She sells expensive things and acts like a man. He likes that."

The reply said, "We need a bill of sale, or a check written by Winchester, or fingerprints, or Winchester's DNA at the scene. Since he likes the woman, I will give you a bonus upon her death."

Manuelita paused. The woman had been friendly to her since the first margarita. She was surprised at the envy she felt as she watched them interact. Wally lit up like a Christmas tree as they laughed. Now she had two reasons to kill her.

The way things are going, she thought, feeling an odd sadness that felt a little like love, he might leave his DNA in her van all by himself.

A pair of well dressed Chicago women walked up to the free table, ignoring the expensive Rohlfs chair behind it.

"What does this mean, *free*?" a stout matron asked.

"That means that you can take anything from that table home without paying for it," Stacie answered sweetly.

"What's the catch?" the other one asked.

"There are no conditions."

The women made faces to each other and walked away.

"See, Wally," Stacie said. "These folks are tighter than a frog's asshole."

Wally was having second thoughts about giving away the Ozark outhouse piece.

A couple walked up, holding a recent purchase, a stick with a balloon dachshund on top, courtesy of Balloon Man. "What's the story with this *free* sign?" the farmer asked, one thumb in a suspender.

"Everything on the table is free," Stacie said. "Take it away with my blessing."

Wally popped the cap of a cold Heineken, amused beyond words.

"How about that fancy chair?" the man asked.

"Everything on the table is free. The chair is fifteen thousand."

The couple focused on the table as though a pile of free items next to a fifteen thousand-dollar chair was normal in a dusty Indiana flea market on a Tuesday afternoon. The woman picked up the teddy bear.

"Might be a Steiff," Wally volunteered from his chair.

She replaced it, a disturbed look on her face.

The farmer held up the single Roycroft bookend. Fine hammering twinkled in the five o'clock light.

"Got the other one?" he asked.

"Nope. Stack the other end of the books against the wall."

He replaced it and mumbled to his wife before urging her away from the table with a stern look and pressure on her elbow.

Stacie cracked a Heineken. They broke out into laughter.

Manuelita watched the episode and reaffirmed her resolve. The tug on her heart as they laughed troubled her. Señor Winchester was an assignment. The fondness she felt was not in the plan. She touched the wedding ring on her finger and shook the warmth out of her heart.

The next ten people who approached the free table left empty-handed.

Balloon Man walked over, tears in his eyes. "It cracks me up, what you're doing," he said. He placed a poodle-dog stick in a carnival glass vase that Stacie had dug out of a carton and added it to the offerings.

The couple with the rat-tainted candy placed a two-pound bag of M&M's next to it. Wally noted a pile of brown bits that had settled to the bottom of the clear plastic sack. He shuddered.

Nike Sock Man added a pair of socks to the pile. "Printed today," he announced, sniffing the cotton. "Love that new car smell."

After two confused shoppers asked about the gimmick and left empty-handed, Wally cracked another beer.

"I haven't had this much fun since Brimfield," he said as he pulled two dollar bills and a handful of pocket change out of his jeans. He put the currency on the table, under the word, *FREE*.

The Chicago matrons returned and noticed the new additions. The stout woman adjusted her designer scarf and asked Stacie, "Really, what is the trick here? There has to be a catch."

"All right," Stacie answered, pulling on a Molson now. "If you take anything from the table, it's yours; if you put it back, you owe me fifty cents."

"I told you it was a trick," she said to her friend. They walked away again. Wally reached for another cold one.

Ten minutes later they were back. "This is the trick," the stout one said to her friend. "If I pull that balloon dog on a stick out of that vase, there'll be an explosion."

Her friend nodded, conspiratorially.

"Watch this," the fat one said. She placed her feet in an escape stance, reached for the poodle dog balloon and snatched the stick from the vase. She jumped back, bracing for the report. Wally and Stacie clinked beer bottles.

When nothing happened, the matron looked at her friend, shrugged, and placed the balloon stick back into the vase.

"Fifty cents," intoned the candy people, Balloon Man, the Nike sock guy, and Wally, all in unison. The befuddled customer found two quarters in her purse and added it to the free currency pile that Wally started.

The next visitor to the free table was an elderly woman, accompanied by a young woman, perhaps a caregiver.

"How much is the rocking chair?" She asked in a quivering voice to Stacie.

Wally jumped in. "That's my chair," he said, "I just bought it today."

The elderly woman looked at the chair, ornately carved in nice quarter-sawn oak.

"You purchased this chair today, and now you're offering it for free?"

"I got it for a really good price," Wally offered.

"How much is it, really?" the woman asked, propped up by her friend.

"All right," Wally answered, "Two dollars."

"Ah, two dollars," the woman said, a look of justification creeping into her tired face.

"That's all I can afford," Wally said. "I'm running low on cash." Beside him Stacie tipped a beer bottle in a salute.

"You're offering to give me two dollars if I take your chair? I don't understand."

"All right," Wally reached deeper and pulled out three quarters. "Two seventy-five; that's all I have without writing a check."

"You want to give me two dollars and seventy-five cents to take your chair home?"

"Stop it," Wally pleaded. "You're breaking me. I need some gas money to get to Boston. Please take the chair." He offered her the handful of cash.

"Well, I came here looking for a rocking chair," she said. "Can I try it?"

Wally realized that he was trying to give away a chair to the only person in Shipshewana this month who actually wanted to buy one. He shrugged at Stacie and lifted the chair off the table to the ground. The woman gingerly put her hundred pound frame into it and rocked back and forth.

"I like it," she announced, pulled from the oak seat to her feet by the attendant. Wally gave her his cash, and they departed.

The neighbors materialized at the free table, eyeing the items and the cash next to the *FREE* sign.

"Back off," Stacie said between sips of her beer. "This table is for the tourists, not for you flea market whores."

A pair of teenage boys walked up, dressed like the Amish of the area, too young for the chin beard.

"This money is free?" the shorter one asked.

"Take whatever you want," Stacie said.

The boys looked at each other then pocketed the money. They bundled all of the articles on the table, including the poodle dog on a stick, under their arms.

"It's OK if we take these things?" the tall youth asked.

"Start an antiques business," Stacie said.

Manuelita and Wally slept in the tent again. She leaned over to kiss him and found him unprepared for the offered affection, his thoughts on the neighbor. She found his hand and held it as he began a low snore. She nudged Wally awake.

"When are we leaving this market for Boston?" she asked.

Wally's mind cleared. "Tomorrow afternoon, late," he mumbled. "After the auction." He snored again. Manuelita calculated her plan.

At eight o'clock in the morning, Wally knocked on the back door of the van next door. Stacie opened the door, wrapped in wrinkled pajamas.

"I thought we should have a discussion about the items we're going to bid on today, since we like the same things."

"I got coffee on, hon. Come on in."

They sat between the ghosts of blanket-wrapped antiques sipping a strong Columbian brew cooked on a camp stove. Stacie brushed her hair and pawed through a suitcase to find a clean shirt.

"Turn your back," she said as she unbuttoned."

Wally inspected a stack of bungeed, blanket-covered objects toward the back door. "Got any early Gus Stickley on board that you haven't uncovered?" he asked over his shoulder.

"No other Stickley. A few Limbert pieces. Nothing outrageous. You'd like my house."

They sat on the back bumper. Stacie said, "The way I work this auction, I find the piece I want most, then talk to the auctioneer of that section just before the sale. Ask when they figure the piece will come up. Then I get the second pick and do the same. Then I race around the craziness, trying to be at the right auction at the right time."

"How about that bidding pool I talked about?"

"Your plan for us to split up and put everything we buy in a pile back here by my van and have our own personal auction? I'm an expert in what I buy, bub. What do I need you for?"

Wally lifted a blanket corner to reveal the oak leg of a tea table. "That's a Limbert #574 drink stand. The through-tenon suggests it's an early piece. Probably has only the Grand Rapids brand, not the Grand Rapids and Holland brand. I've owned three examples of this model. Figure the retail price at eleven hundred to twelve hundred dollars." Wally peeked under another blanket. "Quaint Furniture armchair. I can identify it by the front trumpet stretcher. It's in pretty good shape. What are you planning to offer it for, three fifty?"

"I'll throw it in with an important piece as a *gimme*, but you're right about the price. You know the market."

"You and I know what we want to pay for items in the sale today. With simultaneous auctions, we're going to miss some things if we stick together to compete. I vote for the pool."

Stacie wasn't buying it. "Hey, bub, I come here at least once a month to get stuff cheap. Why should I allow you to get a shot at my booty, furniture or otherwise." She squeezed off a naughty wink.

"How about you not bidding on things I want and me doing the same with you?"

"Because we both want the same stuff."

"Hey, Wally, it's a big room, ten singers at once."

"Watch your ass, then," he said. "I've been at this a long time. I have a pocketful of cash and a hankering to buy something to remember this road trip by."

Stacie said, "I can handle myself just fine in an auction, thank you."

"All right," Wally sighed. "*Mano a Mano*. No quarter."

Stacie smiled and said, "Bring it on."

Manuelita listened to the muffled debate and worked on a plan to kill the neighbor girl as the last act before the racing car resumed the journey toward Boston. She was troubled by the reluctance she was feeling towards her assignment. Killing, for her, was a workplace tool.

She sat in the shade of the *gringa's* van and dressed her knife with an emery board. Her phone vibrated. She opened it and listened: "I'm concerned with your resolve, child. Your assignment leaves no room for your personal whims." She frowned, wiped the shiny blade on her shorts before packing it away.

"I have killed seven in seven days, sir."

"The next target is a woman that Winchester likes, is that correct?

"*Si, señor*, he tells me his dreams have this woman inside them. She loves to drive to strange areas to find old things. He says to me he never met a woman like her."

"I like that. He will be pained by her death. Do you have a plan?"

"I only need a minute with her in her van as the *gringo* and I resume the journey. We are highly visible in a public place; the only opportunity will be the moment of leaving."

"So I don't have to send someone to help you do your job?"

"No, señor."

"Remember, you are an assassin, not Mother Theresa. Cut me off a souvenir from this one that Winchester likes. It will amuse me to show it to him before he is captured, if I get the chance. Good girl."

Wally surveyed the organized chaos in the big hall. Microphone sound-checks peppered the air with "Testing, one…two…three, whadda-ya bid?"

Stacie gave his hand a squeeze and said, "Happy bidding." She disappeared into the teeming crush. Wally acquainted himself with Wednesday morning arrivals, determined to out-buy Little Miss Confidence in her own backyard. A ceiling fan, in the shape of a passenger aircraft, caught his eye. Six-inch propellers on each wing spun to create the breeze. He'd never seen one like it. A woman, with pancake makeup, big hair, and a microphone in her hand, told Wally the airplane fan would be sold about an hour into the sale. Wally wrote *11a.m.* and the room section, then looked for the little table he saw on Monday. A different auctioneer told him the same time-frame. He was going to have to choreograph this sale to the minute.

A walk around the vast chamber told him it would be a frantic day. The middle section held a Stickley magazine stand, the one with the spindled sides. It sat next to the back section auctioneer, wearing a cowboy hat, a bolo tie, and muttonchops down to his chin.

Near the Amish quilt booth, Wally spotted a fat-armed Morris chair that he recognized as the L.&J.G. Stickley paddle-arm recliner. Holy shit, he thought. No wonder the Rohlfs Queen makes this a regular stop. Wally asked the auctioneer of that section when the chair would come up and was told in about an hour. “Everything is set for eleven,” he muttered. “Like I can be in four places at once.”

A buzzer screeched at the ten o’clock start. A collection of amplified voices filled the lofty building with song-like chants. Wally walked around the perimeter. He looked for Stacie and ignored the meaningless first objects, offered all over the room at once. Wally spotted her near the geographic center of the sprawling display of Midwest castaways. She held up a bid card as the auctioneer said, “Sold!”

Wally watched her place a chair next to the tall oak dresser she just purchased then climb up to stand on the sturdy top. He recognized her strategy.

Wally wound his way through the auction cacophony towards the center and watched Stacie, five feet above the crowd, buying at multiple auctions. He bid one hundred dollars for a pine dresser of no interest other than the height. Stacie bid two hundred. Wally let her have it. He next bid on an English, Liverpool-type wardrobe, 1950’s, imported by the ton. Totally boring but six feet high. Stacie doubled it. Wally bid two fifty. Stacie bought it for three.

A stepladder in a perimeter auction was offered for twenty dollars to start. Wally said, “Yes.”

From two auction stations away, Stacie bid thirty. Hardball.

Wally bid forty bucks just to get in the game. She let him buy it. A forty-dollar ladder for the owner of a sports car. He opened it and climbed to the top just in time to see her buy the Stickley magazine stand. Another raised card bought the clipped corner taboret that Wally had his eyes on since Monday.

“Damn.” Wally looked out from the corner of a vast field of objects. From his perch, he knew that all the things he wanted on this side of the schizophrenic Amish auction were sold by the time he climbed his forty-dollar ladder to compete. He abandoned the ladder and raced for the other end of the vast chamber.

He circled the room as the auctioneers sang their songs. He looked for Stacie, standing on the dresser. She was gone. Wally spotted her with the various cashiers as she gathered her new belongings. Score: Stacie, 5. Wally Winchester, 0. He stormed out of the hall, marched out to the flea market, shaking his head.

Manuelita looked up from the shade of the woman's van. "Load 'em up," Wally barked. "I just wasted three days. If we leave now, we'll be in Boston by the fucking weekend."

"What about the *gringa*?" she said. "Are you going to say *adios*?"

Wally said, "Fuck her. The Rohlfs Queen's off my Christmas list."

She looked at the knapsack that held the sharpened blade and shrugged as she tucked it behind her seat. Despite the dressing down she knew she would receive, she smiled as the Cobra negotiated the bumpy, county fair parking lot on its way to the interstate.

In the rearview mirror, Wally caught the image of Stacie, the magazine stand on her shoulder like a hunting trophy. She tossed out a prom queen wave. He shook his head again, grudgingly acknowledging respect. They would meet again, he knew. He vowed to be ready next time.

Chapter Eighteen

Cleveland, Ohio

It was in an antique mall just south of Cleveland, Ohio where Wally decided to take a detour to North Carolina. "When is your sister due to give birth, Manuelita?" he asked as he read the poster announcing the annual Arts and Crafts Conference taped to the wall behind the cashier.

The question seemed to take her by surprise. She stumbled on the date, finally saying, "About a month."

"Great," Wally said. "The lollapalooza of the Stickley collectors' year is a conference in western North Carolina. When I sell this car, I can have anything I want, and this shindig starts in two days. I think I'll scoot across Kentucky, a short distance, north to south, and maybe do some shopping, get me something rare." He traced his finger from Cleveland to Asheville, North Carolina on the travel map.

"That looks like a long journey in the wrong direction, señor," his companion said. "Did you promise a time for this car's delivery?"

"The buyer said June, but I don't think he really cares as long as it gets to him in one piece. I've never picked Kentucky or Tennessee, M. How about it? You up for a southern sojourn?"

"My job is to be a passenger and guard the car as you play. You can say I was hired to make your life more interesting, Señor Wally." She reached over and gave his fingers a squeeze that evaporated any memory of the disastrous auction.

A bearded man in the passenger seat of a dirty Ford Econoline van pulled out a map as they followed the Cobra up an exit ramp for southbound traffic on Interstate 77.

He texted his employer, reporting the change of direction.

Wally turned into Smith Lake RV Park, just south of Parkersburg, West Virginia when he spotted the *Wi-Fi* sign at the entrance. He paid twenty dollars for a space between a fifth-wheel trailer and a Winnebago, down by a man-made lake.

He bitched into the air as he guided the sports car into the slot.

"It's not even summer. All the state parks are full. What are all these people doing camping now?"

As they motored into the opening, Manuelita looked at an overweight Anglo couple grilling meat next to their trailer. The retirees waved to the new arrivals in their sports car and hoisted large insulated mugs in a greeting. She made a note that they wouldn't be the ones to die.

Wally popped out from the low seat. He bent forward, stretching one leg then the other. "Sorry about the digs, Manuelita. Asheville's the goal. We'll get there tomorrow afternoon and then live like a king and queen at the G.P.I."

"I have no desire to live like a queen," Manuelita said.

"Doesn't a little part of you, the little-girl part, still want to be a princess and have everything you desire?"

"I never had that wish. I watched my father killed by men with guns when I was three years old. We lived on handouts and the big hearts of neighbors until my mother moved to Mexico City and got a job. Where is this princess dream? My fantasy was a full tummy."

Wally set up the tent on level ground in front of the car, the ass end of two travel trailers and a glimmer of a man-made lake through tired trees. He powered up the laptop and connected to the internet. He closed the monitor, locked the computer in the car and wandered through trees, down to the lake. He thought about the parking strategy for the next day, picturing the Grove Park Inn parking garage, carved out of mountain cliffs, and relaxed, knowing he could park the race car amid the BMW's and Land Rovers of the millionaires upstairs and be safe while he took a two-day vacation from vigilance.

Manuelita hoisted her pack over her shoulder and went in search of the *baño* She walked through neighborhoods of manufactured vacation homes on wheels, sling chairs around fire pits in the front yards.

A cinderblock structure with men's and ladies' symbols on signboards was tucked in behind the check-in kiosk and a gift shop.

As she pressed her hand to the woman's shower door, she stopped, alerted by a fragrance. She turned and saw Winnebagos nestled amid sculpted trees. She detected coconut.

"Coco," she said to the person behind her.

"Hola, Manuelita. ¿Cómo está?"

"I didn't see you behind me, congratulations *amigo*. What are you doing here? Are you following me? Are you the second team?"

"You taught me well."

An elderly woman, cooing to a black pug that she carried like a loaf of bread, passed them and entered the ladies' room.

Manuelita looked at the muscled Mexican youth and remembered his unshaven chin against her face one night. "I'm in the middle of nowhere. You're here. GPS?" she said.

"I love technology."

"Why are you here?"

"You're not doing your job. We were sent to help."

"Go away. I've killed seven people. This Winchester leads a complicated life. My assignment requires a moment of solitude, and, with this man, those moments are rare."

"You are expected in Boston in three days. Why are you here in West Virginia?" He moved closer. She retreated.

"He makes a thousand kilometer right turn because of a poster on the wall. I'm a passenger. Sue me."

He moved closer, backlit by night insects around a yellow light. She stepped back and felt the door to the ladies' room a foot behind her. She explored her options.

"Señor Braun thinks you have been in the United States too long, weakened by your contact with white-bread Anglos and their materialistic lifestyle," her stalker said. "He is concerned that continuous contact with the *hombre*, Winchester, could cloud your mission."

"The man drives across the United States like a mongoose," Manuelita said. "Leaping north and south to see old friends or attend a thing called an *auction.* He tells me the hotel we're driving to will be filled with important people. High profile targets.

"Claus Braun thinks you've gone soft."

Manuelita locked the eyes of her student. Peripheral vision explored a door beside her. A broom closet. No lock on the latch.

She stalled. The kid was good. Her best. She broke eye contact in the head-bowed act of submission. Checked out the handle to the closet. It was unlocked.

"There are no tools to use as weapons in the closet, Manuelita. I checked."

She raised her eyes and, in slow, measured motions, lowered the backpack to the ground. The gun was two Velcro straps and a handful of clothing away. She stepped away from it, flattening her back against the restroom door. She calculated the distance between them as two meters.

The Mexican youth smiled. He slid the knife back into a sheath on his belt and laughed out loud. He said, "The Macedonia Defense. A two-meter leap with a push off the door behind you. What was your target, my eyes?"

"Windpipe," she said.

"I'm not here to terminate your mission. I offer help, a second weapon. Paulo and I can step in if killing becomes a problem for you."

"Paulo is here also? Who's left to terrorize Mexico City? All of its *banditos* are here on a camping trip."

"Don't ever take a long ride with Paulo. Trust me. Beans, more beans, then beans for dinner. The van smells like an outhouse. Wave to him, Manuelita."

She put up one finger and offered the gesture to the dimly-lit vegetation behind him.

"I don't need your help, Coco."

A tall man with a scoped rifle emerged from a dark hedge. Manuelita knew him, a reckless hoodlum with no conscience. Good on a team if you watched your back. His grin looked pasted. She put out a fist. He met it with his.

"Are you determined to follow me all the way to Boston?"

"That's what we get paid for," Coco said.

"I want you two to back off and let me operate. If you two spook the *gringo*, I can't complete my mission. Stay out of sight or the next two bodies may be yours."

"Señor Braun says if you don't get back to doing your job, the next body is *you*."

Manuelita sized up her former students, and her face turned to stone. She stepped forward and delivered a slap across Coco's face. "I taught you everything you know," she said. "Don't for a second think I taught you everything I know."

Snug in the tent with the laptop, Wally opened his email program and saw twenty messages. He opened one from Yvgeney Ivanchenko.

"Hello, Super Picker: My American culture sources tell me there's a popular television show that features antique doorknockers – blokes like you. Have they found your yard yet?

"I'm in India, in Mumbai, stuck here for three months in a bureaucratic shitstorm. Like that word, shitstorm?" he wrote. "I found it the other day. It describes the hellish bickering I immerse myself in every day here. All politically correct and proper. Rubbish.

"The Indian government has petitioned UNESCO for the return of a number of objects taken from India to England during colonial rule. Great Britain, of course, doesn't intend to give anything back, so it's endless rounds of talks getting nowhere. Lord, give me a villain to battle, not another meeting, and no more paperwork. I miss life on the road with Wally Winchester.

"Chana, yes our Chana, is also in town. She's attending a symposium of religious leaders at the Bombay Hilton this weekend. I'm going to meet her for lunch today. She has a treasure for me. It will be good to see her again.

"The next time you take a road trip, please invite me. I need an adventure to escape this bureaucratic nonsense."

Wally typed back that his current road trip was pretty uneventful except a lady known as the Rohlfs Queen cleaned his clock at a Midwest auction.

Manuelita came into the tent with polished skin and wet hair from the campground shower. Wally looked up from his laptop to see her pull the shirt over her head. Nut-brown nipples on cupcake breasts stiffened in the cool night air. She unbuttoned her jeans, lay on her back next to him and arched her hips to pull the pants off. She wore no underwear. A thick forest of jet-black muff disappeared under a blanket that she pulled up to her waist. She idly pushed at a nipple with her finger.

Wally felt lightheaded, told himself to take a breath.

Manuelita lifted her chin up towards his face. She kissed his lips, opening them with her tongue, then pulled her head back to observe his face. “Isn’t it your birthday, Señor Wally?” she asked.

Wally reminded himself to breathe again. He said, “I believe it is,” as he felt fingers on the buttons of his shirt, then his belt buckle. “Your hand is soft,” was all he had in his answer bag.

“That makes one of us,” she said. “Later you can tell me about the important people we will meet at the big hotel.”

“Later works for me.” He left the light on.

Chapter Nineteen

Asheville, North Carolina

Wally wheeled the Cobra, like a favorite pinto pony, through well-paved curves that led into the hills above Asheville, up a winding road to the Grove Park Inn.

A red-suited reincarnation of Robert E. Lee bowed as the Cobra arrived under a terra cotta tiled porch that shaded the old hotel entrance. Wally looked at the pair of massive Roycroft lanterns that flanked the front door and sighed. Again. He held a fifty dollar bill in his hand.

The doorman leaned down to the window as Wally lowered it, holding the fifty out of sight between two fingers.

"Welcome back," Robert E. Lee plus fifty pounds said. "You remember me? I remember you. I remember a night in the Magnolia Lounge a year ago when you told me about Stickley furniture, the stuff I'm surrounded by everyday here, and we watched the twenty year-olds play the dating game, us the oldest two people in the room. Nice car, by the way."

"And you sent a drink over to a woman sitting alone, intercepted by a six-foot fullback from a local college. That pair of tickets to the Duke/North Carolina playoff game saved your sorry ass," Wally said as he tucked the fifty under his thigh and brought up his hand for a shake. "Listen, I need a favor," he continued. "I don't want to park this car in the garage. It's too valuable. Parking on the outside is totally out."

"I assure you, the security in the parking garage is top notch." An indignant frown crossed the bearded face. He stepped back.

Wally pulled the fifty out from under his leg, motioned the man back and waved the bill in the air as the gold-lapelled greeter leaned in and said, "Now, how is it again that I can be of assistance?"

"I need a safe place to park this masterpiece for three days. What else have you got?"

Bushy white eyebrows compressed. "The curator at the old car museum over there…" He gestured to a series of buildings partially hidden by trees. "He's my buddy. I might talk him into letting you park this…what is this anyway?"

"A Cobra," Wally said. "Tell me about the parking."

"There's a fair amount of parking space in the garage behind the museum. A bunch of old jalopies parked in there now, waiting to get worked on. Everyone's gone for the weekend. Place is closed up tight."

"Perfect," Wally said. "I won't need the car till Monday."

"Excuse me, sir," Robert E. Lee said as he stepped away and made a cell phone call. He listened and wrote a phone number on a scrap of paper he pulled from a gold-lapelled pocket on the red vest. He returned to the window. "Got you a parking space at the museum. Problem is, you've got to get someone with a key to unlock it. If you get the notion of a midnight drive in the next four days, you're probably out of luck."

"Thanks! You did great." Wally said. He frowned. "What's this parking space going to cost?"

"Four days parking, that will be five hundred dollars, cash."

"Five hundred dollars for four days parking?"

"Sir, this is the Grove Park Inn."

Wally looked for options. Saw none. "How about four hundred cash?" he asked, "For old times' sake."

The grey-bearded man laughed and said, "Sure. This is the phone number of the fellow with the key. You call him if you want to get your car. No guarantees when he gets back to you, but he lives around here. After 5:00 p.m. you probably won't get anyone to open the garage for you on short notice."

"I'm here for the conference," Wally said. He pulled his picking wad out of the left pocket and pulled out four hundreds. The pile was thin. He handed the cash out the window and received a phone number in return.

"Welcome back," Robert E. Lee said, assuming the posture of a southern gentleman. "Better bring everything you need into the hotel on the first trip 'cause there may be no getting back in till Monday when they open up. Toss of a coin, this number, but he's local. If he's not at a car show, he'll be around."

As he was about to lock the door, thrilled that for the next three evenings he could put his car-sitting chores aside, Wally said, "Be sure you bring anything you're going to need in the hotel for the next four days, Manuelita."

She felt the weight of her knife and the bulk of the heavy handgun as she hoisted her bag on her shoulder. "I'm good," she said.

Wally sauntered into the great lobby, looking for people he knew in a sea of V-back Stickley chairs that surrounded a monumental stone fireplace. He gazed skyward at hammered metal and glass fixtures, made for the inn in the early 20th century by the Roycrafters, a successful community of artisans in upstate New York at the turn of the century. He thought about all the flea markets, antique stores, auctions and yard sales he'd been to and knew that, in all his years of paying attention, he'd never come close, face-to-face, with a light fixture that wonderful for sale.

Manuelita surveyed the great hall's massive stone fireplace, perfect for a shaped charge, and wondered if Coco was packing a handful of C4 in the backup van. She noted the exits: A door near the front, which looked like the office; two hallways leading to the hotel wings; and six doors that opened to a porch and a vast panorama of the town below. She followed Wally to the front desk as he pulled out his wallet.

He whispered, "See that beautiful painting on the back wall?" An impressionist landscape, cradled in an enormous gold frame, showed a sunset through an oak grove. "I tried to buy it right off the wall last year. They laughed at me."

She shrugged, uninterested, with mayhem, not merchandise, in her thoughts. The point of her assignment was to link every killing with the *gringo* – through a sales receipt, a credit card swipe, a fingerprint, even the man's DNA, a sample of which she'd harvested under her fingernails from his buttocks during lovemaking in the tent the night before. How to pin a murder on him, here at the inn, surrounded by a mass of white-bread antique collectors? That was the problem yet to be solved.

The desk clerk's smile turned into a French waiter's sneer as he handed back the credit card. "I'm sorry, Mr. Winchester, this card cannot secure your room. Insufficient funds. Do you have another?"

"That's impossible," Wally said. He pulled out another Visa card.

"Not enough on this one either." The clerk's eyes darkened and looked past the shaggy-haired guest like Wally had become invisible.

Wally handed over three other credit cards. "Between all of these, there has to be enough to book our room. We've driven a long way, and we're tired. I was here last year. Tried to buy the painting behind you, remember?"

"Apparently you were unsuccessful because it's still here. Did you run out of funds then as you did today?" The smile was not genuine.

"You probably won't believe this, but in a week there's going to be two hundred G's to back up those bad boys. Soon as I get that race car outside up to Boston."

"You're right, I don't believe you."

"Can I just write a check?"

"Based on what you've shown me so far, no."

"I'm sure there's enough money in all the cards together. You could run all four. Take five hundred off of each. There's your room charge plus enough to use the mini-bar."

"We don't do that here. Perhaps you could find a cheap motel in Asheville. Maybe down by the river."

"Let me speak to the man in charge."

"I am the day manager. That's all you get."

Wally analyzed his awkward moment and looked at Manuelita. She displayed no emotion, no reaction to this mini-nightmare played out in public. He took it as a blessing and turned back to the check-in desk where he saw the manager with an intern and another guest, his empty station a rejection. Wally fished out a twenty and handed it to her, along with his backpack. "There's a bar over in the corner," he said with a nod toward the other side of the vast hall. "Buy yourself a cocktail. Sit by the fire."

"Can I just go outside instead?"

"Good idea. Get some nature."

Wally surveyed the crowd sipping wine and networking as they sat on Stickley-style chairs under Roycroft chandeliers. The room was a *Who's Who* of Arts and Crafts superstars and collectors. Amid the handshakes, hugs, false cheek kisses, back slapping, and family reunion smiles were quiet appointments for big sales that would take place in private suites, out of the public eye.

He saw Harry Hagopian, a stockbroker and collector of early Stickley, huddled with Bill Copeland from Buffalo. Copeland pointed to an item in a catalogue. Wally saw Hagopian's eyes go wide, then a handshake.

At a round table near the bar, San Francisco dealer Russ Gostrom inspected the bottom of a pot with a jeweler's loop while a handsome gentleman and a beautiful woman on his arm waited for a response. Wally recognized a movie actor whose name he couldn't remember. Russ opened a checkbook and scribbled on a check as he rewrapped the plum-colored ceramic and placed it carefully in his shoulder satchel, taking his leave.

Wally followed Gostrom with his eyes. Watched him interrupt Hagopian's chat with a whisper. The stockbroker peered into Gostrom's canvas bag and nodded his head. Wally recognized the gesture as a sale.

He spotted Will Suter from Connecticut, now divorced, according to the grapevine, his ex getting half of his collection, the poor bastard. His arm embraced a redhead half his age. Wally sold him a Harvey Ellis drop-front desk two years ago, the plain one without the veneer. A month later, a similar desk, this time with the classic inlay, fetched eighty thousand at a New York auction but was returned due to "condition problems." Wally had always wondered whether his sow's ear had morphed into a silk purse with the help of Suter's skilled repair shop, but the auction world was mum.

Russ Gostrom, a glass of water in his hand in a room full of overpriced beverages, spotted Wally and smiled. Wally admired his perfect hair as he approached.

"Nice to see you here, Wally," Gostrom said. "Didn't think I'd see you after the ruckus you caused at the front desk last year."

"I didn't mean to drop the painting. I was just trying to get a look at the stretcher. It's not my fault the canvas was so brittle. I'm sure those tears were simple to mend. There was hardly any paint loss."

"What on earth led you to believe you were allowed behind the front desk to begin with?"

"All the clerks were busy with checkouts. It wasn't like there was a gate at the end of the counter that said, *Employees Only*. Besides, when I mentioned the painting to the manager just now, he didn't even remember the incident."

"That manager is new this year. He replaced the poor bastard who was in charge when you broke the painting."

"Speaking of the front desk, Russ, you know that Gus Stickley wall sconce over my bed that you always wanted?"

"The one you promised to never sell? The one you bragged you'd be buried with?

"It's available today for two thousand, cash."

Gostrom tilted his head and said, "You laughed at my offer of twenty-five-hundred last summer."

"I need something to stick up the ass of this year's manager, and I think a roll of twenty hundreds would just fit. Besides, I need a place to sleep this weekend. Next week, I get a big paycheck. Perhaps I buy it back for double the money."

"In other words, I'm nothing but a pawnbroker to you." He pulled a wad of green from a side pocket.

"It's a dirty business, but ain't it fun?"

Manuelita moved to the row of chairs on the porch that overlooked the spa. She watched tiny figures work on a construction project far down below, where a distant town straddled a meandering river. Sounds of a distant airplane mixed with a spring breeze.

"Hey, you!"

Manuelita traced a thin line of asphalt as it skirted the tops of the surrounding hills and guessed it was the skyway that Wally told her was one of the most scenic highways in the world.

"Hey, *you*!" Louder and closer. She looked behind her toward the massive hotel and saw a *gringa* with a nameplate. "Yes, *you*," the angry faced woman repeated. "*You* know the rules about domestic help sitting in the guests' chairs out here."

"I don't work here," Manuelita said softly.

"Damn right you don't. You're fired."

Manuelita stood slowly and looked down at the wood deck chair she'd almost fallen asleep in. "I can't sit on this chair?"

The woman put her jowled face up to hers. Manuelita read the nameplate, *Alice Johnson, Spa Manager*, and committed it to memory.

"Guests here pay five hundred a night and they don't want to be elbow to elbow with a Dominican housekeeper while they admire the view."

"I am from Mexico City."

"Mexico City, San Salvador, what's the difference."

"I'm a guest of this hotel. My husband…"

"I'll believe it when I see it. What'd your spic husband do, rob a bank?"

Manuelita smiled in a way that took the matron aback. "Thank you for clarifying my status, Alice. Where is this 'spa' that you manage? Is there a pool?"

"Listen, Consuelo, or Rosie, or whatever you call yourself. The spa has pools, hot springs, underground cavern swimming, massage therapy and a beauty shop, not that you'll see it. We charge one hundred fifty a day to keep the likes of you out."

"The likes of me are not allowed? How interesting."

"Your old man is going to have to mow a lot of lawns for you to drop one hundred fifty for a foot rub, dearie."

"Underground caverns. You don't say. Do they have a ventilation system?"

"What the Sam Hill are you talking about? Get your spic ass out of here before I call Security. What's your name?"

"Manuelita."

"Manuelita what?"

"Manuelita Guevara. Perhaps you've heard of my husband, Che."

"You can tell Che you just lost your job 'cause you were thinking you were as good as legals."

"Thank you," Manuelita said. The matron followed her through the lobby, past Wally at the counter again, and out the massive front door. Manuelita blew her a kiss and shot her with forefinger and thumb, as the door slammed shut.

The doorman walked over and asked, "Problem, Mrs. Winchester?"

"No, a solution, she said. "Where's the nearest pharmacy?"

"This is the finest bed I have ever slept in," Manuelita said, a sheet to her waist.

"Five hundred a night, it better be good," Wally murmured.

"I met an interesting woman today," she said, her head on Wally's shoulder.

He mumbled an acknowledgement, followed by a gentle snore.

"She invited me to the spa."

Wally's eyes opened. "They charge an arm and a leg for a swim in a cave and a pedicure," he said. "Probably more cougars down there than at Yellowstone National Park."

"She didn't warn me of the danger."

"The only ones in danger with these cougars are the pool boy and maybe the masseuse. If you want to try it, we can charge it to the room. I'm going to be up to my neck wheeling and dealing for the next couple days. We can afford it if we don't open the mini-bar. Want to try the spa, just give them the room number."

"I'd rather ride that bus housekeepers take down to the village. Pick up some things at the pharmacy. Save the spa visit for the day we leave."

Manuelita stood up, leaving the sheet in a bunch. At the closet, she pulled a white, terrycloth robe off a hanger, turned back to the bed, the robe open to her nakedness. She walked seductively toward Wally and straddled him like a cowgirl.

His fingers cupped the brown areolas as she reached below her and guided him.

"That movie we watched after dinner, señor, the one with the pay per view. Can you make yourself have sex on my chest like that large Negro woman?"

"Gonna make a mess," Wally said. "Better take the robe off if you're going to wear it to the spa."

"So what? It's a big towel with sleeves." She arched her back and uttered a high-pitched cry. Wally groaned.

"Tell me when you're ready, my stallion," Manuelita said, "I want to be your whore."

Standing in line at the entrance to an exhibition hall, filled with what Wally told her would be the nicest collection of antiques she would ever see, Manuelita picked a book off a pile on a skirted table. The man behind the tablecloth explained, "This is a novel about an obsessive Stickley collector and his very patient wife."

"Interesting," she said.

"Got any photos of Stickley furniture in it?" Wally asked.

"Just a picture of me on the back cover," the author said. "It's a work of fiction."

"Too bad," Wally said. He took the book from Manuelita and replaced it on the pile. "I'm not buying anything I can't sit on or park a lamp on. Good luck, son."

After an initial meander through ten million dollars worth of brown furniture, glistening art pottery, and mica-shaded lamps, Wally asked Manuelita what she thought.

"How can you know all these people?" she asked. "You are three thousand kilometers from your house, and these shopkeepers treat you like a lost brother."

"It's the network, hon. I've been screwed and back-stabbed by half of these assholes and made a lot of money from the rest."

"Is there anyone here you're so mad at that you'd like to see dead?"

"All of them. No, there's a handful of dealers I'd let into heaven if I had St. Peter's job. The rest would get the *down* elevator."

"Show me a bad man."

"Just close your eyes and point."

She did. They followed her finger to a bearded man, sitting on a bench priced at $35,000. A matched pair of drop-arm spindle Morris chairs sat on the corners of his booth like concrete lions. The man noticed the gesture, looked at Wally, and frowned.

Wally sent off a prom queen wave and flashed a grin. Through clenched teeth, like a ventriloquist, he said, "That son-of-a-bitch once bought a Frank Lloyd Wright house in northern California. Came in with a bulldozer a week later and dismantled the whole fucking structure so he could sell the building for parts. He tripled his money and left a hole in the ground.

"The bastard even clearcut the orange trees on the property, sold them for firewood. Then he sold the empty lot. Got half the purchase price for the raped land. View property."

"Is that wrong?"

"He destroyed a national treasure for a few shekels. The city passed a law after that to keep it from happening again, but the damage was done. I had a chance to purchase one of the lanterns, one to die for, and passed on it, knowing the next buyer would snap it up."

"I wonder if he uses the spa," Manuelita said to no one. "Show me another one."

He did, at a booth displaying hanging fixtures. Wally said to Manuelita, "This motherfucker once agreed to trade me the lamp of my dreams for a little tile-topped table I had $12,000 on. Two weeks later, he told me the trade was off. I said, give me my table back. He told me he sold it. I find out later it brought fifteen five. He said he decided to keep the lamp. He says, chose something else. He had nothing else I wanted. He told me, tough shit. It was a handshake deal. No paperwork. Haven't seen a penny to this day. Watch this."

"Mr. Winchester," the chandelier man said. "They let you in again after that stunt you pulled last year?"

"Where's my twelve thousand dollars?"

"That table was a mess. I sold it for under a thousand just to get it out of the shop. It was embarrassing. Can I write you a check?"

"For a thousand dollars? A Grueby tile table? You're out of your fucking mind. Where's my fixture?"

"In my living room. You're not invited."

Wally made a fist, took Manuelita's hand and led her under the glowing shapes of art glass lighting.

"I'll take this one," Wally said. "Call it even." He reached up to touch a brass-clad panel that depicted fir trees and mountains at sunset.

"You think I'll trade an Albert Berry scenic lamp for a run-down table. It had been refinished, you know. Nice try, Winchester. By the way, don't touch my lighting. I don't want your fingerprints on my products."

"Fuck you," Wally uttered. He walked out of the booth in three strides. Redness flowed to his cheeks. Manuelita saw a vein on Wally's forehead swell and throb. She grabbed a business card from the table and flipped the lamp man the finger. He laughed. She drew an imaginary knife across her throat and pointed to him. He smirked as she turned away and took Wally's arm. "Cheer up, señor," she said. "Show me another bad guy. This is fun."

"Any more of this and I'm going into your backpack for our gun, Manuelita. Let me introduce you to one of the good guys." He walked into Russ Gostrom's circus of rare pieces and said hello.

After making love, Manuelita lay back and dabbed the puddle on her chest with the robe.

"You can hang that jiz rag you call a robe out for the laundry service and they'll bring it back fresh, you know, Manuelita," Wally said as he traced the contours of her face with gentle fingers.

"I kind of like it," she said in a sleepy voice. "It turns me on."

Wally shrugged. He asked her what she liked most this afternoon in the show downstairs.

She said, "I don't know. Was I supposed to like something? I saw many interesting and beautiful things. I didn't know you would like me to make a choice."

"Which object do you remember enough to describe?"

"These are hard questions, Señor Wally. I saw many objects today. I don't know how to like objects. In my world, you use them, you sell them, and you trade them. Then you can buy something to eat. If I can use the language of the computer, none of those files of my mind were opened when I walked around the show. What am I going to do with a thirty thousand peso chair? Nothing. I didn't save the memories of these things. They were data I didn't need on my hard drive. I hope that's OK."

"Describe something that you remember."

"I'm tired of this game. All right. Just to keep you from asking again, I saw a chair that was painted black. Simple and plain like a poor man's chair. Yet it rose to a great height. I read, in that chair, a message: The simplest creation on God's earth can walk up on a ladder to heaven." Manuelita stopped, smiled and said, "My goodness, a chair talked to me today. How interesting. Thank you for bringing it to my attention. Are you a shaman?"

"I have a good friend who is a shaman. She's in India while we speak. No, Manuelita, I'm not. A devil maybe." He put out his cheek. "Kiss me right here," he said. As she pursed her lips, he spun his mouth to hers. She opened her teeth and let him in.

"I'm glad a chair spoke to you tonight," Wally said. "Furniture speaks to me all the time. Walking through a high-end antique collection is like sitting in the bleachers of a Yankees game in the ninth inning."

"I don't understand this Yankees game. Your people are all Yankees to me."

"Can I tell you the day when a Chippendale desk talked to me? People seem to cringe when I suggest an interesting reminiscence, I'm not sure why."

"Sure, I want to hear your story. Every word. Tell it twice if it pleases you, but first I need to call my sister and give her a guess of my arrival. Exactly when do you expect to leave here? And when do you expect to be in Boston?"

"Tuesday morning sometime we should hit Beantown. I gave a Stickley lantern away for this fucking room. I damn sure intend to sleep in it. Besides, we'll get a fresh start on an all day drive. Tell your sister Wednesday or Thursday. We may take the parkway north and avoid traffic."

Manuelita nodded. "I have one more request, but to show you I really care, tell me your story now, I love to listen to you talk. I've learned so much on this trip. Tell me the story, and then I'll ask my favor." She moved her hand softly over Wally's sparse chest hair as he began.

"Central Massachusetts. 1970's. A folk collector invites me to his house. Shows me a pine drop-front desk in the Chippendale style. 1820's. Tells me it came from a little hamlet in upstate New Hampshire."

Manuelita stopped him. "Wally, you're not texting. Put the little words back in. My English is like a child."

"Sorry, trying to not bore you, Wally said, then continued.

"So this guy tells me that the original owner was a notorious North Country fire and brimstone preacher. In the sparsely populated White Mountains, he was the recognized moral authority. My buddy pulls out a drawer and says 'look at this.' The back of each drawer had penciled confessions: sins of the preacher. We spent the afternoon, drawer by drawer, reading his transgressions, apparently lifted from his conscience with a sharpened pencil and plunged into darkness for all time."

"A purge."

"Exactly. Guess what? This righteous old coot was out of

control. He was doing the neighbor's wife. He was diddling the neighbor's kid. He confessed to having his way with their cow. I swear to God, I read it myself, and he admitted longings for the sheep. The pious bastard took the pulpit on Sunday and fucked everything that moved on the other six days. The furniture told me the story."

Manuelita nodded. "In Mexico, that concept is understood immediately. We carry our sins like saddlebags. A dark place to unload your transgressions would be a big hit there. In our country, you'd need to attach a plastic chalkboard to the back of the drawer to use with a dry eraser marker, so many sins to put to rest."

"What's the favor you wanted?"

"Can I go to the spa tomorrow and also Monday?"

Dressed in the unsoiled bathrobe, Manuelita wandered down a sloping tunnel lit by indirect lights, a passageway carved through the hillside.

On a Saturday morning, white-robed women preparing to spend a pampered day in underground caverns populated the entry to the spa. Manuelita marveled at the power of Mother Nature to carve out chambers like this. She touched the wall. There was no contact with a thousand tons of Mother Earth. She tapped the wall with her knuckles and heard a hollow sound. Disenchanted, she walked over to a well dressed white girl, who sat behind the machine age reception desk. She introduced herself, told Manuelita her name was Kristal, "with a K."

"Is Alice Johnson here today?"

"She's off to somewhere for the weekend. Back on Monday."

"Perfect."

"Since Alice is not here, can I help you?"

"Alice said when I came down here she would show me all the parts of the spa. The layout, she called it."

"I can do that for you, hon. My break is in fifteen minutes. If Alice promised you a tour, I'll be your guide."

Manuelita thanked her and pocketed the room card since there would be no charges this time. All her questions, thanks to Alice, would be free. She had an odd thought: Wally Winchester would be proud of me. It troubled her.

Krystal bounced over, handed her a brochure. Manuelita opened it and saw pages that described decadent mud wraps, massages, facials, waterfall showers, foot rubs, pedicures, couples treatments, cave swims, and a gift shop for unctuous oils, available to the hotel guests for an additional five hundred dollars a day, charged to the hotel room.

The names of these services amused her: A Mica & Hot Towel Massage, Couples Retreat, Mountain Honey Wrap, Waterfall Body Experience, Blue Ridge Bliss, Gentleman's Getaway, Carolina Mud Pie Wrap, Sanctuary of the Senses Body Treatment for Women, Ageless Hands, Gentleman's DeStress Body Treatment, Gentleman's Mountain Stream Foot Treatment. Manuelita smiled. She gave a mountain stream foot treatment to a guy once in Mexico City in the back of a taxicab. All she got was twenty pesos and a soiled pair of fishnet stockings.

She made a mental note to send these words to her friend, Marie, in Mexico City, who could use a new set of titles for the services she provided in an alley near the government buildings in the center of the city.

"Can I keep this?"

"Of course," Krystal said. "You're an honored guest here."

“Show me the massage rooms,” Manuelita said. “Also, as an afterthought, I note that clean air is important at this wonderful place. Do you have a ventilation system?”

“We just spent fifty million dollars on a remodel. Everything is state of the art.” Krystal brought her face close. “I’ll show you the technical room, where they make all these effects happen. These aren’t real stones on the cave walls you know. They made ‘em.”

“I know,” Manuelita said.

“I’ll show you the tech room. But don’t tell anybody.”

“I promise.”

“Did you enjoy the spa today?” Wally asked as he flipped through the TV channels on the big flat-screen.

“I saved us two hundred dollars by pulling a Wally Winchester.”

“I’ve damaged you, haven’t I? I’m sorry.”

“In more ways than you know, señor. Here’s what I did. When you were having trouble checking in, I sat out on the porch. I met the woman who runs the spa. Today, when I entered the cave,I mentioned the name of the woman to the girl in charge and was given an extensive tour of the whole amazing place for free.”

“Didn’t you want to use any of the services? The massage, the mud thing?”

“Why? I know a brothel when I see it. Read the names of the events that you can purchase for five hundred additional dollars. I have friends in Mexico City who perform sex acts in alleys for twenty pesos. Here they get five hundred dollars.”

“And they don’t even have a happy ending.”

“What do you mean, *happy ending*?”

Wally said, "When you go to a massage parlor near the airport – any airport – you can buy a thirty-dollar massage or a hundred-dollar massage with a happy ending. That means after the backrub…"

"I know the rest, Señor Wally. *Happy ending*."

"Hey, Manuelita there's an acting group called the 'Craftsman Players' and they will be on the stage tonight at the lecture hall."

Manuelita looked to the closet.

In downtown Asheville, a ten dollar taxi ride from the Grove Park Inn, Manuelita sat at Dunkin' Donuts, where she noted all the employees except the manager were Dominicans, east coast Mexicans the way they told it, handing over the muffins and coffee.

Coco and the other youth were at the table when she sat down with her tray.

"You didn't bring us a coffee?" Coco asked.

"Have Claus Braun bring you a coffee. You're not on my payroll." She spread butter on the muffin in front of the hungry pair whose life lately was the back of a van.

"We have C-4 for you," Coco said. "Half a kilo. You could take down that whole building with what we've got if you place it properly. The spa you mentioned, built into the hillside, you could flatten that grotto like a pancake, with all the people providing the filling." He laughed, bumped knuckles with his partner.

Manuelita ate a buttery fragment, sipped her coffee and said, "My sweet Coco. You are a chainsaw in the forest. I am the master woodworker who fashions a masterpiece out of what you cut down. Remember that. My job is to link this *gringo* to a string of murders – not to do mass killing of innocents. We have no cause. I have no statement that I want to pin on the dead bodies of children."

"How about just the spa, not the hotel?"

"No. I've chosen people linked to the *gringo* Winchester, plus one special new friend, Alice."

"What do you need from us?"

"I need you to leave me alone. Read the paper on Tuesday."

Chapter Twenty

Mumbai, India

Yvgeney Ivanchenko, USESCO stolen art recovery investigator, met Chana in the luxurious entry hall of the Mumbai Hilton. She looked the same as when he kissed her goodbye on a Moscow street corner two years before. Her hair was longer now. A forest of dark tresses, parted in the middle, framed the face of a freckled Amazon native with almond eyes.

"You look great," he said. "The life of a shaman becomes you."

"You look like you've gained weight," Chana said. "It becomes you. Fills up all those lines on your face."

"Thanks," Yvgeney said. "I think."

"What do you hear from Wally?"

"Emailed yesterday. He's driving a sports car from Seattle to Boston to deliver it. Right now he's in North Carolina, at a Stickley fest that happens once a year. I'm sure he's like a kid in a toy store this weekend. Trolling for brown furniture in a sea of predation."

Around them in the vaulted lobby, clusters of long-robed religious leaders were involved in animated discussions. Yvgeney gestured with a sweeping hand. "Last time I saw this many clerics was on car number four on the Trans-Siberian Railway."

Chana nodded, "The young priest from Baikonar who received the *Kazanskyia* is attending the conference. He told me our icon is filled with miracles."

"Kept his church from being invaded?" Yvgeney mused, not expecting an answer.

"The reason I invited you here today has to do with this conference, eighty leaders, eighty paths to God praying together to actualize a reduction of the hate and anger that covers our planet like a crown of thorns."

"Amen to that."

"Something wonderful happened yesterday during the first session," Chana continued. "As part of the opening convocation, every leader was to bring a magical object to place between us in the center of the meditation room."

"Let me guess, a stolen cultural artifact turned up."

"An imam from Iran brought a chair fragment. A very old chair, part of the Peacock Throne."

Chana continued to talk but Yvgeney was still on the last words. *The Peacock Throne.* He tuned back in as she said, "The jewels are long gone but the empty settings suggest a poem – just a few words – spelled out in emeralds, diamonds, or pearls."

"The Qudsi couplet," Yvgeney said. "This is astonishing. Do you know why I am in India?"

"I gathered you are here to do your UNESCO sleuthing for stolen cultural masterpieces so you can return them to their rightful place."

"I wish it were that exciting. I'm a paper-pusher here in Mumbai. A paper-pusher, referee and a go-between. India has petitioned the UN to get its heritage back from all the outsiders that have looted its national treasures for a thousand years. The most famous diamond in the world, the Koh-I-Noor, was once embedded in the very same Peacock Throne. Now it resides in the Tower of London. My job for UNESCO is to tell the Queen of England that the Indian government wants the Koh-I-Noor diamond back. My job is to ask the Queen to pluck the jewel from the Maltese cross on top of her crown and send it back to India. How do you think I am doing with *that* mediation?"

"Sounds worse than being chased by flesh-eating pigs in Serbia."

"Trust me, Chana. I'd choose a pig chase into a minefield any day over this exasperating bureaucracy. How did this fellow get his treasure out of Iran?"

"The fragment's existence was never made public by the people who passed it down through generations. It has no paper trail attached to it. It's not in a government data bank. To anyone in the world, except the ten people who know what it is, it's only a broken piece of wood at any customs inspection."

"Will this cleric agree to return this fragment to the people of India?"

Chana looked into his eyes without blinking. "My feeling is that if you can provide a compelling argument for its return, and more importantly, guarantee him that the fragment's recovery will not be publicly announced, India will recover part of its heritage."

"India, I fear, will want this return to be shouted to the world," Yvgeney said.

Chana shook her head. "The Iranian government doesn't know of the fragment's existence. A public spectacle will endanger this man and his family and his mosque."

"Let me work on that one," Yvgeney said. "When can I see it?"

"I can take you to his room now."

Chana noted the crowd in the vast lobby had gone silent. A native of the Amazon rain forest, she knew that silence in the jungle signaled a predator. She looked toward the big front doors; saw black clothing and masks. Then the weapons.

She grabbed Yvgeney's hand and said, "Run."

Automatic weapons fire erupted at multiple points. Chana watched the head of a white-collared priest snap back and spray brains as a volley shattered his skull. She scanned the vast entry for predators, counted seven hooded assassins screaming obscenities as they gunned down waves of screaming guests.

"Get to the stairwell," she said.

"Too far," Yvgeney answered. "Too exposed. Hit the deck, Chana. If you're standing, you're the target."

Gunfire continued while the screams faded. Face down on a floor full of bodies, Chana opened one eye to see a black hood kick the prone body of a whimpering cleric, his white robe stained with blood. Two shots and the man lay still. A woman beside the corpse pleaded in French, as a wicked dagger opened up her throat.

A shadow crossed Chana's eye and she closed it, heard the footfall, felt the nudge of a running shoe probing for signs of life. She heard muted noises of mutilation, a gurgle, a stomp, the unmistakable sound of a blade, tearing through flesh. The pressure from the foot increased in an attempt to roll her onto her back. Eyes closed, she had no strategy, only instinct. She yielded to the foot. As her seemingly lifeless body was flipped onto her back, she opened her eyes, looked into the dark, enlarged pupils of her assailant, standing above her with an old Uzi in his hand. She winked, pursed her lips and blew him a kiss. She read a second of confusion, all she needed. Her foot snapped up and made hard contact with the gunstock. She catapulted to a crouch and sprang at the man above. Her fingers sank into his throat as she grabbed for the weapon. The assailant tried to suck air into his broken windpipe as she pulled the gun from useless fingers and shot him in the heart.

"Yvgeney," she yelled. "Head for the stairwell. I'll cover."

The loud English sentence echoed over the lobby. She spun around, counted six others in masks and shot the closest one in the head as he wiped a bloody knife on his pants. She sprayed the room with automatic bursts and ran for the metal stairway door. Return fire ricocheted off a granite column. She emptied the last of the magazine and leaped through the door that Yvgeney held open.

Gunfire rained on the metal door as it closed. “Up the stairs, quick,” she ordered.

“Use this,” Yvgeney shouted back. He tossed Chana a long-handled mop. She looked to jam the door handle and didn’t see a way. “Just run,” she said.

Confusion filled the third floor hallway. “Get back in your rooms and lock the doors,” Yvgeney screamed. “Don’t let anyone in.”

“We have to do this on every floor,” Chana told him as they raced back to the stairwell.

“I guess just escaping is out of the question,” Yvgeney gasped as they took two stairs at a time. Foreign voices drifted up from the shaft below.

On the eighteenth level, Chana said, “We make a stand here.”

“Why here?” Yvgeney’s face was red from the staircase scramble.

“The Peacock Throne is on this floor,” was her answer.

Yvgeney shouted to panicked guests who banged on the elevator buttons: “Go to your rooms and lock them now. Don’t use the elevator. They have automatic weapons in the lobby.”

A chime announced an arrival. A group of screaming guests ran to the door as it opened. Chana shouted, “Get back!” and sprinted into the hallway. She flattened against the wall by the elevator doors as a burst of rifle fire cut down the helpless throng. She flattened her back beside the open door, watched the tip of another Uzi cross the threshold toward the bloody pile of moaning victims.

One more step, she thought.

The terrorist looked out the door to his left as he exited the elevator, stepping on a dead man's hand. She leaped onto his back, clamping an arm around his throat as he fired wildly into the ceiling. Her wrist pressed into soft tissue. The sound of little bones breaking increased his frantic gyrations. He slammed his back against the wall in an attempt to knock her off and swung the gun hand over his shoulder for an impossible shot. Then his legs buckled, with Chana riding him to the corpse-littered carpet.

Yvgeney emerged from behind an ice machine with bullet holes in its stainless steel box. "Thank God for ice," he said. Chana retrieved the machine pistol and tossed it over. He checked the clip. "Almost empty."

"Set it for single shots," Chana said. "We need every bullet."

She stepped gingerly over a sea of twisted arms and legs, avoiding pools of blood. She looked at all the faces. "Our Iranian is not among the dead," she said, "Perhaps he stayed in his room."

"Maybe he was in the lobby,"

"I would have seen him. It's a pretty big room. I would have noticed the flow of people when they came near the Peacock Throne fragment."

"That's right, Chana, you can do that. I remember."

She stepped over the body of a woman wearing an elegant beaded dress, ruined, like her last moment of life. At a door marked #1822, she stopped and knocked.

No answer. "That's the right response," she said. "Stand back, Yvgeney, so he can see us through the peep-hole in the door. Hide the gun."

She knocked again, then stepped back to reveal they were alone, unarmed in the quiet hallway.

The door opened to the safety chain.

Chana said, "You know me from the conference. I'm Chana. It's safe for you to let us in. Please hurry."

A grey-bearded man with fearful eyes let them enter.

"Lock it now," Chana said. "These people still control the hotel." She introduced Yvgeney in hit or miss French, describing him as a UNESCO art expert who was trying to repatriate stolen objects to India. The cleric turned to a table near the door and donned a headpiece. He bowed. "I am Farouk Nadir," he said. "I brought this sacred artifact out of Iran because its keepers wanted me to attend this interfaith conference for peace. We believe it belongs in India where it was created. The knowledge of the relic's existence lives in the minds of only ten people, now twelve."

Yvgeney stepped forward and spoke in French, "If your intention is to return the fragment of the Peacock Throne, I would be your ideal conduit."

The grey bearded man glanced out the window. "The television shows our hotel under attack," he said. "I've hidden the fragment. I heard gunfire. What's going on? Has the hotel been taken over by terrorists?"

Chana said, "I saw seven masked men in the lobby. They control this hotel. Now there are four. By now, they have acquired the master key and are going floor to floor, killing anyone they find in the rooms. I taught this tactic as an insurgent strategy in Brazil a long time ago."

Yvgeney said to the Iranian, "Can I see this fragment?"

"I'd rather wait until it is safe."

The building shuddered as a concussion rattled the windows. A ragged plume of smoke and debris rose over the rooftops in the direction of the railway station. "It's a repeat of the 2008 attacks," Yvgeney said.

Chana agreed. "Worked the first time. Get the name and manifesto of your fledgling Pakistan splinter group spread across the world on CNN and Wikipedia at the cost of twelve martyrs plus collateral damage."

"One hundred innocent people," Yvgeney said.

"One hundred seventy-three," Chana said. "I paid attention to that attack. I used to do it for a living."

"Memories of Claus Braun," Yvgeney said as they looked out from the eighteenth floor at the rooftops of one of the great cities of the world.

"There's chatter that Claus Braun is alive, hidden in deep layers of cover," Chana said.

"Braun, alive? How good is your intel?"

Another flash of light lit the sprawling finger of a city below them. A mushrooming cloud appeared three blocks and three hundred feet below, followed by a concussion. The windows caught the shock wave and transmitted the jolt into the room.

Chana studied the billowing plume, felt a flash of nostalgia, and said, "I don't know the intentions of the people below us. If the relic is in this suite, hidden, I respect that, but I believe the structure of this building is in jeopardy. If we leave, which I think we should, we should take it with us."

"The relic is with us now," the cleric said. "It is fastened to my body with tape. We can leave now."

"I'd love to see it," Yvgeney said.

"We have to go," Chana said. "Yvgeney, your ideas? Up to the roof, stay here, or go down?"

"How many rounds left in your gun?"

"Five," she said. "It's on single shot. How many *banditos* are holding this hotel hostage? I'd figure four. One in the lobby. That's a given. Three left to roam with a master key."

Yvgeney thought quickly. "I vote *no* to the lobby. *No* to this room. *Yes* to the roof. Our best defensive position with five rounds of ammo is open space."

Chana nodded, "Take this pistol with you and keep this man and the artifact safe. Go now. I'll follow. Make sure the stairwell's empty above you."

"Where are you going, Chana?"

"We need another weapon." She opened the door to the hall without a sound and eyeballed the corridor. "Now," she said. They skirted the carnage at the elevator doors. Chana patted down the dead terrorist, pulled a knife from his waistband. Yvgeney opened the heavy stairway door and listened.

"*Merde*," Chana cursed in French. Yvgeney looked back. "What?" he whispered.

"He's carrying a detonation cord. Go now. Trust no one." She wiped the bloody knife on the intruder's black shirt. He shuddered and blew a ragged breath. She plunged the blade into his solar plexus and ripped a path to his heart then wiped the blade again. Yvgeney and the cleric stepped into the stairwell. Chana pushed the *down* button and dragged the dead man to the door, which opened. Inside, she propped him against the back wall. The door began to close. She stopped it with her foot and reached for the buckle on the dead man's trousers. A minute later, she wiped the blade again and pushed the buttons for each floor, all the way to the lobby. As the doors closed, she ran for the stairs, heading down.

On the twelfth floor landing, Chana looked through the wired glass window in the staircase door and saw a masked man in the hall turn when the elevator door chimed and opened. She watched him physically react when he saw the tableau she'd arranged. When he entered the car, she opened the door to the twelfth floor.

The bandit pulled a pair of woman's panties from his naked compatriot's slack mouth when she drew the blade across his neck, flooding the splayed corpse below him with spurting blood. He tried to turn his masked head to look at the devil that killed him, but the muscles didn't work anymore. He collapsed, the last breaths gurgling from his ragged neck wound. Chana grabbed his pistol and took another knife. She searched for bomb materials and found three detonating caps and a cell phone, which she put in her pocket. She stripped the second killer, gave him her A-cup bra as a hat, replanted her panties and sent the elevator down. She checked the clip. It was full.

Bodies littered many of the carpeted hallways that Chana viewed as she chased the elevator, floor by floor, to the lobby.

Two insurgents left, plan for three just in case, she figured as the elevator left the massacre on the mezzanine and headed for the ground floor.

When Yvgeney and the cleric opened the door to the roof, they entered a killing field. Bloody bodies littered an elegant rooftop garden. A line of crumpled forms at a railing, installed to avoid a twenty-story fall to the street, reminded him of a form of execution used in Serbia called, "Jump or Get Shot."

"Please, stay behind me, sir," he whispered in French. They walked through manicured avenues of rare plants and stepped over sprawled human forms, frozen in their last gesture, framed in red. A man on the ground groaned. After a three hundred sixty degree sweep of his head, Yvgeney stopped to feel the pulse on the white-suited body. It was strong. The man, Middle Eastern, turned his head and spoke in broken English, "Thank God you are here. Are you the police?"

"We're guests," Yvgeney said, "but I have a gun."

The prone man grabbed at Yvgeney's feet and hugged them. "Please save us," he said.

"How many were here?"

The man sat back, blood on his fancy shirt. "Only one!" he said. "The masked man found a group of us up here on the roof, hoping for a helicopter rescue. He walked around killing one at a time, like cows at the slaughterhouse. He was methodical, sang a song when he pulled the trigger. I played dead. Watched him order victims to jump to their death or get shot. A frightful choice."

Yvgeney looked around at scalped skulls, women posed and mutilated, the sad pile at the roof-top edge that chose a bullet over a fall. "Why are you still alive?" he asked.

"I have not moved or opened my eyes since the shooting began," the man said as he stood and tried to pat the wrinkles out of his suit, a white Armani cotton blend.

Yvgeney saw a rip in the fabric of the shirt the man was wearing, tinged with red. He said, "You're wounded. Let me help you."

"I'm all right." The lone survivor groaned and turned away as he sank to his knees. The cleric instinctively reached out to keep him from falling and the wounded man snapped back to life with an arm across the cleric's chest, a knife in hand, eyes on Yvgeney and the gun.

Neither man spoke. Yvgeney trained his weapon at the knife-wielder's face as it ducked behind the head of his captive.

"What's on your chest, dead man?" White Suit asked his captive in English, eyes still on Yvgeney.

"Something that is the opposite of you," the cleric said. "Something important enough to hide. I want to see it."

"Excuse me," Yvgeney said. "Over here. I'm the guy with the gun. Are you a terrorist, or am I watching a mugging?"

"I expect to die today," the terrorist said. "Our work is almost done. The question is, do you want me to slit this holy man's throat before I die? Or do you want to save his life?"

"I've seen your work," Yvgeney answered. "What's left? Do you plan to take the hotel down? We recovered the blasting caps, you know. Oh, I have some other bad news for you. I expect that all your pals down below are dead by now."

The knife pulled a red line on the cleric's throat. Yvgeney held the gun steady.

"My people are very good. Why do you think they are dead?"

"They're dead because I know who's after them. There won't be any explosions unless you're the guy with the button, motherfucker! My problem is you."

The assassin said, "Lower your pistol towards the ground. I want to see this artifact before I die."

"I want to see the artifact, too," Yvgeney said. "Let's take a look."

"I won't take it off," the cleric said to his captor. "Kill me, infidel, then you die, then the relic is safe."

Yvgeney intervened. "Please sir, bring this fragment into the light. Your scenario is still intact. I believe its power will create a solution to the Mexican standoff we find ourselves in."

The cleric looked into Yvgeney's eyes and nodded that he understood. He unbuttoned his shirt and reached inside it. To his captor, he said: "I have to pull some tape off, sir. If I make a jerky movement, please understand."

"Peel your tape, meat," the terrorist said.

Yvgeney, despite the tense situation, marveled that, ten thousand miles away, he'd heard the same sentence years ago in a Pacific Northwest warehouse. He lowered the barrel of his gun.

When the cleric opened the cloth, reverence fell over an already silent roof. The gilded surface of the nine square inch fragment caught the last of the Mumbai sunset. The killer in the Armani suit tilted his head in wonderment.

Yvgeney shot him between the eyes.

Chana bounded down the mezzanine staircase to the lobby floor and found herself enjoying the game. She chased the thought away. As a child growing up in the Brazilian rainforest, she played *Linguadope*, a language game in which the player who could visualize the contest from a distance always won. She saw her prey in the lobby. That would be the easy one. She was concerned about the parking garage with its exposed architecture.

A lone terrorist wandered between lifeless victims in the lobby. Armed with a satchel full of clips, he shot a burst through broken windows into the street, a routine he repeated every few minutes. Chana entered the big hall silently. A view outside told her that no police had yet assembled. She watched as the sound of the elevator door opening caught the killer's attention. He readied his gun for a carload of guests, but instead witnessed two of his team, splayed out in a ghastly insult to his vision of heaven. He ran to the elevator oblivious to the dark movement by the staircase.

Chana didn't need the gun. She preferred the persuasion of a knife against the jugular. She pounced, legs around his waist, her right arm around his shoulder with the knife. She drew the blade once.

"Don't move, or I tear your head off," she whispered in French. Her prey winced, and stood still, the devil on his back.

"Funny," Chana said as she straddled him like a pony. "You're here on a suicide mission, but the threat of death still works. Where are the bombs?"

"We are soldiers in a holy war…"

Chana sliced his neck again, avoiding the death-cut, severing a tendon. He yelped.

"The bomb. Where is it?" The knife pressed deeper.

"Level one in the parking garage, devil. You're too late." He threw himself backward into the elevator car. Chana hit the polished brass wall as she finished her cut. She held on like a rodeo bull rider and felt the legs buckle. She pressed the button for Parking Level One, dashing for the stairwell as the door closed.

In the vast cavern that housed Jaguars, BMWs and Mercedes sports cars, Parking Level One, Chana walked silently through a dimly lit sea of luxury vehicles, looking for something out of place.

She saw the bombs, a necklace of white rectangles that surrounded a huge square column near the auto ramp. Ten kilos or more. Was it enough to take out one of the four building supports? She couldn't be sure.

She wove her way closer until only a Mercedes Town Car stood between her and the pillar. She looked for movement. Saw none. She dropped to the concrete and searched under nearby vehicles, a rodent the only sign of life. Satisfied, she approached the chain of plastique, eyes wide for a radio frequency receiver to drive the detonator. In the darkened concrete corner, she spied a model toy truck with its antenna up. Wires linked it to the explosives ringing the support.

"Too easy," she said to herself. "A trap."

The interior of the remote control toy lit up. Tiny headlights blazed. She moved without caution to the C4 necklace and began yanking wires from the plastique.

She'd just finished unplugging the third face of the massive column when the toy truck whined and the last side exploded. A concussion knocked her off her feet and slammed her body into the car behind her. The world went dark. She found herself in the rainforest, at the mist covered lake she went to often in dreams. The fog glowed above still waters. It floated toward her. She put a hand up to shield her eyes. It was the hand of a child.

A soft arm cradled her tiny body. The comforting voice of her mother took away her fear and showed her other beings that lived above the water when the moon was full.

A voice she knew broke through a crack of her dream. "Chana" it said, "Chana, Chana," like a song.

She opened her eyes to a sprayed concrete roof and the wind-etched face of her Russian friend. She coughed up dust.

"There's one more out there, Yvgeney," she said.

"The place is crawling with police. They'll find him."

"Tell them the attacker may be dressed in the clothes of a victim."

"I already have. He's on the roof."

Chapter Twenty-One

Asheville, North Carolina

As Alice Johnson, manager of the spa at the Grove Park Inn, left the Monday morning staff meeting, she scowled when she recognized the Hispanic she'd fired on Friday, now walking around the underground pool wearing one of the hotel's white robes.

"Got a lotta nerve coming down here, Maria. I told you you're fired. Where'd you steal the robe? The laundry?"

Manuelita smiled. The matron shut her mouth, stepped back, unnerved by the response. She glanced around the chamber. They were alone. Manuelita closed the distance between them and pulled her hunting knife from her robe. She raised the blade slowly, like a hypnotist, until it met the manager's neck. Alice stepped back, found the lap pool at her back.

"You and I," Manuelita said, "are going to massage room four, Alice Johnson. And you will tell the girl to take the day off. That is my room today. Do you understand?" The blade nicked throat flesh. A red line flowed blood.

"Yes," Alice said through a shudder of absolute fear.

"Let's go. My knife is at your back. I'll rip your heart out if you fail me."

When the dealer who dismantled the Frank Lloyd Wright house knocked on the door, Manuelita said, "I've been expecting you. Come in."

An overweight, tanned Caucasian walked into the room in a hotel robe.

"My name is Manuelita," she said, her robe unfastened. She watched the flash of Mexican bush set the hook. "My job today is to guide you to paradise."

"Gonna cost me a day on the road, honey, but maybe a good massage would do me good."

"Hop up on the table, big guy. Off with the duds, as they say."

"Face down?"

"Cute. Yes, face down. This is a massage you know. Don't worry, though. I plan for you a great finish. Something I call a Mexican bowtie."

"Sounds good to me, honey. Hurry it up will ya? I got a truck to pack."

"Yessir," Manuelita said. She approached his prone form, a squeeze-bottle of lotion in her right hand, watched his sidewise gaze at her body. "Can I sit on top of you while I rub your back?"

"You bet, little lady, I'll be your bronco."

"You're here to relax," Manuelita said. "Put your head in that hole and I'll take all your cares away."

Astride him, naked with the knife in her hand, Manuelita marveled at how easy this death would be. She squeezed some lotion on the fat ridges of his back, rubbed some in, leaned over and cut his throat.

She held the thrashing body till it bled out and lay still, then dragged the corpse off the table, thankful that the remodel included showers for the massage rooms. Reaching into the dead man's slashed throat, she pulled the tongue out through the gash as she'd promised. Bare feet slipped on the scarlet floor as she pulled the awkward bundle into the closet to join the body of Alice Johnson, propped up against the wall like a Raggedy Ann doll.

She surveyed the trail of carnage. A blood-soaked bed and floor. She checked her watch. Fifteen minutes till client number two.

She pulled off her Wally robe and let it fall into the puddle of her crime. Naked, she walked to the shower.

"Come in," Manuelita said to the knock at the door. She was naked, with her knife behind her.

The door opened. A squirrel in a hotel robe smiled and stepped in.

This is too easy, again Manuelita thought. She walked up to him, pert breasts in his eyes, and said, "I'm sort of in a hurry, señor. Do you want to get to the happy ending?"

"Suits me," the small man said. "I've got a truck to pack."

She closed the door, aware of the eyes on her body. Her arm swung out and parted his throat.

After all, she thought, Wally's waiting.

"How was the spa?" Wally asked when Manuelita returned to the room at noon.

"Just what I needed," she said. "Thank you. When can we get going?"

"I've been waiting on you, darling, the car is in the front parking lot. All warmed up."

She kissed him chastely and brushed his hand away from her breasts as she stepped into her clothes. "Let's go," she said. "Show me America."

Chapter Twenty-Two

Wheeling, West Virginia

For the drive north to Boston, Wally chose the Blue Ridge Parkway as far as Virginia. Manuelita watched lofty, tree-studded hills fly by as Wally pulled the Cobra through the sweeping mountain curves. She reached over and placed a hand on his thigh. He sped up.

Wally made a brief side trip to West Virginia and bought a bookcase in Wheeling, and Manuelita had to go back to work.

"I should go pee, Wally," she said as he settled into the driver's seat, elated with his recent purchase. "Yes, yes, yes. 1901. *Gus in the box* mark. Hot damn."

She entered the used furniture store and wandered through rows of dressers and wood closets till she found a human to kill.

A smiling grey-haired woman behind a counter greeted her. "Hi, hon. How can I help you?" She stood up in the greeting.

Manuelita said, "My friend, Wally, just bought something from you. I thought I should use the ladies' room before we leave."

"Your friend was so excited about the way the wood was cut on the front of the bookcase. It's always fun to have a happy customer. The ladies' room is right over there. And, honey," she said, calling Manuelita closer, "there's a switch on the wall. Heater lamp on a timer. Give it a whirl."

Manuelita stood in the ladies' room and turned the heater switch. It sent a warm glow into the room as the dial clicked toward *Off*.

She didn't pee, and thanked the woman on the way out, thinking that her assignment was indeed becoming difficult.

Chapter Twenty-Three

Central Pennsylvania

Manuelita bounced into the low passenger seat with a smile on her face. "Nice old woman," she said. "I liked her."

"I liked her also. She just sold me a rare bookcase for five hundred dollars and helped me drag it into the back room to keep it hidden till I get back down here to pick it up after the car sale. She's now on my short list of favorite people I know in West Virginia."

The mountains flattened into undulating valleys as Mr. Shelby's racer ate up the Pennsylvania interstate at eighty miles per hour. Wally watched in the rearview mirror as a tiny spot grew into a vehicle, closing the distance between them. "Son-of-a-bitch behind us is really smoking, Manuelita," he said and slowed to the speed limit, drifting right to make room. A ratty Ford van zoomed past at what he guessed was 90 miles per hour. He nodded a greeting to a large Hispanic man at the passenger window. He received a finger salute in return.

Manuelita knew the van and its occupants. She shook her head slowly. She said, *"Mal hombres, señor."*

"Assholes, anyway."

The van slowed, allowing the Shelby to catch up.

"He's playing some fucked-up game, Manuelita," Wally said.

"It's the car," she lied. "You piss off those *cholos* in your expensive car. Please get away from here. You have the fastest car in the world, Señor Wally. Step on it."

The van had slowed to 40. The passing lane was wide open, leading to another Pennsylvania ridge climb. Wally pulled left and began to pass, but the van cut back into his lane. He slammed the brakes and narrowly avoided contact.

"Motherfucker!" Wally screamed as the dirty transport wobbled back across the dotted lane markers.

"Take him on the right, señor."

Wally drifted to the right lane and noted a wide gravel roadside that looked drivable in a pinch. The van moved back to the driving lane to block his path.

They passed the sign for a rest area ahead. Wally hit the turn signal. "I've got too much to lose in a game of chicken with some fuckheads," he said as they rolled to a stop at a cinderblock restroom, featuring a large map of central Pennsylvania.

"They're not done, señor. Look."

The van entered the parking lot from the north end exit and parked a hundred yards away. It rocked slightly as the driver gunned the engine.

"Hey, that's a one-way exit." Wally observed. "That's against the law."

Manuelita said, "I don't believe those asses are worried about *gringo* traffic signs, señor."

Wally opened the door. He said, "I'm going to tell those dorks to leave me the fuck alone. I have no beef with them."

Manuelita stopped him. "You're out of your league. You're a middle-aged white man. Did you see the size of that passenger?" She put her hand on his shoulder. "Let me talk with them. I will not look like trouble."

"It's my duty. I'm the man."

"When you get your ass kicked, who'll protect the car?" Manuelita said, "Hand me my backpack. If you see me in trouble, drive up fast with the door unlocked and rescue me." She stepped out, cutting off further debate, and walked in measured strides toward the rumbling vehicle at the other end of the lot.

At the driver's window, she stood five feet away. "Coco, you fucking bonehead," she screamed. "What the hell you think you're doing?" She extracted the handgun.

"Claus Braun called," Coco said. "You're fired."

"Didn't you read about the murders at the Grove Park Inn?"

"I don't get the local paper," Coco said. "That last antique store. We stopped to check after you left. The old hen was still alive. Acted happy to see us till we took out the tazer."

"That nice old woman?" Manuelita exclaimed. "She didn't need to die."

"She wasn't in favor of it, it's true. She begged and made chirping sounds when we shot her."

"Bastards."

"You've gone soft. The plans have changed. Get in the van. We'll take it from here."

"Fat chance," Manuelita said. She pulled the gun and aimed it at Coco's head.

"We have two guns on you, teacher. Get in, perhaps the boss will give you a job in the kitchen when we get home."

"Or the nursery," the passenger added. "Take care of the bambinos."

Manuelita held her aim at the Mexican face and heard the rumble of Wally's car, accelerating toward the dispute. As it pulled alongside, she jumped in, holding the pistol aim as Wally floored it, leaving twenty yards of rubber on the pavement. In the side mirror, Manuelita watched the van keep pace.

"Drive as fast as you can," she shouted into the wind. "Those boys are crazy." Her hand rested on Wally's as he shifted into fifth gear. The speedometer wobbled at 110.

"Why were they such assholes?"

"Mexicans," she said. "Go figure."

At a riverside campground in upstate New York, just across the Pennsylvania line near Binghamton, Wally lit the Coleman lamp and opened the Julia Margaret Cameron box. "Can I read you another letter from Alfred Lord Tennyson?" he asked.

"Sure." Manuelita thought of Coco and his threat, wondering if her job was indeed over. Part of her hoped it was. As Wally opened another yellowed handwritten document, excitement in his deep blue Anglo eyes, she felt an odd pull from her heart. Warmth covered her like a blanket, and she rested her head on his shoulder as he stumbled over odd-sounding words in a language Wally called *Old English.*

"Dearest Julia," he read from the letter. "I've heard that the vessel carrying another shipment of my photo chemicals for you was lost around the Horn of Africa..."

Manuelita heard the stream of words, but her mind was on her mission. Coco was right, she thought. She was losing her focus. Wally put his arm around her shoulder and held her in a gentle, comfortable embrace, reading the English letter, commenting on parts he found interesting. This was part of the problem, she knew: Wally Winchester was getting under her skin. She tilted her head to kiss his ear.

Wally's lips spoke the words in the letter. Inside his head, he asked himself what he was getting into. She's a gal to whom you offered a ride across the country and now you're lying together in a tent, your hand on her titty. She's wearing a wedding ring you gave her, you now own a gun – a big one. She's already stuck it in a guy's face, though he probably deserved it. What are your intentions with this sweet, savage, complicated woman? Do you want to continue this relationship when you sell the car in Boston, she continuing up to Nashua, New Hampshire? Is she just a cute piece of ass that you've manipulated into fucking you? What do you feel about her as a person? Are you falling in love?

He folded the letter, returned her kiss and found an eager mouth.

At midnight, Manuelita disengaged herself from Wally's arms and got dressed, choosing dark clothing. Light snoring vibrated the tent as she melted into the underbrush. Ten minutes of reconnaissance led her to Coco's van, quiet and dark inside.

Her lips were pressed into a firm, tight line as she tapped softly on the driver's window with her knife blade. She watched the big Mexican's eyes open. She smiled at him as he looked into the darkness for the source of the intrusion. His eyes widened when Manuelita put her finger to her lips for silence, then used it to invite him outside. He opened the door to another reminder to be quiet, a Glock in his right hand for insurance.

"Coco is planning to kill you, Manuelita," the big youth whispered. "Your mission has been terminated."

Manuelita shrugged and held both hands, palm up in surrender, mindful of the cold steel blade in her belt loop, pressing against her bottom. In a low volume, she said, "I did a good job. This *gringo* lives in a world of unpredictability. Claus Braun is making a bad decision."

She moved closer as she sized up her prey, a man-boy she had known in Mexico City when he was ten years old, a street rat who ran with a pack of barracudas – ghetto children with box cutters as weapons who grazed on the *touristas*, harvesting wallets with a slice and a tear. Even then he made her nervous, with his angry, sociopathic stare.

He aimed his pistol at the former instructor. "Coco will be happy if I save him the chore of killing you. Thanks for stopping by."

Manuelita shook her head and smiled. Confusion wrinkled his ham of a face. She said, "You can't use an unsilenced gun here in a campground full of *gringos*. Didn't I teach you anything? You'll wake up half of New York and alert the man, Winchester, as well."

She watched big brown eyes shift back and forth, searching his brain for an answer. She helped him. "Here," she said, drawing the knife from the waistband. "The knife is the correct weapon for this situation."

As her arm snapped the blade into the soft tissue under the rib cage, she put the other hand over an outraged mouth and muffled the surprised grunt. She moved the blade up into the heart until blood shot out of his nose and the corners of his clamped brown lips.

The pistol left his fingers. She arrested the weapon's fall with her foot, like a soccer ball, and then assisted the big killer's collapse as his knees buckled and the eyes rolled back.

Strong hands circled her throat. Coco. Manuelita felt her hypoid bones crackle and heard the deep Spanish voice on her way to unconsciousness. "Good night, bitch," was the sentence she carried into sleep.

A huge sound woke her. It reminded her to breathe. She coughed and sucked in a gallon of air. Beside her, on the ground, was the shattered face of Coco, forehead burst like a watermelon, his killer smile now pasted forever on his brown face. She tried to turn her head and felt the damage to her throat. In the corner of her eye, she saw Wally, holding their gun.

"You crazy little Mexican, I figured you'd sneak out to try to be a hero. You didn't even take the gun." Wally looked at the big steel weapon, then at the body. "Oh my gosh," he stammered. "I just killed a man."

"We have to leave this camping ground immediately," Manuelita ordered. "Leave the tent. You can't afford to be caught here."

"It was self-defense! The son-of-a-bitch was strangling you, Manuelita."

"Trust me," she said. "It's not a good time to be in the hands of police. Run, please."

A line of blinking cruisers flashed by as the Cobra headed into the starless New York night. Manuelita said, "Thank you for saving me, Wally." Her hand held his in a tight grip. "You were very brave."

"It was nothing." Wally's mind was on fire. He'd just killed a guy. Holy shit. Blew his fucking head off, no less. He couldn't wrap his mind around that one. Sure he'd seen people die. His life for the last couple of years had been a chockablock with some pretty hairy shit, most of it, he believed, not his fault. Taking a life was new. He didn't like it at all. Why, he asked himself, was he grinning?

"Is that your first kill, my hero?" Manuelita asked as she watched the speedometer hover at 80 on the toll road to Albany.

"My belt has a lot of notches," Wally said. "No, I'm making it up. It is my first kill, and I don't like the way I feel." He decelerated to a crawl and stopped on the side of the road, opened the door and threw up, careful not to get any on the leather seat.

Manuelita stroked his back. She said, "I threw up after my first also. It's normal."

Wally used a receipt from the bookcase sale to wipe his mouth, then refolded it and added it to the trip log parked on the dash with a magnet.

"That's disgusting," Manuelita said.

"My bookkeeper has seen worse."

The bridge over the Hudson River carried the sports car with the killers inside, over the twinkling lights of the city of Troy.

"We shouldn't have left the tent, Manuelita." Wally was working on a defense for his trial. "What if they find our fingerprints?" He squeezed her hand. "Our DNA?"

Manuelita placed a kiss on an unshaven cheek she was growing fond of. The thought disturbed her in a world spinning out of control. "There's a lot you don't know, my love," she answered, surprised by her choice of words. She thought of Claus Braun, his powerful outreach, and his ruthlessness. "There are worse things out there waiting for us."

"What do you mean?"

"I'll tell you everything when we're safe. Right now my job is giving you some cover."

"Soon as I get the payoff for this car, we can buy our way out, baby," Wally offered.

Manuelita bit her lip. "This is not good timing, you selling the car right now," she said.

"Hey girl, shooting or not, I've dropped four or five grand on this trip. The money to pay for all the fun we've had is under our butts thanks to Mr. Carroll Shelby. How's your neck? You should get it looked at. You were already unconscious when I showed up. I thought he'd broken it."

Manuelita felt the exquisite pain of tiny fractures in the throat skeleton. She attempted a swallow and stopped, said she was fine.

"When we get to Beantown tomorrow I'll pay for a checkup and X-ray for you. If nothing else, it could be useful for a defense if they track us down. What were those jokers still doing in our life? How'd they end up in the same campground? How'd you know they were out there? Is there something about this trip that you're not telling me?"

"There is a lot that you don't know. Right now you need to find a safe place to hide before the police find us or worse," she said.

"What could be worse than being arrested for murder? I shot that man, you know. In self-defense for you, but that motherfucker's dead nevertheless, and you killed the first guy, that brown giant. We're both in shit city."

"Sweet Wally." Manuelita touched his cheek again, looked in the sideview mirror – an automatic reflex now. "There are places much worse than this *shit city*. Please take my advice. I can't tell you more right at this time. You have to get away from here. They'll be waiting for you, and right now, me also."

"I'm not afraid of coppers," Wally mimicked an Edward G. Robinson line.

Manuelita wasn't amused. "The people I'm afraid of are much more dangerous."

As they passed the turnpike exits for Worcester, Wally made a decision, one that had been building for a long time. "I'm flying to Sri Lanka to door-knock Julia Margaret Cameron."

He paused and added, "We haven't talked about us."

"Is there an us?" Her finger went to his knee and she played with the fabric of his jeans. "I will admit I thought you were an odd old *gringo* with a fancy car when I said yes to this journey. I still believe that, Señor Wally, but I've been captured by your big heart and not so crazy craziness. You are not the fool that you wear over your shoulder like a winter coat. I think you are a brilliant thinker, who lives, as they say, outside the box."

Wally asked, "*Is* there an *us*?" His right hand played in the short forest of hair at the back of her head. His fingers traced a light footed path over her shoulder to the first button of her shirt. He opened it. She brushed the hand away and said, "Two hands on the steering wheel, horny toad." She laughed, then turned serious. "Where I grew up, the concept of *us* was a luxury item. I could barely afford the concept of *me*. There were few happy endings in Mexico City. I've known many men, señor, had my share of boyfriends. I must admit it, *us*, to me, is like other words I've never experienced, like *millionaire,* or *fulfillment*, or," she paused, "*love*. The wish list in my world is less complicated. *Full tummy* is right up there, along with ideas like, *this is a safe place to sleep tonight*, or *it only hurts when I pee."*

"Come with me to Sri Lanka. We can leave in a couple days."

"No passport, señor." Manuelita said. "I wish I could go, and I agree that you should travel there. As soon as you can. Even tonight. You have hellhounds on your tail."

"What will you do?"

"Go to the region Nashua, like I planned. My sister will hide me."

"Can I look you up when I get back?"

"Señor Wally, you have thrown my heart into what you call a spin. I didn't expect that. When you get back, don't look for me. You will soon find out that I am not good for you. I am sad about that now, but the past cannot be replayed."

"Give me the phone number or email for your sister."

"No," she said. "Actually, I have no sister, at least not in Nashua. I will disappear. Don't try to find me."

"You have no sister in New Hampshire?" Wally's hand left her shoulder. "This entire trip for you is just a lie? Are you a fabrication also?"

Manuelita reached for Wally's hand on the shifter. He pulled it back to the steering wheel. She said, "I have done you great harm, señor. You will know soon enough."

"You're freaking me out," Wally said. "Has any of our experience been real? Is our lovemaking part of this…this fake-out? I was feeling my life come together again, and now I can feel it tearing apart."

"It started as a deception, *si*. I'm so sorry. I didn't know you. But believe me, my sweet Wally, I didn't know you then; you were an assignment."

"I was a freaking assignment?"

"Only at first. I've never known a man like you. Men in my world are either users or they want to be used. There is always a price. Falling in love is for suckers. Now I know a man who accepted me unconditionally, wanted nothing from me but my heart. I don't know what to do with that feeling you gave me. You showed me emotions I read about in books but didn't believe in."

Wally flipped the right turn signal at Exit 12, the Framingham exit. His lips held a straight line where they met.

"Señor Wally," Manuelita said, "I'm sorry. Don't throw me off your bus. You will need me if you try to sell this car. The man at the other end is not your friend. I can help you. Protect you. Please keep me."

Wally saw the Greyhound Bus sign and screeched to a halt. He reached past his passenger and opened her door. "Time to get out, whoever you really are," he said.

"Please, señor. There is so much you have to know. You are in grave danger. For my part in it, I am ashamed. Let me watch your back."

"Get out." Wally handed her the murder pack. Tears welled up and flooded her brown cheeks.

"Get out." He pulled a twenty out of his pocket. "Here, find yourself a new patsy. Do me a favor and throw the gun in a river."

"You should keep the gun, Señor Wally," Manuelita said. "At least let me tell you about the terrible spider's web you are tangled in. Maybe you'll have a chance when you know my assignment."

At the repeat of the word, "assignment," Wally's face fell another inch. "Out," he ordered.

She climbed out slowly, hitching her backpack on a shoulder. She offered him the gun and two boxes of ammo. He waved them away, then said, "Wait."

She turned her face into the little car, a tiny light in her eyes.

"Give me back my ring."

Manuelita's shoulders crashed. She pulled herself upright and looked at another street in another town she didn't know. "No," she said and walked into the station.

Wally looked behind the seat for the box with the Cameron photo and the letters with God's gift of an address, trusting nothing. All was there. He cried all the way to Boston, wiping the salty tears off the perfect leather seat with a tissue as he drove. With his cell phone low to his shoulder, in case there was a law against them in this state, he booked a flight to Sri Lanka, leaving the next day, one passenger, no luggage.

Chapter Twenty-Four

Spokane, Washington

Detective Kelly watched the queue of noontime customers waiting for the pizza shop to open on the street below his window. His State Patrol search turned up no new killings along the I-90 / I-94 corridor toward Boston -- Illinois, Ohio, and Pennsylvania. No knife attacks that matched the pattern.

"Where are you, Wally Winchester?" he typed into the Google search box.

He got a pageful of nothing but telephone directory ads and people-search databases.

In interview room number three, the donut box was down to plain cake rings, and the coffee smelled old. Kelly made a face as he refilled his mug and sat down. A muted voice on CNN mumbled a weather report. Kelly idly noted thunderstorms were predicted over the Midwest. The TV image shifted to ambulance shots, followed by file footage of a grand hotel. A map box in the corner of the screen showed a star where North Carolina meets Tennessee.

Kelly searched for the remote and kicked up the volume: "Authorities have not released the names of the victims, two men, believed to be guests of the Grove Park Inn, and a woman employee of the hotel, known for its fabulous antiques..."

He dialed 411 and had a desk clerk in Asheville, North Carolina on the phone in half a minute. Yes, Wally Winchester had been a guest of the hotel, he was told. Checked out Monday morning, *day of the crime.*

"Hello, Wally Winchester," Kelly said out loud. Back at his desk, he contacted the Asheville Police, and got the lead detective on his cell, still at the crime scene. From him, he got the details: Cause of death was multiple knife wounds. No witnesses. Kelly asked if there was a leave-behind like a business card, and drew a negative. On a hunch, he asked about a Mexican girl. The answer was affirmative. One person of interest was a Latin American woman who was seen with the female victim before she disappeared.

Kelly widened his internet search to Florida, Georgia and the Atlantic states. He found a homicide at an antique shop in West Virginia, gunshot wound. He filed it as a "maybe" and scrolled north.

He got a possible with the New York State Police, double homicide at a campground near Binghamton. Two Hispanics, no ID's, presumed illegals. One death by gunshot, one by serrated knife.

Kelly called his boss; he got an out-to-lunch message. Then he called the FBI.

Chief of Detectives Ned Farrey relaxed his frown into a straight line and pursed his lips when Kelly entered his office. He motioned him to sit.

"Kelly, you're a fucking nightmare," he began, the frown returning.

Kelly said nothing.

"Why did you involve the FBI without consulting me?"

"I called you first. Check my cell phone. Check yours. When I saw the murders in North Carolina, West Virginia and New York, I knew my suspect in the Hindu church…"

"Temple."

"Temple. I knew this guy was not done killing. What am I supposed to do about it? He's a suspect in our temple murder. He's in the wind, on a wild drive across the United States. There's a bunch of murders that have followed his route, Ned. How do you want to handle it?"

"Keep your nose on the Spokane murder. Somebody with resources greater than ours will track the lunatic down. Then we get a shot at him. Make sure we have a case."

Chapter Twenty-Five

Mumbai, India

Yvgeney met Chana at the Old Calcutta Lounge at six o'clock. He ordered vodka, neat. Chana had some local tea.

"I have good news," he announced.

"India has its Peacock Throne back?"

"Heavens, no. The minister wants to announce the return of the fragment to the media. Believes it will push the return of more stolen art. The cleric positively refuses to have the transaction made public. I don't blame him." He sighed. "I have another series of meetings tomorrow. God, give me another gun battle. No, Chana, the good news is that Wally Winchester emailed me last night. He's flying to Sri Lanka. In two days, we'll see his smiling face. I've convinced him to arrive in Mumbai and take a day to recover before hopping over to Colombo."

"Why on earth would Wally Winchester want to travel to Sri Lanka? Oh, let me guess, he has a lead on something fantastic, the golden ring he sees just ahead."

"Claims he has the home address of an Englishwoman woman photographer from Victorian times, yes. He believes she left him a portfolio in the plantation where she died in the 1870's. He expects to knock on the door, convince the present owners to allow him to search the crawl spaces in the attic, and then walk away with a million dollars of old photos under his arm with the current owner's blessing. Can you believe that?"

"I know Wally. Only he would believe he could pull off such a long shot."

"Knowing our boy," Yvgeney said, "I believe he has a chance. Says he'll have a pocketful of money from selling a fancy race car."

Chana held her head and said, “Wally Winchester with a lot of cash is like dynamite and an open flame.”

Chapter Twenty-Six

Boston, Massachusetts

The buyer's suggestion of making the exchange in a crowded parking garage made no sense to Wally, who'd spent the last week and a half avoiding such tight places. The voice on the phone seemed surprised to hear from him but recovered quickly and made the arrangements for a meeting the next day.

He walked around the Cobra and inspected it for damage, found none except a handful of miniscule chips in the blue paint by the nose. The cell phone vibrated. Wally heard the buyer change the meeting place. He cursed. The kamikaze drivers in this town were crazy fuckers. Every encounter at the street corner with another car was a jousting match and Wally knew he had a glass horse.

The new meeting place, the caller told him, was in Woburn, a suburb Wally had picked in as a novice New England antiques dealer. The location, a wooded area called Forest Park. Wally told him he wanted cash. The buyer told him that was impossible. He would need more time for cash. Wally told him he had enough money to drive the son-of-a-bitch back to Seattle, suggested the buyer might like to reconsider before he canceled his flight and found the Massachusetts Turnpike. The buyer agreed and called for a 5:00 p.m. exchange, connecting at a Little League diamond in the park called Weafer Field.

Wally sat in his race car while the big motor idled and rocked the hood at one hundred fifty rpm's and watched a stretch limo with darkened glass roll out of the woods on a gravel road. He sighed, his thoughts on Manuelita all over the map. Part of his heart told him to reach out and find her. His brain scolded him for being so gullible that she could have played him like a violin. No, he thought, not a violin – a ukulele. A violin had too much class.

The driver's door opened and a short Latino stepped out with a satchel. Another man, wearing the short blonde hair of a German shock trooper, came out from the passenger door. He wore the smock of an engineer or a super uptight German car mechanic, a BMW genius who could go to dinner wearing the lab coat he changed your transmission oil in.

Wally hopped out, put a loving hand on the deep blue finish and patted the last thing he cared for goodbye. As the mechanic inspected the engine, yanking the throttle and listening, Wally counted out eighteen packages of new hundred dollar bills. The currency was fresh and in a numbered sequence. To a tired veteran of 5:00 a.m. skirmishes, used to grimy wrinkled wads of twenties exchanged at flea markets, the crisp certificates seemed unreal. He sniffed a bundle as he fanned it with his thumb and concluded it smelled like real money.

The mechanic stood up and nodded approval, and the driver sneered as he handed Wally the heavy leather bag.

He said to the driver, "Can you call me a cab?"

The sound of a ratchet reminded Wally of a shotgun cocking. He turned around and saw a face that he'd never expected to encounter again. The tall figure stood with his back to the grandstand. Teutonic features reminded him of Dolph Lundgren, the classic German villain of the 70's cinema.

"Hello, Mr. Winchester. Thank you for returning my car to me," the backlit figure said.

Wally stuttered, "Claus? Claus Braun? You're supposed to be dead. Drowned like the sewer rat you are under the Deception Pass Bridge. You look good. Nice suit."

"You ruined the last one, the one I wore on the bridge. Saltwater and silk don't like each other."

He stepped closer, the double barrel of a 20-gauge looked to Wally like subway tubes. "I've waited three years for this meeting," Braun said. "I expected it to feel sweeter. You've been my hobby, Winchester. Planning your total destruction is the reason I get up every morning. Dreaming of the pinprick when they hook the needle to your arm helps me to sleep at night."

Wally searched his vast storehouse of positive solutions, hoping to use one or two right now to get out of this man's crosshairs. He saw nothing he could use, save the stall, a temporary fix, but all he had. Besides, he was curious.

"Whadda-ya mean, *your* car? I bought this Shelby at a country auction a year and a half ago."

"Good old Harry Roble. The most corrupt auctioneer I've ever known," said Braun.

Wally's face tilted sideways, confused. He measured the distance to the relative cover of the forest, knew he was dead meat if he attempted to run. He looked at Braun and felt a chill at the glazed look of happy madness on the German's face. Thought he'd better start a conversation before the crazy fucker pulled the trigger.

"This car was inside a padlocked dilapidated barn. Roble told me it hadn't been opened for five years. He pulled me aside and suggested that I bid on the contents, sight unseen because I was his favorite dealer. He acted surprised as the rest of us when they torched the old lock off and we saw my Shelby."

"*My* Shelby," Braun corrected. "Roble wanted to place the car in a public sale, excited about what news of the auction would do to his reputation."

"What reputation? The man was a snake; all of us dealers knew it. At his funeral, they say the only person who showed up was his wife, hoping for some crumbs."

"Exactly why I chose him, Winchester. You never would have bid on this car in a public sale. You don't have that kind of money. Roble was happy to pocket ten thousand dollars to make sure you got the car at the price you could afford."

"I thought it was odd that he said *sold* after my first bid on a barn and its unknown contents," Wally said. "The guy used to suck every nickel out of an estate, after salting it with his own dead merchandise."

"He had some misgivings about the financial arrangement after the sale. Too bad his health failed so quickly after that."

"Yeah, Claus, he falls out of his own boat." Wally's eyes looked to the treetops, the baseball dugouts, and a brick cinderblock concession stand. No rescue from those quarters. "You killed Roble? That could be the only good thing you ever did."

"Killing you will feel infinitely more sweet," Braun said. "The Cobra sale was the first block in my plan to destroy your life, Winchester. Destroy it in a manner more drawn out and humiliating than death. Death for you was too easy."

"And Manuelita worked for you?"

"Silly bitch lost her nerve. Had to let her go. Tell me where you dropped her off and I'll promise you a quicker death."

"Fuck you and your plan to ruin my life," Wally said. "Those Mexicans we killed in New York State. That was self-defense. I can prove it."

Braun laughed, "I'll be happy to go into more detail about the destruction of your good name once we get you tied up. I want it to be your last memory of me. Boys?"

The mechanic and the driver grabbed Wally by each arm. Both were younger and stronger. He struggled, held by two vices.

The sound of tires spitting gravel filled the glade as a police car rumbled up the lane. Braun motioned the thugs to release their captive.

He winced as he stripped off his immaculate linen suit jacket and covered the shotgun in the dew-soaked grass.

As the driver's window dropped, Braun stepped forward. The policeman spoke through the microphone. "Sir, stand back. Do not approach the vehicle." Braun stepped back, a ticket-taker's smile plastered on his high cheek-boned face.

At the passenger door, the window also dropped. An officer with an oversized hat covering the face motioned Wally forward. The captors pushed him ahead of them. The loudspeaker barked, "Not you two. The old one."

Wally took a tentative step, felt the hands on him relax. The car's door opened. Under the patrol hat, he saw a familiar face. Manuelita winked.

"Get in quick, dumbass," she whispered.

Braun looked like he smelled something bad.

"Step away from the vehicle," blasted from the speaker.

He hesitated.

Wally leaped through the open door, pulling it closed behind him as the cruiser kicked rocks against the limo in its escape. Manuelita leaned out the passenger window and peppered the Cobra with single shots. The fifth one hit a tire. Braun screamed. Even Wally winced as the sheet metal shredded blue shrapnel. She was aiming at the limo tires when the shotgun blast knocked her back into the car. The driver, a man Wally had never seen, gunned the cruiser through the woods, onto the asphalt on Route 38. Wally's shirt was soaked with blood as he lifted Manuelita's head and looked into her eyes. She smiled and, through pained half-breaths, said, "Thank you for showing me what love is." A gurgle clouded her lenses and she was still.

"Holy shit," the driver screamed. "She just hired me as an actor. Who the fuck *are* you people? He pulled the cruiser to the road edge and leaped out, shedding the police clothes as he ran. Wally sat in silence, his lover's head in his lap. He stroked her hair and sobbed. He saw the make-believe wedding ring and knew it should stay on her finger.

Chapter Twenty-Seven

Mumbai, India

The Wally Winchester who walked off the plane into the concourse was not the person Chana remembered. Deep bags lined red downcast eyes. She bounded over to hug him and he looked at her with a faint smile.

Yvgeney held back, wondering if this was the same old friend who'd emailed him earlier in the week with a head full of outrageous expectations and a big box of cash. He walked over to Chana and the goofy dreamer he'd hunted antiques with in South America, the guy who still claimed he was bitten by a quarter-ton salmon in a Mongolian lake, his head down.

"As they said to the presidential candidate John Kerry," Yvgeney, a student of things American said, "Why the long face?"

"I can't talk about it yet," Wally managed to choke out. A part of his brain that was not yet functional screamed to tell them Claus Braun was alive and filled with revenge, but he didn't hear it, grief bogarting all the thinking parts. They walked in silence to the baggage claim area.

In Yvgeney's hotel room, Wally brightened slightly as the pair filled him in on their week. "Haven't paid attention to news for awhile," the weary traveler mumbled. "I guess life's a bitch all over." He tossed down another shot of scotch, his seventh.

Chana pressed him for details of his sadness. He shook the queries away as he sucked on his glass. "Tell us why you're here," she said.

“I bought a box of old letters at a church sale in Spokane a few weeks ago.”

Yvgeney knew the details from a long email Wally posted the week before, but let him talk about his score, knowing it was therapeutic.

At breakfast Wally brightened as he sketched his plan on a napkin. He opened a map of the island nation off the southeast coast of India and pointed to a region south of Columbo marked in green along the yellow-colored shoreline. “The address on the Tennyson letters is Kalutara Province. *Here*.” Wally stabbed the map with a knifepoint with more emphasis than the gesture required. Chana looked at Yvgeney, who shrugged.

“My first stop is Colombo. There, I hope the newspaper has a morgue where I can look for stories from the 1870’s that concern Julia and her photos. Also her obituary. There may be clues to her activities here in the obit. The next stop is the museum, any museum I can find. She was well known enough in the seven years she lived there; her photos might have ended up in the ancient holdings. Perhaps they’ll be for sale.” Chana winked at Yvgeney as they watched their friend come back to life.

“The big reason I’m here is her plantation. I have the address. It should be a cinch to find.”

“You expect the owners to let you snoop around?” Chana asked, knowing the answer.

“I’ve never set foot on this island before. These people have no immunity to Winchester charm.”

“Want some company?” Yvgeney said. “Give me a chance to duck the paperwork for a couple of days. I have some time off due…about a year.”

Chana said, “The Tamil Tigers are quiet now, with their leaders killed. Still, you could use someone at your back. It’s not a stable nation these days. Anger runs there like water. Old wounds are not forgotten.”

“I’d rather be alone,” Wally answered. “I have a lot of thinking. I have an image that needs some time in the fixer bath. I don’t want to lose it.”

Chana looked at Yvgeney and knew that something was really tweaking their friend’s psyche, something that knocked him out of his shoes.

Chapter Twenty-Eight

Columbo, Sri Lanka

Wally left alone for Colombo on the afternoon flight. He carried a notebook, ten thousand dollars in cash, an extra shirt, clean pair of socks and a picture of Manuelita in his shattered heart.

The coastal city of Colombo showed no indication of the recent tsunami that came to this island on quiet feet and swept one hundred thousand citizens into the sea. Wally had followed the disaster in 2004, along with the rest of the world. The guide he hired at the airport was named Punjab.

"Named after the tree Buddha slept under during a hailstorm, right?" Wally said.

"It means 'five waters,' referring to the rivers of India," Punjab responded politely.

The guide told Wally he lost two cousins and a sister to the wave. "I was in Colombo when the sea entered the city," he said. "My car was ten blocks from the water and I heard nothing, saw no ocean at my feet. The radio station told me a disaster was occurring. When I drove closer to the shore, I noticed that the buildings and the people were gone. Just gone. The sea took them. People here still don't eat the fish caught offshore, afraid they'll be lunching on a family member. It's not really a choice anyway, all the fishermen lived on the shore and they're gone."

Wally took this thought and put it away as a band-aid for his next pity party.

He paid cash for a hotel room at the Holiday Inn for a week's research. Punjab told him not to rent a car because one of his cousins who survived had one and needed the work. Money given to the locals, he said, was better than giving it to a superstore of millionaires in the United States: Mr. Avis, Mr. Hertz, Mr. National, Mr. Budget and the rest. Wally agreed on twenty dollars a day plus gas with the cousin's wages as a driver included.

Two purple-faced langurs chattered from a windowsill above them as Wally and Punjab entered the colonial-era building that housed the *Colombo Times*.

Punjab engaged the receptionist in a Sinhalese conversation and reported back. "She says that the newspapers, available to view in the archives, go back to 1985 but no more, boss Wally."

Wally said, "Ask for microfiche or another method that saved older issues of the newspaper. I have to get back to 1873, at least."

Punjab translated and returned. "She says the newspaper was founded in 1922."

"Damn. Ask her if there was an older newspaper in this town – something that was publishing as far back as 1870."

The guide relayed the query. He returned and said, "She has answers to your questions but now she is on a break and would be glad to answer your questions upon her return."

"How long is her break?"

"In the city, it is usually two or so hours. It's a cosmopolitan center here and time is rationed."

"Damn," Wally said. "Ask her if I can buy her a coffee or a tea while she is away from her desk and ask more questions." He did.

Ten questions and a short drive to the city library later, Wally had an antique microfilm reader turned on. He fed brittle, 1920's archive transparencies into the machine. He scanned every newspaper page from 1872 to 1888.

"Here is an article," he said to the disinterested guide. "1877. Says an exhibition of Julia's photographs was scheduled for July 7th at the Ceylon Exhibition Center, wherever the fuck that is." He looked to his guide and asked, "Can you take me to this place?"

The address was not easily found. Street names had not survived one hundred forty years of change. Punjab's best guess brought them to a vacant lot where a boy and a tethered elephant sold melons. Strike one.

To the driver Wally said, "Here are letters sent to Julia's husband's plantation in 1876. Can you find this place?"

The surviving cousin squinted at the old English words on faded yellow envelopes and shook his head in a confused "no."

Punjab held them up and pointed to the address, penciled in old Sinhalese by the Ceylon postal magistrate. "This," he said, "indicates a place outside the city, a rural zone to the southeast. We can drive to this region and ask."

The address on the letter sent to Julie Margaret Cameron from her friend Alfred Lord Tennyson was a farming region where manicured bushes dotted rolling hillsides in orderly rows. Outside the crowded city, the road was quiet. A group of children walked in silence past the entrance to an old plantation. Bird sounds and the chatter of an unseen primate competed with the distant drone of an invisible jet. A gap between two huge trees led to a colonial-era mansion at the end of a tree-lined path.

Punjab told him the property belonged to the Tamil Cultural Center. Wally expressed concern.

Punjab said, "In Ceylon there are two main religions, Hindu and Buddhist. The Tamil culture is the Hindu segment and represents many of the intellectual and cultural sectors in Sri Lanka.

"What about the bombings? The atrocities?"

"The last fifty years have seen a civil war with violence on both sides."

"Who's fighting whom?"

"The Tamils versus Sinhalese …Europeans have a two-sentence attention span when it comes to our country. I'll put it in a paragraph. The Tamil people, Hindu, arrived on the island twenty four hundred years ago, and so did the Sinhalese, a Buddhist group. The Sinhalese outnumber the Tamils three to one. When the island got sovereign rule in the 1950's the troubles began."

"I heard about some atrocities on both sides," Wally said. "It's not a pretty war. Lousy PR for all you people."

"A lecture from the mouth of an American who invaded Iraq. You weren't the audience the message was intended for," Punjab said coldly. "This year is a new nightmare for the Tamil people. News sources have been curtailed. Reporters are not allowed to speak of government crackdowns and the abuses that have increased since the death of Prabhakaran."

"Sounds a bit like that ethnic cleansing in Yugoslavia," Wally said.

"Worse," Punjab answered. "We are an island. The government has vowed to push all the Tamil people into the sea. Where do we go with the ocean at our ankles? Do we swim to India? To the United States?"

"We?" Wally said. "You are a Tamil?"

"I'm the smartest tour guide in Sri Lanka. I'm who you want. No more questions, please."

Wally's mind still wobbled between his picker's buzz and the image of a dying Manuelita saying goodbye.

A child with large brown eyes looked up at him as she exited the path from the cultural center. Images of Julia Margaret Cameron's enigmatic Victorian waifs replaced his memory of a blood-stained Mexican face. He took a breath and decided to get back to work.

The plantation looked abandoned. Curtains of flowering orchids hung from unpruned trees on both sides of a pebbled walk that had once been a driveway.

Punjab pointed to the peeling stucco mansion covered in flowering vines. "The times are not good for the Tamils," he said. "Nature flourishes on neglect."

Something soft hit Wally on the back. A second small turd dropped to the ground behind him, accompanied by a chorus of monkey screams from the overhanging trees.

"Is anyone here?" he asked.

"The level of trust is low in these times," Punjab said.

At a heavy oak door with a green bronze Victorian knocker in the shape of an elephant's head, the guide rapped once and spoke loudly in a high-pitched song. It opened and an ancient matron, wearing a sarong, engaged Punjab in conversation. He nodded and smiled, patting Wally on the back as he spoke.

To Wally, he said, "The center is closed now due to the troubles, but I have introduced you as a professor of art, here to see the last home of the famous English photographer who once lived here."

The matron invited them into a dark, dusty, oak-paneled hall that opened to a high-ceilinged portico with the rotting remains of a grand staircase sweeping up the wall to a second floor.

Wally was impressed. "Old Man Cameron lived large back then," he said. Punjab nodded agreement to the nonsense.

Above them, a door opened and a bearded man in a turban walked slowly down the ancient steps. He spoke to Punjab, who nodded and bowed frequently and then said in English, "P. Ponnambalam is the current director of the center. He tells you that the center is not a safe place right now, on the eve of Veska-Buddha Day."

Wally bowed to the elder, then he said to him in English, "Are there any objects that remain in the house from the first owners? Any old photographs perhaps? I have a great deal of money…"

Punjab interrupted him, and pulled Wally aside, apologizing to the director and bowing.

"The offer of money is an insult in this special place, sahib," he whispered. "This man is a respected scholar, and he expects that you are the same. Please speak to him as a colleague and not as a merchant. I suspect he speaks English as well. Show him respect."

Wally again faced his host. "Please excuse my mistake, sir. I have come a long way to see how Julia Margaret Cameron lived in the last years of her life. Her photographs are national treasures and I can only hope to find examples of her last works here."

The man in the turban smiled. He said in perfect English, "We here in the center are fully aware of the importance of Julia Margaret Cameron to the Western world, but nothing of her times remains. The climate here eats a newspaper in a month. A book left outside will turn to pudding in a matter of weeks. Mrs. Cameron's photographs would have turned into dust or soup a hundred years ago. I'm sorry your trip was wasted. Can I offer you some tea? We grow it here on the original trees from the Colonial times."

Disappointed in the answer, Wally accepted and watched the elderly woman shuffle away.

"Did any old cameras or darkroom equipment survive?" he asked.

"Since we purchased these grounds five years ago there has been constant turmoil between the Tamil people and the Sinhalese overlords," the director said. "The estate covers a vast area with many outbuildings that have not received any attention. I'm sorry I can't answer your question. The main building here, I assure you, has nothing that you seek."

Wally's eyebrows rose. "Outbuildings? Is there a building with no windows? A room that is underground, cool and dark?"

"There are storerooms for crops scattered around the plantation."

A flash preceded the sound of an explosion, then a concussion as the big front door fell inward with a thud. The director put his bearded chin out, his brow creased in a defiant stare.

Punjab grabbed Wally's arm. "Come quickly," he said, and pulled him through a Victorian kitchen, past the wide-eyed matron, into the overgrown plantation behind the old mansion. Gunfire erupted behind them as they melted into a forest of old-growth tea.

Wally risked a backward glance and saw uniformed men in pursuit. Punjab yanked him forward, pointing to a low bunker that looked like a root cellar, accessible from a heavy riveted iron door. He pulled at a rusty metal ring. The door creaked and opened. Two rifle shots ricocheted next to Wally's ear as the tour guide pulled him inside into darkness. He heard the guide fumble with something. "Reach straight down," he said, out of breath. "There's a wooden beam at our feet. Help me lift it up to secure the door."

Wally felt the heavy timber and lifted his end up and forward into an unseen bracket just as muffled voices pounded on the door from the outside.

Punjab uttered a curse and exhaled as rifle fire rattled outside of their pitch black tomb.

"What do we do now?" Wally asked.

"We thank all the Gods for British colonial engineering and hope the army only came with small arms."

The sound was familiar, but he couldn't place it, a metal-to-metal scrape and then a ratchet noise. The flame from a Zippo lighter lit Punjab's face.

"Nice lighter," Wally said.

"A tour guide has to be prepared to aid his guest in any fashion," Punjab whispered over the commotion outside the iron door. He held the flame up and revealed a jumble of old wooden crates with branded tea labels that Wally would have put on eBay in a minute at another place and time. "There," Punjab said, and reached over to a candle stand with a brown bit of wick, sprouting from the last of the wax. He lit it and a flame sputtered to life.

As Wally's eyes adjusted to the faint illumination, his heart soared. In a dusty corner, he saw a stack of large glass plates, nestled with apothecary bottles with old cork stoppers – dark room gear from the early days of photography.

He recognized another relic, similar to one he'd purchased on eBay for his photographer wife, Rae, in the days when she loved him. The flat wood container was designed as a traveling dark room and held a hollow glass sleeve with space inside for a photo plate and the developer. She'd bitched about another online auction item showing up at the door until she saw it was for her. The gratitude lasted for a week. Here, in a tea cellar off the coast of India, with a gang of soldiers outside intent on mayhem, was another one – the portable darkroom of Julia Margaret Cameron. Holy shit, holy shit. The door behind him groaned as a heavy vehicle hit it with the bumper.

Punjab said, "Pay attention, sahib. Look for a solution. This is no antique store – it's a tomb if we don't find a way out!"

The candle flame flickered as the wax puddle in the bobeche grew smaller. Wally looked through the gloom for anything, a second door, a weapon, a miracle. He saw an oak icebox, a fancy one with bracket feet and Victorian hardware, top of the line, he figured. England, 1870's. As the door buckled behind him, he looked heavenward at the earth and wood ceiling. He said a prayer as he pulled on the latch. Suction from the old rubber gasket made a tearing sound as the old chest gave up a 140-year grip on the top door. Wally shrieked at the sight of a leather-wrapped package inside.

Punjab muttered a foreign curse and said, "Here it is." He pulled a tattered cloth off the earthen wall to reveal a low opening, deeper into the soil under the old growth tea. Wally didn't notice. The guide slapped him hard on the face. "If you stand here with that silly look on your face, you'll die with it," he shouted. "Follow me."

They ducked and entered a hand-cut passage, the candle holding its light in a losing battle as the wax ran low.

One hundred feet in, the passageway merged with two others in a chamber high enough to stand in, supported by gold-mine beams under a plank roof. Punjab watched the candle ebb. "sahib," he whispered, "Find us something to burn."

Wally looked at the leather-wrapped folio in his hands saved from a century and a half of tropical entropy by an airtight icebox. The light dwindled to near black. He began to whimper. Jesus, no, he said to himself, convinced by the weight and circumstance that he was holding priceless photographs, perhaps an unseen Ceylon suite. Photographs never recorded. Photographs that shed light on a brilliant career. Photographs that could command an entire catalog at a New York auction, no, London. A London sale. Photographs he hadn't looked at yet. He unwrapped the leather over the pages inside.

The first page was blank, an ancient yellow sheet. He handed it to the tourguide-turned James Bond, who tore it into strips and got one burning just as the candle's flame was giving up.

A brightening glow showed three tunnels in the direction of the mansion and one headed out into the plantation.

Punjab cursed. In English he said, "I see a trip wire on the escape tunnel. Give me more paper, now, please."

Wally looked at the next page, penned on linen in an elegant quill, **Julia Margaret Cameron Introduces a Folio of Native Children.**

He went to the next page, a tissue of vellum. He handed it up, cringing as he viewed the photograph beneath. A soft-focused child with liquid eyes against a sepia jungle stared up at Wally and took away his breath.

"Hurry," the tour guide said, "I have to find our way around this trap while we have light!"

Wally looked at the page behind the photo. Another vellum. He handed it over, watched the tour guide approach the exit tunnel with the flaming rag and motion him to follow. He did, closing the portfolio of his dreams to step over the wire that Punjab motioned to with the last of the tissue.

Punjab said, "OK. Now we're over the trip wire but there may be more ahead. Hurry. Give me more to burn."

In the dim light of a flickering vellum torch, Wally opened the folio. He flipped ahead to the next separation page and passed it to Punjab, who caught the flame as it died. "I need more than ten-second pages, sahib."

Wally groaned. He went to the back of the folio and pulled out the back page, a blank sheet of bond paper. He offered it up. The tunnel brightened.

"I refuse to burn a photo." Wally said. 'I'll take my chances with another trip wire. We can follow this tunnel to the end in the dark. These images need to be unveiled. They're new to the world."

"Pull out the other tissues then, look for a wire, high or low. Let's go," Punjab said.

After six more pages, the light went out. Darkness was total.

Wally said, "I've thought about this moment as we ran."

"As I have, sahib." The sound of the Zippo opening preceded the ratchet and the flame, a small one. Punjab said, "My fuel is also low. Choose a photo: the paper is thick. We cannot walk in a booby-trapped tunnel with our eyes closed. It's suicide. Just choose one. Close your eyes and choose."

"I can't do it," Wally said into the dwindling flame. "Close the Zippo, Punjab. Save the gas." The tunnel went black. "What I have in my hands has to be saved. I don't care by whom, damn it. I'll go first. You take the photos and hang back. The lead guy can't be holding these photographs. You hold this package and I'll go forward with gentle feet. Give me a couple yards ahead. You have the prize. Give me the lighter."

Punjab, his flickering image ghost-like, said, "I was thinking entirely the opposite."

"We could play Rock, Paper, Scissors," Wally said into the blackness around him. "But who's to say who won?"

After a pause, Punjab said, "I am a Tamil. This is my struggle. You are a guest. How could you ask me to put your life before mine?"

"The stuff's that important, my friend. If I die saving it for posterity, that's a good exit for a picker." He thought of Manuelita kissing him goodbye.

"It's my duty to lead," Punjab said. Wally felt strong hands push him aside as the guide walked forward, flashing a lighter flame for seconds as he inspected the next five feet.

Light filled a rectangle far down the shaft. The tour guide shouted out in a language Wally didn't understand.

Voices came back.

The rectangle enlarged to a strong flashlight held into Wally's eyes. He heard the ratchet of a shotgun. Punjab's shouted a response that sounded like an order. Wally turned his head out of the flashlight's blinding beam. He felt the tour guide's firm hand on his shoulder, heard him say, "Best that you don't see these men, sahib. We're going to cover your eyes. Relax. I won't let them harm you."

As a blindfold was pulled over his face, Wally heard a tremendous explosion, felt the concussion roll as a blast of pressure threw him against the wall.

He woke up with a blinding headache, lived a panic-filled second until he realized the sack over his head was the reason he couldn't see. His mind was on *reset*: You're in India, no, Sri Lanka. A tunnel. Bag over the head. Explosion. What? Are you sure you're awake?

He felt hands pulling the portfolio from his grasp and held on fiercely.

A voice from above said, "Let them have the papers, Wally."

He relinquished his grip. "Don't scratch the photos," he shouted through the bag.

Punjab said, "Don't trifle with these men. Your life means nothing to them."

Wally said, quietly, "When they realize I'm just a tourist from Washington State, please collect the photographs and return them to the bound portfolio. The photographs are a national treasure."

More discussion in another language, then, "Your portfolio is intact, sahib. Now shut your mouth; I'm trying to save your life."

Unseen hands grabbed Wally under the arms and pulled him to his feet where he rocked unsteadily and thought about the safety of the photographs.

After a half hour march in the tunnel, Wally, hooded, blind, and prodded from behind, tripped over three unseen obstacles before a flow of fresh air from above signaled the exit.

The tour guide spoke in English, "Don't resist. We're headed north." Then, in a small voice next to Wally's ear, he added, "These men know you are no threat. It's up to me to convince them you are valuable to them. Otherwise, you'll just slow everyone down and they'll kill you for their convenience."

Wally gulped. He ran through a mental list of his useful talents and came up short in the category called, *Tamil Tigers.* His hooded head shot up. Wally exclaimed, "The photographs."

Punjab shushed him. "The truck is here. You'll ride in back. Say nothing."

"But the photographs belong to the Tamils, since they own the property. I can sell them for the Tamil Cultural Center. Could be worth a million."

"Quiet."

After a ten-hour pothole-filled ride in a vehicle with no springs, Wally had a full bladder. He asked Punjab for permission to go to the bushes. Unseen hands hauled him from the truck-bed. The tour guide warned him not to remove the hood.

A hand on his arm guided him through underbrush.

Punjab spoke to the American as he squatted and moaned in relief. "The movement is nearly bankrupt. The idea of a large cash infusion by sale of the photographs is more than the soldiers can digest, but they understand the term *cash* and have agreed to keep you alive until you talk with a regional commander on the Jaffna Peninsula."

Wally groaned and asked, blindfolded, for a leaf or two. Later he said, “You still have the portfolio?”

“Right here in my arms. The Tiger soldiers now look at its protection as their new mission.”

Wally said, “Get some paper between the photos with the burned up vellum before they stick together. I don’t trust this climate.”

“First chance I get, sahib. Paper is not easy to find on the peninsula. There’s a blockade. For now, keep your mouth closed.”

The truck decelerated, then stopped. Wally heard faint sounds of creatures in the forest in the sound dampened canopy that surrounded them. He felt the hood pulled gently off his head and blinked red eyes at the noonday sun. His abductors were nowhere to be seen. In the cab, a lone driver, a pimple faced youth barely out of his teens, tapped the steering wheel impatiently as Punjab opened the truck door and ushered Wally inside.

“There’s a checkpoint ahead,” Punjab said. “This man is Valenporr. He will drive us through.”

Wally reached a hand over in a greeting, saw an automatic pistol in the driver’s lap, pulled his hand back and settled for a nod.

“You will be interviewed by the Sinhalese guards,” Punjab said. “Tell them you are a reporter from CNN, a friend of Wolf Blitzer. And Wally?”

“Yes?”

“Say nothing else.”

“Let me see the photographs,” Wally said.

“There’s no time. They are safe and dry.”

At a fat chain barrier next to a cinderblock guardhouse, two armed soldiers approached the truck. As one of them peered into the driver's window, the guard fired a barrage of questions to the young driver. Punjab took control of the conversation. Wally caught the word, *CNN*, in an unknowable sentence.

The guard looked at Wally with less of a sneer.

Wally smiled and said, "I'm a friend of Wolf Blitzer." The guard grew cautious and pointed the gun barrel inside. "Larry King," Wally added. "Anderson Cooper, Rachel Maddow."

"That's enough, sahib," Punjab said, and he shot the man in the forehead as he leaned in. The driver pulled the trigger on the gun in his lap and shot across the cab at the passenger window. A burst of lead whizzed past Wally's nose. A wisp of gunpowder-scented air hit his face. The other guard crumpled.

With the sound of gunfire, more soldiers rushed out of the office, shooting randomly at the truck and into the forest. One by one they fell to unseen snipers, the last one killed by Punjab as the soldier moaned on the soft, bloody ground. The dead guards' two-way radios croaked questions that no one answered until the rest of the team emerged from the underbrush to turn them off, kicking the bodies on the way to the truck.

Wally was dumbfounded, unable to catch his breath as the Tamil force climbed back on the truck with the checkpoint's weapons and extra rounds from the guardhouse. Punjab smiled at him as the vehicle continued its journey.

"Good work, comrade," the tour guide said. "It looks like you are part of the family now, till we reach the northlands. Now you can see our beautiful country."

Wally took short breaths and looked at a valley of deep green treetops, undulating like ocean waves down to flat, green lowlands with blue water of the Indian Ocean on the horizon. Driving fearlessly on the narrow hillside road, the young driver reached out and patted Wally's back and smiled to expose a mouth of black-stained teeth. "He likes you, sahib," Punjab laughed. "He says his new name for you is Wolf."

Wally learned a Sri Lankan card game called 532 as he and his new friends ate bowls of rice mixed with mystery meat around a small campfire in a dense jungle. Played with the top half of a fifty-two card deck, the sevens through aces, the game involved trump cards and bidding, not unlike *Hearts* or *Bridge*. Wally figured out the strategy quickly. Soon he and the tour guide were an unbeatable team, with old age and youthful bluffing a winning strategy.

By midnight, with the help of a local intoxicant that tasted like fermented Moxie, Wally had shared three of his best British Columbia bear stories and listened to a handful of Bengal tiger tales. "Tomorrow, late, we will meet in Jaffna with the highest ranking Tamil Tiger still alive," Punjab told him as they finished the last of the local brew and threw plastic cups into the fire. "There you will prove your worth to the insurgency."

"The process of getting these photos verified and into a museum's or a collector's hands could take a long time. Auctions don't happen overnight," Wally said.

"Our struggle has no end. We have lost most of our financial support. We will be patient. Is the portfolio really worth that much?"

"Maybe a lot more. Can I have my cell phone back?"

"It won't work here. This region is dark to phones."

The road to Jaffna Peninsula ended at a heavily guarded bridge that Wally approached on foot, passport in hand, carrying the portfolio under his arm like a school child going to class. A dilapidated taxi took him to a coastal village, a cluster of modern concrete living quarters that the taxi driver said was the world's response to the tsunami.

Punjab met him at the door of one new home, a thirty square foot unpainted box with tiny windows. "How was your passage into Jaffna, sahib?" he asked.

"They like Wolf Blitzer. You were right. Got me right over the bridge. I told the guards my photographer was due in today. I have a list of their names they expect their family will hear on the satellite feed. Where's the big cheese?"

"Inside. And he fancies himself a photographer. He's interested in seeing the photos."

"I came up with a strategy to get these photographic masterpieces out of the country, all the way to New York City, but you've got to get me some cell service on this bloody island."

"The commander has a satellite uplink, sahib. You can make your call after the meeting."

In an empty, windowless interior room with a desk and folding chair, Wally saw a young soldier, phone to his ear, penciling red marks on a map. He smiled and stood, extending his hand. "My name is P. Rajagopalachari," he said. "I am looking forward to viewing these pictures of my countrymen taken one hundred forty years ago."

"So am I, actually," Wally said as he felt a firm handshake signal respect. "I've not had a chance to look at most of them myself in the four days since I discovered them."

The portfolio was comprised of thirty-five large-plate images in the soft focus that the English genius mastered in the early days of photography. Wally was blown away by the subtle moods, captured in the eyes of the Ceylon natives that Julia used for the images. The commander saw grandparents of people he knew, caught as innocent youth in the days when fixer and developer took eight months at sea to deliver to a land without chemicals.

Rajagopalachari, a thirtyish, dark skinned pencil of a man, doing his best to grow a moustache, ordered a young soldier standing guard to bring tea.

"Who owns these images?" he asked.

Wally looked down at the biggest score of his long life. As the commander passed over a teacup, he said, "I found it at the estate run by the Tamil Cultural Center in Kalutara. I assume they are the owners, if there was anyone left alive when we escaped."

Wally saw disapproval on the intelligent face. He added, "I was there with the center's approval. I had tea with the head guy, Pananablam, I think his name was."

"Ponnambalam?"

"That's it. Ponnambalam. The portfolio was in my hands when the army attacked. I couldn't leave it there. It could have been lost forever. I assure you, sir, that I make no pretensions to ownership. Your region has been stripped of its national treasures by outsiders like myself for a thousand years."

Wally noticed that his attempt to bond with the Tamil Tiger was having the opposite effect. He threw in another sentence as the commander caressed his gun. "I'm not one of them. I wish to be an agent for the owners, the Tamil Cultural Center, in exchange for a commission for my services. I can navigate the complex network of the fine art market for you to maximize the sale price."

The commander brought his hand from the gun on his hip back to the teacup. He asked, "What do you think this portfolio would fetch? The strike team relayed a figure of a million dollars. Is that an accurate number, or one you invented to save your life?"

Wally looked into the man's eyes and said, "Now that I've seen all the images, I would guess more. By the way, sir, I had to burn up some of the vellum sheets that separated the photos. Can you get some acid-free paper to separate the photographs? You're the boss. You can make this happen. Even here. It's important. The value of the portfolio will be lost if this climate melts them together. It's your million. Forgive me for bringing it to your attention."

The commander barked and a young man in civilian clothes ran in. He spoke at length to the lad and sent him on his way.

"We'll get the paper you need to protect our photographs, Wally Winchester. What do you propose?"

Wally thought of the tortuous path to get a picked item to the most advanced collector and realized he only had to contact Christie's or Sotheby's and offer it out. "I need to take these photographs to New York," he said.

"That may be difficult in the event we reach an agreement," the Commander said as he spread the photos out to reveal another 1875 Ceylon face. "The Sinhalese own the island now. All of it. They control the customs offices, even here in Jaffna, our heartland. We can't export them. Even an untrained customs agent could recognize these as cultural artifacts. And then the government takes them away. Everyone loses."

Wally smiled, marveling at how a thirty-five year-old kid in five minutes had come up with the problem he had wrestled with for days. "I have an answer to that excellent question," he answered. "Not far from here, in Mumbai, I have an associate who is an inspector in the UNESCO Cultural Properties Restoration Division. He rescues stolen art. He can fly here and take the portfolio out of Sri Lanka in a diplomatic bag."

"This person will do that for you? At what cost?"

Wally said, "He owes me. He'll do it for free if I can talk him into it. He's bored. They tell me, sir, that you have a working phone line. If I can use it to make a call, I can arrange passage of the portfolio to New York. He can do that. He's a big shot at the UN."

"What collateral do you have to take the portfolio away from the Tamil Cultural Center?"

"You can have my life," Wally answered, images of Manuelita dying in his arms again in his head. "I'll give you my home address. You can GPS it. I know you guys are badasses. I respect it. Deal with me as you will if you are not satisfied, a bad auction day not included."

"What is your fee for us taking this big chance?"

Wally looked deep into the commander's eyes and saw a savvy brain. "I flew twelve thousand miles to this island to search for this portfolio. No one knew it existed. I rescued it from a moldy end, lost to history. I can take it to top money. My fee is fifty percent."

"Thirty."

"Sir," Wally said, "This is free money for you. Would half a million dollars help the struggle?"

"Forty percent, assuming we can find a way to get the money through."

"Forty-five and I'll get you the money, even if it's a personal bequest to the Tamil Cultural Center. And you have my life as collateral."

"How's your health?" the commander asked.

"Top notch. Blood pressure 130 over 90. Like a teenager. I have a long future at stake. I want to introduce these photographs to the world."

"Here's the phone."

Wally dialed Yvgeney's cell.

Yvgeney answered. He said, "Speak."

Wally said, “Gustav Stickley, calling from Sri Lanka.” He saw consternation on the commander’s face, mouthed the word *code.*

“Chana and I were about to send out the cavalry. Are you all right?”

The commander pressed a red button on the handheld communicator and Wally’s voice echoed as the conversation filled the room.

“You know I’m indestructible, but I do need your help. Are you free to travel?”

“My appointment book is empty. Chana is still in Mumbai also. She has twice suggested hopping over there to rescue your sorry North American ass, sure as she is that you’d stir up a hornet’s nest.”

“I found something extraordinary, Yvgeney.”

“Of course you did. What else is new?”

“There are complications. I need you to fly to the Jaffna Peninsula. They have a jetport here. Bring your diplomatic bag.”

Chapter Twenty-Nine

Spokane, Washington

Amber light in the hundred year-old booth cast brown shadows. Detective Kelly faced his chief. Fresh bread and dark vinegar in a dipping bowl separated them across an old oak tabletop. A waitress said, "Hello, Ned."

Farrey sent her away and asked, "What have you learned?"

"Two more murders, both Mexican, one found in a stolen police car near Boston. No details. Gunshot victims. No knife. It might be a stretch to link it unless I go to this town – Woburn – and look for a link to the Spokane murder.

"We don't have two thousand dollars to send you to the East Coast for clues. Stay on your computer. You seem good at it."

"I believe I'm the only person who has put these crimes together as the work of one killer. Think about it, Ned. A Hindu cleric in Spokane, a couple of tweekers in Montana, four juveniles with records in North Dakota, a triple murder in North Carolina, a dead West Virginia antiques dealer, two Mexicans at a campground. They're all connected to a knife, probably Navy SEAL issue."

"It's the FBI's problem," Farrey said. "Solve our case."

"I've been after Winchester, our guy at the temple murder, for five days. I spent two days on Camano Island. I told you that. I got a lucky break when I looked into those Spokane tweekers who died in Montana. The cops there mentioned a Wally Winchester business card. That's when I put Wally Winchester on I-90 and I-94, headed east. I told you that also."

"You just described a serial killing spree from Spokane to New York. I knew nothing about this till you called the FBI. Now it's on the news."

“It’s all on your phone, boss. You should listen to your messages. This isn’t our fight, Ned. I had to share this as soon as I realized it.”

“I understand, Kelly. If you’re right, we’ll be up to our ass in Feds by tomorrow. Fill me in on what you know.”

“First thing you should know, Ned,” Kelly said. “I’m convinced there is a second suspect, a Mexican girl. They could be traveling together.”

“What about the Hindu temple. Any other developments?”

“DNA samples of all the blood on the scene were from the deceased. Nothing mixed with the killer. Heard that yesterday. I believe Winchester’s our boy, but I can’t imagine why.”

Chapter Thirty

Mumbai, India

On the eighteenth floor of the Mumbai Hilton, at a table covered with a portfolio of Julia's faces, Wally spoke about his cross-country drive.

"I shot a man in New York State last month. I killed him," he said, sipping an Indian attempt at a Merlot that reminded him of Boone's Farm. Chana's expression remained unexpressive. She said, "How did that feel?"

"I don't know yet," Wally said. "I haven't allowed myself to think about it."

Yvgeney, a veteran of Soviet dark ops, asked if the man deserved to die – "or were you just being a middle American white-bread bad ass?"

"He was choking my girl."

"Your girl?"

"She later died in my arms," Wally said in a gulp of air that watered his eyes. "Beautiful Manuelita."

Chana's jaw dropped, a reaction that surprised Yvgeney as much as Wally's unlikely role as a killer. She asked: "Was she dark haired, a slight figure, and had, no, you'd never know this."

Wally interrupted, "Two moles, low on her tummy, down by the belt line? Two moles that resemble the eyes of Osama Bin Laden when she pulls her pants down? Yes, Chana, we were close." He looked up at her and said, "Wait a minute. You knew her? My Manuelita? From Mexico City?"

"I knew her, Señor Wally, I knew her well. I guarantee you, she was not yours. No one would ever own Manuelita."

"There's more," Wally blurted.

"Claus Braun is alive," Chana said.

Wally's jaw made it three for three. He asked, "How could you intuit that from a name?"

"It's a rare name, even in Mexico, a boy's name with a female tail. I trained her. She was the best. How did she die?"

"She was saving my life. Braun shot her."

Chana raised her eyebrows for the second time in her life. "*He* killed her? She was his favorite, his sword."

"Manuelita wasn't working for Braun at the end. We...," Wally hesitated, "became fond of each other. I believe we were falling in love." The image of Manuelita's eyes as they lost their vision filled his with tears.

Yvgeney bit back the easy reply. He said, "Let's focus on what's important right now. Claus Braun is alive and in the United States. Take us back to the beginning, Wally. How did you, a guy who searches for pocket change under the divan cushions, get your hands on a valuable sports car?"

"Luckiest day in my picking career," Wally smiled. "Old man Roble calls me one day. Tells me he's running a farm auction in the hills above the town of Index. Lots of outbuildings. Selling the barns still locked for salvage rights. Tells me it might be a good idea for me to show up with all the cash I could get my hands on, which wasn't much that week. Funny, I thought then, he'd never invited me personally to one of his sales before. I asked him if there was mission oak at the auction. He said no, come anyway."

"The auction turned out to be a bunch of crap – 30's mahogany and farm vehicles. At the second barn, a falling-down building out in an apple orchard, he gives me such a look that I bid on the contents – sight unseen. On my first bid he says, *sold*. Tells me to come back the next day to open it, see what I own."

"At eight the next morning armed with a bolt cutter, I found that I owned a Caroll Shelby Cobra – in perfect shape under a dusty tarp."

"What did you pay for the contents?" Yvgeney asked.

"A thousand dollars. My luckiest bid. When I called him a few days later to say thanks, his wife told me he went to the Okanogan on a fishing trip. That's where they found him a week later, drowned, floating near his Boston Whaler with a fly rod in his hand."

Chana asked, "How did last month's buyer contact you? Did you have any indication the purchaser was Claus Braun?"

"Heavens, no. He emailed me initially. He said he had three cars like it already. Wanted to see me drive the car three thousand miles to Boston."

"Where does Manuelita fit in?"

"She was working in the long-term storage where I kept the Cobra. Now that you mention it, she told me that the regular gal, a dumpy grandmother no less, had been hurt skiing in South America."

"Manuelita was a big asset on the trip. We took turns guarding the car as we shopped and camped out. She even faced down a van of Mexican thugs on the way north from Asheville. She risked her life. How could she be a part of this?"

Chana looked at Yvgeney, who shook his head sadly, knowing. She said, "If Claus Braun is still in the United States, you are in grave danger when you return. I know how this man thinks."

Yvgeney probed, "It was Braun who met you in Boston."

"In Woburn, actually. About twelve miles out."

Yvgeney resumed, "In Woburn, he met you with a bag of cash but tried to double-cross you?"

"That's when they shot Manuelita. As we tried to speed away."

Chana said, "Then you used some of Braun's cash to hop a plane to Sri Lanka. Braun, buzzing around Woburn like a wet hornet, looking for you."

"I left that night. Paying thirty-five hundred in cash for a last minute seat, my heart broken."

"Good move," Chana said. She asked, "Where is Manuelita's body?"

"I left her at the shore of a local pond in the police car she'd stolen. Didn't know what else to do. She saved my life. The entire day is a blur."

Yvgeney sighed and he asked, "What do you plan to do when you return?"

Wally squared up the pile of photos on the table and tucked the prize into the leather portfolio. He said, "First of all, I'd like you to use your office to get these beauties to the United States. After that, I'll buy a beater van in Boston and drive home to the Pacific Northwest. I purchased quite a bit on the way east. I need to get my hands on that stuff on my return."

"You bought antiques as you traveled with Manuelita?" Chana asked.

"We had a blast. We did some door-knocking, found the box of letters that lead me to these photos, hit a couple auctions and crashed the Grove Park Inn for the Stickley fest. Oh, and bought a killer early Gus bookcase from a nice old lady in West Virginia."

Chana frowned.

"If she left the racing car, say to use the bathroom, did you stay behind?"

"The rule was someone had to stay with the Cobra at all times."

"Merde," escaped her lips. "How would you like some company on your four thousand-kilometer drive back to Camano

Island? I believe Yvgeney and I can find the time to attend your road trip."

Yvgeney pressed a button on his PDA and looked at the little screen. He said, "After a meeting tomorrow I'm free to travel. It would be a pleasure to get out of this paper chase."

"Hey," Wally said, eyes brighter. "We can swing down through Kansas on the road back, stop in on Johnny at his farm."

"It will be like old home week," Yvgeney said through grim lips, thinking about facing Braun again.

Chana said nothing. She looked at Wally and knew he had no idea what lay ahead.

Chapter Thirty-One

Boston, Massachusetts

Wally Winchester, U.S. citizen, accompanied by a freckle-faced woman whose Chilean passport read only, *Chana*, and Yvgeney Ivanchenko, Russian citizen traveling under a UN diplomatic umbrella, entered the United States with no fanfare.

Yvgeney felt the reassuring heft of the Cameron portfolio in the padlocked United Nations shoulder bag around his neck. He saw the headline, *FBI Searches For Cross-County Killer* at a newspaper kiosk and steered Wally toward the doors to the ground transportation.

Chana noticed the airport's blanket of heightened vigilance. She suggested to Yvgeney that they grab the first available vehicle, destination unimportant.

The thunder of an ascending 747 woke Wally out of a series of terribly sad dreams. He thanked it. Chana, in a tank top, brushed her teeth in the bathroom alcove. Yvgeney was tucking in yesterday's shirt, his hair wet from the shower, combed straight back from his crenulated face. A two-day beard showed more grey than black.

Wally asked, "You going to use that coffee ring over there, Chana?"

A mouthful of foam said, "No."

Sipping black coffee, Wally announced, "First thing, I figure, I'll buy a van."

"I've taken care of that already, old friend," Yvgeney said. "I rented a brand new Dodge cargo van on my United Nations' credit card. My gift."

"Knowing you, we'd end up with a broken transmission halfway to Kansas because you got a good deal on a tired old transport van from an old friend you remembered from the flea market. Our van has a guarantee, and it's in my name, not yours. Your name is too hot."

Wally smiled. "I've got a reputation here in New England, I'll admit."

Chana said, "Wally, please be quiet. Sit down."

Wally did, legs draped over the rumpled bed, coffee cup in hand.

She began, "Everything you've told us about the Shelby car suggests a well-planned effort to destroy your life."

Yvgeney stepped in, "The cruelest Roman punishment was called *Victus Crux*, where the victim lived a long life chained to a wall while his good name was vilified in his community until it was uttered like a curse."

"That's a bitch," Wally said.

"Chana and I believe that Claus Braun planned that punishment for you, Wally. With Manuelita as his sword."

"My Manuelita?"

"She was a trained assassin, Wally," Chana said with no expression. "She had fifty kills when I knew her three years back."

"Manuelita, with the cute moles under her tummy?"

"The same. I've seen those marks myself."

"She was a killer?"

"The best I've ever seen."

"She loved me. I make a living reading faces. Her eyes told the truth."

Chana softened. "You are an interesting human being, Wally Winchester, a mixture of goodness and guile that Manuelita had probably never encountered. Perhaps, during her assignment, your big heart corrupted her, and she felt the love that she never expected to find. Perhaps you turned her around with Wally Winchester charm, but that's not important now. You are a wanted man, I suspect all over North America. We kept these conclusions from you so you could get through customs without freaking out."

"You're shitting me."

"We're not shitting you," Yvgeney said. "I just got off my computer. On the internet, you're a celebrity, a person of interest in a string of killings from Spokane to Woburn, Massachusetts."

"Killings? Like dead people?"

"It's on the web. A Hindu priest in Spokane, two Spokane residents at a lakeside resort in Idaho, four street punks in Fargo, found slaughtered with your business card in their dead fingers, a massacre at the spa at the Grove Park Inn, matched by your DNA on a bathrobe, a retired antiques dealer in West Virginia."

"No," Wally interjected, "Manuelita told me she loved the old gal. She even smiled."

"Then the murders north of Boston. They're speculating a terrorist connection."

Wally said, "Excuse me, what the fuck are you talking about? Murders? I drove a fancy car across the country. We got into some scrapes near the end and I had a face-to-face with Claus Fucking Braun. I didn't kill anybody except that guy in New York State. I saved Manuelita's life that day, Chana. I shot the son-of-a-bitch in the head. Had to. You would have been proud of me."

Chana said, "I am right now."

"Let's get back to the murders," Wally said. "What the fuck is that all about? I drove a sports car across the county. I didn't kill anybody…until the end. Why are these people dead? I liked some of them."

"Manuelita, the sword," Chana offered.

"Holy shit."

Chapter Thirty-Two

Boston, Massachusetts

"We are invisible in America," Yvgeney said to his tired companions, stuffed with fruit and pastries from the Continental breakfast offered in the lobby. "Wally will have a satchel full of cash once we get to his locker, so we don't need credit cards We're under the radar. The vehicle is in the cradle of the UN, according to the credit card. We can travel the country at will. The visit with Johnny in Kansas can be made under this cloak. As far as saving your ass from this mess you're in, I don't have a clue."

"Murders. Me, a killer. How can I go home to Camano Island?"

"As of right now," Yvgeney observed, "you can't."

The journey to nowhere with Wally Winchester, America's favorite fugitive serial killer, began where Old Route 128 meets the Mass Pike in West Newton. Wally, in the passenger seat, scowled at the photo used by the Boston Herald on page three.

"That's such a shitty photo," he said. "Where'd they get that, Facebook?"

Yvgeney drove. He picked a ticket from the kiosk and entered the six-lane highway that started in Boston and ended in Seattle. "Do you truly understand that you are a wanted man?" He asked. "Subject of a national and soon to be international manhunt, my friend? You seem so unconcerned."

"I'm totally freaked out," Wally said. "I didn't kill anybody, except for that guy in New York. I still don't believe it."

“You were traveling with a professional killing machine, Wally,” Chana said.

“It’s just nuts. We were so close. Who do they say I murdered again?”

“You’ve got the paper in your hands. Read it.”

Wally skimmed the Herald story. “A Hindu cleric in Spokane? That guy? He was a sweetheart. Manuelita killed him?”

“I taught her,” Chana said.

“Two meth heads in a campground? I did that? Where the fuck are they coming up with this? Teenagers in Fargo? I don’t kill teenagers. Why would I? How could they think I did it?”

“I suspect your business card or your DNA was easily found at the crime scene,” Chana offered.

“DNA?”

“Spit, sweat, semen, skin cells.”

Wally’s face clouded. He read on.

“The Grove Park Inn massacre? What massacre? I sold a wall sconce to Russ Gostrom. Who did I kill?” He read on. “*Him*? Really? Wished I had. This is crazy. Is this Manuelita’s hand?”

“Sadly, yes,” Yvgeney said. “And it sounds like she died trying to save you. I don’t understand it. I’ll chalk it up to Wally Winchester charm.”

“I loved her.”

At Exit 4 to Interstate 91, Wally asked Yvgeney to head north.

“Why?”

“They have great pizza in Northampton. Each slice is so big it takes two paper plates. And there’s a photo expert in town who should see the Cameron portfolio.”

“Your best bet at this point, my friend, is to keep your head down until we can find some solution, some exit from this trap that you've been caught in. You're lucky you got back into the United States."

Wally said, "We're out here in the middle of Massachusetts. Anonymous. This dealer is discreet. He has to be at his level. He could save us a trip to Christie's and Sotheby's in New York. And the pizza is that good."

It was lunchtime. Yvgeney turned north.

The man who met them in Northampton emerged from a door between two tired, mid-century emporiums. A sign above him stated, *Stanley Solomon, Rare Books. By Appt.*

"It's nice to see you, I think," the robust greybeard said. He offered his hand warily as Wally introduced his mates. Solomon glanced out at the street before he invited them upstairs. At the door to his office he stopped, turned to Wally and said, "There's a lot of bad press out there about you on the internet. Am I in any danger? Tell me now."

"I'm on the internet, already?" Wally laughed, "You? Hell no. I didn't kill any of those people, Stanley. It's a big setup, but we don't have time for that now. I have some photographs you may want to see."

"Your phone call mentioned Julia Margaret Cameron."

"Can we go in?" Wally asked. "If promise I won't kill you?"

"You have five minutes, then I want you to leave by the back door."

Sweat ran from Solomon's brow at the third photograph, a tightly focused face of a Ceylon native girl. "These images are not catalogued. These are one-of-a-kind, new to the planet, absolute miracles. And you just carry them around in a bag?"

"Where do I go from here?" Wally asked.

"Are you hurting for cash?"

"No," Wally said, "I've got huge cash. I'm here because you're the highest guy in the fine art hierarchy that I know personally and trust. You have to agree the provenance is impeccable, from Julia's own darkroom to your gallery. I represent a Sri Lankan charity. My job is to get them what they deserve."

"Before you go to New York, I might have a private client who may enjoy owning something…this fresh. What are you asking, Wally?"

"What's a good number? A million? Twenty million? Fifty million? What will your client pay? You get your percentage."

Solomon said, "I know my customer's limits. I expect I can ask eight hundred grand, half to me. Will your charity be comfortable with four hundred large bills if I make the sale?"

Wally carefully folded the leather flap and tied it. He said, "Those photos have more in them than that, Stanley. Another ballpark."

"In better times perhaps," Solomon said. "Can I offer safe storage of these photographs with addresses of your next of kin before you resume your flight from the law?"

"I'm good, thanks." Wally said. "You have my cell. Remember I came to you first."

In Room 104 of the Troy, New York Holiday Inn Express, they feasted on Chinese takeout. Between bites, Yvgeney said, "On the internet, they say you bought a gun in Wisconsin."

"Yeah. Manuelita suggested we get it to protect the Cobra."

"That gun is linked to three murders on the East Coast. It's your gun. How do you expect to get out of this?"

Wally parked his feet up on the bed, shoes off. "I don't have a clue. I'm innocent for Christ's sake. The only one who could clear me is dead, damn it." He bit his lip.

Chana looked at Yvgeney. "There is one other person alive who can take the blame for these crimes and clear Wally's name: Claus Braun."

"I don't think we can convince Claus Braun to testify at my trial," Wally said.

"Trials," Yvgeney corrected.

"Claus Braun is in the United States. He's here for Wally." Chana spoke without expression. "He is Wally's only defense in a trial. I like the irony. I agree with you, Señor Wally, good luck getting him to the witness stand."

Wally said, "We need a plan, Yvgeney, you're the military expert. Chana, you're the…overseer. How are we going to find Claus Braun?"

"He will find us," Chana said.

Chapter Thirty-Three

New York City

Wally mugged a face into the brass mirror interior of the elevator.

"Please stop," Chana said. "I'm not happy that we're here, exposed."

"We're more invisible here at Sotheby's than we were at the MacDonalds in Albany. These people don't have time for headlines. They don't read the *National Inquirer.* I don't have to give my real name; I'm an agent from the Tamil Cultural Center in Kalutara, Sri Lanka, offering them an object for sale. They don't care who I am. Their eyes will be on Julia."

"I am uncomfortable with this unnecessary exposure," Chana said. "I suggest again that we return to the van and become invisible."

Yvgeney agreed. "Wally, until we disappear into the vast American unknown, we are not safe. If you are successful here, you will put yourself in the spotlight again."

Wally stared into the elevator's mirrored walls. He moved sideways to watch his bronze reflection wiggle. "My name is Smith. I represent the Tamil Cultural Center. I have something we wish to sell. What part of that says, *Wally Winchester?* We're invisible, even here. These guys don't have time to read the tabloids."

In the office labeled *Fine Photographs*, Wally and company entered a sitting room. He saw Corbu's comfy cube chairs and smiled as he approached a twenty-five year-old with great teeth behind a modern tubular chrome desk. "I have an appointment," he said. "Mister Smith."

The receptionist looked up from the screen and said, "Have a seat."

Wally felt the leather sides of the most comfortable chair in the world in 1928 suck him in. He saluted the decorator.

Out of the light a figure emerged. A young man, Wally thought, too young to understand what he had in the portfolio.

"Hello, Mr. Smith," the youth said. "My name is Nathan Collver. Your message said you have a set of Julia Margaret Cameron photographs. Follow me please." He opened the door to a simple conference room, four chairs around a glass-topped table.

Wally unwrapped the portfolio and pulled out the top photograph, a doe-eyed teenager wearing a sari. The auction agent nodded and said, "That's nice," and opened his laptop to type.

"That's *nice*?" Wally said. "Are you familiar with Julia Margaret Cameron's work?"

"Sir," the young man said as he looked at the monitor. "I have a master's degree from the Wharton School." He glanced at his screen. "She was a Victorian photographer born in 1815."

"Wait. Don't read it. Look at me. Tell me about her life. I seem to know more about her than you – the expert."

"We have an extensive database, I assure you."

Wally tucked the photo into the stack and stood up. He said, "Is there anyone in your department who is familiar with her work, personally?"

"This is an intake interview, Mr.... Smith. I'm not accustomed to defending my competence."

Wally tucked the portfolio under his arm. "Sorry," he said to Chana and Yvgeney. "I thought we'd get to show these to an expert, someone who knew the significance of the discovery."

The agent frowned and spoke on his cell phone. "Please wait," he said in a flat tone that didn't hide his annoyance. "Alice Wagner will meet with you in a minute."

He gave Wally his back and exited the room. A muffled argument beyond the door ended as a tall grey haired woman entered the chamber. She wasted no time on introductions. "I have extensive experience with Julia Margaret Cameron photographs, Mr. Smith," she said. "Whom do you represent?"

"A private party," Wally answered as he sat down again. "In Sri Lanka."

"As an auction agent, I require a full provenance. That includes the consignor's information. I assure you, we are discreet."

Wally opened the leather flap and showed her the front page in Julia's handwriting. He extracted six photographs from the stack and spread them on the table. The woman's eyes widened. Wally said, "I found these on the plantation where Julia died."

The woman said, "Holy shit."

"I think you're the person I'm looking for," Wally said. He told her the story as she uncovered the remaining images with reverence.

"Do you understand the significance of these works?"

Wally sat back. He said, "I was hoping you did."

"These photographs should be studied," the woman said. "They add a chapter to her distinguished career. A number of unanswered questions, blank spots in her history, could be answered on these pages."

"Bingo," Wally said. "Can you give me an estimate?"

Sweat beaded on Alice Wagner's forehead. Chana observed the reaction and looked to Yvgeney, who nodded. They watched the power of the art animate the woman's appearance as she spoke: "There is no precedent to compare with. Individual photographs have realized two hundred thousand dollars, but this volume is unique. One of a kind. It's a whole chapter of art history that's never been written. If your story and the provenance check out, I would expect this portfolio to realize five million dollars, at least. There is no upper number. That depends on buyer interest."

Wally let out his breath. "That's the answer I wanted to hear," he said. "Let's get some paperwork started, Alice. My friends are itching to see America."

"We'd like you to leave these photographs with us, Mr. Smith. We have a rigorous conservation intake process. Authenticity requires a battery of non-invasive tests, chemical, spectral, and aesthetic, though I can already testify to the third element."

"I will rest easy with these pictures in your hands," Wally said. "We're sort of traveling light and I'd hate to be responsible for any harm."

"You handled that well," Yvgeney said as he drove the van south into New Jersey. "I agree, Señor Wally," Chana said from the backseat. "Good work. I've never seen a five million dollar negotiation."

Wally said, "Neither have I." He caught the grainy image of his face again on the front page of the Boston tabloid, folded at his feet with the McDonalds bags.

"Should I change my look?" he asked the two dark ops experts in the van. "A beard perhaps? Shave my head, stain my skin?"

Chana entertained the image of Wally Winchester as a bald, bearded Negro and shook the thought away with a shudder. "Yes, Señor Wally," she said. "I think you should adopt all of those disguises." A smile escaped her lips.

Yvgeney caught it in the rearview mirror, filed it away as a notable moment. The unfocused flight toward the anonymity of a Kansan farm seemed a bit lighter.

"If I did all that, I'd look like an ugly version of Dick Gregory," Wally said.

Chana said, "I don't know this man."

"Go with the image you already created, Chana, the one that caused you to smile," Yvgeney said.

At the entry to I-76, the van headed west into the setting sun. Yvgeney held the speed exactly to the posted limits. In his job with UNESCO, he'd read the homeland security briefing on highway surveillance which said vehicles traveling ten to fifteen miles under the posted speed were either elderly, disabled, timid, or people with something to hide.

Chana opened her phone and called a number in Kansas.

"Hello, this is Johnny," a youthful voice answered.

"Chana here."

"Wow. Chana. How nice to hear from you. I knew you guys were loose in America. That's all."

"We are in Pennsylvania, heading to Kansas. Can we visit?"

"Of course. We even have a bunkhouse."

"Johnny, I ask a favor," Chana said.

"Anything. You saved my life in Mongolia."

"I threw you off a moving train into water with man-eating salmon."

"How can I help?"

"Wally has been put into a trap, and he is wanted for murder."

"I know," Johnny said. "It's on the news. You are invited anyway. I accept the risk."

"It sounds like you've grown up in the two years since we met at a train station in Harbin," Chana said. "I'm asking you not to use the name, Wally Winchester, in any idle talk, even with relatives. His safety is in your hands. If you don't use his name, he will remain invisible at your farm."

"I told my grandparents that I may have friends stopping in, but I don't believe I used Wally's name. Thanks for the heads-up."

"I expect to see you in two days, Johnny, but traveling with Wally, you never know."

"My door is open," Johnny said. "Call when you get close. We're not easy to find."

"That's good."

In a Holiday Inn Express remake of a failed motor court halfway across Pennsylvania, Wally dreamed of Manuelita and the light in her eyes when he finally got her to laugh. He woke up covered in sweat. The bedside clock flashed 2:30 a.m. He sat up and saw Yvgeney's lump on the other bed and Chana in her bedroll on the floor. Wally dressed in stealth mode. He found the room card in his shirt pocket and soundlessly stepped into the corridor.

Chana watched him leave. She calculated the risk of Wally Winchester alone in the rolling hills of Pennsylvania, at a truckstop exit at 2:30 in the morning, and sighed as she climbed into her pants to follow.

Fay's Café, a twenty-four hour truckers' rest, had the bling that drew Wally to a restaurant amid fueling stations, its neon blazing in the dark. Food held no interest. He watched unfocused as country girls smiled at new arrivals while compiling fuel receipts from the pumps. He wandered through aisles of handy gadgets, pep drinks, and amusing dashboard figurines, missing Manuelita, thinking of her face.

The magazine rack was twenty feet long. Wally zombie-walked past trucker mags, *Playboys* covered in plastic, and fix-it magazines. Near the bottom, in a wall slot, he spied a copy of the *Antique Trader,* fat as the Sunday New York Times, with a Queen

Anne tea table on the cover. He grabbed it, paid the three dollars, and headed for the parking lot.

Two men in flannel shirts passed him on the way through the doors. One opened a folded newspaper and looked inside.

"Hey, buddy," he said towards Wally's back.

Chana's voice spun him around. "Sir, is that your vehicle on fire?" she asked as she pointed to a billowing cloud of smoke behind the cinderblock café.

The trucker ran to the corner where a trash can was fully ablaze. He looked back but the man he recognized from the front page photo was gone. He reached for his phone.

"Two-minute drill, Yvgeney," Chana shouted as she flooded the room with light, she and Wally by the door. The Russian was dressed, waiting, his bag on his shoulder.

"We're exposed," she said and wiped the countertops with a towel, polishing the remote control and the faucet handles as she pocketed a used tissue from the wastebasket. She wiped the latch as the door closed and caught up to the men by the elevator. "Use the stairs," she said, erasing their passage to the lobby as she ran. "No freeways."

Yvgeney drove south under the six-lane overpass as a string of angry police lights zipped by overhead.

As he nursed another scotch, Nathan Collver, unemployed art appraiser, looked at the help wanted classifieds. He snarled and highlighted another low-level position and closed the newspaper, shaking his head. A photo on the top of the fold caught his eye, a feature on the front page, a face he knew, the asshole that got him fired. He googled Homeland Security on his i-phone and placed a call.

Deep in the basement of a Federal office building in Portland, Oregon, the bulletin flashed on a computer screen. A sleepy operative copied the report, a link between Wally Winchester and the Tamil Cultural Center – a suspected terrorist front. He added the data to the suspect's extensive folder, and was brewing coffee when the file expanded with the addition of a sighting at a truck stop on the Pennsylvania Turnpike.

Back with a steaming mug, the G-6 trainee returned to his Facebook page and turned up the country western music on the radio.

Claus Braun didn't miss the bulletins. A Mexico City hacker caught the Tamil connection as well as the truck stop report and alerted him in a Tweet. Hello, Mr. Winchester, he said to himself as he unfolded a road map of the United States. His finger followed Interstate 70 westward, tapping on heartland cities like he was squashing bugs. He called the Kansas City Auction House and asked if there was any new interest in the Austrian chair he'd consigned.

Wally looked at his shaved head in the visor mirror. He fingered bumps on his head that he had been unaware of thought he looked like a plucked chicken. The beard itched where the spirit gum pulled at his skin. A map was open on his lap. "Take the next right onto Route 16," he said casually.

"Why?" Yvgeney said. The traffic on the rural highway, connecting dying mining towns, was light, and that suited him fine.

"There's a bookcase that I bought on the road from the Grove Park Inn, an early one with the mitered front."

"No," two voices said as one.

"It wasn't part of the killing, I'm sure. Manuelita told me she liked the old gal, even bought something. Her death has to be a coincidence."

"You have no clue to the level of deception Manuelita was capable of, Señor Wally."

"How about this?" Wally suggested. "We give the store a drive-by. If everything's normal, you two can go in and haul it into the van. I have the receipt. It was a cash sale. It has no name on it. Tell them you are shippers, hired to pick it up. They should expect you."

"I say leave it," Chana said.

"It's 1901, for God's sake." Wally pleaded. "Year one. Earliest piece I've ever owned. Thick as a brick wall. Black finish."

"You have so much more to worry about than another piece of furniture." Yvgeney added.

"It's only a mile from here," Wally said. "What's the harm to drive by?"

Seven miles later, the van entered a quiet village. "There." Wally pointed to a used furniture store, front door open, no vehicles parked nearby.

As he parked the van, Yvgeney cursed. "Anything weird and we're out of here," he said. "Chana, watch the street. Wally, stay put."

Wally fished into his wallet and unfolded a sales slip, handed it to the Russian.

"Smells like vomit," Yvgeney said as he palmed the receipt and entered a dimly lit showroom. A young woman, nodding to an iPod, looked up and smiled.

"Nice store," Yvgeney said.

"Thank you, it belonged to my grandmother."

"Belonged?"

"She died a couple of weeks ago, murdered by the serial killer, Winchester. Bastard."

"I'm sorry about your grandma."

"Is there something I can help you find?"

"No," Yvgeney said as he closed his fist on the receipt. "Just passing through."

"I'm going to miss that bookcase." Wally said as the van resumed its westward meander.

"You can carve one in prison," Yvgeney said. "You'll certainly have some time before they insert the needle, Wally."

He didn't answer, head down amidst a sea of Midwest auction news.

"Stop the vehicle, Yvgeney," Chana ordered.

"There's a county park in a couple of miles; I saw a sign back there."

"No. Stop it now."

The van bounced as it hit the roadside rubble at 20 mph and came to rest in a dusty cloud.

"We need your attention, Wally," Chana began. "All of it." She leaned forward and grabbed the antique weekly off his lap and threw it behind her in back. Wally's mouth formed an objection, but he closed it.

"Listen to me," she continued. "A trap has been triggered, a clever trap with you in the middle."

"Tell me something I don't know," Wally responded. "Ever since we landed in Boston I've been living in a surreal nightmare. I can't get my mind around it."

"You have help." Yvgeney joined the intervention. "Chana is a brilliant warrior, emphasis on brilliant. I have training, dark skills that I've never told you about. I have access to the UN database. I can negotiate with criminals as easily as prime ministers. We've been *on our heels*, as they say in America, since we landed. It's not just you, Wally. We're involved now also…as aiding a fugitive."

"Sorry, you guys," Wally said. "I thought I was only facing a sad drive back to the west coast."

"The trap was designed by a master and executed by another, Señor Wally. You had no chance. The plan appears, even now, to be flawless. When you are arrested, assuming that you live, you will face the death penalty – or, at best, life without parole. I haven't heard details of the crimes. Yvgeney's spent more internet time on it than me. I suspect that each scene is an easy connection to you. A signed credit card slip, a fingerprint."

"My DNA," Wally offered.

"With Manuelita gone, the evidence points to you alone. It's a perfect box."

Wally gulped. Felt like he'd been told he had incurable cancer.

"I'm really screwed, aren't I?"

Yvgeney answered. "You're fucked, my friend."

"I didn't kill these people. Except for that Mexican near Binghamton. I'm innocent. Doesn't that count for anything?"

Chana said, "The only defense now is to find a flaw in the box. Right now I don't see one. I hate to say this, Wally. Please tell us the tale of the Cobra and the cross-country trip in great detail. Again. Leave nothing out. Sorry, Yvgeney."

Wally sat back and began with the odd call from the auctioneer who sold him the car in the locked barn. He mentioned the man's death after the sale.

Chana said, "How did he die?"

"Fishing accident. The guy was dead. I read it in the paper."

Chana said, "Claus Braun's hand begins here. What happens next?"

"I get an email a year later."

"Do you still have it?"

"I have them all. I don't delete."

Chana said, "There's another crack in the box."

Yvgeney's laptop displayed a vertical list of Wally's alleged murderous spree. "What's the first purchase you made on the trip?" he asked.

"Ah, some light fixtures from a Hindu church garage sale where I found Julia's letters and a snapshot. A good day."

"Cleric found with throat cut, gutted like a fish," Yvgeney noted.

"Mercy," Wally said. "He was a nice man."

"What did you buy next?"

"Nothing till we got to Butte, Montana. I bought a marshmallow sofa off a third-story porch."

"No deaths in Butte," Yvgeney said, "Two Spokane area men, with extensive criminal records, murdered at a lakeside campground in Montana."

"Never met them; certainly didn't murder them. There was a couple of yahoos who followed us out of Spokane to the freeway, but the Shelby won."

"Sounds like Manuelita doing housecleaning," Chana said.

Wally said, "I bought some lights at a factory auction in Fargo, North Dakota."

"Four murders there. Teenagers with gang affiliations."

Wally said, "I was inside, in a fight for my life for a bunch of mirrored lamps. Manuelita guarded the car. Maybe they pissed her off."

Yvgeney glanced at his laptop. "Next are the spa murders at the Grove Park Inn."

"Crazy business. I never set foot in the spa – too fucking expensive. I did give Manuelita a free ride on the room charge. Shit. She really did these things. How many were killed there? Three?"

"Two dealers and the spa manager."

"I was up at the old car museum retrieving the sports car on Monday morning, pissed off cause no one could find the garage key."

"Your DNA says you were there, according to the internet," Yvgeney said.

"Don't ask."

Police lights flooded the inside of the van. A spotlight beam found the rearview mirror and danced around.

"Don't talk, Wally." Yvgeney barked the order and dropped the driver's window.

"Evening, sir," said a voice behind the flashlight. "Would you all pass your identification out the window? How many people you got in there?" A beam caught Wally in the eyes. He smiled.

"Three, including me," Yvgeney answered.

More flashing lights lit the interior. A third cruiser u-turned and lit the windshield.

Chana, expressionless, extracted her passport. Wally, lip buttoned, pulled the brand new ID out of his wallet. The documents disappeared into the darkness behind the flashlight in Yvgeney's face.

"You folks on vacation?"

"Yes," Yvgeney said in his best version of the King's English.

"Get out of the van please, one at a time." Chana nodded to Yvgeney. She signaled Wally with a palm down gesture that said, *Chill*.

The pat down was intimidating. Wally felt rough hands under his armpits and between his legs. He looked at Chana, stone-faced, as her breasts endured a thorough search. The hands moved to her hips. He looked away.

Yvgeney brushed the intrusion out of his mind as he looked into the eyes of an overweight policeman, wearing body armor. "Why are you doing this to us?" he asked. "We are tourists."

"There's a serial killer on the loose in these parts. All suspicious vehicles are being searched. You folks, you from France, and what's this, Russia? And you…." He pointed to Wally. "Where are *you* from?"

Wally nearly fainted. His mind raced back to the back room of a tattoo parlor the day before when he invented a personal history for his new ID. What address did he invent? Seattle? Portland? All he could remember was it didn't lead to Camano Island. "The USA," he answered. "I live in the United States of America."

The fat officer walked over to Wally, skewered in the high beams of three vehicles. "Where," he asked, looking down at the new driver's license, "is your home in the USA, Mr. Smith?"

Into the lights, Wally said, "Seattle, Washington," a wild guess, his memory lost in fear.

"That doesn't seem to match up with the address we have here," the officer held the ID up between them.

Wally snatched it, glanced at the address – *Snohomish* – that's right, Bickford Street, my favorite shop.

"Hey," the policeman grabbed the card back, pulled out his wand.

"That damn divorce," Wally rambled. "She got the house in Snohomish. I got the antiques. I live in Seattle now. Guess I better update my license. I usually wait till it's time to renew, you know, on your birthday."

Wally looked at the meaty hand that held the wood baton as the trooper raised it into the air. "That's a Masonic ring, isn't it?" he said.

That baton turned inward and up as the cop glanced over to his hand.

"What's it to you?" he said.

"That's a 32nd degree ring. Looks like it's from the 20's. My grandfather was a 32nd degree Mason. He gave me his ring. Looks like yours, double-headed eagle design with a diamond in the middle. I keep it in the safe deposit box."

"Your granddaddy was a 32nd degree Mason? This is my granddaddy's ring."

"You're taking a chance wearing it around every day, sir. Do you know what that ring is worth?"

"Never thought about it." The baton was in the belt again. He looked at his finger.

"I'd say nine to eleven hundred dollars. That's what my granddaddy's ring is insured for, though I'd never sell it."

The policeman said, "I'm sorry we interrupted your road trip, Mr. Smith." He returned all three ID's and called the militia away to their cars. The headlights turned, leaving the van in the dim light of the shoulder.

Chana said, "What did you say to the fat man that changed his chi? I saw his aggression melt into trust."

Wally watched the last of the police cars re-enter the highway. "The guy was wearing a gold art deco 32nd degree Masonic ring. I just sold one on eBay for nine seventy-five. I told him my grandfather had the same ring, meaning that he also had been a 32nd degree Mason, a top position to achieve, I'm told. That made us brothers, grandsons of 32nd degree Masons. I even appraised it for him. Knew the number from the eBay sale."

"That was nicely done, I'd almost say brilliant," Yvgeney said. "I was impressed by the ID snatch and glance. And then that lie. You turn his ring into a bonding experience with another series of lies. In the blinding lights of the cars, yet. Wally, there may be a spy in you yet."

"I'd call it a lot of shit luck, piled into one weird moment," Wally said.

"That's why they call us *spooks.*"

It was 10:00 p.m. in the Super 8 motel on a blue highway in eastern Ohio when Wally noticed the chair in the auction listings of the *Antique Trader*.

"Holy shit. It's a *Sitzmachine*. And it's getting sold this weekend at a Kansas City auction. A *Sitzmachine*. Yvgeney, look at this beauty." Wally carried the page to the Russian, feigning sleep on the other bed. He sat next to the pillow and made him look. A second eye opened and Yvgeney's unkempt head of brown hair emerged from the blanket. He sat up and looked at the auction photograph. "Chana," the Russian said, with no sound of sleep in his voice.

From a blanket roll on the floor, she said, "Claus Braun is sending Wally an invitation."

Chapter Thirty-Four

Central Missouri

The rolling hills flattened to undulating swells of cornfields, then a straight-line meeting with cumulus clouds on the horizon. A grey ribbon of two-lane asphalt cleaved the cornstalks.

Wally fingered the wrinkled trade paper. He traced the dramatic bentwood curves of the chair in the picture. He counted the square cut-outs and tried to remember the shape of the original he saw in Claus Braun's Chilean mansion years before. The chair in the picture seemed identical to the memory. He said, "We have to stop at this auction house. It's right off the road to Johnny's farm. What luck."

"Too much exposure," Chana said.

"You will be walking into Braun's rifle sight when you show your face, you damn fool," said Yvgeney, left arm out the window as he kept the speed at 40.

"The auction's not until next weekend, guys. This is the perfect time to check the thing out. Before he expects us. Under the radar. I'll just walk in and check it out without putting the big eye on it. Tell them I'm there for the pile of dumb mahogany they have in the sale. My appearance shouldn't alert anyone. Not now." In the rearview mirror, Wally looked at his tan, bearded, bald head and turned his chin to catch another angle, then frowned.

Chana said, "Why do you insist on sticking your Anglo head out of the gopher hole, señor? We're one day's drive to the safety of Johnny's farm."

"You and Yvgeney agreed that meeting Braun himself was the only way out of the predicament he constructed for me, Chana."

"Meeting Braun solves nothing, señor. It's true he is the key, perhaps your only living witness. How to use him to save your sorry white-bread butt, I have no clue, yet. We're not armed, we have no strategy. We're just Monopoly pieces at this point on his personal game board. Meeting him today would be suicide."

"He won't recognize me," Wally protested. "I suggest we buy a used baby carriage, dress you in an Amish scarf and put me in a Mennonite hat. We'll be two locals with a little one. I can learn all I need from six feet away. If it's real, I'll agree Braun placed it there. If it's bogus, the whole thing may be a coincidence. Maybe I should get another gun."

"Merde."

The auction house was on the south side of the sprawling city, west of the Missouri River Bridge and down near the stockyards. The smell of livestock and manure tweaked Wally's nose as he wheeled the baby buggy through the front doors with an Amish version of Chana gripping his arm like an obedient wife. He'd removed the moustache, going with a line of chin hair that seemed more in keeping for a Midwestern elder. Yvgeney sat in the van, engine running, shaking his head at the folly he'd been talked into – again.

On Tuesday at 10:00 in the morning, the small desk in the old lobby was unmanned. Two French doors opened to a hall full of folding chairs facing a stage. Furniture and tables piled with bric-a-brac lined both walls.

A worker talking on a cell phone polished a Duncan Phyfe table. He ignored the visitors as they strolled past items waiting for next weekend's hammer.

Wally spotted the *Sitzmachine* over on the other side but kept his slow pace down the line of offerings, mostly low-end junk and 1940's attempts at Chippendale furniture.

"I'm sorry, we're closed today," the man said as he pocketed the phone. "Viewing hours are Friday 6:00 to 9:00 p.m. and the Saturday morning preview before the sale."

"Can we walk past the other side on our way out?" Wally asked. "Mother doesn't get off the farm often and I promised her a look-see. We need a dining room set. Like the one you're working on. Isn't that pretty wood, mother?" Chana, under a polka dot kerchief, nodded.

"Suit yourself. As long as you're headed for the door. Should be a good sale." The guy yawned, squeezed a puddle of dark brown scratch cover on a tired mahogany finish and rubbed it in.

The Wally family squeezed by behind him and crossed the room in front of the stage to exit on the other side.

As he passed the dark bentwood Morris-style reclining chair, he reached a hand out to touch it. Chana slapped it down. He dropped a pen from his pocket to the floor and tried to catch a glance at the label under the seat as he retrieved it.

Chana nudged him onto his feet with a knee to the butt.

The man with the dark polish was watching. He reached for his cell phone.

"Run, Wally," Chana said. They bolted from the hall through the front doors and into the waiting van.

"Go," Chana ordered the driver. "Get lost in a hurry."

Yvgeney inserted the van into the traffic flow. At the stoplight, he turned left onto an avenue of liquor stores and fast-cash emporiums. Five blocks down he entered a sad neighborhood that flanked the stockyards, dilapidated bungalows-turned-crackhouses and crash pads. Wally scowled at the lack of maintenance, peeling paint, lounging prostitutes, unkempt landscaping and littered lawns. "There's some beautiful architecture in this slum; what a waste. Give me a thousand yuppies and we could turn this place into a garden," he said.

Yvgeney found an empty slaughterhouse parking lot with three exits. He backed the van against a wall and shut the engine off.

"We're dark," he said. "I don't believe we've been followed. Our location is highly improbable. What happened in there, Chana?"

"Wally acted oddly when he was near the chair. He vibrated his interest to the worker inside who made a phone call, I suspect to Claus Braun or his network."

"The chair's real," Wally said into the quiet van.

The backroad to Johnny's farm was seven hours of cornfields pierced by occasional towns and stoplight villages. The van followed a rocky rut, down into a mini-valley, a circular depression in the flat prairie that reminded Wally of a meteor crater. A turn-of-the-century farmhouse and barn sat behind a row of tall poplars. He looked at a dimple in the landscape that descended into a wind-shadowed respite from the winter storms and saw a sanctuary.

At the front door, under a wrap-around porch canopy, a lad with oriental eyes stood with an elderly couple at his side. Wally leaped out the passenger door to the porch where handshakes and hugs were passed around.

"Farm life has made a man of you, Johnny," Wally said in greeting. "Look at you. You're buff. Mr. Beefcake. Nice to see you."

"Five a.m. milkings build up the upper body," the young man said.

"Don't let him kid you," the grandfather said. "We have machines for that. Johnny goes to the gym every day."

"Good job," Chana said. "You took my advice."

"Never forgot it, m'am. "I'm taking a forensics course at the community college. Closest thing I can get out here to spy training."

"Keep collecting the tools," she said.

Over fresh coffee, Fred and his wife, Amelia, told their guests about the heartbreak of losing their son to a toxic accident that wiped out half the town, and the joy they experienced when his child came to America, to live on the family farm. They thanked all three of their guests for their help getting Johnny to the United States.

Yvgeney knocked the love fest down. He said, “Thank you for the coffee. We can’t stay here, you know, although we do request your help. We need a place to sleep away from your farm. Something with a roof and a bathroom. Maybe a shower.”

“You want a place with open space around it, a commanding view,” Fred said. “I worked for the Army in Vietnam, Intelligence Corps. I’ve read *The Art of War.* You can have all of what you need here. We have the bunkhouse, and the perimeter of our valley has a commanding view.”

“We’ve all agreed not to put your farm at risk.”

Amelia said, “We know Mr. Winchester is a wanted criminal. The whole world does. He gets five minutes every hour on Fox News.” She zeroed in on Wally. “Johnny tells us, Mr. Winchester, of your good heart. He tells us you couldn’t kill any of these people you’re accused of and that murdering people would never occur to you.”

“He’s right,” Wally said. “I love everybody.”

Yvgeney stepped into the conversation. “There is another threat out there: A powerful man, bent on revenge, more dangerous than the authorities. We can’t put your family’s safety at risk. I refuse to involve you or your farm. If you want to help, find us a place to take a stand. A fortress on a hill.”

The small, grey haired farmer looked up at Yvgeney’s face. Johnny stepped in to intercede. His grandfather brushed him away.

“Do you know the designation *tunnel rat?”*

Chana turned to the question.

Yvgeney said, “I know the term. I respect the tunnel rat above all soldiers.”

“In Nam, I did three tours. My unit used to brag we’ve been in more holes than Wilt Chamberlain, the basketball player.”

“What was your casualty rate?” Yvgeney said.

“One out of four,” the spry farmer answered.

“One out of four killed.”

“One out of four came home. You think we can’t handle ourselves here? This little valley is a natural citadel. We have half a mile of open space, plenty of weapons, even a few tunnels of our own.”

Wally stepped back in. “I’m a wanted man. If I’m captured here, your property could be in jeopardy, you folks would be in trouble for aiding and abetting. I can’t do that to Johnny’s future.”

It was Johnny’s turn: “This land is rented from Archer Daniels Midland, a lifetime lease. We lost the farm last year to the bank. Now we are sharecroppers, workin’ for the man. My future is worth nothing if I don’t pay you back for bringing me to my family, to the USA. We have all you need in the bunkhouse, even satellite broadband. Park your van in the barn and come in and catch your breath. You’re officially off the radar, Wally.”

“I have a hot roast in the oven,” Amelia said. “Don’t make me waste it, times being what they are.”

Chana looked at Yvgeney. “I must admit the property is ideal for a stand if it comes to that,” she said. “If Wally can keep his head down for ten minutes, our location is still dark to the authorities.” She looked up the winding gravel path that connected the farm to the Kansas City road. “I’m more worried about Claus Braun.”

As Wally enjoyed the best meal he'd had in a month, he looked at the Chinese lad across the table. Two years before, thirty pounds lighter, as a half-breed street orphan in an airport in northern China, Johnny had sweet-talked his way into a job as tour guide and shared a slow motion, five-day escape to Moscow on the Trans-Siberian Railway. Yvgeney's UN connections found the lad's American grandparents in Kansas. Now, here he was, a rugged youth, strong cheekbones finding their place on his face. Wally thought Johnny looked comfortable at the head of the table and told him so.

"Chock it up to farm life," the grandmother said. "And four-egg breakfasts."

Over a dessert of fresh apple pie with cream, Wally narrated the story of his cross-country trip, a fancy-free picking adventure, filled with tales of great scores and auctions won and lost.

He pointed a finger in the air before him, following an imaginary eastbound interstate highway to the dinner audience. Wally's take on his road trip was a tale of things purchased, auction betrayals, and rude hotel desk clerks. Then he recounted the shootout in New York near the Pennsylvania border. "I shot a man, Johnny, when he tried to kill Manuelita."

"How did it feel?" Johnny asked.

"Terrible. I've never even liked hunting. Catching a fish and keeping it gives me a guilt trip. I rescue spiders.

"The news reports say you killed your Mexican companion in Massachusetts."

Wally took a breath. "She took a shotgun blast meant for me. I loved her."

Chana stood up without speaking and walked outside into the deepening night.

"She's an odd one," Amelia said.

"She's a soldier," her husband said.

He looked to Yvgeney who said, “She’s a very competent human being.”

Johnny added, “I’ve seen her stop a full grown man in his tracks with a look.”

“Where’d she get her training?” the grandfather asked.

“South America,” Yvgeney said. “She was an orphaned rainforest child, recruited off the streets and trained by an Al Qaeda-like group in Brazil.

“This outfit had training centers all over South America called *Future Clubs,* the brainchild of a man called Claus Braun, the same man who built this trap that Wally’s in now. He’s totally ruthless, brilliant, and well-funded. Chana was his security chief when we first met.”

“So this Braun character is out there in the prairie night looking to do you people harm, and your primary defender used to work for him? Are you sure of her loyalty if the shit hits the fan?”

“Chana’s world view has changed since her South American days. I trust her totally. I hope it doesn’t come to that.”

Wally jumped in. “He’s a crazy motherfucker, Claus Braun. Thinks he’s Hitler’s son.”

“No shit?” Fred said. “Adolf Hitler?”

“Claus Braun. Eva Braun. He certainly thinks so,” Wally said. “I had a chair that was signed by Eva in pencil under the seat. Claus really wanted that piece. So did I, as a matter of fact. It was the coolest chair I ever owned, a rocker.”

“What happened to it?”

“I threw it off a bridge. Fuck him and his revenge plans.”

“Braun went over the bridge also,” Yvgeney explained. “His body was never found. Presumed drowned. I work with UNESCO and have access to the active insurgencies database. I use it in my job of recovering stolen art. After he fell from the bridge, Claus Braun went dark. All chatter ceased. Four years off the radar and now he surfaces to spring a Wally Winchester trap that seems to have no way out. Are you sure you want to put your family in harm's way?"

"Hitler's son. Is he really Hitler's son?" Fred sat at attention.

Yvgeney said, "Whether he is or just believes he's the Fuhrer's child, he represents the same threat."

"Hot damn, a shoot-out with Hilter's son. Wouldn't miss it for the world."

The spry senior sprang from his chair and sprinted up the stairs. He walked back down with an armful of weaponry.

"Grandpa!" Johnny said. "I've never seen these."

"Never had a reason to show you till now. I'm not proud of these, Johnny. After Vietnam, I got involved in some shady groups. Militia. I was smart enough to get out when Amelia and I purchased the farm, but I kept my guns. I have 5,000 rounds of ammo in the closet upstairs.

He looked at his wife who cleaned the sink. "Amelia," he said, "I want you to take Johnny and go to your sister's in Topeka."

"You'll be worthless without me, Fred."

"Wally is the guy who plucked me from the streets of Harbin, China and helped me find you," Johnny said. "I'm not leaving. I can fight. I'm a street rat."

"OK, Johnny," Fred said. "I figured you'd want to stay. It's time for your first lesson with automatic weapons. Mr. Yvgeney, do you know how to use these guns?"

Yvgeney walked to the couch. He commented, "M16 and a M4 carbine, American guns. That's wild, a Chinese QB2-95. Nice rifle, never shot one."

"I try to keep up. Call it a hobby. Come over here, Johnny, and I'll show you how to break down an M16."

Chana's gaze swept the rim of the valley, looking for intrusions. A starry sky with moonlit clouds filled the airy dome above her. She watched a pair of tiny headlights turn from the crest and enter the depression. "Car approaching," she said into her cell.

"Hide the hardware, Fred," Yvgeney said. "But keep it handy. Are the guns loaded?"

"Ready to fire when you switch off the safety."

Chana, at the doorway now, said, "It's a police car. One man approaching. A large man."

"Probably Floyd," Amelia said as she poured coffee and passed out plates of steaming apple pie. "Come in, child, and have some dessert."

Fred opened the door. "Hello, Floyd," he said. "What brings you down into paradise valley at this time of night? He blocked the doorway with his small body, remembered they were friends. "Forgive me," he said. "Come in. Amelia, do we have one more piece of pie?"

"We do." Amelia said from the stove. "Come on in, Floyd. You want coffee?"

"Black, thanks." The large man took off his hat, ambled to the harvest table, and sat down amidst three strangers eating pie.

"So what brings you here on this fine night?" Fred asked as he adjusted his ample bottom on the dining room chair.

Chana watched the large policeman ignore the question as he eyeballed the strangers. "My name is Chana," she said to him across the table.

"Oh, excuse my manners," Amelia said as she placed a plate of pie in front of the large belly. "Let me introduce our guests. This is Chana. She's from Russia." Chana created a smile.

"This gentleman's name is Yvgeney. He works for the United Nations."

"I'm on holiday," Yvgeney offered. "Here with Chana to see America."

"My name is Floyd. Floyd Fenwick. I'm the law in these parts."

"Hello, Floyd."

"What do you think of our beautiful country, Yavgenie?"

"Flat as a pancake, I think, is the correct American phrase."

"You got it, comrade. Do you know what flat land is good for?" The sheriff eyed Wally, hiding behind a fork. He didn't wait for Yvgeney's guess. "Topsoil," Floyd said. "Six feet of God's brown sugar. Iowa claims eight feet of topsoil but east Kansas's bottomland is the best growing surface on earth. Right, Fred?"

The grandfather murmured agreement as he pulled the fork out of his mouth. He swallowed, then said, "How's that old question go? How many Mississippi River floods did it take to lay all this fine dirt down?"

"All of them," Floyd answered. He and Fred laughed at the local joke. The rest of the table was silent. Wally began to laugh.

"I get it," he said accepting a second wedge of steaming pie. "Ten thousand floods since the last Ice Age. Ten thousand years of silt to get six feet of loam. That's a good one." He slapped his knee, noting Chana's disapproving scowl.

"Actually, the earth was created in 4004 B.C.,according to the best evidence we got, the *Holy Bible,*" the sheriff said.

Wally began to speak. A look from Chana buttoned his lip.

"What's your name, son?" The sheriff's red face darkened. His body twitched in response to some internal conversation. His meaty sheriff's hand slipped below the table and touched his side arm holster. He undid the snap.

Chana watched the lawman's dance. Yvgeney calculated the number of steps to reach the guns, hidden under the settee's skirt.

Time to get a finger on a trigger, he figured, three seconds. He calculated the time to leap over the table, unarmed, at the officer. Figured half that. He worked on plan two but didn't like it.

Fred stood up and put his hand on Floyd's shoulder. "You never told us why you're in the neighborhood, old friend. What in blue blazes gets you out here so late?"

The sheriff wasn't done with Wally: "What country are you from, junior?"

Wally finished a swallow, cleared his throat.

"The USA, boss."

"I didn't get your name."

"Er…Smith. Call me *Smitty*. Everyone does."

"Where you from, Smitty?"

Amelia floated over to the table. She said, "You're in our home, Floyd. We've known each other for thirty years. You went to school with Johnny's dad. Why are you acting so…so official?"

The sheriff said, "There's a serial killer loose in these parts, Amelia. I'm hitting all the outlying farms like yours, keeping you safe."

"Safe?" she said. "This is an interrogation."

"Where you from, son? Can I see some ID?"

Wally pulled the Washington State driver's license he'd purchased in a back room in western Pennsylvania and passed it to Yvgeney who handed it over.

"Snohomish, Mr. Smith," the sheriff read. "Know any people from Camano Island?"

"Never been there," Wally answered. "I hear it's a nice part of the state."

"What do you do for a living?"

"Floyd," Fred said. "You're upsetting my wife."

"Answer the question, Smith."

Wally gulped, swallowed at the unexpected question, told himself to put some distance between him and the word *antiques.*

"I sell used cars," he said.

"Sports cars?"

"No, clunkers. Beaters."

"What brings you to Kansas, Smitty?"

Chana watched the inquisition, saw a mind of a policeman in the body of a broken down, overweight Anglo. "He's our tour guide," she volunteered.

The big man turned to her and said, "So you wanted to see America, and you chose a used car dealer from Washington State as your guide?"

Johnny stepped in. "We all met in China. At the train station in Harbin. I was an orphan, a street kid. These people are responsible for me finding my grandparents here in Kansas. I am in…Smitty's debt. This is America, isn't it? Right now it feels like Communist China."

The cop stood up, his gaze still on Wally. "There's a dangerous man out there. I'm doing my job. Sorry, Fred. Keep your doors locked, folks. Call my cell if you see anything suspicious." He handed a card to the farmer, retrieved his hat, and exited into the warm Kansas night.

"Wow," Johnny said. "You've got the country all riled up."

"Thank God," Yvgeney said, "that you didn't ask the sheriff if his grandparents left him a Morris chair."

"That was my next question," Wally said as he finished his second piece of pie. "You know, this part of the country is loaded with Stickley."

In the bunkhouse, Wally watched Chana return from her perimeter patrol. He offered to take his turn on guard. Yvgeney smiled and said, "What part of *America's Most Wanted* don't you understand? You're better off inside."

"How am I going to bid on that chair Saturday if I have to stay hidden?"

"The auction is an exposure we can't afford. It's only a chair."

Wally's face wrinkled. "It's not just a chair. It's the *Sitzmachine*!"

Chana spoke. "Claus Braun will be there. We have to attend."

Yvgeney said, "What good will that do? Braun's the mastermind of Wally's dilemma. Why would he be of any help?"

"Because he's the only flaw in his own trap."

"But what on earth would compel him to go to Wally's defense?"

Chana said, "I have no idea, but we have to play it out. I suggest we invent multiple back doors on Saturday and have them all in play.

Chapter Thirty-Five

Kansas City, Kansas

The street was damp from an early morning downpour as Johnny's Ford crew cab parked two blocks from the auction house after two drive-bys satisfied Chana it was safe to stop. Wally, in bib overalls and a Kansas City Chiefs cap, felt like a local.

Chana returned to the truck after a walk-around. The passenger window lowered. "There is no increased police presence," she said. "No signs of Braun or surveillance. I think the risk is acceptable. Señor Wally, promise to keep your mouth shut. If you run into anyone you know, don't acknowledge them. You and Johnny got your phones?"

Both held up their Nokias. Yvgeney shook his head. Chana shrugged. Life with Wally.

The auction crowd was robust as Wally wandered past items that lined the wall. He passed his *Sitzmachine* without apparent interest, though he trailed his fingers across the arm as he walked by. He saw no interesting Arts and Crafts objects. He looked at a pair of ornate gas light fixtures, items without a market these days. He stopped to inspect a stainless steel, wall-mounted drop-down sink from a vintage train car, and returned to a chair near the back row, keeping his head down as ordered. From under the brim of his cap he rolled his eyes up to look for the face of his adversary, saw Yvgeney instead, searching faces in a roomful of previewers. He watched Chana return from a visit to the street. Then he caught sight of Stacie Morningstar.

Shit, he said to himself. Competition.

Yvgeney hadn't seen Claus Braun's face for a few years, but he knew the piercing blue eyes and pronounced Germanic cheekbones would be easy to spot. He looked into eye shadows of baseball caps, past facial hair, beyond skin color, and under body shapes. Not present, he concluded as the auctioneer began the sale down the right hand wall. An older Mexican man with a cell phone to his ear got his attention, then lost it as Yvgeney watched him bid on a ceramic 50's television lamp that depicted a cactus and burro. He searched the room for heater vents, holes in the old pressed-tin ceiling, anywhere a sniper could gain access to the hall. He saw none.

Chana returned again from the sleepy, industrial zone street as two farm boys in suits and ties held up the Austrian chair.

"An old Morris chair," the auctioneer spoke from the room speakers. "European. Pay attention, everyone, this object has had a lot of interest. *Thonet*, it's branded under the seat – the bentwood people. *Vienna*, it says. Looks like it's about a hundred years old. Long way from home. Should be a couple thousand. Can I have a thousand dollar bid?"

Johnny looked back at Wally in the back row. Wally typed, "Don't look at me. No bid yet."

"Five hundred, we got." The auctioneer pointed to a clerk with a phone to her ear. "Do I hear six?" Wally typed, "bid." Johnny raised his number. "Six, we have. Do we have seven?"

Wally watched his nemesis, Stacie, the Rohlfs Queen, lift her finger to her ear.

"Yo," a spotter shouted. "Seven, we have," the auctioneer said. "Alice says we have eight hundred on the phone. How 'bout nine?"

Wally saw Stacie rub her ear and push the phone bidder to a thousand. His text to Johnny said, "Wait."

"Told you folks it was a dandy," the auctioneer barked, acknowledging the phone call. "Back to you folks. Who's next?" Stacie scratched her head. "Twelve hundred on the floor," he said.

Chana stood on the outside stoop, re-read Yvgeney's text saying her former mentor was not inside. She looked across at four-story brick structures, built when the cowboys still drove cattle north from Texas, saw no familiar German face staring out the vacant windows or watching from a rooftop perch. It didn't make sense.

"Hello, Señor Braun," she said softly into a warm Kansas morning. "I know you're out there." Sidewalks steamed as the rising sun spilled into the urban canyons. Her memory of Braun held no anger. It was his school of insurgency that plucked her off the dangerous streets of Manaus, taught her the skills of terror craft and brought her to Chile to learn from the great man himself. True, she recollected, he had his faults, like the plan to burn down the great South American cities, killing thousands, to launch a Fourth Reich, to put his feet into his famous father's shoes. Braun had always treated her well, taught her spy strategies and gamesmanship to match her killing skills, and trusted her eventually as head of his security.

Everything changed when Braun vanished after a deadly fall from a Washington State bridge, presumed drowned. Yet here he was, somewhere in Kansas City, now an adversary. As she snapped a Polaroid filter onto her field glasses and peered through window reflections, she marveled at the whimsy of the gods.

Wally ordered Johnny to bid when the price reached twenty-four hundred, watched Stacie look at the youth in surprise. She answered at twenty-six and heard the auctioneer credit twenty-eight hundred to the bidder on the phone.

Chana re-entered and caught Yvgeney's eyes, watched him shake his head to say *nothing's here*. The price of the chair was now three thousand. It didn't make sense. Braun was the phone bidder; that much was obvious. Where was he?

He wasn't in the room. Yvgeney texted, "He not here. I'm thinking bomb."

Chana typed back, "Too messy. He likes elegant solutions."

Wally answered, "The chair's mine soon. Good we have a truck."

"The chair," she said out loud. She texted Wally, "you looked at the chair. Did you see repairs? Replaced parts?"

He answered, "All original. I know bentwood. The fabric on the padded seat was new. Gotta bid."

The auctioneer shouted, "Four thousand, two hundred dollars from the young gentleman in front."

Chana texted all: "Get out now."

Wally answered, "I'm still bidding."

Chana's answer, "There's a bomb in the seat cushion. A Wally trap."

Johnny texted, "Do I bid? We're behind."

Chana texted, "Run."

"Sold," the auctioneer said, "Five thousand dollars. To bidder number…"

Wally saw Stacie raise her paddle for the clerk. She smiled broadly and stood up to retrieve her prize. "There's a bomb in the chair," he shouted to the winner. "A *bomb*. Don't touch it!"

Yvgeney saw panic flood the hall. "*A bomb*," someone screamed. The doors jammed as people clogged the entrance doors. A fistfight broke out.

Wally stood still in the back of the auction hall as terrified bidders ran for the exits. He looked at the chair – bold squares cut into polished beachwood– and felt outrage at the thought of destroying it. He noticed Stacie standing above it. "Get away from the chair, Stacie," he shouted.

She looked up, oblivious to the screams. "Wally? Wally Winchester? Was that you bidding against me using the Chinese straw man?"

From the crowd pushing through the exit doors, a voice shouted, "Wally Winchester, the killer!" The name of a serial killer was now loose in the room. The last of the exiting patrons screamed louder.

"There really may be a bomb in the seat cushion," Wally shouted to the Rohlfs Queen. "There's a madman out there trying to kill me!"

Stacie Morningstar stepped back. "Look, Winchester. I'm not afraid of you. I don't care how many people you killed, but you're not going to get your hands on this chair with the old bomb-in-the-seat-cushion lie. You could have had your Chinese teenager bid again. Better luck next time."

The hall was nearly empty. Wally felt a hand on his shoulder and turned to the angry red face of the auctioneer, who shouted, "Look what you've done to my sale!" His hand swept the empty seats. Police sirens sounded through the exit doors.

An arm appeared from nowhere and locked on the auctioneer's throat. Wally watched Chana ease the unconscious man to the floor with a sleeper hold. "Grab an arm, Wally. We have to get him outside." To Stacie, she said, "Believe what you want, *gringa.* Wally's leaving and so are you."

Stacie, broke from the stare, let go of the chair, and bolted for the door.

From a darkened warehouse window, Claus Braun saw a stream of panicked customers and reached for his other cell phone.

The *Sitzmachine* blew up and knocked Wally into the wall.

Wally regained consciousness inside a settling cloud of plaster dust, looked up to see Johnny and Yvgeney lifting him into the pickup truck. "Where's the girl, Stacie?" he asked. "The one who bought the chair?"

"She's alive, Wally, in the back of the truck. Drive, Chana!" Yvgeney shouted. "Anywhere but here!"

From his warehouse window, Claus Braun had watched Chana, *his* Chana, drag an unconscious body toward a parked truck. He recognized Yvgeney, the nosy Russian he met in South America, carry another body over his shoulder like a sack of potatoes and place it in the pickup bed. He made a call.

Chapter Thirty-Six

Chadsworth Hollow, Kansas

Johnny's grandfather met the truck as it screeched to a halt in front of the farmhouse. He carried a carbine and a frown. "What in Sam Hill have you gotten our grandson into, Mr. Winchester?" he said, drill-sergeant-close to Wally's nose. "The news says you blew up an auction house, three folks wounded. The auctioneer is critical."

"Wally saved lives at the auction house, granddad," Johnny jumped in. "He cleared the hall and then dragged the auctioneer and the lady we have in the cab away from the chair before it exploded."

"Jumping Jesus, Johnny, get these people into the house and get the truck out of sight," he ordered. "Mother," he yelled to his wife on the porch, "get the first aid kit."

Darkness found Chana in dark clothes and a watch cap, high up on the slope behind the farm. From here, the interstate highway was a necklace of tiny lights, twenty miles away on the horizon. The snap of a twig breaking brought her attention to the valley. A figure that walked like Yvgeney, backlit by farmhouse lights, walked up the hill to her position.

"Good job finding me, Yvgeney," she said as he drew near.

"You're not the only tracker on this team, Chana." He sat beside her and produced a bottle of vodka and two glasses.

"I expect a visit from Claus Braun tonight. Are you sure you want to dull our swords with alcohol?"

"I suspect you know more about the history of battle than I do, Chana. They say the ancient Scythians smoked hemp before fighting an opposing tribe that drank a concoction called *trauma* that caused frenzied aggression. I'd pay a dollar to see that fight."

"I knew Yanomamo people in the rainforest who would ingest a special hallucinogen before a battle. It's a fun drug. I've tried it."

"Before battle?"

"No, before sex. In Manaus, all sex was a battle."

"I was taught that Chinese troops in the time of SunTzu drank wine before warfare and watched gyrating swordplay."

Chana, beside him in the dark, watched a jetliner headlamp at thirty thousand feet fade as it passed behind a cloud. She sipped the alcohol and asked, "Would you like to see me do some gyrating sword play before our battle tonight?"

Yvgeney hesitated, said, "Yes, as a matter of fact, I would."

"Forget it." She laughed. "Can we talk strategy?"

Yvgeney poured another measure for himself. He said, "Please do. I can't remember ever being in a fight that has such poorly defined objectives."

"What are our givens?" Chana asked.

"One: Wally is actively wanted by every law enforcement office in America. He's nearly as well known as the Northwest teenage burglar."

"Colton Harris Moore," Chana responded. "I'm on his Facebook page, a friend" "Figures. The thing is, Wally will be captured. It's inevitable. America is too transparent. There will be a trial. He has no defense. Manuelita did her job well. She is dead. The auctioneer who sold Wally the Cobra was Braun's first contact. He's gone. Claus Braun is the only living connection to Wally's innocence."

Chana said, "I have given much thought to my reunion with Señor Braun."

"What did you figure out?"

"I've concluded that, though we may meet tonight under adversarial conditions, I have no interest in causing him harm. I owe the man a great deal."

"He turned you into a professional killer."

"Claus Braun taught me how to excel on any path. In Manaus, professional killers had a lot of growth potential. These days I favor professional healing."

"So instead of fighting Hitler's son to the death tonight, you plan to thank him for your life's successes and ask him for a notarized confession of his role in Wally's frame-up to use in his trial?" Yvgeney asked.

"Now we have a strategy. Thank you, Yvgeney."

"Can we now work on a default strategy, one that will keep us alive?"

"Absolutely," Chana said as she offered her glass for a refill. "There are two roads into the valley and numerous footpaths. Fred has plenty of firepower at the farmhouse and that tunnel system he dug to connect the outbuildings is a good back door."

"Tornado protection, my eye," Yvgeney said. "Leave it to a tunnel rat to build his own underground nest."

Chana swallowed the second vodka, tossed her glass into the chaparral. She said, "You and I outside tonight on a hundred meter circle. Hand weapons and walkie-talkies. Fred and Johnny inside with five thousand rounds. Wally and the ladies in the tunnel. See what happens."

"First one to get a signed confession from Claus Braun wins." Yvgeney said. He tossed his glass in the opposite direction, heard the smash. "What do we have for side arms?"

"A Glock, the two Sig-Sauers that Fred bought this week, the two Navy SEAL assault knives you ordered, a jar of something I call

Chana's Botox Surprise, plus a handful of plastic zip ties in case we take prisoners."

"I'm good with that," Yvgeney said. "I'm going to relay this to the people in the farmhouse, help them set up a safety zone. I'll see you on the perimeter."

"If I'm doing it right, you won't."

Wally looked into the spare bedroom and saw Stacie Morningstar, sitting unsteadily on the edge of the bed.

"Where am I?" she asked. "Who are you?"

"You're in a farmhouse sixty miles west of Kansas City," Wally said. "You're safe."

"Who the fuck are you?"

"Wally Winchester. We met in Shipshewana. You kicked my ass at the auction. I look different with a shaved head and this fake beard." He lifted the corner of the beard off his chin.

"I don't know you from Adam, buster. I've never heard of this Shipshewana and I don't know anything about an auction. What the fuck is going on?"

Chana watched a shelf of high, flat clouds drift from the west and occlude the remaining stars, taking the thin crescent moon with them. A hunter, she approved.

A pair of headlights across the hollow turned into the valley. She watched the vehicle's progress as it stopped halfway into the bowl and went dark. "It begins," she said into the phone.

Inside the farmhouse Fred passed a rifle to Wally and Johnny. "We have tons of ammo, kids," he told them. "Put a few clips in your pockets."

Amelia touched her husband's arm. His posture softened. "Getting a flashback, babe?" she said.

Fred relaxed his grip on the M-16. He dropped his head down on his wife's shoulder. "How many years have we had, Amelia?"

"Fifty-two, last time I counted."

"When was that?"

"Last night."

"Remember when I came back from Nam?"

"I remember the first time, the second time and the third time."

"I feel like I'm back there again. I have to admit I love it. I'm alive again. A big part of my life, a part that I'm proud of, has been hidden, even to me, hon, in a grey cloud of trying to forget.

"Back then, I was superman. I had to be, or I couldn't dive into a manhole designed to kill Americans. I put that feeling in a coffin in 1971. Never looked back. Sealed it tight till now. It feels good to let some of the superman out of the box. Problem is you. You and the wounded woman. I'd like you to take her into the shelter and lock the doors."

"I can help here, Fred. Fetch ammo, make sandwiches. You don't really know an attack is imminent. Four days ago we had a happy farm. Today we're an outpost, told we're about to be overrun by unknown killers. All of this from the mouths of strangers."

Fred said, "Johnny is our beloved grandson. These people are family."

Yvgeney walked quietly between tree trunks. Below him, the distant farmhouse windows winked out. He heard the sound of careless walking. Flattened against a tree, he pulled the SEAL knife from the sheath.

The suggestion of a human figure, carrying a rifle, moved past his position toward the farmhouse. What the fuck, he said to himself. Yvgeney Ivanchenko, Cultural Properties Investigator for UNESCO, leaped and made his first kill on American soil.

It took Chana ten minutes to reach the car that parked on the opposite slope. Nearing it in the darkness, she knew it was a police car. Old training.

At the driver's window, she stepped on broken glass. A penlight from her back pocket revealed Sheriff Floyd, her pie partner, a red wound oozing blood above his ear. The flashlight went to his right hand, still grasping the microphone. "You get to ask God about the age of the earth, yourself," she said as her finger closed his eyes. She ran down toward the farmhouse to intercept the invasion.

A dark shape before her stood, crouching in a grove of trees. Chana pulled a dart from her fanny pack, her little Botox surprise, and closed on the nearest shape. She leaped.

The intruder's shriek leaked into the night between the fingers of her left hand. The other jabbed the dart where the neck met the shoulders. Chana smelled feces as she watched the body sag. She looked for another.

Yvgeney noticed movement in the grove of poplar trees behind the farmhouse. A window shattered. He heard an order, whispered in Spanish.

As an operative in the super secret Soviet GRU a couple of lifetimes before, Yvgeney's training screamed at him not to fire the first shots in a battle that was not yet defined, but he saw no alternative, him against four. He emptied his clip into the group, who spun and gyrated as the bullets cut them down.

Scattered gunfire now erupted from the darkness in front of the house. Windows shattered. Yvgeney loaded a fresh clip and began a silent walk up the hill.

Chana heard the gunfire and scattered return fire that broke windows behind the farmhouse. She trusted the old man, the tunnel rat, to take care of things inside. She trusted Yvgeney's ability to handle behind-the-lines mayhem, something she enjoyed herself. Somewhere on the ridge above her, she knew, Claus Braun was orchestrating the assault. It was time for them to meet. She placed her weapon up against a tree and headed up the hill to find the command vehicle.

When the windows broke, Fred was behind the upturned oak table that last night held pie and coffee. Johnny sat in the hall, deep within the house, with a view of both bedrooms as access points. Wally was miserable. He sat in a folding chair just inside the entrance to the exit tunnel, the massive door closed and camouflaged in front of him. His orders, *Shoot anyone except us who tries to enter*. He was out of the action, and he hated it. Muffled reports told him a gunfight was underway on the other side of the door, and he wanted to join in.

Johnny heard glass breaking in his grandparents' bedroom. He looked in to see a black-garbed form in a ski mask, halfway through the window. He shot him four times as the invader raised his weapon.

The body fell into the room and lay still. Johnny heard voices outside. He took a breath, tried not to think about what he just did.

As he peered from behind two inches of quarter-sawn oak, Fred watched the front door casing splinter and break. Three figures burst in, firing a spray of bullets into the room. China in the hutch behind him shattered and fell. He watched the floor crack and collapse, dropping the intruders into the pit that Fred, living in a Vietnam dream, had created in 1974 to stop intrusions exactly like this one.

Screams of anguish rose from the hole in the floor.

"You're lucky there's no shit on my punji sticks, motherfuckers," he shouted into the darkened front room.

"Johnny," he shouted. "You all right?"

"I'm OK, granddad," a voice from deep within the house said. "I killed a man."

"How'd it feel?" he yelled back.

"Terrible."

"Good."

Chana spotted the van, parked near the top of the long entrance into the bowl, a hundred yards from the county road. Circling the vehicle, she identified three sentries. She wished for her blowpipe and little arrows, hunting tools she used in the rainforest a million years ago.

Tonight she had tavern darts, coated with a month's worth of Botox, a dark, gritty paste. Not pretty, no happy ending; it was all she had.

The first was a big man, tall for a Mexican, no body armor. He was an easy takedown with a dart between his shoulder blades. Gagged with a scarf, he tried to stand up and failed.

The second man was lighting a cigarette when she clamped a hand on his mouth and jabbed the dart into his back. She left him with a cigarette in his lips that useless arms couldn't reach.

Access to the last sentry was limited. He stood, serious, by the passenger door, guarding the side opening.

Chana walked out of the darkness, weaponless, hands out.

The close perimeter man stopped her with a word, "*Alto.*"

Chana froze. "I'm here to see Claus Braun," she said in Spanish.

The sentry held a cell phone against a bushy Latin face. He turned to Chana. "What do you want?" He leveled the machine pistol at her midriff.

"My name is Chana."

His countenance sagged. "Chana," he said softly. "Please forgive any insult."

Her face was empty. "I want to go inside," she said. "Make it happen."

The man spoke to the phone, "*Chana quiere verle*."

The side door opened to a bank of computer monitors. A tall thin man stepped out. "Hello, Chana dear," Claus Braun said. He made a gesture to close the gap between them. Both stepped back. Braun laughed. He said, "This must be an awkward moment for you, child. You, the adversary of the mentor who introduced you to the world."

"I am not your enemy. I hold no malice toward you. You are and will continue to be the person who gave me my life."

"Why do you back away?"

"I don't trust you. I know you too well, sir."

Braun laughed. Chana thought he looked weary. He said, "Good for you. I taught you well, didn't I?"

"Yes, sir."

"So you're not here to kill me, sided as you are with Winchester?"

"Killing you never entered my mind, Señor Braun. I bear you, personally, no ill will."

Braun sat back on the extendable van step. He relaxed his shoulders, looked up into the sky. "There are no words that can express how much I have missed you, Chana. I searched for you. Found nothing. Finally discovered you in Siberia, a shaman no less. Long way from *three ways to kill with a toothpick* isn't it?"

"Yes, Señor Braun, I've moved forward on an interesting path. I thought of you often also, although I believed you were dead."

"What do you think of the puzzle that I built?"

"It is brilliant. I see no flaws in it, except that you lost Manuelita."

Braun sighed. "Manuelita was my sword, after you. She changed. A week on the road with Winchester ruined her mind. She fired on our own men outside of Boston – she, the assassin for hire. We fired back. I'm sorry she's gone. I have a great fondness for her spirit."

"I have a request for you," Chana said. Her face was blank, an empty shape with eyes.

"What can I do for you? Does it involve my assault on your client Winchester?"

"He's not my client, he's my friend."

"Your friend, Wally Winchester, ruined my life. He crashed an empire ready to ignite South America. He destroyed my dreams and ambitions."

"This is your payback," Chana said.

"I've spent four years and a couple hundred thousand dollars for a car to weave a public trap around Wally Winchester that he could not escape, one that makes his very name a curse."

"If you look in the newspapers or on TV or on the internet, I believe you will find you succeeded."

"I wanted Winchester alive to see his good name destroyed. Now I want him dead. Excuse me." Braun listened for a voice in his ear. He barked a command. "Go." Gunfire below them increased.

"Excuse me," he said. "Where were we?"

"I came to ask you to stop this attack."

"Good request. If I were in your position I would be asking that."

"Can I tell you my dream scenario?"

"Of course, Chana."

"In my dream scenario, you take a piece of paper and describe the box you constructed to frame Wally Winchester, describe your role in the car sale and explain Manuelita's role in the murders."

Below, the pop, pop, pop reports ceased, then resumed. Chana resisted the urge to join it. She watched the familiar face break into a smile.

"You want me to confess?" Braun said. "After four years of planning, the loss of my most valuable operative, hundreds of thousands of dollars? You expect me to undo all this? Why would I do such a thing?"

Chana's face was the same mask as the one Braun first saw on a plucky teenager in his training facility. "I have no idea," she said. "Your plan was a beautiful conception. Wally's reputation has been devastated. His name is now linked with Jeffrey Dahmer, BTK, and the Zodiac Killer. A nationwide manhunt is underway. You won. He's ruined."

Braun said, “I was content to see him rot on death row with his reputation destroyed until he ruined Manuelita. Now, I just want him to die.”

“Is there anything in the world that would make you change your mind?” Chana asked.

“I’m sorry, child. This is an eye for an eye. No, wait. There may be one thing.”

Chana said, “Tell me.”

“Come back to Chile. Take your old position, head of security. Then I’ll call off my dogs.”

Chana closed her eyes to hide a reaction that she couldn’t mask. She said, “I don’t share your goals. Our paths lead in opposite directions.”

“You don’t have to become a true believer, Chana. Just agree to watch my back like the old days.”

Chana surprised herself when she asked, “For how long?”

“This would be a permanent position. By the way, where are my remaining sentries? Did you kill them?”

“I find it more interesting to solve problems in a non-lethal manner these days. They’ll be fine tomorrow.”

“My security chief has to be able to kill without thinking. Can you still take a life if need be?”

“Every situation is unique, sir. What exactly are you offering?”

“You will leave your group of fools and accompany me back to South America, to the house in Osorno that you remember well. You will be available seven days each week, your salary…room and board.

“In exchange, I will radio my small force and withdraw. Mr. Winchester will be free to protest his innocence to the police. I hear they have now issued standing shoot-to-kill orders.”

“Will you admit your role in the Winchester frame-up?”

"To you dear, I'll admit to anything, but I won't do it in writing."

"Promise me you'll walk me through your entire plan some day."

"I look forward to it. You are the one person in the world who would appreciate the elegance and the timing."

"Yes sir, I recognize your brilliance."

"So it's done then? Are you back on board? I'll call off the attack."

Chana stood up, walked over to Braun and held out her hand. He took it. "It's been an honor to know your mind, Señor Braun."

"You're saying no?"

"I'd rather face your troops," she said. With that, she turned, and in one step, melted into the inky night.

Braun stabbed his cell phone with finger jabs. "Kill them all!" he shouted.

The explosion knocked Johnny back into the hall. He stood up and retrieved his rifle in time to see a gang of men pour into the bedroom through a ragged gap where the window used to be.

"Grandpa," he shouted. "The house is breached." He fired a burst at the bedroom door. A hand with a pistol reached around and fired into the hall. Johnny hit the floor. The hallway erupted with gunfire behind him.

"Get to the tunnel, son. I'll give you cover." His grandfather's voice reached his ears between bursts. Johnny rose to a crouch and ran to his side.

"We can hold them off from here," he said. He emptied his clip at the doors at the end of the hall.

"Get to the tunnel, John. Lock it behind you. Protect Wally and the women. And Johnny…." He fired a trio of bullets into the bedroom. "After you lock the door from the inside, press the red button on the console on the wall. Never use that exit again. It will be armed. Leave from the barn or the other ports in the system."

"You and I can hold them off here."

"Go. Now. Protect the others." He fired again. "I'm having the time of my life, John. Forty years of bustin' sod, making nice at the church social, today I'm alive again. Go now, John. I'm proud of you. I know what I'm doing. *Go*."

As Johnny secured the metal door and pushed the red button on the console, he heard a furious gun battle outside.

Yvgeney spotted the flame from a cigarette lighter in the shadow of the farmhouse. When it lit the tail cloth of a Molotov cocktail, the flame illuminated the attacker as well. Yvgeney shot him five times as he fell. The bottle burst and a violent blue plume flowed out over the writhing body as it brightened the night.

He turned from the furious blaze and peered into the darkness of the backyard. He willed his irises, tight from the fire, to open. He saw another cocktail lit. He fired all the ammo in the clip into the flaming tail, watched the figure drop the bottle, and saw the blue flash as the gasoline hit the air and the flame.

Chana heard gunfire from within the farmhouse and saw the truck-sized hole in the bedroom wall. She retrieved the M-16 from the place she hid it before her meeting and stepped over splintered wood into the ragged gap.

The house was silent. No lights lit the interior. She stepped on a body, then another. Counted four as she entered the hall. Flashlights ahead in the common room lit the way. She heard a conversation in Spanish. They were looking for Wally.

She came to the prone figure of the grandfather warrior, Fred. He had a pulse but wasn't moving. She continued down the hall.

At the great room, she saw the upturned table and imagined old Fred reliving an attack in the Mekong Delta. She hoped he enjoyed it. A flashlight swipe revealed a gaping hole in the floor by the front door. Anguished moans filled the room. She smiled.

Movement in the kitchen pulled the gun to her shoulder. She aimed at a flashlight beam and cut somebody in two with half the clip.

Muffled voices in the pantry suggested at least two more.

Chana spoke into the kitchen area, now dark, her nose full of the familiar twang of recent gunfire. She spoke in Spanish. "There's a back door behind you. If you leave now I won't kill you."

A hand, holding a machine pistol, snaked around the corner and sprayed the room with gunfire.

Chana felt the impact of a slug shake the big tabletop she crouched behind.

"My name is Chana," she said in a quiet voice. "Do you want this fight?

In the darkness, she heard the door open and the sound of feet exiting into the night.

The house was silent now. She found her way to the body in the hall, felt again for a pulse.

Fred spoke in a gurgle of forced breath. "Good times," he said.

"We have to get you into the tunnel,"

"Too late. The booby traps are hot. Meet them at the barn."

"How badly are you hurt, sir?"

"Bad. Save yourself," he coughed. Chana heard air whistle from his chest. "Wasn't it the time today? We showed those gooks a thing or two."

"Yes, sir, we did. They're going to burn the house. Can you make it to the back door?"

"I'm done, honey. Go save the family." A muffled explosion filled the living room behind her with light. Flames consumed the curtains and raced across the ceiling. Chana found the shirt collar and pulled the limp form into the kitchen, now ablaze. The tunnel rat was surprisingly light. She exited the back door in a crouch, minimizing her silhouette.

Flames lit the orchard where she pulled the old warrior. His breathing sputtered and stopped. Chana closed his lids and wished him an enlightened journey.

The voice behind her was Yvgeney's. "They just cleared out, Chana," he said. "Soon as the fire started." Beside her, he crouched, mindful of the conflagration that consumed the farmhouse at his back. "Shit," he said. "It's Fred."

"He's gone."

"We brought this to the farm. This death is on our heads."

"I know."

"Did you get your meeting with Braun?"

"Yes."

"Did you get the signed confession?"

Chana pulled a tape recorder from one of her commando pockets, held it up in the light of the fire. "In a way, I did," she said.

Amelia didn't crumple when Yvgeney told her about Fred. She stood taller. Johnny went to her arm. She said, "He told me last night that your visit, with 'the hounds of hell on your tail,' as he called it, was a dream come true. He had the cancer, Johnny, we didn't tell you. Had it bad. His head has been in Vietnam since he came back in 1972. I knew he hated pushing a plow or driving a tractor. I've watched him build the perfect defendable outpost for thirty years. His biggest disappointment was that he was dying and hadn't got to use it. Then you came and made his day. In a terribly sad way, I'm grateful."

"We have to go," Chana said.

"I'm so sorry, Johnny," Wally said. "I brought this upon your family."

"You heard my grandmother," Johnny said. "We have fire insurance. You granted my grandfather a soldier's death."

"There will be police here soon," Yvgeney said to Amelia. "Tell them we drove down your road, followed by the Mexican killers, and your family was caught in the firefight." To Johnny, he said, "Remember, son. You never knew Wally Winchester. These people who drove into your valley were strangers."

"Floyd saw us having pie," Amelia said.

"Floyd's dead," Chana said, "I found his car. He was the first Mexican kill. Your family has no links to serial killer Wally Winchester if we leave now."

Stacie Morningstar woke up again and found herself in a van, traveling at high speed. She closed her eyes and tried to open them into a different dream. She looked up and saw a four-lane interstate out the front window. "Wally Winchester," she spoke through closed eyelids.

"Right beside you, Stacie," Wally said. He picked up her hand for a squeeze of support. She pulled hers away. "I don't know you," she said, opening one eye to look at him. I see you at an auction. I wake up in a farmhouse. Then I'm in a tunnel. Then in a bomb shelter with a flat-screen TV. Now we're on the road. Where are we going, and why are you doing this to me?"

"We're going to the nearest hospital."

"Second nearest," Chana added.

"You have a concussion and need a good look-over," Wally said. "It's been a busy weekend."

"I'm all right. Just get me back to my truck in Kansas City."

"We're too hot to be seen near the auction site," Yvgeney told her. "You really need medical attention."

Wally kept his mouth shut as they passed two antique shops in Emporia.

"We're going to drop you off at the front door, if you don't mind," Yvgeney said as the hospital campus loomed.

"How am I supposed to get back to my rig?" Stacie objected.

Wally peeled off a hundred. "Take a cab," he said and passed her a card. "Here is my phone number, in case I get out of this. I still want to show you the Pacific Northwest."

They left her standing, confused, at the emergency room door.

Two hours later, the Highway Patrol had Wally's cell number and a search radius that included most of Kansas.

Chapter Thirty-Seven

Somewhere in Kansas

Yvgeney talked to Chana as they drove west on a two-lane blue highway in Kansas. "Tell me about the signed confession you got from Claus Braun."

"We met. I told him he won."

"Were you in danger?"

"No. I don't fear Claus Braun."

"Did you consider killing him?"

"Never."

"Where did you meet?"

"In a command van, near the top of the ridge. Up near the sheriff's car, Floyd's."

"He must have had security."

"I put two sentries into frozen statues using that Botox concentrate."

"So it worked? Did you throw the darts?"

"I went for the neck muscle under the collar."

"So you rode them down like a rodeo rider."

"Not much of a ride when your muscles stop talking," she said. "It was an interesting meeting. Braun offered to call off the attack if I went back to work for him."

"Holy Cosmos, Chana," Wally chimed in. "What did you say?"

"I knew the farmhouse was secure. I trusted old Fred, liked his defenses. I knew Yvgeney was at the attacker's backs. I told him we'd take our chances with his killers."

"How did he react?" Yvgeney asked. He marveled at the string of words from Chana's normally quiet mouth, then remembered it was a debriefing.

"Poorly," she said.

Yvgeney kept the speed at fifty-five. Flat fields of wheat spread a tan blanket to the horizon. Traffic was a mix of farm vehicles and SUV's. "What did you capture on your recorder?"

"You tape-recorded your conversation with Claus Braun?" Wally said. "Hot damn. Did he confess?"

"We discussed the details of his campaign against you, Señor Wally, but I don't believe they will help you at the trial."

"I hate the way that sentence ended," Wally said. "You got a confession. Just what I needed."

"What I have is one man's voice on a recorder. That's not much of a defense against a string of eleven murders, an auction house bombing, and a Kansas farmhouse killing field."

"Ouch," Wally said. "Here they come."

Far ahead, the lights of a police cruiser flashed wickedly as it closed the distance at 80 mph. Yvgeney pulled the van to the fog line as the car blew past. Wally peered up from below the dashboard.

Yvgeney regained the pavement and resumed a practical speed. "They're going to run you down, Wally," he said softly. "Chana and I have discussed it. We have to separate soon."

"What? You're bailing out? That's OK. I don't blame you, either of you. This is my problem."

"It's not the heat, Wally," Chana added.

"We're still dedicated to finding a way to vindicate you," Yvgeney said. "Right now we're not linked to you by name. We are legally free to roam the USA in your defense. If we're with you when you get caught, and you surely will, we'll be stuck in the same jail as you – accessories to your latest crimes. Then you have no support, no investigative backup on the outside."

"What am I supposed to do, take a fucking bus? I'm beginning to get nervous about my predicament."

"About time," Chana said. "Yvgeney thinks you should surrender to the authorities. Walk into some small town station and give yourself up. That would be safest for you out there alone. There must be a shoot-to-kill order. Some trigger-happy rookie will get a medal for picking you off."

Wally said, "Thanks for the vote of confidence. I'm perfectly capable of living on the lam. After all, I'm a picker. I live by my wits already."

"It will be something you never anticipated that is your undoing."

"You guys are leaving?"

"We're still at your back," Chana said. "I voted against surrender. My idea is for you to hole-up in some isolated cabin and go dark. No phone calls. No internet. No credit cards. No flea markets where you might be recognized."

"No flea markets! Shoot me now. Wait a minute. I know a place. It's on Vancouver Island, a cave, way up on the west coast, above Tofino. Remember, Yvgeney? Susan's project. It's livable, totally off the grid. They'll never find me there."

Yvgeney frowned. "Don't involve another family," he said. "Death follows you like a shadow."

"That seems to be the theme of this whole fucking trip."

"I still think you should turn yourself in before you are shot. How do you expect to cross the border without a passport?"

"I still have my passport. Oh, that's right, I can't use it. I'll steal a boat. There are a million little coves on Vancouver Island. I'll travel at night."

"Have you ever piloted a boat on open water, Wally?"

"When you're in Port Angeles, you look across the strait and you can see it – the coast of Vancouver Island. You start the motor and drive it across."

"Turn yourself in," Chana agreed.

"Take that right turn up ahead. I'm getting off this chicken train," Wally said. The signpost read, *Cawker City 6 miles.*

"There ought to be a police station there," Yvgeney said as he angled the van onto the secondary road.

"It's not the police station I want," Wally said. "It's the bus station."

The Greyhound bus station at Cawker City was a 1940's grey box next to a shuttered Western Auto Store. "Yes," a friendly grandma said from behind a banded aluminum counter that Wally would have shown interest in if it wasn't fifteen hundred miles from Camano Island. "There's a bus heading to the west coast that passes through around 4:00 p.m."

"Anything sooner than that?" Wally asked. He looked at uncomfortable hardwood benches under a collectible mid-century clock that read 10:30 a.m.

"There's a 12:30 local that goes to Omaha."

"Forget it," Wally said.

"I got a 2:15 bus going south, last stop Dallas."

"Why would I want to go to Dallas?"

"These are questions you have to ask yourself, sir. I'm going on a break." She turned and opened a door behind the desk.

"Wait," Wally said, "What's there to do in this town till four?"

"Well, we have a big feed store down the street. You look like you need a new pair of Carharts."

Wally looked down at his tan cotton overalls, a uniform he'd worn since the auction. Red stains spotted the big front porch and the knees.

The woman asked, "You must be in the livestock business. A packing house?"

Wally changed the subject. "Anything else worth seeing in this berg?"

"Cawker City used to be the county seat in the old cattle drive days. There's a beautiful old courthouse."

"I'm not into antiques." Wally felt stupid as he spoke it, as if a simple lie would throw the authorities off his trail.

"Well, we have the world's largest ball of twine on Wisconsin Street. Walk three blocks. You can't miss it. That's in the *Guiness Book of World Records.*"

"Wow," Wally said, despite his best efforts. "Right here in this town? I saw a snippet about it on the Travel Channel. It's here?"

"Three blocks over. The twine's out in public view. The city built a shed roof to keep the weather off."

Wally said, "I'll take the four o'clock ticket. Now I need a lunch place that has at least four calendars."

"The only meals in town are at Shirley's Lunch unless you get back to Route 24 and the White Castle. I don't know how many calendars Shirley has."

"Close enough." Wally pulled two hundreds from his pocket and bought a ride to Portland, Oregon before heading into the sun-washed main street.

Yvgeney and Chana sat under the partial shade of an old elm tree, windows down, the heat of a Kansas summer morning collecting in the back of the van.

"Where's he going, the idiot?" he said.

"He doesn't understand the consequences of needless exposure," Chana said.

Yvgeney started the engine, grateful for a push of air conditioned coolness from the dashboard vents.

Wally was unprepared for a tourist mecca dedicated to twine in a backwater town on a late spring afternoon. He walked past an art gallery. The front window displayed El Greco's reclining nude, protecting her modesty with a ball of string. A trail of well-worn painted footprints on the sidewalk meandered past gift shops that offered twine collectibles that would be a hit on some future eBay page. He was impressed. Under the pavilion roof, he walked up to a haystack of yellowed string. A park sign told the story of old man Stoeber and his obsession. Wally read it; sent the crazy coot a silent salute.

"Wonderful thing, this ball," a voice said behind him. Wally turned to see a bearded gentleman in a plaid jacket and nice tie.

"It's a wonderful thing and a wonderful story," Wally said.

"Bruce Johnson," the man said, offering his hand.

"Call me Smitty," Wally said, accepting. He felt a farmer's grip that he couldn't match.

"Where you from, Smitty? We get visitors from all over. There's a map with pins on it over at the welcome center. A world map.

"Back east," Wally said. "New England."

"Been to Maine once, lousy soil. It's amazing they grow anything."

"Potatoes like it," Wally said, looking for an exit line.

"Would you like to add a few feet of twine yourself? We keep a supply for visitors to join in."

"Sure," Wally said. "Does it cost anything?"

"We have a contribution box if you choose to donate. This is a town enterprise, and Cawker City, like every town out here, is out of money."

Wally accepted a six-foot strand of twine and applied it to the sweet smelling mass. It was the most fun he'd had in weeks.

"Don't bother with the contribution," the man said. "The ball is going for sale next week. It's that or we fire the mayor."

"No shit," Wally said, aware of Kansas's noontime temperatures as the spirit gum lost its grip. He casually touched his beard to press it to his face. "What are you asking for it?"

"Some of the committee wants to try it on eBay, but I think twenty thousand dollars would own it, damn it," Bruce said. "The loss of this tourist attraction will decimate a thriving neighborhood, but the mood of city council members has shifted to tax cuts and belt tightening. The ball is one of the casualties."

"I hate to see your town lose this wonderful treasure, but I know a guy who would buy it in a New York minute," Wally said. He watched the man's face fall, defeated. "If you want to keep it, and I think you should, I'd rather make a contribution to its upkeep. How about five hundred dollars?"

Bruce answered, "We had a fundraiser. It brought two thousand dollars. We need forty thousand a year. Here's my phone number. Have your friend call me."

"Can I take some pictures on my phone?"

"Of course. Stoeber's ball is one of the most photographed objects in the state."

Three networks were alerted when Wally sent pictures of Stoeber's Ball of Twine to Crazy Danny, a Seattle dot-com millionaire who collected extreme objects.

In Quantico, an FBI agent caught the phone call in an alert prompt and sent it to his supervisor, who sent out a be-on-the-lookout bulletin: The fugitive, Wally Winchester, was in the vicinity of Cawker City, Kansas.

In Portland, Oregon, the Office of Homeland Security was short-handed again. An operative logged the information into Wally Winchester's file under a recent post concerning a bombing in Kansas City. Above that was an alert about suspected money laundering for a Sri Lanka terrorist group, which he didn't read. He lingered a moment and looked up to see his replacement, a cute recruit, fresh from a three-week training session. She wore a short leather skirt and white knee-high boots. He closed the file and logged off.

A Mexico City geek caught Wally's call also. He tweeted Claus Braun.

Wally, with a backpack full of cash plus a toothbrush and second pair of socks, climbed on the westbound Greyhound at 4:00 p.m. He found few choices. A large woman near the driver spilled into the empty seat beside her. He walked deeper into the bus. There was an empty seat next to a soldier in uniform and one farther back with a pretty girl against the window. He stopped at the soldier in a desert uniform, a beret perched on a shaven head. Wally extended his hand and said, "Thank you for your service," then moved to the empty seat with the window babe. He stuffed the backpack by his feet and said hello.

She was twentyish and blonde. Her reflection in the window suggested a pretty face. She didn't return Wally's greeting. He sat back and closed his eyes as the bus resumed the road. His mind raced with scenarios and questions, none of which cheered him or suggested a solution. He willed himself to sleep and it came.

Chana and Yvgeney kept the bus in sight a quarter mile ahead on the long, flat highway.

Chana said, “How long have you known Wally Winchester?”

“About a year longer than you. Do you think he will escape this crazy frame-up with his skin intact?”

“Logic says no, but he seems to have many lives, like a cat.”

They watched a state police cruiser as it blew by them at 80 and closed on the bus. Lights flashing, it passed the Greyhound and disappeared over a low incline in the wheat fields.

“It’s just a matter of time,” Yvgeney said.

“Somewhere in North America, there exists a way out for our friend. It’s our job to find it,” Chana said.

“I hope he survives his capture.”

Chapter Thirty-Eight

Cheyenne, Wyoming

The sun rose over Cheyenne, Wyoming. Wally felt a thousand aches and pains. A blanket covered the sleeping form of his seatmate, her face to the window. He unbuckled himself, stumbled to the restroom at the back, and threw water on his face.

A chill in the early mountain dawn hit him as the Greyhound stopped at a terminal in the heart of the city for a one hour layover. By the time the bus emptied, the restaurant next to the station was full. He looked up the quiet, early-morning street for another, spotted an antiques shop with big windows. Beyond it, a café's neon sign glowed brightly in the rosy dawn shadows. It was an easy choice.

Baby buggies and Victorian chairs populated the antiques store window, nothing that suggested he take a later bus and wait for the store to open. He walked past, toward the café, thinking about chicken fried steak. A roar of powerful engines behind him reverberated in the quiet Cheyenne street. A speeding police car shot by. Wally flattened against the café door. He watched the patrol car close on the bus, now surrounded by black and whites. He saw uniformed officers herding breakfast diners out onto the sidewalk. He ducked behind the corner building and walked to the next intersection, head down.

Three blocks from the scene, he saw a taxi, hailed it, and told the driver to take him to an internet café on the other side of town. One that served breakfast.

At *Ruby Montana's Wi-Fi Café*, Wally ate a breakfast sandwich and emailed Yvgeney. "Where the fuck are you?" he sent. "They jumped the bus. I'm on foot in Cheyenne."

He had a second cup of coffee and waited for a response. Got none. He went back online and BING-searched for a municipal airport outside of town. Something small. The anonymity of the café cubicle felt comforting, like a womb. He emailed for another taxi, savoring the formica niche, paid his bill, and walked out as the car arrived. "Take me to Matthews Field," he told the cabbie, a pimple-faced Latino, as he hopped into the backseat.

"Are you sure you don't want Jerry Olson Airfield?" the driver asked. "That's the only real airport we got in this town. The drive to Matthews will cost you more than fifty bucks. You OK with that?"

"Drive," Wally said.

Matthews Field was three buildings, an airstrip, and seven hangars on a flat plateau forty miles west of Cheyenne. Wally walked up to a pole structure that looked like it could be the office and entered. A spectacled matron ambled out of the interior and met him across the desk.

"Can I charter a flight from here?" Wally asked, creating his best smile.

"Well I don't know, hon, where do you want to go?"

"Portland," Wally said. "Actually, Port Angeles, Washington. They have an airport."

"Jerry Olson Field can connect you to Portland, I'm sure. Port Angeles, I don't know. How'd you get way out here? Our planes do local flying, skydiving, sightseeing, prospecting, crop stuff."

"I'm sort of an eccentric traveler," Wally lied. "I like to take short hops to my destinations, hate the crowds. The seats in coach can cripple you. First Class is just the front of the bus. Do you have anyone who wants to take me to the Pacific Ocean in a two-seater, one airport at a time?"

"I hate coach myself," the attendant said. "A small plane would be a great way to see the Rockies up close and personal. Go down to hangar five. Ask for Mike. He's the outlaw out here and I know he needs the money."

"Is he a good pilot?"

"Stories about his flying go back twenty years."

"Perfect."

Chana said to Yvgeney, "He's buying a flight. We lose him at this airport."

Yvgeney said, "I know where he's heading, Port Angeles, Washington, to steal a boat. We can get there tomorrow night if we drive all night."

"I'm sure a city of Cheyenne's size has a real airport. Why don't we fly there and beat him to his destination?"

"By the time we get lucky and find a flight to Seattle or Portland and then charter a small plane for Port Angeles, we might as well have driven," Yvgeney said. "Let's start driving now. We can take shifts. My job is to find Wally in Port Angeles before he starts stealing boats and committing actual crimes. Our friend never showed much interest in following authority or rules. I'd hate to see him lose sight of the line that separates antique dealers from criminals." He paused and added, "If there is one."

The van had been rented on a UNESCO credit card. Yvgeney had ordered the vehicle loaded. Now he was glad he did. He fiddled with the GPS transponder, punched in Port Angeles, Washington, pointed out the directions on the dashboard monitor to Chana, the driver, and crawled into the back to sleep.

Wally glanced around at the bare interior of hangar five, looking for old industrial metal tables that might have found their way to an isolated airport in the highlands. He saw an airplane with two people working on a tire.

"Is Mike here?" Wally asked.

"That would be me," a burly, bearded man said. He put down a wrench and approached.

"I want to hire you to take me to Port Angeles, Washington."

"The airport's fifty miles east," the stocky pilot said. "Fly to Seattle and take Horizon Air to Port Angeles. Save yourself a lot of grief." He turned away and picked up the tool.

"I have cash and I want to cross the Rockies in a small plane. Do you want my money?"

The pilot walked over to Wally. "This is my plane, a Cessna 172, an antique built in 1961. It has a range of eight hundred miles. That's it. Port Angeles is fifteen or sixteen hundred miles. That's three stops to refuel with some hairy passes to fly through. And then there's the weather. When we arrive, I have to repeat all those landings and refuelings to get back here."

"How much is that?" Wally asked.

The pilot searched into Wally's eyes. He said, "You seem a bit desperate. You're not a tourist who wants to see the Rockies up close. Don't fuck with me."

"There's people after me," Wally confessed. "They'd find me at the big airport back in Cheyenne. I'm innocent."

"I'm all right with that," Mike said. "This is going to be an expensive trip. You found the right guy."

"What's expensive?"

"I'll have to land and refuel six times. The time on the engine I estimate at fifty hours. I estimate the flight charge at…." He closed his eyes in calculation, then said, "Ten thousand dollars."

"Is that a guarantee that you will deliver me to Port Angeles?"

"Depends on your schedule. The plane can't handle serious weather."

"My trip to Port Angeles is not time sensitive," Wally said. "The price is fine. I have cash."

Despite a head filled with panic and a heart on the edge of despair, Wally found himself amused and delighted with the airplane ride over the northern Rocky Mountains, passing cliffs and notches like an eagle, snowfields just beneath the wheels. His stomach retched as they flew over knife-edged ridges with three thousand-foot drop-offs under the wings. His blood pressure dropped and the tension in his shoulders relaxed as they spooked a herd of elk in a high mountain meadow. Late afternoon sun backlit the knife edges of a hundred mountains. Wally smiled, and for a moment forgot his fear.

Nightfall found him and the pilot in a nineteen dollar motel room near the Yakima Municipal Airport. "The weather's turning sour, pardner," the pilot told him. They sipped cold beer outside on a rickety second floor porch. "See the red ring around the moon? That's some high level shit blowing in from the Pacific Ocean. By the morning, I expect pea soup fog. Might shut us down for a day or two."

"Can't we just fly through it?"

"We're flying in an old plane. A classic. I don't have the ability to fly through clouds – particularly over the North Cascades. That requires a different instrument package. If you want to get there tomorrow, hire a 747."

"How far is it from here to downtown Yakima?" Wally asked. The room had two single beds and an old fashioned TV with bare bones cable. It reeked of mold. Two days in this room, he thought. I may reconsider turning myself in.

"A five dollar cab ride will take you downtown," the pilot said. "But don't leave yet. I might have a way out to the coast. To try it, you'll have to strap on a second set of balls."

"I'm no stranger to strap-ons," Wally said. He opened another beer.

"The Columbia River," Mike said, "is a natural venturi. It's a wind tunnel that sucks clear air into the gorge. If we follow the river close to the water, we can fly under the weather to the other side of the mountains. It's a hairy ride. I've done it twice."

"Sounds like fun," Wally said. "Beats sitting in this petri dish."

"It won't be fun. We're flying through a canyon with hills and cliffs on both sides in a tube of clear air. Sometimes the cloud cover collapses the tunnel. Then we turn around and go back to Yakima and wait the weather out."

"You're shitting me," Wally said.

"You don't want to be between two walls when all you can see is white."

"How often does that happen?"

"Mister, I'm a crop duster from Cheyenne. I've been around the West a bunch, as a pilot, so I know about this back door. I'm not Wiki-fucking-pedia. I don't know the odds, son. I made it through twice, as I said. The decision's up to you."

"When do we leave?" Wally asked.

"Dawn is the best bet."

The Cessna rose toward a hundred-foot overcast ceiling and flew under it at tree-top altitude over empty prairie until a cliff edge dropped to the Columbia River.

"Hold on," the pilot said.

The plane nose-dived into the canyon. Wally felt early morning coffee rise to his throat. The Columbia River loomed as a fat blue ribbon as the pilot flattened the descent. Wally saw waves and small boats. The river was wide. The walls on either side of it rose into the clouds.

The Cessna rose from the wave tops to fly over a bridge. Gentler slopes replaced granite canyon walls. The pilot pointed ahead, where steeper walls rose vertically into low clouds.

"This is the entrance to the gorge," the pilot said. "See the tube?"

Wally did. The river canyon steepened and remained clear under a white cloud.

The Cessna hugged the river, flanked by walls. The passage bent left and widened at the head of a dam. Wally pointed downriver to the next bend. "The ceiling's dropping, Captain Mike," he said. "We're going to duck our heads when we round the bend."

"I don't like it. You buckled in tight?"

"Yes, sir."

Fifty feet above the fat blue river, the Cessna banked right as it entered another canyon. White strings of mist cascaded down the walls like frozen waterfalls. The pilot craned his head to see what lurked around the corner. He saw a wall of white and yanked the controls to his chest. The plane shot straight up into the cloud.

Wally yelped as he felt the lurch and roll. Visibility dropped to the wingtips. A surge of vomit threatened. He willed it down as the Cessna completed a twisting barrel roll and broke out into the clear air over the dam they just passed.

"Back to our honeymoon suite, Smitty," the pilot said.

Wally nodded, the image of their plane flattened against a granite cliffside like a paper spitball stuck in his head.

It took Wally three days to reveal his Yakima location to the FBI. It was a simple mistake, a request to a sales clerk at Sarah's Timeless Treasures. Wally, in disguise, asked, "Can you open that case over there? I need to look at the Van Briggle pot."

The clerk looked at Wally, tilted her head and scratched her temple. "Do I know you?" she asked.

Wally knew her from the Midway Flea Market. Karen somebody. He averted his face to look at the underside of a chair. "Spent some time in Grand Rapids," he said. "Have you? That's my home base."

"Something about your voice," she said. She handed Wally the vase, ten inches high in a nice plum glaze. He turned it over to see its bottom, the color of chocolate pudding. A faint, incised date of '04 under the stylized shop mark quickened his heart. The price on the tag was one hundred sixty dollars. "I'll take it," he said, handing it back while he slipped a couple of hundreds off the roll in his pocket.

"Got a tax number?" she asked.

Wally did. He said, "Afraid not. I'm just a tourist. I'll pay the tax. Lord knows the states need all the money they can get these days. Michigan, in particular."

Karen said, "Are you sure you haven't been to the Midway Market on a Sunday?"

"That's near Chicago?"

"South of Seattle. I could have sworn…" She looked up after relocking the case. He was gone.

She was wrapping a glass plate with the front page of the Yakima Gazette when she came across the Wally Winchester story on page two. She snapped her fingers and called her best friend who told her she was lucky to be alive. The third friend who heard of Karen's brush with destiny called the Feds.

Yvgeney walked into the main building of the Port Angeles Airport and asked if any flights from Cheyenne, Wyoming had landed recently. The manager looked at him like he was crazy. He flashed his United Nations ID and got some answers.

In the van, he told Chana he might have guessed wrong. She reminded him that his intuition was the only tool in their bag. "One of us needs to sleep," she said. "Give me the field glasses. Crawl in back. You'll be more helpful with a clear head." Rain battered the windshield and pounded on the roof, bad weather for a small plane. She closed her eyes.

The Cessna re-ran the gorge during a late afternoon break in the weather and climbed to five hundred feet where I-5 crosses the river. The bridges and buildings of Portland passed by them on the left. The pilot turned north to follow the ribbon of rush hour traffic.

Breaks in the overcast showed the orange of a fierce sunset to the west. The pilot pointed to monumental dark towers of cumulus clouds that covered the peaks of the Olympic Mountains across the blue-grey fingers of Puget Sound.

"Another bad one," he said as the white dome of the State Capitol passed under the left wing. "We don't want to be on that side of the pond when those clouds drop down over the Hood Canal."

"Again?" Wally asked.

"I've been flying twenty-five years," Mike said. "Haven't killed anyone yet. Don't want to spoil my record. I got some friends up in Snohomish – Harvey Field. We can wait it out there. You like antiques?"

"No," Wally said, in automatic.

"Too bad, the town's full of shops."

"All I want is a motel room where we are the dominant life forms, one that has HBO."

As the plane passed over the ribbon of cars streaming north from Seattle, Wally saw the familiar shape of Camano Island, a forested sausage backlit by reflected sunset on Puget Sound.

"Hey, Mike," he shouted. "Can you fly over Camano Island?"

"Thought you was an Easterner," the pilot said.

"Um, I used to vacation on Camano Island, back when I was a kid. I went to summer camp there."

"Make up your mind, son. I know who you are. You're the most wanted man in America. My momma didn't raise no fool. Who else would pay ten thousand dollars for a fifteen hundred dollar plane ride?"

"Fifteen hundred dollars? You thief!"

"You didn't blink. I never expected a *yes* answer."

"What are you going to do about it?" Wally asked.

"Got any interest in killing me?"

"I didn't kill anybody. This was a frame-up. The thought of killing you never crossed my mind. I don't kill people."

"Why do you want to go to Port Angeles, sonny?"

"I want to get into Canada. I have a place to hole up there, if you want the truth."

"The truth, plus the ten thousand dollars you gave me, is all I need. It's not up to me to judge you. I'll get you to Port Angeles, if that's what you want."

"I want to do a fly-by of my house," Wally said. "Since we're speaking freely. It's on the west side, just south of the state park. I've got a lot of valuable shit in that cabin. I expect there have been people snooping around. It freaks me out. Strangers looking into my windows. At the paintings and collectibles. I feel helpless to stop it. Pray that no one's broken in."

"There's just enough light, as long as we stay east of the storm front, if I fly over now," the pilot said. He tipped the wings and the Cessna angled into a westward turn.

As he looked down at his cabin from fifty feet over the treetops, Wally was aghast at the scene. "Get the fuck out of my driveway!" he yelled out the window at the gaggle of vehicles parked on the gravel path and up on the road above it. He saw the satellite crane of a local TV news crew and cringed. How would he ever be able to have breakfast again at the Elger Bay Café with all this publicity?

"You got a cell phone, Mike?" he asked as the plane veered eastward in front of the storm.

"Here you go." The pilot handed an iPhone to his passenger.

Wally had racked his brain wondering whom he trusted with the information that he was back. He dialed Alfred, one of the kids with whom he'd started an eBay club. They still met once a month when Wally was in town. The enterprise was wallowing, like everything else this year, but holding its own.

Alfred answered. "Who are you? I don't know the name on the phone."

"It's Wally, Alfred. I'm on another guy's cell."

"It's Mr. Winchester!" Alfred shouted into the room. Wally heard it as an echo.

"Alfred, I would like to ask a favor."

"Where are you?"

"I'm probably flying over your house right about now."

"Wow," Alfred exclaimed. "That's so cool."

"I just flew over my cabin, Alfred. That's why I'm calling."

"Did you really kill all those people?"

"No, Alfred. I've been framed."

"You didn't kill *any*?"

"I killed one in New York State at a campground, but that was in self-defense."

"One's still pretty good, Mr. Winchester."

"Alfred, I need our group to take some money from our savings account and hire a lawyer to keep people off my property. It freaks me out when people are peeking into the house at all my stuff."

"Me and Ron already keep people out. Ron's good with a baseball bat."

"I just flew over. My property is a zoo!"

"Ron told me he was overrun by a big crowd and the cops. Sorry."

"Don't get involved. I'm poison. Hire me a lawyer to keep people off my land. If he's a defense attorney, all the better. I think I need Perry Mason."

"Ron has attorneys all the time, Mr. Winchester. I can ask him."

"I don't need a public defender, Alfred. Get that lawyer in downtown Stanwood. A guy named Caughlin. He bought me lunch once."

"Sure, Mr. Winchester, but me and Ron will still hang out around your cabin and keep intruders and thieves away. I think Ron would enjoy being your security guard."

"Don't hurt anybody, Alfred. Tell Ron. Tell him twice. More importantly, don't ever tell anyone that you spoke with me. And secondly, if Danny can manage it, go down to my cabin and grab my G-4 computer tower before someone grabs it. If he can find another relic like it, have him replace the whole unit with a look-alike. I don't want the world snooping in on my hard drive."

"The eBay Club is here in the room. I have you on speaker. Want to say hello?"

"Hello, Wally," the voice fell into a phone echo.

"Wa…Wa…Wally, it's me," said the voice of Kenny.

"Hi, you guys," Wally said. "Thanks for helping."

"We're landing," the pilot said. "Time to hang up."

"All of you," Wally said into the phone, "Listen. Any contact with me could get you arrested. A person who helped me in Kansas was killed. Forget you ever heard from me."

"But we want to help," came the voice of Kenney, the diminutive former student whose dream was to be the perfect janitor.

"All of you, listen," Wally, tried again. "Start a chat line. Design a Wally Winchester web page. Open a defense fund and ask for donations. You guys can help me on the outside if I'm captured, a fate that everybody seems to think is just around the corner, but *listen.* You can't tell anyone about this conversation. No one. I'm too hot. You'll all be under suspicion. Don't call back. It's not my phone." He hung up and passed the cell back to the pilot, who placed it in his pocket without looking, his eyes on the runway of Harvey Field.

A freshening breeze with light raindrops hit the pilot's face as he exited the airplane. A hooded figure met him as he helped Wally out of the aircraft.

"You still owe me that drink, I believe," a woman's voice said from within the parka.

"I owe you more than that, Tammy," the pilot said over his shoulder. He had a hand on Wally's back as the fugitive climbed out on unsteady legs.

"Tammy, this is Smitty, a guy from back east. I'm his tour guide. We're headed for Port Angeles."

An attractive redhead peered out from a yellow rain hood. Wally extended his hand.

"This is her airport, Smitty," the pilot said. "Act nice."

"Lovely airport you have here," Wally said. "Call me Smitty"

Tammy said, 'Welcome to the Northwest." To the pilot she said, "Need a place to sleep tonight?"

"Me and my client," Mike said.

"I think there's a bed in the hangar for your client," Tammy said. Her smile glowed under the rain hat.

Wally woke up at nine in the morning on a cot next to a row of rusty lockers in an unfamiliar hangar. He did his best to pat out the wrinkles on the shirt he'd slept in and grabbed the backpack that held the cash. A gust of stinging rain hit him in the face as he walked to the tower.

In the office, Tammy produced a plate of eggs with fried ham. "You boys got in just in time last night," she said with a nod and a glance at flat slaps of rain hitting the window behind her. A windsock, visible from the office, was fully extended. "You like antiques, Smitty? The town's full of 'em. You won't be heading west for a couple of days, at least."

"I'd prefer to hang out in the hangar," Wally lied. "Got any books I can read?"

"I got a full set of Louie L'Amour westerns," Tammy said. "That'll keep you occupied.

"Oh boy," Wally said. He calculated how well his shaved head and beard would fool people he bought antiques from every week and told himself to stay put.

After the second day of horizontal rain, Wally adjusted his beard, folded the page of the second of the westerns he'd read, and donned dark glasses, despite the gusty gloom. He walked over the iron bridge to the group of antique shops that dotted the main street like crystals in a geode he thought. Main Street, Snohomish, was the clearinghouse for new finds north of Seattle. Wally was a regular buyer, hitting the street twice a week on his many sweeps.

He walked into the first shop after the bridge, Black Dog Antiques. Wally remembered the owner as British Boy because of his accent.

He perused the new inventory on British Boy's floor, hoping, as he always did, to see an early Stickley table that was grossly underpriced at four hundred dollars. The owner, Stanley, behind the counter said hello. Wally dropped his baseball cap and mumbled something about Teco pottery.

"Wally? Is that you?" British Boy said, "Why the fuck are you dressed like that? Are you in disguise? You better be. The whole world's after your ass. Did you do those killings?"

Wally noticed the shopkeeper's hands were under his counter.

"The whole thing's a set-up," Wally said. "I didn't kill anybody, except a Mexican in New York, and that was self-defense. I was hoping to pick the town in this disguise."

"You are Wally Winchester in a beard," British Boy said. "Where's the disguise?"

"I'm bald."

"You have a hat on. Who can tell?"

"Don't' tell anyone we met," Wally said. "Your life could be in danger if you do." Wally stopped as he exited onto the sidewalk of rain-soaked Snohomish, looked back and said, "You'll never get two thousand dollars for that Limbert chair in the corner, Stanley, not this year. The right price is more like half that."

"From a serial killer's lips to God's ear," British Boy said back.

Wally raised his collar, tipped the rim of his cap down and skulked back over the iron bridge for another afternoon with Louie L'Amour.

Sunshine hit him in the face. Wally rubbed sleep out of his eyes. The hangar door squeaked as it rose in front of Mike's Cessna. "We're leaving in two minutes, Smitty, or Wally, whatever your name is."

Wally mumbled a protest.

"You want to wake up, sonny? Take a look at the scene across the river."

At the window, he saw three helicopters hovering over antique row. Flashing lights reflected off the walls of old brick storefronts. Behind him, he heard the prop sputter and spring to life. "Hop in, Junior," the pilot yelled. Wally grabbed his pack and waved goodbye to Tammy as she pulled the blocks from the wheels.

As they caught air at the end of the runway, Wally looked back to see a black and white patrol car at the hangar door. "I need a cup of coffee," he moaned.

"Tammy gave us a thermos," the pilot said. "It's behind the seat. You can pour me one, too."

As the plane passed the Everett waterfront, Wally saw new snow at the tops of distant mountain peaks that rose behind his destination, an hour's flight away. He wondered which of the fellow antique dealers that British Boy told about the visit had turned him in.

Chapter Thirty-Nine

Camano Island, Washington

The young men who met the rental car at the top of Wally Winchester's driveway held baseball bats. As the passenger window lowered, a British-accented voice asked if this was indeed the home of Wally Winchester. The lad leaned his wide face in for a look inside. He saw a woman sharing the backseat with camera gear.

"Who wants to know?" The other youth, tall and well-built, had hostility in his voice.

"We're with BBC America," the passenger said. "Here to get some background footage of Mr. Winchester's lair."

"This road is closed," the tall boy said.

"Are you a relative? I'd like to interview you."

"I'm not related."

"Then I don't believe you have the authority to block this drive, sir."

The youngster walked to the front of the car and calmly smashed a headlight with one right-handed swing.

The reporter lurched out of the car. "Fantastic," he squealed. "Get out here with the camera, Jenny." To the youth he said, "Can you wait for my crew before you do the other one? What's your name?"

"My name is *Fuck You*," Ron said, and he took out the other headlight, switch-hitting now from the left.

"And yours?" The reporter asked unfazed to the moon-faced child.

"My name is Alfred. You people should leave. Wally didn't kill anyone. Not that many, anyway." The camera zoomed to Alfred's face as confusion raced across it.

"Are you telling us you've been in contact with Mr. Winchester, Alfred?"

Alfred struggled to frame an answer. A crashing sound spun the camerawoman around to catch Ron pulling the end of the bat out from a hole in the windshield.

"Did you get that, Jenny? Hit it again, son."

"Eat me," Ron said. "Quote that." He slammed a foot against the driver's door; a size 14 Doc Martin boot buckled the sheet metal.

"The camera is next," the big youngster snarled.

The camerawoman shot footage of two kids flipping the bird as the rental car limped away.

Chana looked up as Yvgeney returned to their surveillance post above the tarmac of William R. Fairchild International Airport. He carried a take-out breakfast of burgers and onion rings. "The airport's been busy this morning," she said. "A break in the bad weather brings them out."

"Any sign of our boy?"

"Not yet."

The drone of a small plane signaled another landing. Chana watched it come to a stop. Field glasses to her eyes, she said. "He is here. He's shaking hands with the pilot. The plane's taking off. He didn't refuel."

"If he knows who he just dropped off, he's smart to get some distance ASAP."

Chana reported more. "Wally's entering the terminal. No, he's back outside by the airplanes. Looking around. He's acting like prey. Someone's after him. A policeman. Now another. He's running this way," she said, "gaining ground. The policeman has pulled out his handgun. *Merde*. He fired." The report reached the grove at the side of the runway. Yvgeney had the van motor running.

"Do we help him? This is the capture scenario you were afraid of."

"We can't drive into the middle of police pursuit. That's an automatic conviction for aiding and abetting."

Glasses to her eyes, Chana said, "He's pointing the pistol again - in full stride."

Another gun report echoed off the hangar doors. "Wally's down. Damn. No, he's up again."

"Is he hit?"

"Doesn't seem to be. He's almost to the trees," she said. "If he gets into cover, I want to help."

"We can't get involved."

"Move the van out of here," she said. "We can meet later. Don't worry. I can give Wally a fighting chance. No one, even our friend, will know I'm there."

Yvgeney looked at the running figure as he tumbled and fell on a snow fence that bordered the field. "Text me if you need a rescue or a lawyer, Chana. I'm not going far."

Wally's legs were rubber when he tried to scale the fence at the edge of the airport. He fell like a sack of potatoes and willed his burning lungs to take another gulp of air. He risked a glance over his shoulder, saw the fat cop who, two minutes before, had looked up from a photo in his hand and made eye contact when he entered the tiny terminal. The guy was flagging, his face beet-red, but other uniforms were catching up. He heard a siren and considered raising his hands in surrender. The fat guy fired again. Wally felt a 600 mph whisper crack a branch near his shoulder. He dove into the underbrush and plowed through young blackberry thorns that stabbed his legs through the denim till he reached a clearing.

His options were a neighborhood of tract houses along the airport road or the backyards of a handful of farmhouses holding their ground against the sprawl. He jogged down the hill toward outbuildings that bunched around a small barn.

Chana entered the thicket as the first of the armed pursuers climbed over the fence. She'd watched Wally's flight and turned around when he angled down toward the abandoned farm. In the blackberries, she faced multiple targets, saw no chance of success in direct contact. She pulled a handful of cash from her jump pants. Dropped a twenty on a thorny stem. Another bill, a five, ended up in a clearing nearby. A ten-dollar bill fluttered onto a mossy stump. She ran out of cash at the airport road and texted Yvgeney she'd be attending a yard sale on M Street.

Wally maintained a casual gait as he picked a muddy path through rusty farm equipment. Shoulders tight, he braced for the impact of a high-powered slug and the sound of the rifle that would follow. No bullet exploded his heart as he gained the wraparound porch. He risked a look behind him and saw no evidence of pursuit. It puzzled him as he cupped his eyes and peered inside.

A pile of letters and newspapers under a nice old brass mail slot fanned out behind the front door. On vacation, Wally thought, gone to see the grandkids. He found an unlocked window into the kitchen and climbed in. The sound of helicopters thundered in the sky.

Wally Winchester, America's most wanted killer, felt awful about breaking into a stranger's house, even one on vacation. He tiptoed around the comfortable home as he looked into spare rooms and the attic space to make sure he was alone. Distant sounds of police sirens pierced the stillness.

In the refrigerator, Wally found nothing but condiments and a carton of eggs. The kitchen window above the sink had a clear view of the hillside, up to the airport. He saw no activity, despite the sound of traffic on the airport road, as he cracked three eggs and heated some olive oil in a skillet.

After washing the pan and dish, he risked exposure to check for a drivable vehicle in the barn. A key holder by the back door held a loop with the same type of key that his Pontiac Firebird used to start with. He dropped it in his pocket and snuck out into the yard.

A farm truck sat in the barn, a classic Chevy pickup. Wally tried the key. It worked. The engine roared and settled to a 283-cubic-inch gurgle that sounded like the voice of God.

He walked back to the farmhouse and folded two hundred dollar bills into the egg carton in the fridge before aiming the pickup down the hill for a two mile drive to the harbor.

Yvgeney and Chana observed Wally leaving the farmyard in an old truck. They knew where he was headed.

Wally drove down Race Street on the way to the waterfront, intent on stealing a boat and motoring to Canada. He pondered his life on the other shore. Exile, he thought, holed up in a coastal cave till his friends performed a miracle and saved his sorry ass. Fat chance of that.

On the shore of the Strait of San Juan de Fuca, he saw the imposing shape of the ferry Coho as it began its passage to Canada. Beside the ferry, a landing dock on pillars reminded Wally of the best breakfast he'd ever had. He craved one hour, a Dungeness crab omelet from Smuggler's Landing, a *New York Times* on the table next to the salt and pepper. Fresh-brewed coffee. An hour of *everything is all right*.

The waitress looked happy to have a job. Wally said, "I want the crab and shrimp omelet. Hold the shrimp, I'm allergic."

"White or wheat toast?" she asked. A steaming mug of coffee arrived on the table.

"Russian rye if you have it. The wine bar still running?" Wally asked. The waitress turned. She said, "The wine bar is kicking ass. No one has work in this town, and they're selling wine to a full house every night at ten dollars a glass. They're not open this early."

"We'll see," Wally said, and left his coat on the seat.

Upstairs, through a gap in a wall of rare vintage bottles, he approached an attractive, shorthaired woman, typing on the computer.

"We're closed till 3:00 p.m.," she said with a smile.

"I want to buy a bottle of your best Cabernet, something that wakes up my mouth," Wally said.

"There's a nice shop back on Second Street."

Wally said, "I'm sorry. I'm going to catch a boat within the hour. I have breakfast cooking downstairs."

"The crab omelet?"

"You bet. What's your best red wine?"

"We just got in three bottles of a Shepherd's Crossing Cabernet. I think it's amazing."

"I'll take what you have left," Wally said. "Uncorked. I have cash."

Tummy full of Dungeness crab, Wally wandered up the landing, looking for a boat to steal.

He passed a bold kiosk that displayed large format paintings, pseudo-historic fancies that depicted Northwest history. "The guy has talent," he thought and made a note to come by later when he could spend some time.

The dock had one boat, a sailboat. He wanted a skiff, a Boston whaler, a boat with a motor. He heard a commotion inside the parking garage behind him, saw a cruiser, its lights flashing. Wally looked back at the sailboat.

The vessel was large. Wally guessed forty feet. He found a button by the steering wheel. It started the engine. A rumble under his feet erupted in exhaust bubbles at the back end. He undid the ties and aimed the craft at Canada. As he left the calm waters inside the spit, he remembered his escape vehicle's name, *Bijoux de la Mer*. The words made no sense, but she sure steered well.

The waters of San Juan de Fuca were more bumpy than they appeared from shore, the grey coast of Vancouver Island not much closer than it was when he took off from Port Angeles an hour earlier. Behind him the steep cliffs of Hurricane Ridge gleamed with a whitecap of late spring snow.

His stomach lurched as he saw a series of house-sized waves, remnants, he figured, of the big tanker that passed in front of him on its way to the Pacific Ocean ten minutes before.

The water began to rise. Wally debated riding over the top or taking it at an angle like a surfer. He hated all the choices and chose a compromise angle that launched him over the swell and plunged the boat into a dark trough that rose to another mountain of green. The engine sputtered. Wally cursed. It regained its rhythm and pushed the boat up the next rolling hill.

The shore of Vancouver Island was a thousand yards away when the *Bijoux de la Mer* ran out of gas. As the sailboat bobbed in place, sanctuary at arm's reach, Wally pondered the phrase, *dead in the water*. He wet a finger and held it into the end of the day's breeze, felt a coolness that said *the wind is pushing you back into the straight*. So much for wind power, he thought, as he looked up at the towering mast and wondered which of the lines made the sail unfurl. He walked to the stern and looked over the rail for a dinghy, saw a bracket and wet lines in the water. He looked at the deepening orange of a Northwest sunset and gave himself half an hour to nightfall.

A search of the cabin offered no new ideas till he was leaving. Two steps up the ladder, headed topside, he saw a locker with the stenciled word: *Emergency*. A canvas sack that held the inflatable was heavy, but Wally managed to drag it up to the deck. He opened it, pulled a rip-cord, and watched the raft unfold.

Darkness engulfed the inflatable soon after he pushed off into open water. Wally managed to snap a set of plastic oars in place and began to pull toward the twinkling lights of Canadians. A gust of wind hit him in the back, then another. Wally rowed with more determination as the sea became choppy and a wave splashed over the raft. Knapsack between his knees, he fought to make headway. He looked over his shoulder to get his bearings and saw no indication of a friendly shoreline as rain stung his eyes.

The light beam that hit his face was a blessing, a rescue. Wally makes it through once again, he congratulated himself.

A voice from a loudspeaker said, "This is Canadian Customs. Hold up your hands while we board your vessel. Please have your paperwork ready for inspection."

Wally raised his hands and gave up. For the first time in ten years he wished he had a cigarette.

Chapter Forty

Stanwood, Washington

Detective Kelly's search warrant had teeth. With the story in the headlines, he carried a comprehensive, open-any-door order. Winchester's financial records lay open beside him on the seat as he turned off I-5 to the hamlet of Stanwood, the mainland side of the Camano Gateway Bridge.

At the local branch of Winchester's bank, he sat with the manager who was clearly flustered at the national spotlight aimed at the area. She described him as a nice guy, usually one step ahead of bounced checks, but not always.

Kelly asked about other assets -- stocks, real estate, and other businesses. She pulled up a mortgage on a Camano Island home, built in 1945 at a cost of forty thousand, now valued at four hundred thousand. "He makes payments of six hundred dollars a month on the note," she said.

"Any other investments? How's his cash flow?" Kelly asked. He waved the search warrant like it was a magic wand that makes truth appear. She looked into her monitor. "He was late twice last year with the house payment. Always came in with flowers to beg for another week." She smiled and said, "I can't believe he's a murderer."

Using a local antiques store handout, Kelly visited all the shops on the brochure's map. He began to form a picture of his subject-of-interest. Everyone knew Winchester. He came across as a likeable fellow, a guy with a reputation as an honest dealer with really high hopes who never seemed to have any money.

Kelly knew about charming killers. Ted Bundy was handsome, a rising political star in Olympia when he began a cross-country killing spree that started in the hills outside Seattle and ended in Florida. He wondered if Wally had a dark side.

The captured voice of Peter Falk, speaking from the windshield GPS, directed the detective to the home of Winchester's ex-wife.

Rae Roberts answered the door.

She was tall. Kelly noticed blonde hair to her shoulders. She blocked passage to the interior as he explained his inquiry.

"I haven't spoken to Wally in over a year," the woman said, her arms crossed in defense. "I know zero details of his present life. The press has been merciless since this FBI story hit the airwaves. Wally is no murderer. He has no anger in him. He doesn't care enough about money to kill for it. I have no information for you. Please leave me alone."

She was shutting the front door when Kelly asked, "Do you know anything about him dating a Mexican woman?"

Rae stopped. "Come in," she said. "I'm sorry I was so guarded. There was a BBC crew, complete with a camerawoman, at my door at noon today. They wanted to know about Wally, the serial killer's sex life. I told them to bother someone else."

Kelly entered a well kept modern interior with photography on the walls. Rae Roberts offered him a beverage. He declined and said, "I asked a similar question as the television crew. Why did you invite me in?"

"I want you to know you have the wrong man," she said. "Wally emails me once a week with tales of his endless quest for the big score. I ignore them, but his obsession is strangely compelling…like watching a train wreck in slow motion. A couple weeks ago, he texted he was headed east to sell his Shelby. Said he planned to travel with a Mexican girl he just met. I forget her name."

"Wally Winchester is no killer. He used to capture spiders that scared me, in juice glasses, then let them free outside."

Kelly said, "I have a search warrant in my pocket that's pretty broad, but I don't believe it reaches your computer. If you want to help Wally's case, you could make me a copy of his messages."

Rae sat at the computer. She said over her shoulder, "If you want the Mexican girl email, I can just forward it to you. What's your email?"

"I want all your correspondence with Wally Winchester."

Rae turned. The monitor backlit high cheekbones on her Nordic face. "Even the early stuff?" she asked. "There's some sensitive material. We were new."

"I'm a professional," Kelly said. "If you want to clear your friend, I have to see everything."

"Ex-friend," Rae said. "But I want to help him clear his name." She stuck a thumb drive into her tower and copied a large file.

A large youth, wielding a baseball bat, stopped the cruiser at the entrance to Wally Winchester's driveway. "This is private property," he said.

"Turn on your roof lights." Kelly said to the deputy sheriff.

The blue flash lit the youngster in regular intervals. Kelly and the deputy exited the car and gave the bat-wielder space.

"We have a warrant to search the property and to seize the computer," the deputy sheriff said. Kelly held up his badge and the writ.

The boy seemed confused. He raised the bat like a hitter at home plate.

"Who are you?" the deputy asked. "And why the fuck do you think you can restrict access to a county road, young man?"

"There's a bunch of us," the young man said. He identified himself as Albert. "We're an eBay club, and Wally's the president, sort of."

"What makes you think you can stand on a road in front of cops with a baseball bat?" the deputy sheriff asked.

Kelly whispered, "Let it go. I want to get my hands on the computer down there." He handed the youngster a scrap of paper and said, "Write your name and phone number here and go home," then walked down the driveway to the cabin on the cliff.

The door was indeed unlocked. Kelly entered and smelled the stale air of an unused beach house. He walked silently through corridors of dark oak armchairs, his focus on a computer.

A noise in a dark interior hallway stopped him in his tracks. He unbuckled his pistol and crept up to a room on the right, his fingers on the stock. He stuck his head in low and saw a figure hunched over the monitor.

A shriek from behind him stopped Kelly's entry. Alfred brushed by him into the room, a heavy oak chair in his meaty hand. Kelly watched the man-boy hurl the chair like a projectile at the interloper. The window smashed as the intruder ducked and ran for the outside door.

Kelly watched the boy lift an oak desk and heave it in the direction of the exit. It shook the little house as it hit the doorframe.

"What are you doing in the house I'm supposed to guard?" Alfred screamed at the fleeing figure.

Through the window, Kelly watched a black-garmented figure run toward the water and disappear where the lawn stopped for the cliff below. He looked behind him and saw the deputy sheriff, shotgun in hand. He waved it down.

"Good job, Alfred," he said to the large red-faced boy. You saved the files. He saw a delete program on the computer screen as windows winked out. He looked for a stop command, then reached under the table to unplug the computer.

Chapter Forty-One

Seattle, Washington

Victor Jay Moriarti lifted the brim of his cowboy hat and looked at the strange collection of people in his office, high up in the Smith Tower with a view of the Seattle waterfront. He saw a group of oddly-sized teenagers and two adults.

A five-foot ball of youth with Brylcreemed hair spoke up. "We wa…wa…want to hire you to defend Wally."

"What's your name, son?"

"Kenny," he answered.

"Who are these people with you, Kenny?"

"The other kids are members of a club, an eBay club that Wally helped us start a couple years ago."

Moriarti nodded. "Very commendable, the serial killer with a civic conscience. I may use that. And, Kenny, who are these older people with you?"

"Th…Th…Th…They are friends of Wally's. They were his first phone call from jail. We were the second. He put us together."

The attorney turned to the adults. He said, "I'm familiar with the case. How could I not be? The entire world has followed the string of murders and bombings. I pity the poor bugger who has to defend him. Why are you here?"

Yvgeney said, "We are here to ask you to defend him and offer our services as investigators."

"Why would I need your services? I have a staff that I've worked with for years."

Yvgeney outlined his job at UNESCO as an investigator of cultural crimes. He mentioned his training with a Soviet group called the GRU. He looked at Chana and said, "This woman is the most dangerous person I know, and the wisest. We know how your client thinks and acts."

"Wally Winchester is not my client," Victor Jay Moriarti said to the room. "I appreciate your loyalty to Mr. Winchester and your desire to hire the best counsel. Frankly," he said to Kenny, "I don't think you can afford me. My retainer for a case such as this would be one hundred thousand dollars, minimum, with more charges later. Sorry folks."

"We have one hundred thousand dollars to hire you," said a dark-haired twenty year-old club member who identified herself as Arial. "Our club has a balance of over half a million from the sale of some rare books. We voted to authorize half of that balance to Wally's defense."

"No shit?" Chana blurted out, startling Yvgeney.

"No shit, Miss Chana," Arial said. "Wally got us interested in antiques, we bought the books at an auction, and he sold them for us."

Chana liked Wally even more. She looked at the lawyer, who reminded her of a North American cowboy with a tie. She said, "We were with him for part of the supposed crime spree. We traveled a thousand miles with Wally, from Boston to Kansas."

Moriarti interrupted her, holding his hands, palm up, in front of him: "You put my integrity in a bunch, young lady, by revealing your part in a felony to a citizen of the United States of America. I don't represent you. I'm not your lawyer, though perhaps I should be. Please keep your confessions to a minimum."

Chana continued. "I interviewed the man who engineered the frame-up, as Wally calls it. I have it on tape. I hope it will help in the defense."

"I'd love to listen to your tape, dear, but I can tell you right now it won't make it into the trial. I am getting intrigued, I'll admit. I'd like to meet with Mr. Winchester. Then I'll give you my answer."

Wally sat in front of an inch-thick slab of safety glass in a Canadian lockup, looking at a hawk-faced man wearing a cowboy hat. He spoke into a microphone. “Are you my lawyer?” he asked

“Not yet, son. I’m just here for a chat. My name’s Moriarti.”

“Victor Jay Moriarti,” Wally said. “I sold you a desk a million years ago. We lugged it up to your office in the Smith Tower in that fancy elevator. A Limbert partner’s desk with original leather. Still have it?”

“I love that desk. I guess I didn’t pay attention to your name back then. I don’t usually remember my vendors.”

“You bought it in my shop called History of the World, Part 4.”

“That friendly store in Stanwood, across from the Norwegian bakery? I wouldn’t have associated Wally Winchester, serial killer and anarchist, with that quaint establishment.”

“I’m innocent,” Wally protested. “Wrongly accused. I’m sure you’ve heard that before.”

“No, that’s a new one. Maybe we can run with that defense.”

“Really?”

“Just kidding, Mr. Winchester. Right now you’re fucked. You’re first job is to refuse extradition until the United States takes the death penalty off the table.”

“Are you my lawyer?”

“Tell me your side of the story. Then I’ll decide.”

“You better get a cup of coffee before I start. And a pillow if your chair is as badly designed as mine.”

When the lawyer returned with a steaming mug, Wally began with the day he bought the Cobra in a locked barn.

The lights flickered to signal the end of visitation hours.

"I actually believe you, Mr. Winchester," Moriarti said through the microphone. No one but a genius could have that much ignorance of that much bloodshed as an alibi. Can I see you tomorrow?"

"You know where to find me."

A huge Canadian Mountie escorted Wally back to his cell. At Wilkinson Prison, high profile inmates were housed in a special wing, separated from the rest of the population. Wally considered himself lucky. He had a single room, one hour on the internet at the library, and no one had tried to make him his bitch. For that alone, he felt grateful.

The solitude was a welcome thing at first. As he slept, the days of drama, close calls survived, the marshmallow sofa snatched from a third floor porch, the fight for mirrored lamps at the factory, the ass-kicking in Shipshewana, the Grove Park Inn fiasco, the Gus bookcase score, the shooting in New York, the Claus Braun meeting, the tragic loss of Manuelita, the Sri Lanka discovery, the auction house explosion, Johnny's farm shootout, the slow motion flight to Port Angeles, and the scariest boat ride of his life all fought for examination but lost out to sweet dreams that featured a beautiful Mexican face.

Wally opened his eyes and saw a grey wall three feet from his bunk. He closed them again and said hello to Manuelita.

Victor Jay Moriarti's first act as counsel to Wally Winchester was to have his shackles removed before meeting again with the Spokane detective who came to claim him. After two weeks of negotiations, they were on a first name basis.

As they sat around a grey metal table in a secure windowless chamber, deep within the prison, Wally looked at the uniformed

Mountie standing at attention with a nightstick and figured it was more than adequate protection against a scared middle aged art dealer in a locked room.

Wally looked, over piles of dog-eared legal documents at the man from the United States who'd been sent to retrieve him. "You look sharp today, Mike," he said, "Get a haircut? Your head looks particularly flat today."

"I did have a trip to the barber this morning, Mr. Winchester. Got my shoes shined also. It's travel day. A lot of people in Spokane are looking forward to asking you questions."

Moriarti looked at Wally and placed a finger over pursed lips. "My client will defer all questions through me." He put his mouth to Wally's ear and quietly said, "It's an eight hour bus ride between here and Spokane, son. This guy's not your friend. Say nothing. Beware of a casual conversation. Anything out of your mouth without me present will hurt you. *Capiche*?"

Wally nodded. The attorney lifted a sheaf of papers, examined a signature and handed it to his client with a pen. Wally signed his name.

"It's official," Moriarti said to the detective. "The death penalty is off the table. My client agrees to extradition to the United States. He is now your prisoner. Let's get the paperwork to the Canadians and I can start on Winchester's defense."

Detective Kelly sat beside Wally, chained by the wrists and ankles to a hook bolted to the floor of a prisoner transport. The policeman was in a good mood. He pointed at an auction house just south of the Canadian border. "Ever shop there, Wally? Looks like a nice place."

Wally stared at his feet.

"How old were you when you bought your first antique?"

Wally looked at the reinforced bus roof, counted forty bolts.

"First thing I found was a South Carolina face jug," Kelly offered.

Wally turned his face, made eye contact.

Kelly continued, "I was fifteen, at a car swap meet with my dad. The jug sat on a table with auto parts. It called to me. The price was two dollars. My father laughed at the purchase, but I still own it. Last year, I looked it up on Google. You wouldn't believe what it's worth. Know who the artist was?"

"*Dave the Slave*, I bet," escaped from Wally's closed mouth.

"Hot damn, you're as good as they say, Winchester. *Dave the Slave* all right. The expert on the internet identified it by the inscription. He offered me five hundred dollars."

"It's worth ten times that," Wally said despite himself. He went back to counting bolts.

"They say you know a lot about chairs."

Wally looked away, remaining silent

"My granddaddy has two chairs I always liked as a kid. *Morris chairs*, he called them. Big as a horse they were to us young ones. Grandpa didn't mind us climbing on them. Indestructible, he said. Called them his *Stickleys*. That was the name of the furniture maker."

Wally counted forty-one ceiling bolts this time, then started again.

"We used to put them side by side, adjust the backs down and pretend we were astronauts."

"How'd the back adjust?" Wally shook his head as he heard his own words.

"There were big plugs that fit into holes in the arms," the detective said. "Hey, do you want me to unhook you from the floor?

I've known you a week now, Wally. I don't see you are a physical threat."

"I didn't kill anybody."

"That's not for me to decide." He produced a key and unshackled Wally's arms. "My sister got the chairs in the end. Still pisses me off. She doesn't even like 'em. Stores them in the barn. Threatens to put them on Craigslist every time we argue."

"What does she think they're worth?"

"She thinks the pair of them are worth a thousand dollars. Can you believe that? Old farm chairs."

"We gotta talk," Wally said. "Did the chairs have slats under the arms?"

As the bus passed the Camano Island exit, Wally looked through narrow windows at the road to his home and felt the chill of fear. He wondered if he would ever see another sunset over the Olympics.

"Did you find any Stickley chairs on your last trip, Wally?" Kelly asked.

"What?" Distracted, Wally looked back to milepost 212. "Bagged a great two-door early bookcase in West Virginia," he said. "Damn. It's still there. How am I going to get my hands on it if I'm in prison?"

"I could arrange to get it shipped back for you."

"Would you do that? Could you get it to my antique club in Stanwood."

"I'll need a receipt"

"Yeah, of course. I kept all the receipts from the trip in my backpack. You guys must have it by now. Figure I'll never see my money again."

"Describe the backpack."

"Tan, *Jansport*, I think, canvas. You put your arms through the loops. Why do you ask? Don't you have it? It was with me on the raft when they boarded."

"Did you find anything else memorable on your travels across the U.S.?"

"We scored a George Nelson Marshmallow Sofa in Montana. Right off a porch. Say, that old couple met Manuelita. They're my first witnesses. They saw her. No one's reported them dead."

"Who is Manuelita?"

"I told you last week, back at the Canadian prison. She's the killer. I gave her a ride to the East Coast to meet her sister in New Hampshire."

"Manuelita was the killer."

"I had no idea," Wally said. "I only found out when I got to Boston."

"And where is Manuelita now?"

"I told you. Dead," Wally said. He bit back a gulp of sadness, looked the detective in the eyes, and realized he opened his mouth in Bellingham. At least, he thought, he'd identified his first witnesses, the old couple who sold him the Marshmallow sofa.

"There was no record of a backpack in the Canadian arrest record," Kelly said. "All those receipts could be a valuable tool…in your defense. When did you last see it?"

"Last time I saw it I had a spotlight in my eyes a hundred yards off the Vancouver Island shore."

"What was Manuelita's last name?"

Wally came to attention. He knew interrogation when he heard it. He returned to his pledge to clam up. "Tell you what," he said. "I can shut my mouth or I can tell you what I've recently learned about Arts and Crafts decorated leather."

Detective Mike Kelly said, "Tell me about decorated Arts and Crafts leather."

Chapter Forty-Two

Spokane, Washington

In the Spokane County Courthouse, Victor Jay Moriarti stood with Wally Winchester as he was charged with the murder of a Hindu cleric in Spokane and two other Spokane men, found dead in a lakeshore campground in Idaho. Other charges in other states were pending.

He pled not guilty.

Bail was denied.

Moriarti touched Wally's arm as a bailiff steered him toward his cell. "I'll see you in the morning. Ten o'clock," he said. "We've got a lot of work to do."

"I remembered some witnesses. A couple who saw me and Manuelita together."

"That's good," his lawyer said. Wally felt the tug from the bailiff. "My backpack never made it into custody. That's important. It had all my receipts, one hundred grand in cash, and my toothbrush."

"What happened to it?"

The bailiff nudged him toward the exit. "Somebody up there in Canada has it," Wally shouted back as they pulled him through a door.

Wally winced as the metal door on the third floor retracted to reveal a small tan box. He walked inside and sat on a metal shelf covered by a foam pad. He tried not to freak out. The door slid shut. He heard shouts and singing. Then a scream. His neighbors.

A metal toilet sat in the corner, exposed to the door. A tilt-down shelf on the wall dropped to become a desk when he sat on the bed. It was beautiful, simple, a Bauhaus nightmare. Minimalist Hell.

Suddenly overwhelmed, Wally lay back on the pad, closed his eyes to his world, and tried to mentally reassemble an M-16 from a lecture he received back in Kansas. He fell asleep with a headful of loose rifle parts.

As he sipped a double white chocolate mocha, sugar free, that his lawyer brought to the meeting room, Wally said, "The food here sucks. "Terrible eggs. Soggy toast. Thanks for something real."

"We have bigger issues," Moriarti said. "Each of the states in your killing spree…"

"I didn't kill anyone."

"Sorry, son, you just have to have a sense of humor in this job. Of course you're innocent. I've listened to the tape recording that your friend, Chana, gave me. It makes me think you really were framed. Your biggest crime is likely being a dupe. We can't use the recording, of course. The judge will never let it in. Here's the bad news."

"What was the good news?"

"The good news is that they don't have your backpack with all the receipts and that cash. I'm sending your friend, Yvgeney, over the border to try to retrieve it. Is he really that good?"

"He'll get it. He's that good. Do we turn it in?"

"Hell no, son. That's their smoking gun. We deep-six the bag and pray."

"What's the bad news?"

"Here it is. Seems each state where someone died wants a piece of you. Then there's the bombing in Kansas City."

"I saved people from that bomb."

"I know, but for them, it fits. And then there's the holocaust at the farm. That's on you, too."

"Holy shit. The world thinks I'm another Hitler. How ironic."

Moriarti said. "I'm sending Chana to Montana to interview the old couple you said met the Mexican girl. Do you remember the address?"

"The marshmallow couch is in storage, damn it. My keys were confiscated. Guess I have to leave it there for now. I can describe my walk to the building and tell you what floor the old folks were on. Apartment 5, I think. Chana's smart."

"One thing you've got going for you is most of the early killings, all the way to the Grove Park Inn, were carried out with a serrated knife, Navy SEAL-type, and it's never been found. That's good for us. No direct link with the killings, like fingerprints on the murder weapon."

"Manuelita kept it in her backpack. Didn't they find it with her body?" Wally's face fell at the memory.

"As your defender, I've seen all the reports. I don't want to burden you with that now. No knife has been found. Did you ever touch it?"

"Heavens, no. She showed it to me. I scolded her. She scolded me back about her being a defenseless woman guarding a two hundred thousand dollar car."

"That knife and the contents of her backpack could save your ass."

"It was pretty frantic in the woods at Forest Park when the shooting started," Wally said. "Manuelita was halfway out the window firing that gun. Perhaps she dropped it there."

"Where is the gun?"

"I have no idea. I never saw it when I left her."

Moriarti said, "Two bad both of your friends are occupied. Finding that backpack and knife would give you a fighting chance."

"Send some of the kids," Wally said.

"Those children who hired me?"

"If the backpack is in Woburn, in Forest Park, I know the people I want to send to retrieve it. I want Danny 'cause he thinks in numbers and this is a search. Arial would hold the trip together, and Kenny has the nose of a janitor. If your office puts the trip package together for the kids, I trust Arial to get them there and back. If it's there, they'll find it. It's my dime."

"I'm glad to see you taking an interest in the predicament you are in, Mr. Winchester."

"It's sort of overwhelming, all this. I was just driving to Boston to sell a car. Now the opposite wall is two feet from my bed."

"The next person you'll see is Detective Kelly. Don't talk with him alone. Call me. I'll be in the clerk's office downstairs with some motions to file."

Wally said. "Kelly's sister has two chairs I want."

Moriarti closed his eyes.

The good thing about criminal proceedings, Wally thought as he entered the conference room again, is that you spend less time in your cell. The guard closed the door behind him. The detective, wearing a wrinkled suit, sat at the table, his posture military-straight, the buddy smile nowhere in sight. He motioned Wally to the aluminum chair across the metal surface.

"Talked with my sister," Kelly said without emotion. "She says she won't sell the chairs to a serial killer. Sorry"

"I didn't kill those people," Wally said. "Should I have my lawyer here?"

"It's up to you," the detective said. "I'd like to get to know you. We're going to spend a lot of time together. The more we know you, the clearer we make your case."

"I'm innocent. Will that come out?"

"I just deal with the facts, Mr. Winchester. If the facts say you're innocent, you win."

"I want my attorney," Wally said.

"That's the right thing to do," the detective said.

Wally said, "I still want my lawyer, Kelly."

"I'll call him whenever you want. You know I am a collector, too. One thing I got from my grandfather is a Roycroft Little Journeys bookstand."

"With the little brass label? You didn't mention that on the trip from Canada."

"That's the one. And I have the books, the entire set."

"Good for you."

"I found one of those in the streets of Stanwood, Washington once," Wally said. "Piled among the trash in the back of a pickup, parked on the street at 11:00 a.m. I located the driver in the first bar I went to. Bought it for a hundred bucks. Gave it to my friend, Ed."

"When did you get interested in the Arts and Crafts movement?" Kelly asked.

"Back in the late 70's. I was one of the first people in America on the lookout for Stickley furniture, never had enough money to do any damage. Arts and Crafts furniture was hard to find back then; mission oak furniture never made it into the auctions. The only buyers in the world were a couple of elusive guys from New York."

"I bought a rocking chair last month. Not a Stickley, a Limbert."

"I love Limbert furniture. Good for you, Kelly."

"I have to ask you some questions about the Hindu church in Spokane," Kelly said.

"I need my lawyer now."

Moriarti entered and interrupted a friendly chat. “Stop talking, Winchester,” he commanded.

Wally was concluding the tale of the Thorndon chairs he scored on Martha’s Vineyard. He shut his mouth.

Moriarti sat down, and looked at Kelly. “Ask your questions to me,” he said.

“OK,” Kelly said, “Were you at the Hindu temple in Spokane on May 17th?” He directed the question to Wally, who whispered a question to his attorney.

Moriarti told him, “Tell the truth.”

Wally said, “I was at the sale at a Hindu church in Spokane. We discussed a light fixture deal. I have no idea of the date.”

“So you met the deceased?”

“I didn’t know he was deceased until I heard about it on the internet,” Wally said.

“Why did he have your phone number in his hand when he was found?”

“We made a deal about some light fixtures. I was going to pick them up on the way back. I’m sure I left my number. Why would I kill him?”

“I’m just taking the facts, Mr. Winchester. “You say Mr…Singh was alive when you left him?”

“We shook hands,” Wally said. “I was going to make a thousand dollars on the lights from his attic. If I kill him, I lose the money.”

“You were the last person to see him alive.”

“Manuelita left the car to pee before we took off. She was killing people behind my back, apparently.”

“Who is Manuelita? For the record.”

“Let me take you back to an email request,” Wally said. “And I’ll walk you across the country.”

Chapter Forty-Three

Sydney, B.C., Canada

The rental car with the United Nations Cultural Property Investigator inside entered Canada without incident. His passport sported entries from Russia, India, Iraq, Mexico, half of the South American countries, and France, but his UNESCO badge opened the border. He followed A-1 north toward a ferry crossing to Vancouver Island to see the head of Canadian Customs.

At the front door of the government structure, he scanned a list of offices and headed for the fourth floor. A secretary brought him tea and cakes as he waited in a carpeted reception area surrounded by vintage paintings of British vessels in the age of sail.

"What brings the United Nations to my humble office today?" a pot-bellied caricature of a bureaucrat asked.

"As I told your secretary, I am a United Nations investigator without portfolio whose job it is to repatriate cultural treasures separated from their owners by war, or ethnic cleansing, or sometimes outright theft. My last post was in Mumbai."

"Were you there during the last hotel attack? Sticky business those terrorist groups."

"I was in the hotel when the bombs went off."

"Goodness. I complain when I have to wait to cross the street for lunch." He offered his hand and said, "Captain Royce Merriweather at your service."

"Yvgeney Ivanchenko."

"Ah, a Russian. Lose any provinces this week? Your nation is down to a couple of acres around Red Square, the way I hear it."

"We still have a big backyard called Siberia," Yvgeney countered. "I'm here about the fugitive, Winchester. About a theft."

"Ah, that bloke. His capture brought more world press to Victoria than the last visit from the Queen. What did he steal? I read he was a murderer, not a thief."

"He was rumored to have had a large sum of cash with him when your boys caught him off the coast."

"At large sum of money? How much? I don't recall that on the inventory. Let me check."

He typed on a laptop and studied the screen.

"No," he said. "The subject's raft was empty when he was processed."

"Can I interview the Customs officers who were at the scene?"

"I'll need some authorization, of course."

"Here's my contact in Lyon, France," Yvgeney said. He penciled a phone number and an email address on the back of his card. "Good luck finding anyone at the office this weekend. Can I speak with them now? The trail gets colder every day I delay."

The bureaucrat expanded the file with his fingertips and commented, "There were four officers at the scene of the capture. One is on duty today, two have been out sick now for a week, and the fourth fellow upped and quit, it says, three days after the arrest." He expanded the monitor screen again. "Says here he was uncomfortable with all the publicity. Took the early leave from the service. How odd."

He opened a phone, hit a number on speed dial and barked, "There's some funny business afoot with the crew that captured the American terrorist, Clive. Why wasn't I informed?" He listened and said, "Two are out sick and one has gone missing." His eyes opened wide. "What's that? Good God. When?"

The captain sucked in his ample gut and reached for a wool overcoat hanging on a costumer. "Hold my calls, Jane," he said, waving for Yvgeney to follow. "They found Ensign Johnson a few minutes ago…dead."

The scene by the customs docks was grim. RCMP officers on the shore formed a phalanx that parted as they approached. An ashen-faced ensign walked with them to a small pier where a body lay covered in a Navy blanket. Forensics techs swabbed the blue face.

"He was found out there near the channel buoy, floating," the day officer said to the commander. "Seems to have been shot. Multiple times."

Yvgeney looked down at the youthful face as the medic pulled the shroud over it.

"What's that in his mouth?" he asked.

The technician opened a stubborn jaw and pulled a currency note from blue lips. "It's a hundred dollar bill," the man exclaimed. "An American bill. Someone left us a message."

Yvgeney knew the sender.

Chapter Forty-Four

Butte, Montana

Chana walked down the hall on the third floor of Heritage Arms Apartments, knocking on doors. She had a photo of Wally she'd printed from the internet, a search that provided eighteen thousand hits this week on a bing search.

The third door opened to an old white man with kind eyes. Chana held the photo up and asked, "Did you sell a sofa to this man?"

"Why, yes, I did, child. Come in. Martha, we have company."

Chana stepped into a small flat. The view out the window was brick buildings and scarred mountains.

"Sit down, child," the senior said. "Are you a friend of Wally's? Do he and his bride like our settee? They were so dear."

"They love the settee. Wally spoke of it yesterday," Chana said. "I'm here to ask a favor."

"Anything, child," the woman said. "Our life is so…quiet."

"So boring," the husband said.

"What can we do for you?"

Chana told them a short version of Wally's mess. The couple retreated. "The serial killer bought our marshmallow couch!" Martha shrieked.

"He didn't kill anyone," Chana said. She looked the woman in the eye, willed her to relax. "He didn't kill you, did he?"

"Well no. He was a gentleman. I never thought . . . "

She asked, "The woman with him. Did she touch anything? Did she use the bathroom? Did she touch a glass?"

"Why are you asking about that sweet young bride? Was she in on it?"

"She was the killer," Chana said. "I need to find her fingerprints or her DNA."

"Well, she came back in after they got the settee into the rental van, told me she needed to use the powder room. For the long trip ahead, she said. I caught her rummaging around in my medicine cabinet. She said she had terrible cramp pain. I gave her a handful of outdated painkillers."

"Did she touch the bottles?"

"She looked at the label of each one. Told me what she wanted."

Chana sat the couple down in their recliners. She asked them to turn off the TV. She said, "Wally Winchester is a good man. He needs your help."

"What can we do?"

Chana said, "A detective will visit this week, I hope, to look for fingerprints and DNA. Please don't touch or clean anything the Mexican woman might have touched till he gets here."

Chapter Forty-Five

Stoneham, Massachusetts

In the motel room at the Holiday Inn, the boys were sitting on the double bed, trying to find the channel with porn. Danny switched to a cartoon when Arial entered.

"You're busted, Danny," she said. "I know what you were watching."

"I found the location of the shooting," he said. His laptop displayed a map on the monitor.

"That's more like it," she said. "Let's go right now. It's only ten miles away. We have two hours of good light. Wally paid for a GPS, let's use it."

The gravel path that marked the entrance to the woods of Forest Park was overgrown and almost invisible from Route 38. Arial turned into Fisher Terrace and pulled a U-turn next to a well kept yard near the interstate. She drove the rental through a canopy of hanging foliage and followed an unmaintained road through the woods and then to a clearing with a ballpark in the middle.

"According to the news reports on the web, the gunfight took place here," Danny said, closing his laptop.

"Let's find a knife," Arial said.

In the glow of an approaching New England sunset, three youths descended on a Woburn forest clearing, eyes to the ground. Kenny cried out, "I found a coin. It has words I don't understand." The search collapsed onto his location.

Arial took it. "It's a peso," she said. "Mexican. Where did you find it?"

"Out there, by the bushes."

"Look for another."

"I have one," Danny said softly from the underbrush. "Another coin."

Arial and Kenny negotiated the brambles to the scene.

Danny looked up. He said, "It's right above us."

A tan bag hung off a pine tree like a branch. He climbed up and retrieved the prize, landing in a triumphant thud.

Arial donned plastic gloves as instructed and opened it, found a knife housed in a leather holder.

"Over here" Kenny said, his back to the gravel road. "I found a gun, a big one."

"Don't touch it. Our job is just to locate it and leave the scene intact for the police." Arial dialed 911.

Chapter Forty-Six

Spokane, Washington

Wally entered the interview room, the door latching behind him, to see his attorney and Detective Kelly sitting at the same side of the table.

"Trading Facebook addresses?" Wally said as he took his seat across from them.

Kelly smiled. He said, "Word is I'm about to lose my job."

"You?" Wally answered. "You're the top dog. You get to investigate a high profile suspect – me."

"Highest salaries go first in a recession, son. I need two more years before I can collect my pension, so I'm on the block. You could be my last case. I want to do it right."

"Ask away," Wally said, "I want the truth to be heard."

"When did you first meet the men killed in the Montana campground?"

"I have no idea who you're talking about."

"LeRoy Long and Billy Watkins, known meth heads from Spokane. Here are the photos."

Wally recoiled from the morgue images. "I don't know these guys. Wait. The bearded man reminds me of an asshole who fucked with us in Spokane. On Division. We blew them off on the interstate." His face darkened.

"Why did he have your business card in his dead fingers?"

"How would I know?" Wally looked to his attorney, silent so far. He shrugged.

"How about this?" Kelly said. "After you kill the Hindu you needed a little pick-me-up."

"Pick-me-up?"

"Don't answer, Wally."

"Methamphetamine, crank. How long have you been a tweeker?"

"What are you talking about? I just learned to text last December."

"Quiet, Wally."

"*Tweeker*. Not Tweeter. The boys you killed were no strangers to the Spokane police, with rap sheets as long as your arm."

Moriarti responded, "My client denies meeting these men. He buys antiques in Spokane, leaves business cards all over. Who knows where these…criminals picked one up?"

"The campground attendant remembers your car."

"Does he remember a Mexican girl in the seat beside me?"

"Quiet, Wally," Moriarti said. He asked Kelly, "Did you ask the attendant if he noticed a passenger?"

"This isn't a courtroom, Mr. Moriarti. You don't get to ask the questions."

"It's my client's contention that his passenger was responsible for these deaths, yet no one seems interested in this line of inquiry."

"This is a preliminary investigation, sir. We have no information on a passenger except from your client's account. Let's go back to the Hindu temple."

"No Kelly, we're done," Moriarti said. "You are judging my client from internet reports. Come back when you've burned off a little shoe leather."

Chapter Forty-Seven

Victoria, B.C., Canada

Yvgeney entered the yard on quiet feet. Light flickering in the window suggested someone was home. He knocked at the door and heard the television noise diminish. No one answered. He knocked again and circled to the backyard, where a figure crept from the back door toward the darkness of a grove of trees.

"Ensign Davis?" Yvgeney shouted. "Going on an evening stroll?"

"Get away from me," said a voice from the shadows. "I have a gun."

"Is it the one you used to shoot Ensign Johnson?"

"It's all over the television. I didn't shoot anyone; I'm afraid I will be next. Who are you? Don't come closer. I know how to use this thing."

"I mean no harm," Yvgeney said. "I work for the United Nations. I'm an investigator."

"Leave me alone."

"Who are you afraid of? Is his name Claus Braun?"

"I don't know his name. Get back!"

Yvgeney sat down on the moist grass. He put his hands on his jacket and opened it up. "See," he said into the darkness. "Unarmed, but I can help you."

"No one can help me. He killed Johnson, probably Peters and Reed as well. They don't answer my calls."

"I'm skilled in the art of personal defense," Yvgeney said. He held up his badge. "I believe I know the man you're afraid of. I've been up against him before and I'm still kicking. I'll stand beside you, but I need some answers. You can talk to me from where you are. Tell me about the day you captured Winchester."

"It had been an uneventful evening," the ensign began after a long pause. "A bit of a blow swept in after sunset and we were checking moorings. The four of us, Reed, Johnson, Peters, and myself were talking about motoring over to Sooke for the chowder at Pelican Pete's when Reed spotted the boat, drifting, then a raft off the bow, beat up pretty well from the squall, a fellow trying to row into a thirty-knot gale and losing the battle. It was a routine event. We tow stranded boats as a public service. Figured his engine conked out. The bloke didn't resist, he handed his wallet over with a Washington State drivers license and no passport. The license failed the smart clip scan. That's when Johnson found the money. Lots of it. U.S. cash in hundreds."

"So you decided to keep the money?"

"I wanted to turn it in. We'd just captured the most wanted man in America, and the backpack was evidence. The others voted no. Said it was his word against ours. That's why I quit the next day. I wanted no part of it."

"How'd you know the man in the boat was Wally Winchester if he had a false ID?"

"He told us, after his license failed the scan. 'You got me,' he said, and told us his real name. Simple as that. He seemed relieved. Johnson hid the backpack in his duffel."

"So Winchester had no idea the money wasn't reported?"

"He was in chains. Prisoners have no rights."

"Johnson took the money home?"

"He called me the next day to tell me to stay mum. I agreed. He offered a share, said he'd hidden the pack. I refused. He called the next day, frightened. Said a crazy German with a carload of Mexican thugs came to his house, told him the money was theirs and wanted it back.

Johnson told him to bugger off. He said the German told him he didn't need his help to find it, but they'd let him live if he gave it up. Save some leg work, the German said."

"Did he give the money back?"

"No. He told the German he'd given the bag to Peters, poor soul. He said the lunatic then penned a bulls-eye on his forehead with a red Sharpie."

"Your commander told me that Peters and Reed were out sick. I suspect they're sending the Mounties around to check. Your commander is madder than hell. You should expect a visit also."

"Peters called me the next day. Asked me if I knew where the money was. He was crying. Terrible thing to hear on the phone."

"Do you know where it is?"

"I have an idea. Johnson had a cabin up in Swartz Bay. Called it his sanctuary."

"Can you take me there?"

"I don't want anything to do with that maniac. I'll take my chances with the RCMP."

Yvgeney said, "I'll find it eventually. In the meantime you're on your own. Don't forget to lock your doors. I've seen Braun kill a man with the rearview mirror of a Winnebago."

"I'd rather be with you," the voice from the bushes said. "I'll take you there. Let's leave tonight."

Chapter Forty-Eight

Spokane, Washington

The freckled South American native who sat in his office caused the hairs on Detective Kelly's neck to stiffen. He stood and then retook his chair as she introduced herself as Chana in a soft voice.

"Chana who?" he asked.

"Just Chana."

"I've got a lot on my plate right now, *Just Chana*. You have five minutes. How can I help you or vice versa?"

Chana said, "I have evidence for you in the Winchester murders." She held up a voice cassette.

"Hold my calls," Kelly spoke into the phone.

To Chana, he asked, "Mind if I record this conversation?"

"I have no problem with that. I'm recording it also."

"Not without my permission, young lady, and I refuse it. I tell you what, why don't I record it and, when you fill out a form, you can have a copy?"

"OK. My name is Chana," she spoke into Kelly's microphone.

"How do you know Walter Winchester?"

"I met him in South America four years ago. We traveled across Asia on the Trans-Siberian Railway two years ago. Last month, we shared some time in Mumbai."

"Our Mr. Winchester was on a serial killing spree one month ago. How could he be in India?"

"He was there and in Sri Lanka for a short time after he delivered the racing car to a man in Boston."

"Well, I'm glad you're here, Chana. You seem to know more about the case already than I do."

"I suspect that is an understatement," Chana said.

Kelly inspected her papers. He commented: “Brazilian birthplace. Chilean passport. Residence on Olkhon Island, Republic of Russia. Why are you here in the US of A? Why are you in my office?”

Chana caught the detective’s tired eyes. She didn’t let them go.

“I’m here to help you prove Wally Winchester is innocent.”

Kelly chuckled. “Innocent? If your friend is innocent, then Adolph Hitler was just another painter, doll.”

Chana said, “You are the lead detective.”

“Your five minutes are almost up, Just Chana, or whatever your name is.”

“Your job is to gather all the evidence and present it to a prosecutor so that it can be used in a trial.”

Kelly looked at his watch.

Chana continued. “I have an address in Butte, Montana where the killer you seek left her fingerprints on the bathroom mirror and on prescription drug bottles.”

Kelly sat back and said, “More of this second-killer story. Winchester tried that, too. Why would fingerprints in Montana change my mind?”

“Because they belong to the Mexican woman, Manuelita, with whom Wally drove across the country. The old couple who sold the divan have agreed to testify.”

“You’ve been a busy child,” Kelly said. “Are you one of Moriarti’s investigators?”

“I’m helping Wally.”

“Just because Winchester had a partner, he’s not off the hook, lady.”

“Will you listen to this tape?”

“Whatever’s on it won’t be admissible in any trial. There’s no evidence chain.”

"What is on the tape will throw your simple minded scenario into doubt, Detective Kelly. I don't care if you use it in court."

He looked again at his wristwatch. "How long is it?"

Chana said, "Eight minutes. I have the playback ready. Press *play*."

Kelly did. He heard: "There are no words that can express how much I have missed you, Chana…."

He stopped it. "Come on, lady. I have evidence to collect."

Chana's face stopped his whine. He resumed the play-back: "…what do you think of the puzzle that I put our soon-to-be-deceased Mr. Winchester in, Chana…Manuelita was my sword, after you… A week on the road with Winchester ruined her mind… She fired on our own men outside of Boston – she, the assassin for hire. We fired back. I'm sorry she's gone…" Chana stopped it.

"Whose voice is that?" the detective asked. "Where and when was it recorded? Who was shooting in the background?"

Chana asked, "Are you interested, now, in the information I wish to offer?"

Kelly smiled, said, "Well, I would be negligent in my duties if I wasn't, don't you think?"

Chana's smile surprised her. She began the tale of Claus Braun, Manuelita, and revenge.

Chapter Forty-Nine

West Shore, B.C., Canada

Yvgeney left the frightened ensign in the car and approached a dark one-room cabin with his flashlight off. Old planks groaned as he tiptoed over a neglected deck and peered inside. Darkness ruled. He felt a door latch, secured by a five-dollar lock, picked it with a spike from his Swiss Army knife, and entered the musty silence. He risked the flashlight and swept the room, shut it off, and thought about what he'd seen. A pair of simple iron beds flanked a small wood stove. He pictured a log table and two folding chairs. An old lozenge-shaped Frigidaire and a metal sink finished his memory of the room's contents. He walked toward the icebox, turned on the light and opened the door to a six-pack of Labatts. He opened the stove door and saw a Jansport label.

Inside the pack, he found an envelope full of Wally's trip receipts, a pair of socks, grimy toothbrush, a small ceramic vase, along with fifteen stacks of hundred dollar bills. He tucked the receipts into his back pocket to share later with the lawyer, and repacked the money.

"Hello, Yvgeney." The Russian's eyes blinked in the glare, but he knew the voice.

"Is that a flashlight in your hand or are you just glad to see me?" he answered.

"You and your North America aphorisms. I've missed those little gems you put to memory. Learned any new ones?" The beam dropped to the floor. Yvgeney saw Claus Braun and four other men, one the whimpering ensign with a gun at his head.

"I heard one the other day, a song title: 'I'd rather have a bottle in front of me than a frontal lobotomy."

"I like it," Braun said. "I have a bottle, as a matter of fact, an excellent Claret. Orlando, get the bottle from the car and find us some light in here."

Yvgeney heard a click, and a wagon wheel fixture with three exposed bulbs lit the room. He sized up the remaining two henchmen, well-built young Latinos with automatic pistols. The ensign's face bled from a cut by his hairline. His legs trembled. His eyes were bruised and swollen shut.

The bottle arrived. Sitting down at the table, Braun passed the cork under his nose, nodded and handed it to the Russian. Yvgeney looked at the cork, sniffed it, and scanned his memory for ways to turn it into a weapon against four adversaries with guns. He gave up and approved. The wine had a big note of plum and opened to wild cherry at the back of his tongue. He told Braun so and watched him brighten and agree.

"Let's see what our friend Wally had in his pack," Braun said into his goblet. The man, Orlando, pulled the strap from Yvgeney's shoulder and emptied the sack onto the table. Money tumbled out with a roll of athletic socks. A purple Arts and Crafts vase fell on the pile and rolled. Braun caught it. The toothbrush fell to the table on a second shake.

"The boy travels light," Braun laughed. He held the toothbrush up and spoke in Spanish to nervous underling laughter. "See this money?" he said to the ensign. It's mine, and you tried to steal it. I'm going to let you keep all that you can eat. Come over here."

The sailor shrank back. Strong hands pulled him toward the table. "Not hungry?" Braun asked. He pulled a hand from under the table, holding a classic Lugar, and shot him in both knees, firing into his abdomen as he fell, retching. Yvgeney smelled his evacuation. Braun shot the wriggling form in the head. It stopped.

"Get this thief out of here, he stinks," Braun ordered.

"How's Wally holding up?" he asked Yvgeney, who'd put down his wine.

"I haven't been allowed to see him since he entered the Federal building."

"And Chana?"

Yvgeney looked into the German's eyes. "Chana's not the same woman you knew, Braun."

"I found that out. Say hello to her for me when you see her, will you?" He stood up while Orlando packed the cash into the backpack. The German snickered as he slipped the vase into a sack. He passed the socks and toothbrush to Yvgeney.

"Give these mementos to our prisoner," he laughed.

"I'm free to go?"

"I'll see you again, Russian, after the trial. I'm not done with you. Today you're a messenger. Tell Chana I'm still waiting for her answer."

"Say, Braun," the UNESCO investigator asked as the killer left. "How did you find the backpack?"

The German stopped and turned with a smile, the vase in his hand. He inserted a finger into the opening and pulled out a grape-sized ball of wax holding a metal chip.

He tossed it over. Yvgeney caught it. "GPS," he said. "Brilliant. How did you get Wally to buy it and carry it with him?"

"Chatter told me Wally was in Yakima, waiting out the weather. We couldn't find him, though we hit every motel in the desert. I found a four thousand dollar vase, stuck the transponder inside, and consigned it with a silly price that Wally couldn't say no to if he wandered into town. He did. We spotted him buying it on the second day. The purchase saved his life that day. I had him in the crosshairs but decided to play with him for a while. It amused me to be able to track him. Sometimes the chase is more enjoyable than the kill."

Braun turned the vessel over and looked at the inscription on the bottom. "The 1904 date was the *worm on my hook* as they say in the USA," he said as he pocketed the vase.

"Never heard that phrase, *worm on my hook*."

"I made it up. See you in court, Russian. Your day is coming. After the trial I'm setting my sights on you. Today I need a messenger."

Chapter Fifty

Spokane, Washington

Kelly sat in the office of the District Attorney. The meeting was not going well.

"I just got off the phone with the D.A. in Boston," a grey-haired Marine face said. He pulled on his Windsor knot and took a deeper breath. "They got the DNA results from the knife some kids found in the woods at their crime scene."

"And?"

"They found multiple signatures. Linked it to victims in North Carolina and North Dakota, the teenage hoodlums."

The detective asked, "Any match to our three?"

"They're testing another accumulation by the hilt. The lab tech said don't get your hopes up."

"Fingerprints?

"All the prints on the knife belong to the Mexican girl found shot in the stolen police car. They found Winchester's prints on the steering wheel and door handle but none on the murder weapon. We can put him at the scene. That's all. This Winchester character is made of Teflon. Nothing sticks."

Kelly said it: "Or he's innocent. A framed man as he claims."

"Do your job, Kelly," the prosecutor yelled. "Winchester's dirty. The whole world knows it. We have him cold at the crime scenes. If we don't get a conviction in the Spokane murders, I'll be the laughing stock of the west coast!"

"I'm developing two other suspects, George, one of them is that dead Mexican girl, the other, a Chilean national, Claus Braun."

"Don't dilute this case with other suspects, Kelly. If we have to run on circumstantial evidence, the slightest whiff of reasonable doubt is an acquittal."

"I interviewed a couple in Butte yesterday," Kelly said. "Pulled a pile of clean prints from the bathroom. I won't be surprised if they match the Boston victim's prints. The couple sold a sofa to Wally and a woman pretending to be his newlywed bride. We'll get some pictures from Woburn of the deceased and I'll run them by the couple. The girl is part of it, George. I have to include her, at least as an accomplice."

"Then forget that Braun character. Concentrate on the couple."

"I don't think I can."

"I think you should."

"You know that story yesterday about the four Canadian customs officers found dead?"

"I saw it. Didn't pay attention."

"According to Winchester, he had a backpack with all his trip receipts inside plus one hundred fifty thousand in cash when he was captured. There was no cash logged in. Now all four of the crew who found him are dead."

"Where'd he get all that money?" the prosecutor asked, interest trumping anger.

"Winchester claims he sold a car to a collector after driving it across the country."

"Let me guess, the Chilean."

"Wally claims the collector is Hitler's son."

The Prosecuting Attorney put his face in his arms on the desk.

Chapter Fifty-One

Seattle, Washington

Victor Jay Moriarti beamed as he held up a folder. "We just received this from discovery," he told the assembled gaggle of Wally's team. "Nice work, Arial."

"Du…Don…Don't forget me and Danny," Kenny chirped.

"Yes, son," the lawyer said. "I hear you found the first clue, a coin. Here's the good news. The Boston police have processed the knife for DNA and fingerprints. It's clearly the murder weapon, or one of them. The only prints are the woman's."

"Manuelita," Chana said.

"This is a blow to the prosecution."

"Do we win now?"

"No, Kenny, we don't win yet. It turns the case against our client into a circumstantial and anecdotal string of evidence. That's much more difficult for the prosecutor."

"What about the gun we found?" Arial asked.

Moriarti thumbed through the file. He said, "A handgun and a cell phone were recovered. The gun is linked to the murders in New York State. It had been wiped clean but partial prints on the remaining bullets have been matched to the Mexican victim."

"That's good," Ron said. "The bitch did it. There's the proof."

"It's not that simple, son, but it doesn't hurt the case. It's not like I can call the Boston Police Department and demand they hand over their evidence. Not now, anyway. I have other news."

"I have other news also," Yvgeney said. "I have all of Wally's receipts from his trip. Right here." He held up a manila folder.

"Put it away," Moriarti said. "We'll talk later."

Chana asked, "What was your other news?"

"The other news," Moriarti said, "is I think I can get all of these multi-state charges put under one Federal indictment to be determined by a grand jury."

"Yikes," Alfred said. "That sounds terrible."

"It's better than what we've got," the lawyer said to the group. "The Feds are hot about the bombing in Kansas City. That's their meat. We might be able to roll all the charges into a Federal beef. That way we get access to all the evidence found by those stingy goddamned states that are waiting for their trial. We're not off the hook with them, unfortunately, but at least we can get a look at what they've found."

Chapter Fifty-Two

Seattle, Washington

Deprived as he had been from lack of stimulation, Wally enjoyed the view from the county prison bus. Above the waterfront on old Route 99, he watched two ferries headed out and one arriving.

SeaTac Airport occupied the right side of the horizon. Wally's bulletproof conveyance turned right at the next light and wheeled into a circular driveway.

Wally looked up at the building that was his new prison. He had to admit, he liked it. Two round towers of concrete rose above him, punctuated by windows in a Wiener Werkstätte fashion. From the towers, two wings of grey showed tiny openings, one of which he figured was about to become his.

Wally swallowed with a jolt of fear. This was real.

The stainless steel lobby was invigorating, retro diner, 1940's hospital chic. A good interior, he thought, to visit and photograph before going home to a comfy chair, a beer and football on a widescreen. Not a nice place to live.

The elevator had no buttons. The guard pressed a code in a wall-mounted keypad and the car rose silently. It opened on a white, tiled, numberless floor. Chained and hobbled by ankle bracelets, Wally stumbled out.

His two guards were six-foot-plus. Wally attempted a conversation.

"Get a lot of jet noise this close to the airport?" he offered.

Silence. They led him to a door that opened with a remote.

Wally entered a gray box, ten feet deep and eight feet wide with room for a tall man to stand up. All his courage spun into circles;

he felt light in the head but gained his composure. The door closed behind him and he felt really afraid.

Chapter Fifty-Three

Bryant, Washington

Detective Kelly sat in a Victorian living room on the Stanwood-Bryant Road under a Tiffany-style light fixture and drank tea with the wife of an auctioneer. He asked, "When the man with a racing car for sale came here, did you meet him?"

The white-haired woman smiled and said, "Just for a moment. I served the men tea. They sent me away."

"Can you describe the man?"

"He had a Nordic face, you know, high cheekbones. German or Scandanavian. A handsome man. I can't tell you more."

"That is enough, Detective Kelly said. "Tell me about your husband's boating accident."

Chapter Fifty-Four

Seattle, Washington

Wally was not happy. He sat on an aluminum bunk and reread the package of instructions given him when he entered the cell. He noted that the law library was open to inmates from 3:00 to 4:00 p.m. weekday afternoons by appointment. He banged his tiny mug against the window and bellowed, “Hello.”

To his great surprise, the door opened to a guard, a giant of a man who stopped to look inside. He said, “You’re new. You’re a high-interest prisoner, I’m your genie, and you have one question. After that, you can bang your heart out. Make it a good one.”

“Is there a law library available to me?” Wally asked. He had no interest in the library. Law books and ledger books bewildered him, but he wanted out of his cell.

“This is your answer. Enjoy it. The law library is open from 3:00 to 4:00 p.m. by prior approval.”

Wally acknowledged the information. He said, “That’s what it says here in the welcome folder. How do I get approval?”

“That’s question number two, son. You’re out. Have a nice life.”

“Wait,” Wally pleaded. “What do you want me to do? Submit a request? Give me a form.”

“You’re out of questions, meat,” the big guard said. “I know who you are.”

“Do you have any antiques questions? I can appraise an estate from a verbal description.”

“My grandpa just died,” the big man said. “He had a big collection of Indian things. A roomful.”

“American Indians or elephant-riding Indians?”

"Pacific Northwest, mostly."

"That's good…"

Wally had a request for the law library in his hands by noon.

At 3:00 p.m., the door opened and a uniformed officer escorted Wally to a windowless room with books filling three walls. Three tables held computer monitors. A woman stopped typing and looked up. He recognized her desk, the new version of a Mies van der Rohe table available in the Scandinavian furniture stores.

She scowled as he handed her the form.

She handed it back and said, "You haven't identified the files you want to borrow."

Wally smiled and said, "I have to get to the files or a database before I can tell you what I need."

"I require a name or a file reference or you go back to your cell." She held her cell phone in her hand like a gun.

"Colton Harris Moore," Wally lied, remembering the notorious Northwest teenage fugitive, now captured and, himself, on trial. "I'm doing research on the Barefoot Bandit."

"Popular topic," she said. She handed Wally a sheet of computer paper. "Go to computer number one," she said. "Enter this code on your sheet. You have one hour."

Wally luxuriated in the open space. Shelves of books around him were a plus. Computer number one opened with the code, and documents appeared that Wally had no interest in. He searched the applications menu on the tool bar above the desktop for access to his email or Google, then gave up.

A tall youngster in a prison jumpsuit that didn't quite fit sat down at the next station.

"I know you," Wally said.

"Hi, Mr. Winchester," the young man said. "You're my neighbor from Camano Island. What are you doing here?"

"I've been wrongly accused," Wally said.

"Boy, howdy," the tall boy said. "What are you in for? I don't get any newspapers in here."

"They say I committed eleven or twelve murders and bombed an auction house in Kansas City."

"Wow, Mr. Winchester, I'm proud to have broken into your house. You humble me."

"You broke into my house, you little shit?" Wally asked looking up into the boy's eyes.

"Your doors were never locked. I just hung out when you were away. You were away a lot. I fed your cat."

"Why didn't you steal anything?"

"What am I going to do with a three hundred pound chair? Open a cigar store? I liked the way it felt in your cabin. You've got a great hot tub. Nothing there I needed."

"I didn't kill anyone, except one guy in New York State," Wally said. "I was framed."

"I hear that a lot here," the young man said.

Chapter Fifty-Five

Everett, Washington

Detective Kelly walked into the long-term auto storage building in downtown Everett and told a middle aged receptionist, sporting a leg cast that he wanted to speak with the owner.

The owner, she told him, didn't like to be disturbed.

Kelly flashed a badge and a smile and was escorted to a cluttered office. Inside he saw auto calendars from the 30's featuring buxom bathing beauties holding hand tools. A short, bald wreck of a man looked up from a dog-eared Penthouse magazine and told him to scram.

Kelly tipped an upholstered chair and sent five pounds of unopened bills and mail order catalogs sliding onto the floor. He sat down, ignored the old man's protest, and held up a photo of the dead Mexican killer. He said, "Her name was Manuelita."

The old face fell. "That photograph. Is she dead? I had nothing to do with it. I never touched her. Maybe brushed into her once or twice. This office is crowded."

"When did you hire her?" Kelly asked.

"Couple of months ago, perhaps three. I'll have to check. I'll get back to you."

Kelly looked at the state of the office; he didn't expect he'd hear from him soon. "Who referred her to you?" he asked.

"She just showed up, just as the other girl took her crazy vacation."

"I can padlock this garage," Kelly said. "Day parking, everything. Call it a crime scene."

"What?"

"Tell me about the Shelby that was parked here."

"Third floor. Long-term storage. Mostly expensive cars. We gave it a section all by itself, owner's instructions. Blue Shelby replica, a pretty thing. The guy kept it under a tarp."

"Why did you change attendants?"

"My girl gets this free vacation in the mail. Breaks her leg skiing, for Christ's sake. Skiing. She's a fucking grandmother. Screws up the schedule. This Mexican gal shows up, looking for work. Lucky for me."

"Go on."

"I was going to give the front desk time to my wife's sister. Then a guy shows up, convinces me to hire the taco."

"Describe him."

"German, through and through. Looked like an actor…Rutger what's-his-name, after a bad day. He had a funny accent, maybe Mexican-like. Ricardo Montalban, I thought. So I hire the cutie and two weeks later she just up and quits. Does this have something to do with the Cobra we stored upstairs?"

Kelly cruised a public housing project in North Everett. He followed a hand-drawn map that Winchester had sketched on a piece of prison stationery. He parked behind a 70's muscle car on jack stands and walked through a haggard landscape of dying shrubs and discarded children's toys to the first door of the block. He worked the project, a mixture of Russian and Hispanic residents, flashing the picture of the dead girl. Twenty shut doors comprised the morning's work.

In the afternoon, an olive-skinned teenager recognized the death-mask photo. She recoiled. "Manuelita is dead?" she said in English.

"You know her?" Kelly flashed his badge, a can opener.

"She lived next door. For a time. Two men were there a lot, *mal hombres*. Then the *gringo* drove up in his fancy blue racing car and she was gone. Is she really dead? She sure looks dead."

"I'm afraid so," Kelly said. "Are the men still next door?"

"We never saw them again. The neighborhood is still talking about the car. We all hoped it was taking one of our own, our Manuelita, to a life of luxury."

"Manuelita?"

"*Si, Manuelita.*"

"Did Manuelita have a last name?"

"I never heard it, just Manuelita."

Kelly struck out at the apartment next door. A belligerent Russian chased him off his porch.

A message in his mind kept blinking. He couldn't grab it. He thought about the Mariners, changed the subject. Five losses in a row. The nagging thought crystallized: *the car*. This fucking Shelby racer. The car was at the center of Winchester's version of the killing spree, yet no one knew where it was.

Where is the car? Kelly asked himself. It must be a forensic Garden of Eden.

Chapter Fifty-Six

Seattle, Washington

Yvgeney sat at his computer in a Seattle hotel room. On the monitor, a map of the United States linked Wally's supposed kill zones, ending at Johnny's farm. He was missing something.

He looked at the Boston murder site. Wally'd told him he left the Shelby in the middle of a firefight at a Woburn park, fleeing in a police car that Manuelita had somehow stolen.

Where was the car? The two hundred thousand dollar Cobra? It must be filled with proof that Wally was traveling with a killer.

He dialed Chana, asleep on the floor in a nearby room.

"I know, where *is* the race car?" she answered.

Yvgeney said, "We have to go back to Massachusetts."

Chapter Fifty-Seven

Seattle, Washington

By the third day of incarceration in his new Federal digs just south of the SeaTac runway, Wally grew tired of the industrial “brute” simplicity of his cell. One piece of quartersawn oak furniture in this space, he thought, would add so much warmth. He ran the options, factoring in that he was not Al Capone, a cartel drug czar, or the Birdman of Alcatraz and decided to think about a more achievable goal.

In the quiet moments between takeoffs and arrivals outside his walls, his cell was noiseless, a spooky silence. His eyes danced around the gunmetal colored walls.

It took four hours to embrace the color. It wasn’t just grey, Wally realized – a simple mixture of black and white – it was a hint of cadmium orange, some yellow, a tinge of brown. He felt better.

Alone with his thoughts, he asked himself, why am I here? A guy wants to buy my car one day and now I’m in prison. I may never see a Puget Sound sunset again. Ever. But, he smiled, wasn’t it fun to drive.

Where was the car? He’d left it in a little town north of Boston called Woburn, Massachusetts. He lay back on the metal bed and allowed himself to revisit the day of Manuelita’s death. Tears ran as he marched through the details in search of something missed.

Wally slapped his own forehead. “We never passed papers,” he said, alone, into the room. “I have the bill of sale and the title still in my wallet, wherever the fuck it is. The car is still mine. Hot damn.”

Dinner was a form of pot roast with mashed potatoes and green beans served with a container of milk and soggy pie. He ate it, and slipped a note to the invisible attendant asking for access to his attorney.

Chapter Fifty-Eight

Boston, Massachusetts

Yvgeney and Chana landed at Logan Airport in the middle of a classic New England nor'easter. The jet skewed a bit and righted itself on the rain-soaked runway as it landed in a 20 mph sidewind.

"Do you want to look for the car tonight?" Yvgeney asked as the line of travelers cleared the aisle.

Chana typed Wally's GPS username and password into her phone and opened up a map of the East Coast that zoomed to a lattice of small roads in the north end of Woburn, Massachusetts.

"The weather is perfect," she said. "We should take advantage."

North of Woburn's center, the elegant Victorian homes petered out, replaced by Cape Cod ramblers. Yvgeney drove the rental under Interstate 95 on a two-lane road that told him that Lowell was twenty miles ahead. Scrub forests and decay suggested that progress and prosperity marched more slowly the farther you got from Boston.

Following the GPS signal, they turned into a sprawling auto junkyard, fenced and locked. A decrepit grouping of tin shacks caught the headlights. Yvgeney parked the rental and watched for dogs as he picked the lock. Hard rain soaked their faces.

The locked door to the second building yielded to Yvgeney's army knife. The Cobra was there, revealed with a flash of the Maglight. They approached the car in the dark. Chana thought about Manuelita and Wally elbow to elbow for a week on the road in the tiny cockpit and shuddered.

Yvgeney played the tiny beam of his pen light across the surface. He stopped at a ragged dimple. "Gunshot," he said in a voice one click from inaudible. "Good sized gun, maybe a .45 or a rifle."

Chana opened the door and a dashboard lamp lit up. She found a toggle and returned the cold garage back to darkness. Her flashlight lit the floor under the steering wheel and revealed a bed of Wally trash. Candy wrappers, spent tissues, gas receipts and fast food cartons that her *gringo* friend seemed to generate wherever he traveled.

Yvgeney, at the passenger door, tilted the leather seat forward to look for anything relevant to Wally's defense. He found a bag of softening tropical fruit, a week's worth of neglect sprouting furry mold hair.

The passenger floor was relatively clean. A crumpled square of notepaper under the seat held a phone number. He spread the folds with a ballpoint pen and a latte straw. The area code was unfamiliar to the Russian. He committed the number to memory and placed it back where he found it.

"A vehicle is approaching," Chana said quietly.

He flashed the penlight across the interior. "That door," he said.

They walked in the dark and found the storeroom entrance with extended fingers.

A strong flashlight outside the garage illuminated greasy glass panes. The door opened and a dark-clothed figure walked in.

From the edge of a door jamb Yvgeney watched the Shelby light up under the strong light beam. The intruder inspected the sheet metal and stopped at the bullet hole, just like he'd done. The driver's door opened and Yvgeney saw the face of Detective Kelly. He was speaking into a tape recorder.

In the dark, Yvgeney reached for and found Chana's shoulder, then touched her head. He felt her nod approval.

"Detective Kelly," Yvgeney shouted out into the dark building shell.

The flashlight spun wildly, then went dark. "Identify yourself," Kelly shouted.

"Yvgeney Ivanchenko," echoed in the cold darkness. "From Moriarti's team."

"So you found the car. How'd you do it? GPS off Wally's computer? The one that was missing?"

"How about you?" Yvgeney asked.

"Old fashioned police work," Kelly said. He switched the flashlight on. "Come on out," he said. "I think we're on the same side."

Yvgeney walked into the flashlight beam and approached the car.

"Your associate, Chana, is invited," Kelly said.

"She is probably on the perimeter by now," Yvgeney said. "She loves that sentry thing."

"I have a guy outside also. A local boy from the Woburn PD with a search warrant. I hope they get along."

"Chana's new hobby is compassionate restraint."

"Looks like a bullet hole in the Cobra," Kelly said. "A big bullet."

"A Dirty Harry gun or a high powered rifle."

"Did you find anything inside?"

"I found a phone number, left it under the seat where I found it."

"Good. Did you recognize it?"

"Didn't know the prefix, but I'd bet it was Claus Braun's."

"The mysterious Claus Braun. The man you say is behind the whole murder spree."

Chana watched the North American plain-clothes detective as he looked into the abandoned building through a foggy windowpane. She determined him to be a zero threat and continued her silent perimeter walk. She found a dark sedan with a driver's side spotlight, hidden behind an outbuilding. It had Massachusetts' plates with an official shield in the upper corner.

She continued to the backside of the rambling collection of shacks and came to a white van, locked. The hood was warm. A yellow license plate was from Ohio, a rental tag in the corner. She called Yvgeney. "We have company," she said.

"Incorrect, Chana," Yvgeney's terse voice said. "The company has us. Come in, please. No weapons."

A body lay by the front door, the perimeter cop, with his throat opened up and still pumping blood. She looked inside and saw Yvgeney and Detective Kelly skewered by a flashlight beam, three silhouettes standing between her and the car. She placed her pack at the entrance and started toward the pool of light, then stopped, still invisible.

"Walk to your friends, Chana. Into the light," Braun's voice said.

"No."

"No? I have three guns aimed at your Russian."

"Señor Braun," Chana said. "You were my teacher. Why would I give up my stealth to march into the sights of your rifles?"

The reverberation of a diesel engine filled the tin structure. A big door opened and the back end of a car hauler beeped as it backed up to the Cobra. Two large men fixed a chain to the car and hauled it onto the flatbed with a screeching winch. Chana watched silently as the men dogged it down and chocked the wheels. Another diesel roar and the transport rumbled out into the dark night, leaving Yvgeney and the detective alone in a flashlight beam.

"My name is Chana," she spoke to Braun's men in the hollow darkness surrounding the flashlight beams. "Put your weapons on the ground and turn off your lamps. If you don't, I will find you after I find everyone you love."

She watched two of the three flashlights shake, then wink out.

"Cowards," Braun's voice screamed. He fired at the fleeing figures.

"So you're the great Claus Braun?" The statement came from the detective in the remaining light beam. "The mastermind."

"Talk to me, Chana," Braun's voice said into the darkness, ignoring the words from the person in his crosshairs.

"If you choose to leave now, I will allow it; you'll be alive and unfollowed." Chana said.

"I have the gun. And I have your friends in my sights. You are weaponless, and according to you, you win."

"You taught me well, Señor Braun."

"I've got some questions for you before you go," Kelly said, still skewered in the rifle sights.

"I'm talking to the lady, not to a dead man," Braun said. From behind the flashlight a shot rang out. Kelly fell to his knees and toppled over.

"I still want you as my Chief of Security, Chana," Braun's voice said.

"If you leave now, I promise not to chase you down, sir," Chana said.

"Hey, Braun," Yvgeney, still in the spotlight, shouted out. "Placing a bomb in a chair that the target person would buy is a brilliant variation on a shaped charge. Congratulations."

"Another person won it. Ruined my plans," Braun's voice said. "Wanted it to be in Winchester's backseat as it blew up. The perfect dart. Instead some panic sent all the bidders out of the building. Someone called *bomb,* I was told. I had to set it off, hoping to catch Winchester still in the room. It's not my best work."

"Some tech writer in Quantico will name it after you, Braun, your whole trap was brilliant. I've never seen a more perfect punishment box."

"The drones around me have no clue. It's taken three years to construct my perfect revenge, part of which involves you, the meddling Russian."

Chana said, "If you shoot Yvgeney I will be forced to act against you, Señor Braun. Please walk away."

The room went black when Braun killed the flashlight. Chana ran in the dark to Yvgeney and the fallen detective.

Chapter Fifty-Nine

Spokane, Washington

For Wally, the journey to U.S. District Court for his Federal arraignment was an elevator ride from the third floor to the lobby of the SeaTac Holding Facility, seven hours travel, ankle irons shackled to the floor of a government van, and a hobbled walk into the Spokane Federal Courthouse where he was met by his attorney in a side room with a U.S. Marshal at the door.

Victor Jay Moriarti handed him a freshly pressed grey suit on a hanger, along with shiny brown shoes and a red-striped tie. "The Constitution of the United States of America guarantees you the right to look your best when you are tried by a jury of your peers," he said.

Wally stepped out of an orange jump suit that hadn't seen a laundry for a week and donned the civilian clothes. "They fit," he said. "Who picked it out for me?"

"That young man, Alfred, from your support team bought you a checkerboard suit coat from a frightful place called *Value Village* but Arial rejected it. She brought this outfit from home, a suit her stepfather grew out of."

Wally checked out his reflection in an interior window; thought he looked sharp. "Let's go," he said.

The bright fluorescent tubes in the modern courtroom were a disappointment. Wally marched through a side door with Moriarti at his side. He looked at the visitor seating and spotted the kids from his antiques club next to Yvgeney and Chana. He gave thumbs up and regretted it when Alfred started applauding and shouted, "Free Wally," an outburst that irritated the judge, a sour-faced man who wore the flat-topped hair of a military veteran. Wally looked across the aisle at the prosecution team. He had met the head guy, a fellow named George Butler, several times during a series of interrogations that they called 'interviews.' His smile was met with a stony stare. Moriarti told him to sit down and keep his mouth shut.

When the prosecution opened the arraignment by announcing charges of crossing state lines to commit a Federal crime, conspiracy to overthrow the Government of the United States, aiding and abetting a known terrorist organization, namely the Tamil Tigers, and the theft of a vehicle and sailboat to cross an international border, Wally nearly fainted.

"Conspiracy to overthrow the government?" he asked in a loud whisper.

"That's the bombing of the Kansas City auction house," Moriarti hissed. "I like that charge. We can beat that one easily. The other ones make me nervous."

The prosecutor sat. Judge Keller asked, "How do you plead?"

"Not guilty," Moriarti shouted out, closing Wally's mouth with an angry look.

"We request remand because of the heinous nature of the crimes," the prosecution said.

Moriarti stood quickly. "Mr. Winchester," he said, "is a respected member of the Camano Island community. He has no criminal record. He is no flight risk. Please allow reasonable bail."

Judge Keller said, "He's accused, among the charges, of flying to Sri Lanka in the middle of a murder spree, and acting as an agent for a known terrorist organization upon his return. And you say he is not a flight risk."

Moriarti said, "Take his passport, Your Honor. He's just a Camano Island small businessman with limited funds and few assets."

"I'll take the passport and a half million dollars for bail, but the defendant has to agree to wear an ankle bracelet with a GPS and not leave the state."

Moriarti said, "Thank you," and sat down.

A note was passed from the gallery. Moriarti read it, written in a childlike scrawl.

"We have the money. From Alfred," it said.

Moriarti shared the paper scrap with Wally who whispered, "That's all they have in their bank account. I won't let them risk the team's money like that. Let me stay in jail."

Moriarti, oblivious to the public venue, said, "Are you going to flee? Bail is to insure you show up. They get their money back if you show up at your trial."

Wally said, "I'm not going anywhere. I promise. Do I get to go home?"

"A couple of weeks, at least. The ankle GPS doesn't keep you in your cabin, just tells the Feds where you are."

"So I can go picking, track down the leads I've been working on, go to flea markets?"

"Please understand, Wally. You are facing life in prison. This time out of jail is to help you prepare your defense. I hope that is high on your priority list."

"It's right up there," Wally whispered. "Right after getting my hands on the Marshmallow Sofa from Butte, Montana and the early Gus bookcase in West Virginia. What do we do next?"

"You go to a holding cell upstairs while the paperwork is worked out," Moriarti said.

"Back to the orange jumpsuit?" Wally asked.

"It's a good look on you, Wally, the orange. I suggest you embrace it."

Soft Focus

Chapter Sixty

Camano Island, Washington

Wally walked into the cabin he hadn't seen in two months. Most of the lights were on, the dark bulbs dead. He cringed at the thought of his electricity bill.

"Where's my computer?" he shouted when he reached his office.

"The kids took it," Yvgeney said. "Danny replaced your G4 with another outdated tower; that's the one the police confiscated. They're still pissed off."

"So I can check my email?"

"Doesn't your phone do it? Mine does."

"What phone? The Feds have everything I need to connect to the network. I have a lot of balls in the air."

Wally cleared the carbon out of the cylinders of his old Ford van on the way south to see his lawyer. The trusty 390 engine fought the negligence for five miles, then remembered its place and purred all the way to Seattle.

"This is how I'm attacking the prosecution's evidence," Moriarti said.

Wally watched passenger ferry traffic out his attorney's window. He said, "How can I help?"

"You can help by listening to my strategies for your defense and telling me anything you can think of that would help."

Wally listened.

After hearing his options he said, “Detective Kelly told me he could help get the early Gus bookcase I bought in West Virginia back to Camano Island. Do you guys talk?”

“Please focus on your trial. Do you have any photographs of this Mexican woman or you and your car?”

“I have no photos of Manuelita, but I took a number of pictures of the car. Those will be on my hard drive.”

“We need them,” Moriarti said. “Can you think of anyone in America who saw you with this Manuelita?”

“Hundreds,” Wally said. “But I don’t know who they are. We drove three thousand miles. Lots of people saw us.”

Moriarti said, “I need people that I can track down who would remember you together. Waitresses who you argued with, dealers still alive who saw you and her and the car together.”

“We bought a Marshmallow couch as a fake married couple. No one died in Butte, Montana, according to the news.”

“Chana’s been there. We have them,” Moriarti said. “Who else?”

“We went to a freaky super patriot’s house in Eau Claire, Wisconsin. Am I accused of murdering anyone there?”

“Not that I’ve heard,” Moriarti said. “Do you have a phone number or an address?”

“This asshole won’t take kindly to anyone of authority looking for information,” Wally said. “I called him from an upholstery shop. The number’s on my cell. Good luck with that crazy motherfucker.”

“Where’d you go next?”

“The next real stop was in Shipshewana. We parked the Cobra there for a few days. A bunch of the flea market crowd should remember the car and us. Find the people who sell rat shit mixed with M&M’s or the guy who makes poodle dogs from balloons and sticks.

Maybe the guy who sells original Nike socks. And then there's the Rohlfs Queen."

Moriarti made a face as he wrote the notes on a pad.

Wally drove north to his home.

Alone in the cabin for the first time in months, he sat at the monitor, like old times. He scrolled through two hundred messages, saved eBay searches, and regular postings, found ten people who wanted to be his friend on Facebook. The message from Stacie Morningstar stood out. He opened it and read, "Hey, Wally, thanks for saving my sorry ass. The doctors in Kansas kept me for a week till my brain swelling went down. They told me you saved my life, though I don't remember most of it. A west coast visit is on my bucket list. Stacie."

He forwarded the message to his lawyer.

Night fell as Wally watched the sun set over the Olympic Mountains. He took some time to sear the moment in his memory.

Chapter Sixty-One

Spokane, Washington

Wally entered the courtroom in Spokane wearing Arial's stepdad's suit for the second day. He was calmer now, somewhat frightened at the reality in which he found himself.

At his client's side, Moriarti removed his cowboy hat as Judge Keller walked in. He'd studied Judge Keller's record, found him an advocate of gun rights, voted Republican. The judge, he'd learned, had a substantial collection of exotic weapons that he kept in his chambers and flaunted to special visitors. Moriarti thought he was perfect for the trial.

The lead Federal prosecutor began the trial with an opening statement of the case against Wally Winchester. He left the chair and spoke to the jury: "The Government intends to prove that the defendant, Wally Winchester, seated over there," he pointed and paused, "in collaboration with the Tamil Tigers from Sri Lanka, a known terrorist group condemned by the UN for their atrocities, drove across our country, killing people in his wake, until he got to Boston where he flew to meet his controllers in Sri Lanka, returning to bomb an auction house in Kansas City. He was caught while trying to sail a stolen boat into Canada from Port Angeles.

"Every crime scene leads to the defendant. We have witnesses and flight records and a paper trail that will prove the defendant guilty of multiple murders, theft, and bombings, designed to undermine the fabric of the United States of America. Did he commit these crimes for personal gain or ideology? That is a question that really doesn't need to be answered. My job is to connect Walter Winchester to a series of crimes. Your job, as the jury, is to determine the truth and to implement justice for the crimes committed against this great country."

The judge asked, "Is the defendant ready with an opening statement?"

Moriarti stood up, asked the judge for permission to don his cowboy hat. He got it.

He walked like John Wayne toward the jury, stood before the twelve and said, "I represent a good American, Wally Winchester." He turned. "Stand up, Wally," he said.

Wally did. The judge frowned.

"Sit down, Wally," Moriarti said.

Wally sat.

"This good citizen made a deal on the internet to sell a car, a Shelby Cobra, a fine work of art, valued at one hundred seventy-five thousand dollars, to a client in Boston, Massachusetts. Mr. Winchester sells fine works of art for a living. He agreed to drive the vehicle to the new owner in Boston, which he did, taking with him a young Mexican woman as a companion. The defendant himself was ignorant of any crimes committed on the journey. I intend to prove that. I intend to prove that Wally Winchester had a murderer in the passenger seat, but didn't know it."

Moriarti took off his cowboy hat and looked at each of the jurors in the eyes before sitting down.

Detective Mike Kelly, wearing an arm sling, took the stand for the prosecution. The prosecutor approached him in the witness box. "Are you the lead homicide detective in charge of the Spokane Hindu temple murder investigation?"

"Yes, sir."

"Please describe your findings."

"Spokane homicide got a call at 11:04 a.m on Monday, May 17th. A body found at 1127 West Division. I arrived at 11:35."

"Go on."

"The victim was male, age forty-seven. Cause of death appeared to be knife wounds to the chest and abdomen."

"Was the murder weapon found?"

"Not at the time."

"Were there any witnesses to the crime?"

"No."

"Tell the court about the evidence discovered."

"I found blood traces on the floor that ended at the front door."

"If it pleases the court," the prosecutor said, "I'd like to submit photographs of the floor of the crime scene." Judge Keller nodded as three large blow-ups were offered to the jury. One showed an eviscerated body, intestines spilling out onto the floor. A juror gasped.

Moriarti leaped up and objected. "Is it necessary to display a four-foot photo of internal organs?" he asked.

"Overruled," Keller said. "Size doesn't matter. It's evidence."

The prosecutor continued, "Can you determine the identity of the killer by the footprints in the blood?"

"Unfortunately, no. They were deliberately scuffed and twisted to obscure a proper analysis."

The prosecutor looked to Moriarti, who raised no objection as he looked into his hat.

"What else did you find?"

"The victim held a business card in his hand."

"Is this the card?" Another large photo was offered and accepted as evidence.

"Yes. I was there when the tech took this photo."

"What was the name on the card, Officer Kelly?"

"Objection, Your Honor. The name is a foot high, the photo's so large."

"Overruled. Please speak clearly for the stenographer."

"Wally Winchester."

"What did you do about this evidence?"

"I drove across the Cascades the next day to interview Mr. Winchester, but he was not home. Word was he had taken a trip to the East Coast."

As the detective described the Montana campground killings and the second business card, Wally's eyes wandered across faces in the gallery behind him. He found Rae's face looking back. His heart lurched. He looked away, conflicted.

On the witness stand, Kelly recounted the deaths in Fargo, North Dakota, and his first suspicion that he was looking for a serial killer. Moriarti took notes on a yellow pad.

Yvgeney leaned forward from the gallery and whispered into Moriarti's ear. Wally turned and watched him and Chana stand up and march out of the courtroom.

"What's up?" He whispered.

"Pay attention to the trial," Moriarti held up the legal pad and pointed to a stick figure drawing. Wally recognized the game called *hangman*. He gulped. Moriarti said, "If the jury thinks you don't care about the testimony, they'll do this to you." Wally got the point and focused his attention on the detective's answers.

It was the defense's turn to cross-examine. Moriarti held his white cowboy hat like a bible to his heart. "Good afternoon, Detective Kelly," he said. "Sorry you are injured. Did you receive that injury while working on the case?"

"Yes," Kelly said. "It was…"

"We'll get back to that injury later," Moriarti said. "I'm surprised our prosecutor didn't bring it up. Let's go back to the Hindu church. What was your first thought as to the motive when you arrived at the crime scene? Robbery, crime of passion, assassination, or a hate crime?"

"I was looking for Doc Martin boot prints because the church, that is, the temple, had received a number of threats."

"Describe the threats, please."

"Phone calls, a number of letters, a swastika spray-painted on the front door."

"You said the footprints were deliberately distorted, Detective Kelly. What would that suggest?"

"It indicated that the killer made a conscious effort to obscure his identity," Kelly answered.

Moriarti walked over to the evidence table, grabbed the giant photo of Wally's bloodstained business card, and carried it over to the defense table. He handed it to Wally and asked him to hold it up over his head.

"Objection," the prosecutor shouted. "My colleague wants to turn this trial into a circus."

"Bear with me, Your Honor," Moriarti said.

"I'll give you one more step out on this branch before it breaks, counselor. Overruled."

"Moriarti turned back to the detective and asked, "You tell me the killer took great pains to hide his, or her, identity by obliterating bloody footprints, yet leaves a business card at the murder scene. Does that make any sense to you?"

"No, sir, it doesn't" Kelly said.

"What does your gut say, Detective Kelly?"

"Objection. Calls for speculation."

Moriarti was quick to answer. "That's all right, Your Honor. I'll drop it, try the question again. Detective Kelly, how many murders have you investigated in your career?"

"Never added them up," Kelly answered. "I'd guess a couple hundred."

"I'll accept that," Moriarti said. "In all your cases, how many murderers tried to cover up their involvement and at the same time deliberately left a calling card with their name on it for the police to find?"

"None."

"Thank you, detective. Have you found any evidence that there was a second person traveling with my client on his cross-country trip?"

"A number of witnesses described a young Latin American woman."

"You said the bloody footprints, even smeared, seem to belong to a small foot. Could they be those of a woman?"

"Objection. Leading the witness."

"Sustained. Watch your step, Mr. Moriarti."

"Yes, sir," Moriarti said, holding eye contact with the detective. "Detective Kelly, you tell the court no murder weapon was found at the Spokane, Montana, and Fargo crime scenes."

"That's correct."

"Was it found elsewhere?"

.The prosecutor cast a wicked glare at Moriarti.

"Yes."

"Tell the court, now, detective, about the weapon that was found and where it was located."

"An assault knife similar to a Navy SEAL weapon was recovered from a Massachusetts crime scene. The Woburn police sent me a photo and the results of forensic analysis."

"Tell me about the forensics, detective."

"Your Honor, this line of questioning is premature. The defense has the list of our witnesses and the forensics through discovery. We plan to introduce this evidence at a later time with an FBI analyst."

“Gee, I’m sorry,” Judge Keller said. “The act of cross-examination has its own rules. You called this witness to testify. The defense has every right to ask him what he knows. Too bad it messes up your playlist. Answer the question, Detective.”

Kelly said, “There was conjoined blood evidence from four separate samples found in or around the hilt. DNA from all three victims of the Grove Park Inn crime and also from a yet-to-be-identified Latin American body found at a campsite in New York State.”

“Is my client, Mr. Winchester, accused of these killings?”

“I’m just the investigator, Mr. Moriarti, but I believe all the deaths listed in the indictment are wrapped up into the conspiracy charge. So, yes.”

“Were any fingerprints found on the knife?”

“The Massachusetts report listed one set of prints found.”

“To whom did they belong?”

“The report matched them to a woman, found dead in a stolen police car in Woburn, Massachusetts.”

“A Latin American woman with small feet?”

“Objection. Detective Kelly has no information about her feet.”

“Sustained. Move along, Mr. Moriarti.”

Moriarti held out his western hat. He looked inside at the sweatband as though he saw an answer there.

“Detective Kelly,” he said. “Is there any evidence on the murder weapon, blood or fingerprint, that links it with my client, the defendant?”

“No.”

“Thank you, Detective Kelly. You deserve a lot of credit for linking this string of terrible crimes together. Let me get this right. The prosecution actually has possession of the knife that killed four people named in the indictment, a weapon consistent with the wounds of six other victims including the Hindu gentleman, killed by a person with small feet here in this fine city. And by your own admission, there are no eyewitnesses that link the defendant to any actual killing? Did I get that right, Detective?"

From the stand, Kelly looked at the prosecutor's table. No objections flew from his tight lips.

"That's why the charge is conspiracy, not murder."

Moriarti looked into his hat again and said, "So, the Government's contention is that the defendant conspired with someone else to murder a string of innocent people and then purposely left his business card at the crime scenes so the police could find him? That would make this the dumbest conspiracy in the history of crime. Sounds to me a lot more like a frame-up."

"Objection."

"I'm done with this witness," Moriarti said. He looked up at the clock, saw it was 4:00 p.m. and started thinking about dinner.

The mood at a large table in the restored Davenport Hotel was cautiously optimistic.

Wally sipped from a glass of water as he checked out the light fixtures and Victorian furniture used in the remodel, thinking he could have done better. He said, "You kicked a little ass today, counselor. I liked the trick of looking into your hat for clues."

"Do you think I wear this thing for looks?" Moriarti said. "I'm Irish. I've been finding answers in this old hat for years. We have a long way to go, son. I may have planted reasonable doubt into the jury's mind, but it's only the first day. The gun you purchased is in evidence. The prosecutors holding that for later."

"I did shoot that Mexican," Wally said, "but it was self-defense. He was going to shoot Manuelita."

"It's not self-defense, Wally," Yvgeney said, "if he wasn't trying to kill you."

"I could probably squeeze a self-defense verdict out of those circumstances, Yvgeney, but we have bigger hurdles," Moriarti said. "The bombing is their anchor crime. Your attempt to sell old photos to aid the Tamil Cultural Center is a problem, but I've got a researcher working on that, a former Homeland Security expert."

Alfred spoke up. "Wally makes a lot of deals," he said. "That's his job. He's still teaching us. He's the coolest teacher we ever had."

"I know," Moriarti said. "The United States has a hard-on about aiding terrorist groups, son. Excuse me, Arial, for my language."

"I'm familiar with the term," Arial said. She touched knuckles with Ron and unsuccessfully suppressed a grin.

"They've got you on stealing a boat and entering Canada, Wally," Moriarti said. He sipped a Glenlivet single malt. "That could cost you a couple of years unless we get lucky."

"What happens tomorrow?" Wally asked.

"Tomorrow they bring out a number of witnesses who met you on the buying trip from hell, according to discovery, a campground attendant, the auctioneer in Fargo, the desk clerk at the Grove Park Inn, and a detective from the Woburn, Mass. PD. Then there's the auctioneer from Kansas City or one of his guys. Finally they have the boat owner in Port Angeles."

Chana spoke quietly. She said, "Yvgeney and I retrieved a month's worth of Wally's mail from the Stanwood Post Office today. *Wally Winchester* is not a popular name there right now."

"What did you find?" Moriarti asked.

"An amazing pile of junk mail," Chana said. "Makes me glad I live in Siberia. I have a package that might be interesting, though. It has no return address and holds a DVD."

"Anyone have a laptop?" Moriarti asked.

Danny spoke, "I have a titanium power book." He pulled the old Mac from his pack, powered it up, and slipped in the DVD.

The image on the screen was Manuelita. Wally held back a sob when he saw her face.

Behind her was a blank wall. The lighting was not flattering as she looked into the camera and spoke. "My name is Manuelita," she said in passable English. "I'm in Boston, Massachusetts. This is my confession."

A waitress came to the big table for the food order. They chased her away.

Chapter Sixty-Two

Spokane, Washington

Day two of Wally's trial began at 9:00 a.m. The prosecutor, as advertised, brought out the attendant from a Montana campground. He pointed to Wally as a guy in a sports car who rented space number 12 by the lake. Moriarti passed on cross-examination.

A detective from Missoula next described the bloody murder scene found near Wally's tent space. The details were gruesome. He told the court about the business card he found next to one of the bodies, throat cut and left in the bushes to bleed out. Moriarti watched the jury's reaction to photographs of the two bodies. He took his turn on cross-exam.

"Are there any witnesses to the crime?" he asked the officer.

"No, just a business card."

"The same card left at the Hindu temple?" Moriarti asked.

"Beats me. This is what I found."

"So the defendant, Wally Winchester, spent a night at a campground and later you found his business card in the site he rented," Moriarti said.

"It was placed next to a bloody corpse," the Missoula cop said.

"Placed?"

"I mean found nearby. Don't twist my words."

"It's my job to find the truth," he said. "I'm done." Moriarti sat down and smiled at the prosecutor's stony glare.

The auctioneer from a Fargo, North Dakota factory sale was next. He pointed to Wally as the guy who shook everyone up with a huge bid on a mirrored work lamp. Moriarti let him leave without questions.

A Fargo cop took the stand, describing the scene of four homicides, ending with a business card. Moriarti asked him for eyewitnesses to the crime, acknowledging his client's presence in the parking lot. The man said there weren't any. Moriarti thanked him.

Next for the Government was the desk clerk from the Grove Park Inn. The prosecutor asked him if he remembered seeing the defendant at the Inn the weekend of the shooting. He pointed to Wally behind the table as if it were a guilty verdict.

Moriarti took his turn on the cross. "So you met Wally Winchester across the check-in desk?"

"He was hard to miss. He bragged about trying to buy the painting behind me even as his credit card rejected the room charge."

"So the defendant, Wally Winchester, didn't try to enter your hotel in a stealth mode. He made his presence known."

"I watched him cruise the grand hall. Five minutes later, he had two thousand dollars cash to pay for his room. I had to give him credit. I take the bus to work."

Moriarti thanked him and returned to the defense table to huddle with his client.

The prosecution entered crime scene photos from the underground spa. Wally winced at the bloody tableau. A Quantico lab tech was sworn in and introduced DNA, found on a hotel bathrobe, left amid the carnage. Wally swept the faces of the gallery and didn't see Rae. He was thankful.

When the prosecution asked the lab expert if the DNA matched any in the database, he said it belonged to the defendant, Walter Winchester. The gallery was still.

On cross-examination, Moriarti asked about the DNA source and was told: *semen*. He strolled to the defense table and returned with a white, terry cloth robe.

"Objection. That garment is not in evidence. Your honor, this is another circus stunt."

"Mr. Moriarti?" Judge Keller tapped his fingers on the desk. He looked annoyed.

"I'm trying to determine who wore the robe at the crime scene, Your Honor. The garment is a visual aid."

"Tread carefully," the judge said.

"With the court's permission, I need someone to put the robe on. How about you, Mr. Winchester?"

Wally looked up from his legal pad.

"Stand up, Mr. Winchester, and put this robe over your shoulders," Moriarti said,

"Objection! The defense can't play dress-up with the defendant. It's a joke. It would prejudice the jury."

Judge Keller said, "I agree. Sit back down, Mr. Winchester, and stay seated."

"May I request a sidebar?" Moriarti asked the judge.

Judge Keller nodded and waived both attorneys to his bench. "You're five seconds away from a contempt citation, Moriarti," he said.

"I can prove my client wasn't wearing that robe, Your Honor. I need a person to wear it for my demonstration."

"You can *prove* that DNA goldmine wasn't worn by the DNA contributor?" the prosecutor whispered. "I'd like to see that."

"So would I," the judge said. "But you're not using your client as a runway model. Not in my court."

"Can I use another of my defense team, Your Honor?"

"You have five minutes. If I feel you've damaged the integrity of my trial, you sleep in a cell tonight. Got it?"

Moriarti nodded and motioned to Chana in the gallery. She approached the bench and slipped her arms into the sleeves. "Thank you, Your Honor," the attorney said as he walked the slight South American native over to the witness stand.

"You personally processed the DNA evidence on the hotel robe?" he asked the lab tech.

"Yes, sir."

"Can you show the court where the…samples…were found?" Moriarti looked into his cowboy hat and pulled a black Sharpie from the inside. "Better yet,' he said, "mark *X*'s on this robe to show the location."

"There was quite a lot of…evidence," the FBI man said.

"We have lots of ink in this marker, son."

"Objection."

"I'll allow it," Judge Keller said, interested.

Wally winced as the forensic expert marked dark crosses on the robe's interior fabric under Chana's armpits on both sides. He stole a look behind him at Yvgeney's disapproving face, mouthed the words, "We were in love."

The witness marked the outside surface. Twenty black crosses covered the shoulders and the top pocket where the name, Grove Park Inn, was stitched in tan thread.

"Was any DNA found lower on the robe?" Moriarti asked.

"A trace amount," the witness said.

"Mark that area, please."

"It would be indiscreet while the young lady is wearing it, sir."

"Describe the location."

"Inside the robe back by the buttock area."

"A big deposit like you found up around the chest area?"

"No sir, just a drop."

"Was there any…DNA…where the robe folded in front, say where the penis would come into contact when the garment was worn to walk around?"

"No, sir."

"In your professional opinion, was this robe worn by a man or a woman when the…contamination…was applied?"

"Objection!"

"Sustained. The branch is cracking, Mr. Moriarti."

"Sorry, Your Honor. Now, Chana…" Moriarti held off the tech's answer with an upturned hand. "Close the robe and rub it against your chest. Now open it for the court."

As she opened the garment like a flasher, the jury's eyes widened at the sight of thirty black crosses.

"Can I answer the question now?" the witness asked.

Moriarti walked back to the defendant's table. "You don't have to," he said. "X marks the spot, as the old saying goes."

In the afternoon session, the Government entered a pistol into evidence along with registration papers from a gun show naming the defendant.

Moriarti huddled with his client and said, "just your luck; you got the one gun dealer out of five who actually turns the registration forms in." He asked the court, "Is there forensic evidence that is linked to this weapon?"

The prosecutor made a face and said, "Yes, we plan to introduce it at a later time."

"Can the court hear it now?" Moriarti asked the judge. "The Government just opened the barn door."

"Your honor," the prosecutor said. "We have choreographed the witness list to best prove our case. My opponent seeks to disrupt the flow of evidence."

"If it would please the court," Moriarti said. "I've seen the forensics. The findings are relevant to the defense and don't help the Government's case at all."

"Objection. That declaration is prejudicial and draws a conclusion. I move to strike it."

"Sustained. Mind your manners, Mr. Moriarti. The jury will disregard the last statement. As to the defense request, yes. I, too, want to get the forensics into evidence. Let's do that now."

"Your Honor!"

"Is the prosecution prepared to introduce the forensic analyst?"

"The analyst is not in the building, Your Honor."

"Where is he, or she?"

"Back in Quantico, I suspect."

"Doesn't seem to be high on your priority list, sir." Judge Keller threw an angry look at the prosecutor. "When can you provide this witness?"

"Quantico's three thousand miles away, Your Honor."

"Tomorrow, then. Good. Let's take the afternoon off while the prosecution calls *Travelocity.com.*"

Wally eyed his attorney with new respect. "I'm glad you're not competing with me for vintage Stickley," he said.

Conroy Lincoln was standing in the shadows of the courthouse lobby when Winchester walked out of the chamber laughing with his attorney. Lincoln's face grew red. His meaty hands formed into fists. As he walked from the courthouse steps across the wide boulevard toward the office he rented last week under the name, Rockwell, he counted his steps, "two hundred one, two hundred two…"

In a top floor suite at the Davenport Hotel, Claus Braun sat in a lumpy Victorian armchair and read the trial details on the front page of the *Spokane Register & Review.* He threw the newspaper at the wall where it dropped to the floor near the *Seattle P.I.* and the *New York Times*. Muttering curses in Spanish, he opened the box of hair color gel and walked into the bathroom.

Chapter Sixty-Three

Spokane, Washington

A tired looking FBI analyst seemed uncomfortable in the witness box. The prosecutor approached. "Is this the weapon found at the Woburn, Massachusetts crime scene?" he asked.

"The chain of evidence is unbroken if the Government entered it," he said. "The answer is yes."

The prosecutor nodded, then asked, "Can I enter another exhibit at this time that is relevant to the questioning, Your Honor? It's a bullet."

"By all means," Judge Keller said.

The prosecutor unveiled a giant photo of a crumpled wad of lead.

"This is a slug found in a murder victim at a New York State campground," he said to the tech. "Did you compare it to the handgun here, registered to Walter Winchester?"

"Yes, sir. We determined the fatal bullet was fired from Mr. Winchester's weapon. 100 percent match."

The prosecutor smiled at Moriarti and said, "Your witness."

"Had a red-eye flight, son? Sorry you missed a night's sleep. The defense thanks you."

"Objection, Your Honor. Prejudicial."

"The court is always partial to civility, counselor. The defense can thank anyone it wants. Proceed, Mr. Moriarti."

"Thank you also, Your Honor," Moriarti said as he looked into the analyst's red-lined eyes. "Tell me, son, did you find fingerprints on the weapon?"

"Yes, sir."

"How many sets?"

"Just one."

"Do you know who they belong to, the fingerprints of the murderer who fired the weapon?"

"Objection."

"Sustained. Keep the conclusions to yourself, Moriarti."

"Yes, sir. To whom did the fingerprints belong?"

"They matched the prints of a dead woman who was found in a stolen police car eight miles from where the gun was found."

"Did you check for prints on the rest of the bullets in the clip?"

"We found one unfired round. Partials on the shell matched the deceased woman."

"Did you find any evidence that the defendant ever handled the gun or loaded it or fired it?"

"No, but it's registered to him," the tech stammered.

"Answer my question directly, please. I know you're weary. Did the FBI find any evidence that directly links the defendant with the shooting? Anything at all?"

"No."

"Thank you very much," Moriarti said. "Go get some sleep."

In the afternoon session, the prosecution shifted gears. The next witness was a Marine officer in uniform. Exhibits M and N were entered into evidence: First, two enlarged photographs of the aftermath of the auction house bombing showing mass destruction and broken windows. The second one showed three of the victims bleeding on the sidewalk.

"State your name," the prosecutor said.

"Major Stephen Roberts, USMC."

"You are bomb site investigator on loan to the FBI?"

"That's correct."

"Did you investigate the scene of the bombing at 3311 Stockyard Boulevard in Kansas City?"

"Yes, sir."

"What did you find?"

"We concluded that the explosion came from one source, a piece of furniture in the sale. We reconstructed the explosion pattern back to the focal point and identified the ignition locus as a European upholstered chair with C-4 explosive in the seat cushion. We found a picture of the intact chair from the auction catalogue."

"Is this the chair?" The prosecutor offered a blow-up photo of the *Sitzmachine*. Wally winced, thinking of the waste of such a great example of the secessionist form.

"Yes, sir. They call it a Morris chair."

"Based on the room, the crowd at the event, and the blast pattern, what would you think were the bomber's intentions?"

"It was designed to kill everyone in the room."

"Objection. How could he know the bomber's intentions?"

"Sustained. Ignore the answer, jury."

The Government called Micky Nestor to the stand. The young man looked nervous as he straightened his clip-on tie.

"Did you work at the auction house at 3311 Stockyard Boulevard at the time of the terrorist attack?" the prosecutor asked.

Moriarti stood, his hat in his hand. He said, "I take exception to that inflammatory phrasing, Your Honor. What happened to that civility you just talked about? Sure a bomb went off. I'm sorry there were people injured. The reason we're here today is to find out who is responsible for this terrible act. *Terrorist attack?* Would Your Honor please instruct the jury to erase that phrase from their minds?"

"Objection sustained, Mr. Moriarti." To the prosecution table, he said, "You jeopardize the Government's case with cheap shots like that." To the jury, he said, "The phrase *terrorist attack* is an unsubstantiated conclusion crudely offered to sway your judgment. Let's put those words behind us and get back to the evidence, OK?"

"You can answer the question, Micky," the prosecutor continued.

"Yes. I've worked at the auction for three years."

"Is there anyone in the courtroom that you recognize from the auction house?"

"That guy," Micky said. He pointed to Wally. "I saw him with a woman and a baby carriage a few days before the sale. We were closed. I was polishing out some scratches, and I let them go through for one walk-around. Halfway across the room, I see this guy fiddling with the underside of that fancy Morris chair. I yelled at him and they ran away."

"So you saw the defendant, Walter Winchester, place something under the seat of a chair that later blew up and seriously injured five people?"

"I didn't say he placed something, but who knows what they could have carried in the baby carriage."

"Objection," Moriarti said. "Flat-out conjecture has no place in this trial."

"I agree," Judge Keller said. "Scratch the baby carriage line."

"Your witness," the prosecutor said.

Moriarti took his turn. "Hello, Micky," he said.

"Hello."

"Tell the court about the appearance of the man who previewed the auction with a woman and a baby carriage."

"What?"

"Describe him as you saw him. What was he wearing? Better yet, turn away from the defendant and describe his face."

"Objection."

"Overruled."

Micky turned to the jury. He said, "Well, he looked to be bald but he had a farm cap on his head. And he had a beard, you know, a chin beard. Looked like a lot of Amish folks I know."

"Describe the woman."

"She was pretty. Wore a bonnet. Had a nice white dress."

"Do you see her in the courtroom today?"

Micky turned back to the courtroom and looked at the faces in the gallery. He said, "No, sir. I don't."

Moriarti's eyes found Chana's. He winked and smiled as he walked back to the defense table and picked up a blow- up photo of his own.

"See this guy?" he asked the witness. The photo was a still from a Harrison Ford movie, *Witness,* with credits printed across the bottom. A bald, chin-bearded Amish farmer, wearing a bill cap, looked at the camera, the shadow of the bill darkening his face. He showed the photo to the jury and the judge.

"Objection," the prosecutor shouted. "This is a still from a movie. It has no evidentiary value here."

"I don't claim it as evidence, George." Moriarti used the chief prosecutor's name for the first time. "I just want a visual aide to ask a question."

"Careful, Mr. Moriarti."

"Thank you, Your Honor. Now Micky, we know this is not the man you saw. This is a movie poster. But tell me, other than the actual eyes, nose and mouth, did the man you saw have this general appearance?"

"Well, sure. That's not the guy, but that's the way he looked, like an Amish farmer."

Moriarti said, "Thank you for your answer. Now look at the defendant." He pointed to Wally, his hair back to a short-haired mop, cleanly shaven and wearing a tie.

"You are testifying that from a brief conversation with a man across the auction gallery who looked like this, you can positively identify him as the defendant, Walter Winchester? Just from the eyes and nose and mouth?"

"Yes, sir. That's the man."

"Interesting. You know, Micky. One of my support team is a computer wizard. Wave your hand, Danny."

In the gallery, Danny grinned as he raised his hand. Moriarti continued. "The other day, I asked Danny to find a photo of a bald Amish man with a cap and a beard. This is the picture he found, a movie promo poster."

"Your Honor," the prosecutor interrupted. "We don't have time for this lesson on computers."

"One more minute, please," Moriarti asked.

"Thirty seconds."

"Well, Danny is good at a thing called Photoshop. I asked him to take a picture of the defendant, Wally Winchester, and insert his face under the cap and beard in the movie promo photo."

He held up the photo to the judge and jury, said, "This is an actual photo of Wally Winchester, bald, wearing a beard and a hat, just the way you say you remembered him. You looked at it and said he was not the man you saw. Then you point to the defendant and say you recognize him."

"You tricked me," Micky shouted. "You said he was an actor."

"You looked at an image of a man accused of a horrific crime and you didn't recognize him, but you swear it's my client?" He pointed to Wally, wearing his best innocent face.

"I'm not done with you, Micky. Sit back," Moriarti said. "Since this is a high-profile case, a Federal affair, we get access to the FBI's data in the case. They have your cell phone records. And so do we." He waited three beats.

"It seems that at 3:47 p.m. on the day you claim you saw my client, you dialed a number. Had a thirty-second conversation. Was that phone call a response to your meeting with the Mormon farmer and his wife? Were you paid to call that number if anyone showed interest in the chair? The chair that later exploded and injured five people? That would make you a co-conspirator."

"How could you know that?"

"We have a phone number." Moriarti recited it. "Who did you call?"

Micky looked at the judge. He said, "Look, Judge, I'm testifying. Do I have to answer these personal questions? Tell him to back off."

"You swore to tell the truth when you sat down," Judge Keller said. "The question is relevant to the case. Answer it."

"Um, I called the owner, to tell him I saw someone fiddling with the sale items."

"I have the owner's home number and his cell," Moriarti said. "They don't match the number you called. Remember, Micky, you're under oath."

"Call me guilty of having fat fingers. I must have misdialed," Micky said. "Sue me."

Detective Kelly, sitting in the gallery, was startled when he heard the phone number. He'd seen that number before, found under the passenger seat of a Shelby, scribbled on a piece of paper. He pulled out his notebook and sent a message to the defense table.

Moriarti read it. He approached the witness stand.

"Well, Micky," he said. "This is my cell phone on speaker. Let's dial that number and see who answers."

Micky's face drained of color. He said nothing as Moriarti typed in the number.

A Wagner melody filled the courtroom. The back door opened and a dark-haired man exited the courtroom.

"Don't leave town," Moriarti said to the witness as he walked back to the defense table.

"Claus Braun was in the gallery," Wally whispered.

"I know."

Chapter Sixty-Four

Spokane, Washington

The prosecutor's case shifted to the charge of aiding and abetting a terrorist organization. The prosecution called Nathan Collver.

A well dressed thirty year-old took the oath and sat down.

"Where did you meet the defendant?" the prosecutor asked.

"At Sotheby's. I was an expert in the Fine Photography department. He came in without an appointment, and I was assigned to appraise the photographs he brought."

"Did he own these photographs, or did he represent a seller?"

"He claimed he was an agent for the Tamil Cultural Center. I didn't pay attention to it at the time."

"Tell the court about the photographs."

"He had a rare portfolio of original prints by the photographer, Julia Margaret Cameron. When I realized the value of the work, I contacted my superior, Alice Wagner, and she took it from there."

"Bullshit," Wally whispered to Moriarti. "The chicken shit had no idea who Julia was. That's why the guy's out of work."

"Quiet. We have that," Moriarti said, "Let me work."

"What caused you to call the FBI?" the prosecutor asked.

"I saw Winchester's face on TV one night, and remembered the meeting. He was on a murder spree, and the Tamil Tigers are terrorists. I put two and two together."

"Objection," Moriarti said. "My client was not on a murder spree. That's why I'm here. To prove that."

"Tone down your answers, Mr. Collver," the judge said.

"So the defendant told you he was the agent of the Tamil Cultural Center and signed documents to that effect?"

"I believe so. It was in Alice's hands. I'm proud that I was the one to link him to terrorism."

"Thank you for your vigilance. The country needs more of that," the prosecutor said.

"Your witness."

Moriarti approached, hat in hand. "Where do you work, presently?"

"I'm between jobs."

"So you parted ways with your employer after you met the defendant? How soon after?"

The witness looked up to the judge, who nodded. "The next day," he said.

"Did your interaction with Wally Winchester cause your termination? Remember, you are under oath."

"There were staff cuts. Who knows?"

"Were you the only staff cut?"

"Yes."

"So instead of a hero, Nathan, you are a disgruntled, fired worker, angry at my client for somehow getting you fired, eager to get payback."

"Objection."

"Sustained."

"I'm done."

The next witness was Alice Wagner, a well dressed woman in her 50's.

"You signed an agreement with Mr. Winchester to sell a portfolio of photographs by Julia Margaret Cameron. Is that correct?"

"Yes."

"Is the person who brought these photographs to sell for the Tamil Cultural Center here in this courtroom?"

Alice Wagner pointed to Wally, who waved.

The prosecutor pulled another giant photo from the pile on his desk. It was a signed document, three feet high. He entered it as evidence.

"Is this the document you signed that declares Wally Winchester an agent for the Tamil Cultural Center?"

"It appears to be."

"Thank you. Cross."

"We have no questions for the witness," Moriarti said. "Thank you for your service to the arts, Ms. Wagner."

Chapter Sixty-Five

Spokane, Washington

Next, the Federal prosecutor marched the boat owner onto the witness stand. Wally, dressed in a white shirt and two-dollar tie fresh from St. Vinnie's, remembered meeting him outside a Port Angeles wine bar the day he stole his boat. He was sixty years old and well tanned.

"State your name."

"Saul Stonaurer."

"Mr. Stonaurer, have you met the defendant, Walter Winchester?"

"Yes. In a little wine bar my wife runs, upstairs in the Landing Mall."

"Did he give you any clue that he was a wanted killer?"

"Objection."

"Sustained."

"Did he show interest in renting a boat?"

"He asked. I took him for a walk onto the dock. Showed him mine. Told him it wasn't for hire. An hour later it was stolen."

"Was it located?"

"They found it over on Vancouver Island, up against the rocks. It sustained some damage. The RCMP told me a suspect was taken from the boat's rescue raft in Canadian waters."

"Do you see the man who stole your boat and sailed it without papers into Canadian waters?"

Stonaurer pointed to Wally, who waved again. Moriarti whispered and he put his hand down. It was his turn.

"Mr. Stonaurer," Moriarti said, "It appears my client borrowed your boat for an excursion over to Victoria."

"They plucked him off my vessel off the Canada coast. I assume he was the one who started the voyage."

"Did you offer your vessel as a rental?"

"I told him on the dock that it would take a truckload of money before I rented her. I assume he took that for a no."

"When you got your boat back, did you find a message from Mr. Winchester in the vessel?"

"I did. In the front sleeping quarters under a pillow, I found a manila envelope with ten thousand dollars in cash and a note."

"What did the note say?"

"Thanks for the rental, it said. It was signed, Wally Winchester. He wrote down his email address and his phone number."

"I appreciate your time," Moriarti said. He sat down next to Wally and conducted a huddled conversation.

The group met again at the Davenport Hotel. Wally ordered champagne. Moriarti vetoed his choice and ordered lemon water for the table.

"You punched a lot of holes in the prosecution's case," Wally told his attorney, raising his lemon water. "Thanks."

"It's a jury trial, son. A lot of high-powered evidence still says you're guilty. My job is to get some of those recordings into evidence, or as a fallback, into their ears."

"Claus Braun was behind us in the gallery," Chana said. "I blame myself. It won't happen again."

"There's a warrant out for his arrest after the killing of the Woburn cop and Kelly's near-miss," Yvgeney said. "I'd love to see him on the witness stand."

"Claus Braun will never be captured," Chana said. "It is written."

"The world is going to hear about him tomorrow," Moriarti said. "Wally will get a voice."

Chapter Sixty-Six

Spokane, Washington

The defense case started with a heart-to-heart talk with the jury.

"I'm going to tell you folks," Moriarti said, hat in hand, "a story about a good man's travel adventure across the United States of America, and of a bad man's effort to destroy his life in a deadly game of revenge. I have films and audio tapes and witnesses to illustrate Wally's journey and his naivety."

"Objection," the prosecutor said. "He's wrapping up in a summation before he starts."

"Sustained," the judge said. "Call your first witness Mr. Moriarti."

"I call Sally Roble."

A thin, grey-haired senior took the stand and was sworn in.

"You're the wife of Harry Roble, an auctioneer from Bryant, Washington."

"Yes."

"And your husband sold a padlocked outbuilding to Wally Winchester, who discovered an expensive car inside. Is that correct?"

"Yes. We've known Wally for years. Everyone was surprised when he broke the lock and found a sports car in the barn he owned."

"Do you remember the model?"

"They said it was a Shelby. The Cobra car."

"How much did Wally pay for the contents of the locked garage?"

"I think a thousand dollars."

"Did you meet the owner of the property that was found in the barn?"

"I did."

"Tell the court about him."

"He was a light-skinned man who spoke English with a Spanish accent like it was his second language. We're a family business, but he insisted in talking to my husband in private. After the meeting, Eddie contacted Wally personally and suggested he attend the sale."

"Where's your husband now?" Moriarti asked.

"He was killed in a boat accident. A month after the sale."

"Was the accident investigated?"

"It was ruled a drowning. No one found any suggestion of foul play."

"I'm sorry," Moriarti said to her. "Do you feel you were manipulated into getting this car into Wally's hands?"

"It was the weirdest auction I ever participated in. Wally sure was happy to find that car. That balanced it out."

"Thank you," Moriarti said.

He called Chester MacAvoy to the stand. MacAvoy sat, his three hundred pounds filling the witness box.

"Welcome to Spokane, Mr. MacAvoy. Are they treating you well out here in the beautiful Palouse?"

"I'm not happy. I'm in a Holiday Inn with basic cable," the big man said. "Hopefully I can get back to Everett this afternoon. The pass is clear tonight, they say."

"Your garage housed the defendant's car, a Caroll Shelby Cobra. Is that correct?"

"He rented storage on the third floor where we keep the classic cars."

"Did you have an Hispanic employee at the time Mr. Winchester removed his car to drive it across the country?"

"Yes. A gal named Manuelita, another pretty face that didn't last."

"How'd she come to be hired?"

"It was odd. My regular gal won a vacation in a contest. Then she broke her leg skiing. Before I could compose a help-wanted ad, this guy with a Spanish accent shows up, tells me he's sponsoring a young woman from Mexico to work in the United States. He says he'll pay half her salary. How could I say no? Two weeks later, Wally shows up to take the car away and she's gone."

The prosecutor passed up cross-examination.

Moriarti called Henrietta Kirby to the stand. The elderly woman negotiated the journey in a walker. "Welcome to Spokane, Henrietta," Moriarti said. "I hope the trip from Butte wasn't too inconvenient."

"George and I love Spokane. We used to take the Chrysler over once a year and stay in the Davenport till it closed."

"The Davenport's open again," Moriarti said. "All restored. We ate there last night."

"Did you hear that George? The Davenport's open again." A nodding senior in the gallery looked up when he heard his name.

"Please confine your remarks to the people asking questions, Henrietta," Judge Keller said softly.

"You and George live in Butte, Montana. Is that correct?"

"Thirty-five years."

"Do you recognize anyone in the courtroom?" Henrietta looked at Wally and waved, then squinted as she searched the faces in the gallery. "Three," she said.

"Three?"

"Actually, four counting you. I recognize the Latin girl over there." She indicated Chana. "The nice detective with the broken arm, and of course Wally."

"Please point out Wally."

A bony finger indicated him at the defense table.

"Tell the court, please, how you met the defendant, Henrietta."

"He knocked on our door one afternoon with his young wife. They were darling. So much in love. Just married, you know. They were interested in an old sofa on our porch."

"Can you describe the woman?"

"Cute as a bug. Mexican girl. She didn't say much."

"Do you remember her name?"

"Mary, I think. Don't hold me to that. I seem to have a hard time with names these days."

"But you definitely remember they were traveling together."

"They held hands. Wally said they were in love."

"Did you notice what kind of car they were driving?"

"We live on the third floor."

"That's a no?"

"That's a no."

"Did you feel threatened in any way when Wally was in your apartment?"

"Heavens, no. We asked them to come back and visit. George and I don't get much company."

"Thank you. I'm glad you can visit the Davenport again."

"So are we," she said as she gingerly exited the box.

The prosecution stayed mum as she wobbled back to the gallery. At the defendant's table, she stopped to have word with Wally. Moriarti smiled as the judge reminded her to find a seat.

The defense called for Eric Langelier. A portly gentleman with a full beard took the oath.

"You work at the Grove Park Inn, Mr. Langelier?" Moriarti asked.

"I've been greeting visitors there for twenty years."

"Do your recognize the defendant, Walter Winchester?"

"Yes." He looked at Wally and nodded.

"When did you see him last?"

"At the Arts and Crafts conference, couple of months ago at the Inn.

"What was he driving?"

"A sweet blue Shelby," Langelier said. "Wally made quite a stink about safe parking. I arranged for him to stash the racer in the old car museum for the duration of his stay."

"Do you remember a passenger?"

"Sure do. A real looker. Latin gal. Didn't say much."

"Did you see Wally Winchester on Monday at 9:30 a.m., the time of the killings?"

"Yes. He was having a conniption because the museum garage was still locked. It took us half an hour to track down the key."

"Was the Mexican woman with him then?"

"No, sir. Wally said she was in the spa."

"Your turn," Moriarti said to the prosecution table.

"Are you still employed by the Grove Park Inn?"

"No."

"Explain."

"I was fired the day after the murders."

"Explain."

"The management found out I was using the museum garage for my personal gain."

"What did Winchester pay you for your creative parking solution?"

"Four hundred dollars."

The prosecutor said, "Four hundred dollars? For parking?

"It's the Grove Park Inn."

"So you and your partner in crime, the defendant, Walter Winchester, entered into a conspiracy to defraud the hotel, and now you're here offering him an alibi?"

"I can understand him wanting to protect that car…you…"

"Thank you," the prosecutor turned and regained his seat.

Moriarti called Fred Franklin.

The bailiff opened the gate, and a portly man in his sixties maneuvered his electric wheelchair to the witness stand. The judge said, "You can sit right there." The bailiff swore him in as he sat in his chair.

"Do you recognize the defendant?" Moriarti asked, pointing to Wally.

"Yes. He was at my auction house the morning of the bombing."

"Was he dressed differently?"

'I've been calling auctions for thirty years. Reading the crowd is part of the job. I watched your boy wearing a fake beard sending instructions to his shill, a Chinese kid in the front row, with his phone. Winchester was dressed like a farmer, but unlike our hired kid, who testified earlier, I'll never forget those eyes."

"Objection. The answer is not responsive to the question."

"Sustained."

"What makes you so sure you recognize the defendant?" Moriarti asked.

"I read people's eyes for a living. Half the bids I take are ear scratches, head nods, and winks. I saw those eyes go wide just before he shouted, 'There's a bomb in the chair.'"

Moriarti looked astonished. He asked, "The defendant, accused of conspiring to overthrow the Government of the United States, using a weapon of mass destruction, yelled out a warning that allowed most of your auction crowd to escape unhurt?"

"He saved my life. Kept trying to pull me away from the chair. He or one of his friends dragged me out near the front door before the horrid thing blew up. I was lucky just to lose a leg."

"Did you meet the chair's consigner, a Mr. Franklin?"

"Sure did. He was a tall fellow. Spoke with a Spanish accent. Called himself Kaczynski, seemed to think that was funny. Left me a cell number and told me to mail the proceeds check to a P.O. Box in Chile."

"Do you have this information to share with the court?"

"Lost it in the explosion and fire."

"Too bad."

"You're telling me?" the auctioneer said.

Moriarti walked over to the prosecution table, touched his opponent on the shoulder and said, "He's all yours, George."

"So on the day of the bombing you saw the defendant in the auction hall, Mr. Franklin?"

"Just said so."

"And you testified under oath that the defendant told you there was a bomb hidden in the chair?"

"He told everyone."

"How would he know there was a weapon of mass destruction under the seat cushion unless he put it there?"

"Beats me."

"Objection."

"Sustained."

"Thank you, Mr. Franklin."

After lunch, Moriarti called Dwayne Anderson to the stand.

"Nice earring, Mr. Anderson," the defense attorney said.

"Thank you, it's an original Spratling from Mexico.

"Did you once work for the Department of Homeland Security?"

"I served as a liaison officer on loan from the Army Intelligence Division."

"What were your duties?"

"I specialized in anti-terrorism till I left the Army last year."

"Thank you for your service. We need more people like you. Are you familiar with the government data bank on known terrorist organizations?"

"I helped generate and update the list."

"How many groups are there on the list?"

"I'm not allowed to answer that question."

"I understand," Moriarti said. "Are you familiar with the Tamil Cultural Center?"

"Yes, sir. We looked into that group extensively."

"Are they on the list?"

"No. We found no connection between them and the Tamil Tigers. Their aims proved to be cultural and political, but they worked with the Sir Lankan government, not against it. The director was a member of the local parliament."

"But the name, Tamil?"

"The Tamil people comprise a third of the population of Sri Lanka, sir. They represent the upper classes of the island society, doctors, politicians, academics, and poets. Until recently the name *Tamil* stood for peace and intelligence. The Tamil Tigers are defunct, now. Their guerilla leader is dead. They did not represent the will of the Tamil population, just a hateful fringe."

"Would a signed contract as an agent for the Tamil Cultural Center represent an act of terrorism against the United States?"

"Absolutely not. No more than representing the International Red Cross or Doctors Without Borders."

"Thank you for clearing that up," Moriarti said. "Your witness."

The prosecutor stood up and asked, "Why were you separated from the armed services?"

"Don't Ask, Don't Tell policies cut our ranks by about a third."

"So you are gay? Do you hold any grudges? Do you hate your country? Did you ever manipulate the database as an act of revenge against those who ousted you?"

"I served one tour in Iraq and one in Afghanistan. I hold a purple heart and two medals for my valor. You insult my services, sir."

"I'm looking for evidence, son. Any question is fair game. Remember, you are under oath."

"The oath I took when I joined the Army supersedes the silly pledge I just took at this Mickey Mouse trial, sir. I suggest you examine your own oath." The witness stood up, his body shaking.

"Your Honor," Moriarti said. "This man is a genuine hero. Can't the prosecution build its case on evidence instead of innuendos?"

"I agree," Judge Keller said. He glared at the prosecutor. "You're excused, Mr. Anderson, with the court's thanks and apologies."

"Your Honor," Moriarti looked into his hat as he spoke. "I'd like to recall Detective Michael Kelly to the stand."

"Objection. He's already testified."

"The state didn't ask the detective how he was injured, Your Honor, I thought this would be a good time to talk about it."

"Is the injury relevant to the case?"

"Totally, Your Honor. It sheds light on the real killer."

"Objection."

"Call your witness, Mr. Moriarti."

"You've already been sworn in," the defense began. "How'd you hurt your shoulder?"

"I was shot in Woburn, Massachusetts in the company of a local detective while executing a search warrant," Kelly answered.

"What happened to the other officer?"

"He was killed. The assailant was never found. The case is active."

"I'm sorry for the loss of another officer in the line of duty. Can you tell the court what you were doing in Massachusetts?"

"The Spokane Police Department tracked the defendant's vehicle to a storage barn in an abandoned sand pit in Massachusetts. We were about to impound the car when we were attacked."

"So the mystery race car does exist? Did you see it?"

"I was looking through the trash under the front seat when I was shot. My fellow officer, from the Woburn police, was killed."

"Was anyone in the barn besides you and the Woburn officer?"

"Two people from the defense support team were with me during the attack."

"Are they here in the courtroom?"

Kelly nodded and pointed to Chana and Yvgeney in the seats behind the defense table.

"Can you identify your assailant?"

"During my investigation, I kept bumping into references to a third party, a person in the background of the murder investigation, a certain Claus Braun."

"And this Claus Braun was the person who killed the officer with you and attempted to kill you?"

"I spoke to him and he admitted his role in an elaborate plot to frame the defendant, Winchester. Then he shot me."

"Objection. Hearsay."

"What part of *he shot me* is hearsay, Your Honor?" Moriarti shouted.

"I have a tape," Kelly said to the judge.

"Objection. We weren't notified of any tape by the defense."

"He's your witness, not ours," Moriarti said.

"I gave the Feds a copy of the tape," Kelly said. "I was surprised you didn't offer it into evidence. Figured you didn't want to muddy up the case with reasonable doubt."

The lead prosecutor looked at three associates beside him. "Did you see a tape?" he asked in a loud whisper. "Did you?"

A sad nod signaled yes.

"Your Honor," Moriarti said, "if the Government can't find its copy, I have the detective's original right here." He reached into the Stetson and lifted out a cassette. "I'd like to present it into evidence."

"Let's hear it," Judge Keller said. He looked to the prosecutor, said, "Your office has a lot of explaining to do, George. Don't think this is over."

Moriarti walked to a box at the defense table, slipped a thumb drive into the driver and pressed *play*. The jury heard, "This is Detective Mike Kelly. The date is May 24, 2011. Eight p.m. I'm looking at a blue car, a Caroll Shelby Cobra, in Woburn, Massachusetts…here's a bullet hole in the sheet metal, large caliber. Inside the car shows litter, the guy was a slob." A recorded voice in the background yelled, "Stand up…"

The mood of the courtroom was pensive when the prosecutor had the last shot: "Did you see the face of this mysterious killer on the night you were shot?" he asked. "Or any other times? The person who said his name was Claus Braun?"

"Not his face, no."

"So you really have no idea who shot you in Woburn, Massachusetts?"

Kelly said, "He was behind a flashlight in a dark room. I could probably identify him from a voice sample, but not by sight."

"So you've never seen your assailant? This mysterious character named Claus Braun is just a voice behind a flashlight?"

"I have other references to this name."

"Thank you," the prosecutor said.

The mood at the Davenport Hotel dining room was upbeat. "I have one more rabbit in here," Moriarti said, touching his hat. "Manuelita's video." Wally looked away. "The prosecution has a copy, but they don't acknowledge it. They'll fight to keep it out of evidence. The original packaging and the cancelled stamps with Wally's P.O. box will get us in the door. After that, it's up to the judge. By the way, where's Chana?"

"She's not one to broadcast her movements," Yvgeney said. "I saw her hop into a cab when court let out this afternoon. She can take care of herself."

Chana entered the phone number that was mentioned at the trial into her phone.

"Hello, Chana," a familiar voice answered.

"Hola, Señor Braun."

"I'm disappointed in the United States Government's ability to conduct a trial," Braun said.

"Señor Moriarti is a clever advisor, sir."

Braun said, "If Winchester is acquitted, my revenge is incomplete. You know, child, it's not a solution I can walk away from."

"I understand that, sir. That's why I made this phone call. I'd like to meet tonight."

"It's always a pleasure to share your company, Chana. You could meet me in my hotel room but I don't trust your allegiance these days. How about the city park down by the river, near the waterfalls?"

"I'm fond of waterfalls," Chana said. "When do you want to meet?"

Braun said, "Just after darkness falls, about nine tonight. Does that work for you?"

"I love darkness also," Chana said. "I'll be there."

Chana enjoyed the musty odor of the dirty brown river as it foamed up at the base of Spokane Falls. It reminded her of yeast. She saw a single figure move through shadows, cast by a half-full moon, and turned away to face the dancing rapids, her back to the well maintained shoreline.

The sound of footsteps behind her stopped at a meter's distance. She turned and looked at the moonlit face of her mentor.

"You've dyed your hair, sir," she said without emotion or a smile. "I liked you better as a blonde."

"It was all going grey anyway."

"I've decided to take your offer," she said.

"Really." A smile revealed teeth that caught the moonbeams. "What caused you to change your mind?"

"I have respect for your determination. You are a powerful man. I know my friend will never be safe from you if he escapes the prosecution's case."

"That's correct, child," he said. "I've already made some calls."

"If you call off your people I will enter into your service again as your personal sword."

"You are willing to walk away from your Siberian life, your new direction, just to save a meddling, irritating North American?"

Chana looked without blinking into the eyes of the man who saved her from a life of crime and prostitution, or worse, in the city of Manaus, the man who introduced her to higher level thinking and taught her a hundred ways to kill. She said, "This *gringo* is not your enemy and never was. He's just a child in a man's body, chasing shiny things."

"An eye for an eye." Braun fought off a frown.

"My choice is one of two," Chana said. "To enter into your servitude or kill you. I choose number one."

"Really." The dark figure stepped closer and put sinewy arms around her. She accepted the embrace and felt a kiss, placed on the top of her head.

"We can leave tonight," Chana said. "I have no business to conclude. I have no one to say goodbye to."

"The trial's not over, Chana. I'm not leaving till justice is done. Tomorrow could be the last day of testimony."

"You're making a mistake, Señor Braun. My first act in your employ is to strongly suggest an immediate withdrawal."

Chana felt him step back. She saw his hand arc up, lit by the moonlight. She didn't stop it as Braun slapped her face. Her eyes teared up. Her expression remained unchanged.

The voice in the dark said, “My first act as your employer is to remind you of your place.”

Chapter Sixty-Seven

Spokane, Washington

The mood in the gallery of Courtroom No. 1 was upbeat. Moriarti chose a buckskin suit jacket over crisply pressed trousers. Wally wore a tie with red diagonals over black, a style chosen by Arial when she saw one on the President of the United States. Wally had argued for a yellow tie with happy faces and had been voted down again.

Moriarti called Yvgeney Ivanchenko to the stand and he was sworn in.

"Mr. Ivanchenko," he stated. "Tell me your occupation."

"I am an investigator for the United Nations. My specialty is cultural property crimes."

"Very impressive. What are you doing here in Spokane?"

"I'm a friend of the defendant, working with you on the defense team."

"Why weren't you in court two days ago, Mr. Ivanchenko?"

"I was at the post office in Stanwood, on the other side of the mountains. I had documents your team prepared that ordered the post office to release all of the defendant's mail that had piled up since he left on his trip to Boston."

"Do you have that mail with you here in the courtroom?"

"All but the junk mail. We didn't have room in the car."

The gallery erupted in laughter. Judge Keller slammed the gavel.

"Did you find anything in Walter Winchester's mail that could cast any light on this case?"

"Objection. He's not qualified to make a judgment on relevance."

Moriarti said, “I’ll let it go, Your Honor. Let’s try another question. Did you recover any mail sent from states where the killings took place?”

“Objection. This is a fishing expedition. Where’s the chain of custody. Anyone could have monkeyed with this mail between the post office and here.”

“Mr. Moriarti?” the judge asked.

“Your honor, I have a list and description of all two hundred twenty-one objects found in Walter Winchester’s mailbox, signed by the postmaster and notarized.” He reached into his hat and extracted three folded pages, passed the package up to the judge behind his bench.

Judge Keller opened it and spent a few minutes reading.

“Answer the question,” he said.

“There was only one letter, a package actually, that was mailed from out-of-state. It was posted in Massachusetts.”

“What was in it?” Moriarti asked.

“A DVD with the words, *Wally Winchester,* written in black marker.”

“Nothing else? No return address or a name?”

“Just the disc.”

“With the court’s permission, I’d like to enter it into evidence and then play it,” Moriarti said.

“Objection. This is one more of the defendant’s circus stunts. Who knows what’s on that DVD? Could be porn for all we know. The jury’s had enough of Mr. Moriarti’s surprises.”

“Sidebar, Your Honor?”

“Come up, you two.” Judge Keller glowered at both attorneys.

Moriarti spoke first. “All I ask is for you and me and George, here, go back in your chambers and take a look. You can decide.”

"The court will take a half-hour recess," Judge Keller announced. He banged the gavel dangerously close to Moriarti's fingers on the edge of the bench.

Sitting at the defendant's table, Wally saw Judge Keller and the prosecuting attorney re-enter the courtroom with ashen faces.

The judge banged the gavel. He said to the bailiff, "Let me see the post office list again. He picked up the mailing envelope and referred to a notation on the documents. He shook his head, turned it to the jury. "I'm going to allow you to see this tape," he said. "I must warn you it will be disturbing."

"Your Honor," the prosecutor groaned.

"I'm allowing it," Judge Keller said. "Bailiff, please bring in a television."

The film had no titles. It opened on a woman's face against a neutral brown wall. Her eyes were red. She spoke: "My name is Manuelita Martinez. I was born in the region of Chiapis, Mexico. I am an assassin. This is my confession." A gasp rose up in the courtroom. The judge banged the gavel.

"I am an agent for Claus Braun from Chile. My assignment was to travel with Wally Winchester from Everett, Washington to Massachusetts and commit a series of crimes to make him wanted for murder."

Wally had seen the tape four times by now. Tears ran down his face for the fifth time.

"This is my first kill, a man in a Hindu church. I stabbed the man with an upward thrust, cut his stomach to let his insides out…"

Moriarti watched the faces of the jury members as the woman on TV outlined her crimes. He was preparing his summation.

She finished with, "I'm sorry, Wally." Her eyes looked directly into the camera. She continued, "I know the meeting site for the race car exchange. I will be there to protect you but I'm making this record to aid you in your trial…," she hesitated, "as a back-up. You don't deserve the evil that was placed behind your back. You didn't feel any of it, so childlike you were on your adventure. From you, I learned to care again. From you I tasted love. *Gracias."*

The courtroom exploded. Keller banged and banged until the conversations ceased.

"The defense rests," Moriarti said. He put on his hat.

Chapter Sixty-Eight

Spokane, Washington

Moriarti was talking with his client on a bench outside Courtroom No.1 when a bailiff appeared and said, "The jury's in."

Wally remained standing as the gallery filled in behind him. He looked into the faces of the jurors and pasted Photoshop smiles on their grim lips in his mind. Silence blanketed the chamber.

In the gallery, Detective Kelly opened his phone, punched in the number he'd memorized from the Cobra floor. A German waltz melody erupted behind him by the back door. "It's Braun," Kelly shouted. He screamed, "Stop him, he shot me!" as a dark haired man bolted through the doors.

Kelly followed, pushing his way through a throng of escaping visitors. He unsnapped his pistol with his good hand.

The dark haired runner disappeared at a street corner. When Kelly rounded it, he saw no one, the lane in front of him leading to the river above the falls. He ran toward the river, looking into alleys that he passed. He crossed a quiet street and headed for the water and a movement he saw in a grove of trees.

"This is Detective Kelly of the Spokane Police," he shouted into the river roar. "You are under arrest. Throw out your weapon and reveal yourself."

A shot rang out. Kelly heard the whining of a headshot miss his ear. He ducked and fired back into the thicket. A figure bolted toward the river, back-lit by the setting sun.

Kelly raised his gun and pulled the trigger.

A figure leaped into the field of fire and crumpled as the bullet hit.

Kelly ran to the body and found Chana. He looked up and saw an empty shore behind her.

Chapter Sixty-Nine

Spokane, Washington

The mood was somber when the trial reconvened. Wally marched into the courtroom and stood with his head down. From behind him, he heard Yvgeney take a deep breath.

The jury leader handed a slip of paper to the bailiff who passed it to Judge Keller.

He read, "As to the charge, *Crossing State Lines in the Commission of a Felony, namely Murder,* we find the defendant not guilty." The gallery exploded in cheers. The judge banged it away. He continued, "As to the charge, *Aiding and Abetting a Terrorist Organization,* we find the defendant, not guilty." The courtroom erupted again. Wally looked up without emotion.

Keller went on, "To the charge, *Conspiring to Overthrow the Government of the United States in the Form of a Bombing in Kansas City,* we find the defendant, not guilty."

A giant cheer rose from the crowd. Keller broke his mallet on the twentieth strike.

"I have one more," he said to the quieting crowd. *"Theft of a Vehicle, namely a Sailboat, and Unauthorized Passage into the Waters of Another Sovereign Nation, namely Canada,* we find the defendant guilty."

Judge Keller turned to Wally, still somber-faced.

The judge said, "Because of the minor nature of the crime of which you were convicted, I'm letting you go free on personal recognizance pending sentencing and appeal. You are free to go."

A rhythmic clapping began in the gallery. A mantra of *"Wall-e…Wall-e"* began and built volume.

Wally entered the main hall and walked toward the light, Yvgeney on his arm.

Sunlight hit him in the face. His thoughts were on Manuelita and Chana.

The bullet hit him in the temple before the sound of rifle fire reached the scene. Wally felt a jolt to his forehead and then nothing.

Chapter Seventy

Spokane, Washington

As he opened his eyes, Wally saw the face of the Rolfs Queen. He tried to speak but phlegm clogged his throat. He coughed it up into a cup someone put by his lip. "Stacie," he gurgled. "Am I in heaven?" He looked around and saw a hospital room.

"Pretty close to it, tiger. Check out the bookcase behind me."

"The early Gus from West Virginia! I thought I'd never see it again."

"And over here," Stacie said, "past the smiling faces of your friend, Yvgeney, is half your internet club. Wave kids." They did. "And a sofa, fresh from Butte, Montana." Wally looked at the Marshmallow Sofa; smiled at the shadow it created on the wall behind it.

"If this is hell, I like it," he said. He felt the Rolfs Queen's hand higher up his leg than he expected. She gave him a wink.

"You've been in a hospital-induced coma for ten days," Yvgeney said. "You were shot in your forehead at the right angle for deflection. The bullet missed your brain."

"It didn't have much of a target," Wally said, happy that his sense of humor had not been erased. His face darkened as a troubling memory returned. Something about Chana. Something painful.

"Chana," he yelled. "What happened to Chana?"

Wally's attention tanked. He looked to his right as his consciousness faded and saw Chana lying on the hospital bed beside him. She smiled. Her image blurred as he lost his grip on paying attention.

Yvgeney's voice broke through the fog. It said, "Don't worry, Wally, the doctor says you will drift in and out till the coma inducer clears."

Wally looked at the face of his South American friend as her freckles dissolved into flesh tones and then to a tan blur as she faded out of focus. For a second he knew the heart of Julia Margaret Cameron.

THE END

Jack Gunter is a prominent Pacific Northwest writer, artist, and antique dealer who specializes in twentieth century decorative arts.

With a degree in biology and graduate training in organic chemistry, he was teaching school in Massachusetts in 1973 when he wrote and illustrated his first book, "The Gunter Papers," which he describes as a futuristic junior high school science curriculum.

A self taught artist using the ancient technique of egg tempera painting, he exhibited his large format works in several New England museums and was included in an Andrew Wyeth and Family show in the Sharon, N.H. Art Center in 1979. That year a studio fire claimed all of his existing paintings and landed him in Washington State with a pick up truck, his dog, and the clothes on his back,
relocating because in Puget Sound he was the only person in a thousand mile radius who wanted mission oak objects and the Northwest was chock full of Mr. Stickley's furniture.

Since moving to Camano Island he has created over one thousand additional paintings, three movies as a SAG indie filmmaker, and four books -- an illustrated guide to Northwest history narrated by a flying pig and three novels in the Wally Winchester adventure series.

He lives in a cliffside cabin with views of the Olympic Mountains, eagles, and spouting whales out his front window